P9-BBN-708

He'll never leave again…

By Eloisa James

WHEN THE DUKE RETURNS
DUCHESS BY NIGHT
AN AFFAIR BEFORE CHRISTMAS
DESPERATE DUCHESSES
PLEASURE FOR PLEASURE
THE TAMING OF THE DUKE
KISS ME, ANNABEL
MUCH ADO ABOUT YOU
YOUR WICKED WAYS
A WILD PURSUIT
FOOL FOR LOVE
DUCHESS IN LOVE

ELOISA JAMES

When The Duke Returns

AVON

An Imprint of HarperCollinsPublishers

This is a work of fiction. Names, characters, places, and incidents are products of the author's imagination or are used fictitiously and are not to be construed as real. Any resemblance to actual events, locales, organizations, or persons, living or dead, is entirely coincidental.

AVON BOOKS
An Imprint of HarperCollins*Publishers*
10 East 53rd Street
New York, New York 10022-5299

First Avon Books paperback printing: December 2008

Avon Trademark Reg. U.S. Pat. Off. and in Other Countries, Marca Registrada, Hecho en U.S.A.
HarperCollins® is a registered trademark of HarperCollins Publishers.

Printed in the U.S.A.

10 9 8 7 6 5 4 3

Acknowledgments

This book is a concerted effort, and I want to offer my heartfelt thanks to all the wonderful people who helped me: my editor, Carrie Feron; my assistant, Kim Castillo; my research assistant, Franzeca Drouin; and the newest member of my team, a brilliant fact-checker, Anne Connell. I love you all!

Prologue

Fonthill
Lord Strange's country estate
February 19, 1784

Women have been dressing to entice men ever since Eve fashioned her first fig leaf. Adam was probably irritable after that business with the apple, so Eve would have done her best with some leaves and string.

So why was it still so hard to decide what to wear? As her maid tossed a seventh rejected gown onto the bed, Isidore, Duchess of Cosway, tried to decide whether her husband would prefer her in a ruby-colored velvet with a low décolletage or a sky-blue open robe with a little train.

The decision would be easier if she'd actually met the husband in question.

"Your Grace looked delightful in the white lustring silk," her maid said, a mulish set to her jaw indicating that Lucille was losing patience with all the tiny buttons, hooks, petticoats, and panniers involved in each change.

"It would be so much less complicated if I only had a few vines to work with, the way Eve did," Isidore said. "Though my marriage could hardly be called Edenic."

Lucille rolled her eyes. She wasn't given to philosophical musings about marriage.

Not only were Eve's sartorial options limited, but she and Adam went *into* the wilderness. Whereas she, Isidore, had lured her husband, the Duke of Cosway, *out* of the wilderness of equatorial Africa, and yet the note she'd received saying he'd arrive tonight sounded just as peeved as Adam. Men never liked to be given directions.

She should probably wear the pale yellow gown, the one embroidered with flower petals. It had a disarming air of female fragility. Isidore plucked it back off the bed and held it in front of herself, staring into the glass. Never mind the fact that docility wasn't her best virtue; she could certainly look the part. For a while.

"That's an excellent choice, Your Grace," Lucille said encouragingly. "You'll look as sweet as butter."

The dress was edged in delicate lace and dotted with pale ribbons. "We'll put flowers in your hair," Lucille continued. "Or perhaps small pearls. We could even add a bit of lace to the bodice." She waved her hand in the general area of Isidore's chest.

Masking her bosom (one of Isidore's best features, to her mind) seemed like taking wifely modesty too far. "Pearls?" she said dubiously.

"And," Lucille said, getting into the spirit, "you could carry that little prayer book from your mother, the one covered with lace."

"*Prayer book?* You want me to carry a prayer book downstairs? Lucille, have you forgotten that we are currently at the most notorious house party in all England? There's not a guest at Lord Strange's party who even *owns* a prayer book except myself!"

"Her Grace, the Duchess of Berrow, has a prayer book," Lucille pointed out.

"Since Harriet happens to be at this party incognito— and dressed as a man—I doubt that she will be wandering around with her prayer book in hand."

"It would give you an air of virtue," her maid said stubbornly.

"It would give me the air of a vicar's wife," Isidore said, throwing the dress back onto the heap.

"You're meeting His Grace for the first time. You don't want to look as if you belong at one of Lord Strange's parties. In that dress you look as young as a debutante," Lucille added, obviously thinking she'd hit on a powerful point.

That settled it. Isidore was definitely not wearing the yellow gown, nor pearls either. She was no debutante: she was all of twenty-three years old, even if she was meeting her husband for the first time, after eleven years of marriage. They'd married by proxy, but Cosway hadn't bothered to return when she was sixteen—or eighteen—or even twenty. He had no right to expect that she'd look like a debutante. He should have imagined what it was like to get older and older while her friends married and had children. It was a wonder that she wasn't as dried up as an apple.

A chilling thought. What if he decided that she really *was* nothing more than a dried-up apple? She was far beyond the age of a debutante, after all.

The very thought made Isidore's backbone straighten. She'd played the docile wife for years, preserving her reputation, waiting for her husband's return. Longing for his return, if she admitted the truth to herself.

And what made Cosway finally come home? Did he suddenly remember that they'd never met? No. It was the news that his wife was visiting a house party more famous for its debauchery than its lemon cakes. She should have thrown away her reputation years ago, and he would have trotted happily out of the jungle like a dog on a leash.

"The silver with diamonds," she said decisively.

Lucille would have paled, but her *maquillage* didn't allow for such extravagancies of emotion. "Oh, Your Grace," she said, clasping her hands like a heroine about to be thrown from the parapet, "if you won't wear the yellow, at least choose a gown that has *some* claim to modesty!"

"No," Isidore said, her mind made up. "Do you know what His Grace's note says to me, Lucille?"

"Of course not, Your Grace." Lucille was carefully displacing the pile of glowing silk and satin, looking for Isidore's most scandalous costume, the one she rarely wore after its first airing resulted in an impromptu duel between two besotted Frenchmen, fought on the cobbles in front of Versailles.

"It says," Isidore said, snatching up the piece of stationery that had arrived a few hours before: "*I discover I have some missing property.* And he added a cryptic comment that seemingly announces his imminent arrival: *Tonight.*"

Lucille looked up, blinking. "What?"

"My husband appears to think I'm a missing trunk. Perhaps he considers it too much work to travel from London to recover me from Lord Strange's party. Perhaps he expected that I would be waiting on the pier for his boat to come in. Perhaps he thinks I've been there for years, tears dripping down my face as I waited for his return!"

Lucille had a hard-headed French turn of mind, so she ignored the edge in Isidore's voice. She straightened with a gorgeous swath of pale silver silk, glittering with small diamonds. "Will you desire diamonds in your hair as well?" she inquired.

This particular dress fit so closely that Isidore could wear only the smallest corset, designed to plump her breasts and narrow her waist. The gown was sewn by a dressmaker to Queen Marie Antoinette, and it presupposed that its owner would grace the mirrored halls of Versailles—a far cry from the smoky corridors of Strange's residence. Not to mention the fact that she would be rubbing shoulders with everyone from dukes to jugglers. Still . . .

"Yes," she said. "I may lose a few diamonds by the end of the evening. But I want my husband to understand that I am no stray trunk that he can simply throw into his carriage and transport to London."

Lucille laughed at that, and began to nimbly lace the proper corset. Isidore stared in the mirror, wondering just what the Duke of Cosway expected his wife to look like. She looked nothing like a pale English rose, given her generous curves and dark hair.

It rankled that Cosway had spent years jaunting around foreign lands, while she waited for him to return. Had he even thought of her in the past ten years? Had he ever wondered what had become of the twelve-year-old girl who married him by proxy?

She had a strong feeling that to Cosway she truly was nothing more than a piece of forgotten property. It made her feel slightly crazed: that she had spent so many years wondering what sort of man she'd married, while he wandered around looking for the source of the Nile, never giving her a second thought.

"Lip color," she said to Lucille. "And I'll wear the diamond-heeled shoes as well."

"*La Grande Toilette,*" Lucille said, and then laughed, a Frenchwoman's sudden laugh. "The duke won't know what happened to him!"

"Precisely," Isidore said with satisfaction. "I had it wrong, Lucille. Eve isn't the right model. I should be thinking about Cleopatra."

Lucille was wrestling with Isidore's panniers and just mumbled something.

"Cleopatra sailed down the Nile in a ship plated in gold," Isidore said dreamily. "Mark Antony took one look at her and lost his heart in a moment. And it wasn't because she looked like a modest wife."

Lucille straightened up. "Modest will not be the word that comes to the duke's mind when he sees you in this gown."

"Excellent," Isidore said, smiling at herself as Lucille dropped a shimmering veil of silver over her head. The bodice fitted as if it were sewn to her body which, in fact, it had been. The fittings had been tedious, but worth every minute. At the waist the silk pulled back in soft billowing folds, revealing an underskirt of blue watered silk. One might not immediately notice the tiny diamonds sewn all over her bodice and skirts, but they made the gown luminescent. It was a gown that turned its wearer into a queen.

Queen Cleopatra, to be exact.

But all the diamonds in the world couldn't stop the cold fear that gripped Isidore's heart when she descended the stairs some time later. She was going to meet her *husband*. For the first time.

What if he were ugly? Well, he was certain to be weather-beaten, at the very least. Likely there wasn't good hygiene in Africa, Isidore told herself. Cosway might be missing some teeth. He might be missing an *eye*! He might be—

But she stopped herself before she began lopping off his limbs. Whatever he was and however he looked, she would finally have a real husband. She could have children. She could be a real duchess, rather than a woman known to some as the Duchess of Cosway, and to others as Lady Del'Fino. She'd longed for this event for years.

The thought sustained her as she strolled into Lord Strange's sitting room. There was a vivid moment of silence as the gentlemen in the room took stock of Isidore—or perhaps more precisely, Isidore's tiny bodice—followed by such a concerted rush in her direction that she actually flinched. No duke was among them. Cosway had yet to arrive.

Men were men, she kept telling herself whenever she felt a pulse of nervousness about her husband. French or English, explorer or juggler, the silver gown brought them all to their knees.

But the sensuality of the gown felt different this time. In the past, she'd ignored men who gaped at her bosom. Now she suddenly realized that a husband's response involved more than just a lustful gaze. To put it bluntly, Cosway had every right to drag her straight up the stairs.

To bed.

Bed!

Of course she wanted to sleep with her husband. She

was curious, she wanted children, she wanted . . . she wanted to throw up.

Her friend Harriet took one look at her and pulled her out of the sitting room—when it happened.

The front door was open and snow was blowing in. The butler was saying something about unseasonably cold weather, and then . . .

A man laughed, and in that instant, Isidore knew. It was Cosway. She could only see his back: he was enormous, wrapped in a greatcoat with a fur hat. She panicked. "I have to go upstairs!" she whispered, stepping backwards, nearly tripping in her eagerness to flee.

"Too late," Harriet said, holding her arm.

And it was. The great mountain of a man turned and then, as if there were no one else in the entry, his eyes met hers and he recognized her. He didn't even glance at her dress, just looked into her eyes. Isidore gulped.

Black hair tumbled over his collar as he pulled off his hat and handed it to a butler. But he didn't take his eyes from hers. His skin looked warm, a honey-dark color that no one could call weather-beaten.

Without saying a word he swept into a deep bow. Isidore's lips parted to say—what?—as she watched him bow and then she curtsied, a moment too late. She felt as if she were caught in the acts of the play. He was—

If Cosway were Mark Antony, Cleopatra would have fallen at his feet, rather than the other way around. He didn't look like an English duke. He didn't have powdered hair, or a cravat, or even a waistcoat. He looked untamed.

"My duchess, I presume," he said, catching her hand and kissing it.

Isidore managed to pull herself together enough to introduce him to Harriet, but her mind was reeling. Somehow in all her imaginings, she'd forgotten to imagine—a *man*.

Not a nobleman, with delicate fingernails, and powdered hair. Not a ruffian, like many of the men attending Lord Strange's house party. But a man who moved easily, like a lion, who seemed to swallow all the air in the entry, whose eyes ranged over her face with a sense of ownership . . . Her heart was beating so quickly that she couldn't hear anything.

He wasn't one-legged, or toothless. He was probably one of the most beautiful men she'd ever met. She had lost track of the conversation.

"The duchess and I leave in the morning," he was telling the butler.

In the morning? Isidore was gripped by a sense of fear so great that she couldn't imagine even walking to the carriage. If she were utterly honest, she had imagined a man who would be slavishly grateful to discover that his wife was so beautiful. But now . . .

She thought she had all the power. She didn't.

She had to take command. *Cleopatra*, she thought desperately. Cleopatra would not allow herself to be transported like a piece of luggage.

"I myself do not plan to leave for several days," she said, smiling at him even though her heart was thundering in her chest.

It wasn't just that Cosway wore no cravat. He wore a gorgeous jacket of pale blue, but it was open straight down the front. Long cuffs fell over his hands, the wrist button undone. He looked as if he were ready for bed. The very thought stoked her nerves.

He took her hand in his, and raised it to his lips again. Isidore watched his lips touch her glove and felt herself shiver.

"Ah, but sweetheart," he said, "I am all eagerness for our wedding."

For a moment, Isidore just thrilled to the sound of

that *sweetheart,* to the way his eyes warmed her, to the secret shiver she felt in her legs.

But then she realized what he had said. "We are wed," she pointed out, withdrawing her hand from his. He looked amused, so she added: "You may have ignored the fact for years, but I assure you that it is true."

That's where it all went wrong.

It started there . . . and it ended with Isidore alone in a bedchamber that night.

Not to mention, Isidore, still a virgin, on her way to London the next day.

He might as well have labeled her, the way they did trunks:

Isidore, property of the duke.

Chapter One

Gore House, Kensington
London Seat of the Duke of Beaumont
February 21, 1784

"*H*e's a virgin."

"What!"

"He's a virgin and—"

"*Your husband is a virgin?*"

"And he won't bed me."

Jemma, Duchess of Beaumont, sank into a chair with a look of almost comical dismay on her face. "Darling, if there ever were grounds for annulment, these are they. Or this is it," she added with some confusion. "Is he some sort of monk?"

Isidore shook her head. "Not that I'm able to see. He

says he will bed me eventually—just not until we're married."

"But you are married!"

"Exactly. I may call myself Lady Del'Fino, but the truth of the matter is that in the eyes of the law, I'm Duchess of Cosway." Isidore dropped into a chair opposite her friend. "We've been married for eleven years, last I counted. And it's hardly my fault that my husband is still a virgin. If he hadn't been chasing all over Africa looking for the source of the Blue Nile, we could be utterly bored with each other, like other well-bred English couples."

Jemma blinked at her. "It's unbelievable. Un-believable."

"I spent the last seven years fending off lechers in every court in Europe, waiting for him to return home, and what does he do? Decide we're not truly married."

"So why didn't he fall directly into your bed, virgin or no?"

Isidore glanced at herself in Jemma's glass. Men had lusted for her ever since she turned sixteen, and the particulars hadn't changed: black hair, pale skin, generous bosom. In short, something short of Venus, but delectable enough to send most men into a lustful frenzy.

"One has to assume that Cosway is fascinated by the exotic," Jemma continued, "and you have such a deliciously un-English look about you. Your eyes are a gorgeous shape, not like the little raisins most of us have."

"I don't think of myself as exotic," Isidore said, "and more to the point, he seems to want someone more skilled in a domestic capacity. Not more than ten minutes after we met—for the first time!—he inquired whether I had been doing any weaving lately. Weaving? Was I supposed to whip out a spindle and sew a fine seam?"

"Even I know that one doesn't sew with a spindle,

which implies that Cosway has a gross disappointment in store if he's counting on your domestic skills," Jemma said, laughing. "Perhaps he's the type that babbles when faced by a desirable woman. It's a surprisingly common affliction."

"Believe me, I was watching him closely, and he gave no sign of being overcome by lust."

"Even Beaumont, who hardly notes anything outside the House of Lords, told me after my masquerade that you had the most beautiful mouth of any woman in England."

"Beaumont said that?" Isidore said, feeling a little thrill of pleasure. "That's nice. Though I have to say, Jemma, I shouldn't like my husband to praise other women to my face."

Jemma shrugged. "According to your own assessment, as a well-bred English couple, we are merely adhering to type. I don't think you should panic, Isidore. I expect Cosway is madly attracted to you and he's just conveying his deep respect by holding a ceremony in front of a bishop."

"He's deranged," Isidore said flatly. "It must have been all that sun in Africa. We married by proxy, but it was still a marriage. I was only twelve years old, but I remember it perfectly well."

"Well," Jemma said, rallying, "maybe the duke wants a romantic ceremony now that he's returned."

"And maybe he's utterly mad and bizarre," Isidore said, putting her fear into words. "What sort of man stays a virgin until he's near to thirty? That's almost disgusting. How am I supposed to introduce him to the bedroom, Jemma? Men do this sort of thing on their own. Honestly, if he's never used his equipment—well, who's to say that it will function at all?"

Silence answered her.

Isidore could feel her eyes growing hot. "I just want to have my husband go to bed with me so that I can be a proper duchess, use my title, and have a child. Is that too much to ask?"

Jemma reached over and took one of her hands. "No. I'm sorry, darling."

Tears started sliding down Isidore's cheeks. "I was never unfaithful to Cosway. The Comte de Salmont told me—in rhymed couplets—that I was more delicious than a 1764 cognac, and given his cellars, that was a true compliment. I finally returned to Italy because Salmont was so extravagant in his pursuit, but I didn't sleep with him, even when he threatened to kill himself." She sniffed, and Jemma handed her a handkerchief.

"I kept to my part of the bargain, although any woman in her right mind would expect her husband to show himself when she came of age."

"Childhood marriages are a huge mistake," Jemma said. "I shall never allow Beaumont to arrange one for a child of ours. People should be adults when they marry."

"I'm not fussy. Truly I'm not. I may have flirted with men as handsome as Salmont, but I like men of other types too. Even short ones. I've told myself for years that no matter how Cosway looked when he finally staggered out of the jungle, I would do my marital part charitably if not enthusiastically. But—"

"Is he unacceptable?" Jemma asked with some curiosity.

"Oh, oh—no," Isidore said. "That's not the point. His looks are irrelevant. He's manifestly odd. Odd!"

"I have another idea. Perhaps Cosway is just too intelligent to have interested himself in carnal matters."

Isidore gave her a watery smile. "Show me the man who's too intelligent to use his tool, and I'll show you a dunce." The words came out more harshly than she intended.

"The most obvious explanation is that he's following some sort of religious law. Did he say anything about going to church? Likely he's a Puritan. Aren't they terrifyingly severe when it comes to base appetites?"

"I spent almost no time alone with him," Isidore said, "and if he has converted to a puritanical sect, he neglected to inform me. He arrived at the house party, scooped me up as if I were a parcel he'd left behind, announced that we were to be remarried, and dropped me in London."

"What do you mean, dropped you in London?" Jemma said, frowning. "Dropped you where?"

"At Nerot's Hotel," Isidore said dispiritedly. "We stayed there last night. I hardly need say that we didn't share a room. He told me—without asking my opinion—that I should wait in the hotel until he returned from his estate."

Jemma cleared her throat. "Obviously Cosway is not *au courant* as regards English customs. What did you reply?"

"Not as much or as sharply as you might expect. He assumed that I would unthinkingly obey him, and though I can hardly believe it, I did. Now all I can think of are the cutting things that I should have said."

"You've discovered one of the primary activities of married life, and so quickly too," Jemma said. "I've lost weeks formulating the witty remarks that I should have said to Beaumont."

"I did manage to tell him that I would stay with you rather than remain in the hotel."

"Why didn't you discuss this hotel business on the way to London from the house party?"

It was humiliating to admit the truth of it. "He barely entered the carriage before he fell asleep."

"Cosway fell asleep after meeting you for the first time? Meeting *his wife* for the first time?"

Isidore nodded. "I believe the truth of it is that I am not what he expected, Jemma, and certainly not what he wanted. When he arrived, the night before, he seemed taken aback by my gown. I was wearing my silver gown. Do you remember that costume?"

"No one could forget the twist of cloth pretending to be a bodice. I've seen larger diamonds."

"It seemed to me that from the view of convenience, not to mention desire, that the gown was the perfect welcome to a missing husband," Isidore said with a deep sigh. "When I wore it in Paris, the Comte de Salmont said—well, never mind what he said. My husband just asked if my taste was always this unorthodox. I did not take that to be a compliment. He then retired to bed. By himself, one hardly need add."

"Few men could resist you in that gown," Jemma said, a frown pleating her forehead.

"The following morning," Isidore said with a sniff, "he ordered everything packed up and I barely said goodbye to Harriet before he bundled me into the carriage. Whereupon he went to sleep rather than talk to me. I've married a monster!"

"If he is indeed a monster, then you needn't stay married to him," Jemma said practically.

"How can I not? He's planning a wedding celebration in the chapel at Revels House. Which means that I have the prospect of seeing my mother-in-law, a pleasure that I have carefully avoided for years."

"He is?"

"Oh, Jemma, I forgot to tell you this part! While he was in Africa, he went to the wedding of a princess. It lasted four days. Or perhaps fourteen, with constant feasts and entertainments. I have a terrible suspicion that he's planning something like that for us."

"He really doesn't seem very English, does he?"

"That's not the most unusual aspect of it," Isidore said, putting down her handkerchief. "I gather the wedding culminated in an orgy, though given Cosway's lack of interest in acts of intimacy—at least with me—I would surmise that he does not plan to mimic this particular aspect of the royal wedding."

"*What?*"

"An orgy. Not to mention the fact that the participants drank warm blood from a sacrificed cow as part of a fertility ritual."

Jemma's mouth fell open. Then she said, "Cosway is holding the wedding celebration at his estate, at Revels House?"

"I expect the Archbishop of Canterbury would look askance at warm blood, don't you think?"

"And his mother will be there?"

Isidore nodded again.

"Warm blood," Jemma said. She covered her mouth but a giggle escaped. "Can you just see him passing a cup of *that* to his mother?"

"The dowager is one of the most upright, English—"

"She could be the queen!" Jemma said. "The queen! She's that rigid. I know this is really crass, darling, and obviously you're going to have to annul the marriage on grounds of pure insanity, but may I have an invitation to the wedding, *please*?"

"It helps to laugh about it," Isidore said with a sniff.

Jemma got up and perched on the arm of Isidore's chair. "Marriage is a great destroyer of logic, but I do think it's a benefit to begin with a sane husband."

"You should have seen the way he was dressed. No

wig, no hair powder. No cravat! He had a lovely coat, but it was open down the front, with no waistcoat."

"I can't wait to see him," Jemma said. "I've always thought it unkind to pay a visit to Bedlam just to laugh at the patients, but if a madman is walking among us . . . Truly, at this point you should probably visit a solicitor, Isidore. Beaumont's offices are in the Inns of Court so he's surrounded by men of that profession. He can point out a good one."

Isidore sniffed again. "I wish my mother were alive."

"I could lend you my mother-in-law, if you like," Jemma offered, giving her a hug.

"Is she the one who populated your house with pictures of Judith holding Holofernes's head?"

"Exactly! She obviously had a fractious relationship with my father-in-law and came up with creative ways to express herself. She might be just what you need to give the wedding celebration an extra little something."

Isidore leaned her head against Jemma's arm. "I didn't realize how desperately hopeful I was until Cosway walked in the door."

"Is it instantly apparent that he's mad?"

"No. He looks like a muscled explorer, all browned by the sun, and rather wild. He has a big nose, but he looks all man, if you know what I mean."

Jemma nodded.

"But then he turned out to be so very unmanly. The virginity, for example, is so disconcerting. I'm afraid he might tell everyone at the wedding," she burst out.

"He wouldn't!"

"He's not ashamed. He says it's the best gift he could have brought me. I'm going to be the laughingstock of all England. Isidore, the Virgin Duchess."

"Now I think of it, Isidore, if my husband had been a

virgin when we married, he wouldn't have had a mistress."

"One has to assume not."

"If that were the case, we would have had a chance at a decent marriage," Jemma pointed out.

Isidore sighed. "I certainly won't have to fend off other women. Believe me, once the *ton* gets wind of his odd ideas, there'll be no competition for his dubious charms."

Jemma's arm tightened around her. "I don't know whether it would be better to initiate annulment proceedings now on the grounds of nonconsummation, or just get the marriage annulled later, on the grounds of mental instability."

"Cosway is probably going back to Africa in any case," Isidore said dispiritedly. "He won't be around for the proceedings."

"Is there a Red or a Green Nile to trace?"

"Who would know? I thought the Nile was in Egypt somewhere, but he talked of Abyssinia. I can't say that I had much education in geography."

"If he's really going back to Africa," Jemma said, "then you might want to stay married."

"Because of the title, you mean?"

"Precisely. Let's hope he'll stay around long enough to create an heir, and then he can wander off for a decade or so."

Isidore got up, walked a few nervous steps before she blurted out her darkest fear. "*If* he's capable of making an heir."

"If he's not, then you know what you have to do. Your first duty to the title is to produce an heir, and if the duke isn't capable, then you find a man to do the deed. That's a fact of life."

"Speaking of that," Isidore said, "didn't you move back to England precisely to give Beaumont an heir?"

"Beaumont doesn't want to engage in heir-making activities until I finish the chess match I started with the Duke of Villiers. But Villiers is still recovering from brain fever and his doctor won't allow him to play chess. Which is actually a good thing."

"Why?"

"Oh, Beaumont and I are getting to know each other," Jemma said lightly.

"And yet not intimately?"

Jemma started laughing. "You would put up with the warm blood, the orgies, and the unpowdered hair, if only your husband would take you to bed, Isidore. Isn't that the truth?"

Isidore felt a pulse of humiliation, but after all, Jemma was her dearest friend. "I'm twenty-three," she said. "Twenty-three! I'm curious! You should see the way Harriet acts with Lord Strange when they think no one is looking. I came across them kissing in a corridor, and the air fairly scorched around them."

"Poor Isidore," Jemma said, meaning it. "Though I feel compelled to tell you that the whole bedroom experience is rather overrated, in my opinion."

"It would have been easier if Cosway expressed the slightest interest in the occasion. At this rate, I'm going to terrify the man if we ever get to a bedchamber." She took another nervous turn around the chamber.

"I think you should probably prepare for the worst," Jemma said. "It seems very likely to me that incapability lies at the heart of this situation. It would explain why he's a virgin, and also why he's making such a fuss out of the wedding."

"Why do you think so?"

"Another wedding delays the inevitable. Perhaps he's

thinking that although he may not have functioned in previous attempts—"

"Sharing a cup of warm blood will make it all better?" Isidore couldn't help it. She started laughing again, a kind of laughter halfway between joy and despair.

"Yes," Jemma said. "That sounds just like something a man would think up."

Chapter Two

Revels House
Country Seat of the Duke of Cosway
February 21, 1784

Simeon Jermyn, Duke of Cosway, expected to feel an overwhelming tide of emotion when his carriage drew up before Revels House. After all, he hadn't seen his childhood home in well over ten years. He arrived just before twilight, when the lowering sun made every turret and angle (and Revels House had many) look sharp and clear against the fading blue sky.

Of course he was poised to quell any such unwelcome emotion. As a follower of the Middle Way, he understood that to live in peace was to anticipate the danger of chaos. Revels House reeked of chaos: even as a mere child he had longed to escape his parents' pitched battles, his father's frenzied speeches, his mother's fierce claims of privilege. They sent him to Eton, but that meant that he had free access to a library full of books describing countries unlike his own. Families unlike his own.

Of course, it was possible that when he came home to the sleepy, tamed English countryside, with Revels House sitting in the midst like a plump teapot, he would be overcome by a sense of righteous pride.

But instead of pride, he found himself looking at the fields as they drew closer and marking their neglected appearance. The gravel on the long drive wasn't just unraked; great swaths of the road were nothing more than ruts carved from dry mud. The trees hadn't been pollarded in years.

Instead of pride—or joy—he felt an unwelcome prickle of guilt, which intensified as he climbed from the carriage to find a broken window in the east wing, and bricks that badly needed pointing.

At least Honeydew, the family's butler, looked the same. For a moment it felt as if Simeon had never left home. Honeydew's three-tiered wig still ended in a stubby tail in the back; his frock was cut in the style of twenty years ago, and lined with brass buttons. Only his face had changed: years ago, Honeydew had a youngish, mournful face, from which his nose jutted like some sort of miserable mistake. Now Honeydew had an older, mournful face. It suited him. He used to look like a boy who had unexpectedly discovered a dead body; now he looked like a man who had judged life and found it wanting.

A moment later Simeon walked into his mother's sitting room. Some of his earliest memories involved interminable lectures delivered in this room. His mother believed in driving her points home with enthusiasm—and repetition. On one occasion she had taken a full hour to inform him that a gentleman does not curl his lip at a portrait of an ancestor. Even if the said ancestor looked like a silly booby in a ridiculous frill.

Like Honeydew, the Dowager Duchess looked the same . . . and yet not the same.

She sat bolt upright on a settee, her skirts occupying whatever space was not taken up by her bottom. He knew little of current women's fashions, though styles had obviously changed since he left England. Yet his mother seemed to be wearing clothing from twenty years ago.

She rose and he saw her embroidered bodice, decorated with a ladder of bows down the front, and revised his estimation: more than twenty years ago. In truth, her costume was precisely as he remembered, from her tall white linen cap to her train. It was only her face that had changed. He remembered her bursting with authority and life, her rosy cheeks and sharp eyes epitomizing the model of duchess-as-general. But now she looked wrinkled and surprised, like an apple gone soft after a winter in the cellar. She looked old.

She extended a hand. He fell to one knee and kissed her beringed finger. "Cosway," she said. "I trust that you recovered your wife from that den of iniquity." He had arrived in London to find alarmed letters directing him to travel immediately to a country house party to rescue Isidore. Which he had done.

"Mother, I missed you these twelve years," he said.

Her eyes sharpened and he saw a trace of the woman he remembered, one who abhorred any display of emotion other than disdain and disappointment.

"Indeed," she said, her voice glacial. Then he remembered how many hundreds—nay thousands—of his comments had been received with that single, damning word. "You will forgive me for doubting your word, since you were at liberty to return at any time."

It was a fair point. "On receiving your note," he offered by way of amelioration, "I traveled to Fonthill. My wife was perfectly fit." He paused for a moment, wondering if he was supposed to report on the state of his bride's virginity.

"I trust you both left the environs immediately."

She folded her hands together. It was almost impossible to see her knuckles due to the flare of jewels. He remembered that about his mother too: she was like a magpie in her delight in shiny things, jewels, gold, silver.

He nodded.

"Where is the duchess? She should be here with you. Your responsibilities to the Cosway line of descent have been sadly neglected."

Simeon couldn't help wondering if his mother intended to monitor how often he visited his wife's bedchamber. "Isidore is in London. She will remain there while I prepare a wedding celebration."

"Wedding! You are married; what need have you for a wedding?"

"We were married by proxy. I should like to celebrate our vows properly."

"Stuff and humbug!" his mother snapped. "That's one and same with those other romantic notions with which you always stuffed your head! Rubbish!"

"Isidore agrees with you."

"Isidore? Isidore? Who is Isidore? Are you, by any chance, referring to your wife, the Duchess of Cosway, by her personal name?"

"Yes."

"Indeed."

Now they were on familiar ground. The groundswell of a lecture rolled toward him. He sat down, remembering a second too late that he should have asked her permission.

But he settled back into his chair rather than spring to his feet. The lecture, which began with his impertinent behavior in referring to his wife by her given name and deviated into the disgraceful, un-English nature of that name (Isidore), swelled like a river in springtime, giving him time to catalog perplexing aspects of his return.

His mother was brilliantly dressed in figured silk. But her chamber had faded, the hangings and upholstery apparently not having been touched since long before his father died three years ago. The house didn't even smell good. There was an underlying miasma that hinted of the privy. Had no one noticed?

He would have returned to England sooner, had there been a problem with money. His solicitor forwarded the estate summary every year and at no time did it indicate a shortage of funds to furbish the house, to pollard the trees, or to keep the fields in good trim.

It was a long hour.

Chapter Three

Revels House
February 22, 1784

"*Where* are you going dressed like that?" The Dowager Duchess of Cosway was no stranger to a shriek, but
on this occasion she excelled. Any reasonable elephant
would have stampeded.

"Running," Simeon answered. For propriety's sake he
had pulled on a simple tunic; he usually ran bare-chested,
dressed only in short trousers.

"Running to what?" his brother Godfrey asked, following their mother into the entry.

It was a reasonable question. Simeon had outrun the
occasional lion (but only with the help of a friendly tree).
He had failed to outrun a crocodile and almost got eaten
as a punishment. There was nothing to outrun in the

prim English countryside that surrounded Revels House; one had the feeling that not even wolves dared intrude on the duchy's herds.

"I just like to run," he explained. "It's excellent exercise and I enjoy it."

His mother and brother spoke at the same moment. "What are those shoes?" Godfrey asked, and "You must stop that practice at once," his mother commanded.

Simeon sighed. "Shall we retire to the drawing room and discuss it?"

"The drawing room?" his mother asked. "With you— with you unclothed as you—" She didn't seem to be able to continue, just flapped her hand in the air.

Godfrey was just the age to be enjoying himself enormously. The only way Simeon could explain the fact that he had a thirteen-year-old brother, when he himself was almost thirty, was to picture his mother and father having a prolonged and energetic marital life. Given that his mother had a look of perpetual outrage and a figure that resembled a cone-shaped beehive, he refused to imagine it.

"You're not clothed," Godfrey said, laughing madly. "I can see your knees!"

"It's easier to run like this," Simeon said. "Would you like to try it? I have several spare trousers of this nature."

"Don't you dare try to contaminate him!" his mother blustered.

"Mother," Simeon said.

"You may address me as Your Grace when we are in public."

"We aren't in public."

"Unless I invite you to my private chambers, we are in public!" she snapped.

Simeon ignored this. "When I return, if you would be so kind as to grant me the honor of an audience for a mere five minutes, I would be most grateful." He swept a bow, a duke's bow.

"The honor of an audience?" Godfrey said. "Do you say that to savages when you meet them, Simeon?"

"Do *not* address the duke with such familiarity," the duchess snapped at Godfrey.

Simeon winked at his brother and pulled open the front door before Honeydew could reach it. Then he tore down the steps, leaving his family temporarily behind.

Two minutes later he was running down a neglected lane behind his estate. The estate could fairly well be summed up by the word *neglected*. He pushed that unpleasant thought away and fell into the physical pleasure of feeling his legs pound against the ground, his heart race, the wind tug his hair back from his head.

He had learned about running for pleasure, rather than for escape, from an Abyssinian mountain king named Bahrnagash. To cross into Abyssinia by the mountain pass, one must appease Bahrnagash. Given that the man was famous for putting strangers to death and dividing their possessions among his tribesmen, Simeon had been a bit concerned.

When Simeon was challenged to a race—the reward for winning being his life and the lives of his men—he thought he had a decent chance. Bahrnagash turned out to be a little man with a close-shaven head, wearing a cowl and a pair of short trousers. He had to be fifty years old. He wore no shoes, and showed no inclination to remove his coarse girdle, into which was stuck a heavy knife. Simeon estimated he could run his way to freedom.

They gathered in the great courtyard of the mountain

fortress. Simeon's cavalcade cheered with all the lusti-
ness of men wildly outnumbered, and picturing themselves sliced open from gullet to gizzard. Bahrnagash's
men cheered with the enthusiasm of men seeing horses
for the first time, and knowing a good thing when they
saw it.

A gun cracked—and Bahrnagash leapt away like a
man possessed. He ran up the pass as if he were a
mountain goat. Simeon ran after, head down, heart
pounding.

Bahrnagash ran straight up, leaping from rock to
rock. Simeon followed, his longer legs allowing him to
cover ground quickly, though his lungs were burning.

Bahrnagash was in his stride now, and they ran on
and on. The air was thin and Simeon's head started
swimming. He thought blearily that he couldn't possibly
win the race, so he might as well die trying.

Three hours later Simeon collapsed. Bahrnagash hesitated, waited, returned. Simeon's chest hurt so much
that he thought there might be blood in his lungs.

After a while, he sat up and asked whether Bahrnagash
intended to stab him and leave his body for the jackals, or
whether they would return to the fortress first.

Bahrnagash was picking his teeth with his great knife.
He grinned, every huge white tooth visible. No chal-
lenger had ever survived three hours, and rather than
kill Simeon, Bahrnagash thought he'd like to have him
in his army.

It took several weeks for Simeon to convince his new
mentor to let him continue into Abyssinia. "No one even
knows why they are fighting in that country," Bahrnagash told him grumpily, "but they always are. They will
have your head for no reason." Simeon didn't bother to
point out that his welcome could hardly be less dangerous than that of the mountain king himself.

When Simeon finally left, he took with him the traditional insignia of a provincial governor, a lasting friendship—and a penchant for running.

Running cleared his mind. It energized his body. He meant to get Godfrey onto the road in the next few days; the poor boy was a bit tubby around the middle. Godfrey needed exercise as much as he needed male companionship.

Simeon let himself run another mile before taking out the fact that his father was dead and thinking about it.

He'd known his father was dead, of course. The news reached him relatively soon after the event, a mere two months after the funeral. Simeon had been traveling through Palmyra, going to Damascus. He had ducked into an English church that loomed up on a Damascene street and offered prayers.

But it wasn't until he walked through the door of Revels House that he really understood. His burly father—the man who had thrown him in the air, and thrown him on a horse, and thrown him out of the hay loft once for gross impertinence—that man was gone.

The house seemed like a dry well, empty and lifeless. His mother had turned into a shrill, screaming dictator. His little brother was plump and indolent. The estate was neglected. Even in the house itself, things were cracked and broken. The rugs were stained; the curtains were faded.

Whose fault is it? asked his conscience.

I'm here now, he retorted.

He was back in England, to clean up the estate, manage his family, meet his wife.

His *wife*.

Another subject that he could examine only cautiously. He'd probably mishandled their first meeting. She was the opposite of what he expected. The Middle

Way taught that beauty was only an outward shell, but Isidore's beauty flared from within, as potent as a torch. She was like a princess, only he'd never seen a princess who had all her teeth.

At the very thought of her he had to slow down, because of confusion in his body about what he wanted to be doing at that moment. Running? Or—

The other.

He adjusted the front of his trousers and started to run faster.

Luncheon began on the wrong foot when Honeydew served bowls of thin broth. Simeon had forgotten that foolish English idea that broth was filling or, indeed, suitable for anyone but a wretched invalid.

He was ravenously hungry, having run an extra hour in a punitive effort to regain control over his body.

"I'll wait for the next course," he told Honeydew.

Honeydew nodded, but Simeon thought he saw anxiety in his eyes. The table was lit with tallow candles fit only for the servants' quarters, so Simeon couldn't see his face very clearly, but the reason for Honeydew's anxiety was soon clear. Next they were each served one paper-thin slice of roast beef.

The following course was even more surprising. Simeon stared down at a sliced hard-boiled egg, across which was drizzled a brownish sauce, and lost his temper.

"Honeydew," he said, keeping his voice even with an effort, "would you be so kind as to detail the menu?"

His mother intervened. "*I* designed the menu, as is necessary and proper. You can thank me, if you wish. This is a dish of *oeufs au lapin*."

"Eggs," Simeon said. "I see that."

"With a sauce made from rabbit."

"Ah."

"Likely you have grown accustomed to rough fare," she commented.

Godfrey was forking up his egg with a sort of desperate enthusiasm that made Simeon wonder about the next course.

There wasn't one.

"You must be joking," Simeon said, incredulous.

"We had eggs and meat in the same meal," his mother said, staring at him. "And a sustaining broth to start. We do not eat lions' flesh in England, you know! Your father and I always kept a moderate table."

"This is not a moderate table," Simeon said. "This is starvation fare."

Godfrey leaned across the table and whispered loudly, "One of the footmen will bring you a large plate of bread and cheese before bed if you wish, Simeon. Sometimes there's drippings as well."

Their mother clearly heard, but she curled her lip and stared at the opposite wall.

No wonder the poor boy was round. Since his mother was not providing the food a growing boy needed, he had learned to hoard like a hungry beggar—and overeat when he had a chance. Simeon turned to the butler. "Honeydew, ask Mrs. Bullock to send whatever she can serve up within a few minutes, and I do not mean bread and cheese."

Honeydew bowed and hastened from the room. His mother huffed and averted her eyes as if Simeon had belched in her presence.

But Godfrey asked, rather shyly, "Have you ever eaten a lion, brother?"

The dowager duchess opened her mouth and Godfrey amended his question, "Your Grace?"

"Not on a regular basis," Simeon said. "There are tribes in the Barbary states who depend on lions as a source of food. I assure you that if they did not eat an occasional lion or two, the lions would multiply and gobble them instead."

It was amazing the way his mother could convey utter disdain without glancing at him or saying a word. He turned back to Godfrey, whose eyes were shining with interest. "I once ate a stew composed of three different lions, as I understood it. It was rather gamey and tough, and not a flavor that I would wish to repeat."

"Have you eaten a snake?"

"No. But—"

"Enough!" their mother said sharply.

That was all the conversation enjoyed at the Duke of Cosway's dinner table.

Chapter Four

Gore House, Kensington
London Seat of the Duke of Beaumont
February 22, 1784

"Do you suppose that if I ordered a particularly enticing nightdress it might arouse him? Or do you suppose
that nothing can arouse him at all? Jemma, do you know
anyone we could ask about male incapability?"

Jemma wrinkled her nose. "*Must* we talk of this over
breakfast, Isidore? Since the poor man has never seen a
nightdress in his life, I advise simplicity. Ribbons rather
than laces, for example. He might not be able to handle
laces."

Isidore looked down at her coddled eggs and felt a little nauseated. "I really do wish my mother were alive."

"What would your mother do in this situation?"

"She would laugh. She used to laugh a great deal. She was Italian, you know, and she thought Englishmen were very foolish. Mind you, my father was Italian and she thought he was just as foolish as the worst Englishman."

"How did she die?"

"They were sailing. A sudden squall came up and swamped their boat." She was able to say it now, years later, without her voice breaking. Which was something of an achievement.

"I'm so sorry," Jemma said. And being Jemma, she looked genuinely sorry.

"At least I have memories of her and Papa. And the aunt who raised me afterwards was truly wonderful."

"Was she from your mother's side?"

"No, she was my father's sister. She accompanied me to the Cosway estate after the funeral; people thought that since I was affianced to a duke, it made sense for his mother to raise me. Since Cosway had reached his eighteenth year, we went through the proxy marriage. But I was clearly miserable living there, so my aunt snatched me away shortly thereafter."

"I can imagine that the duchess must be an appalling companion. I met her only once, but she gave me a strict set-down."

"The duchess—or dowager duchess, rather—does not believe in grief," Isidore said, remembering. "She told me so repeatedly. I think she was quite happy to see the back of me, although she tried to make me return once she learned more of my aunt."

Jemma raised an eyebrow.

"My aunt is a violinist. She told the duchess she would take me to live with my father's relatives in Italy, but in fact we traveled around Europe as she gave concerts. We lived in Venice on and off, but we went farther afield as well, to Prussia, France, Brussels, Prague . . ."

"How unusual." And, after a moment: "The Duchess of Cosway's daughter-in-law in company with a traveling musician." Jemma grinned. "Is your aunt still alive?"

Isidore nodded. "She leads a rather quiet life now. A few years ago she professed herself tired of wandering about Europe. We kept expecting that Cosway would return. So we would say, *one last trip to Vienna!* But somehow there was always another trip, and never a message from Cosway. She moved to Wales when I turned twenty-one."

"By herself?"

"No. She married a painter."

"Really? Anyone I might have heard of?"

Isidore said it reluctantly. "One of the Sargents."

"Not Owen Sargent! The man who painted Lord Lucien Jourdain in the nude with just a bunch of violets?"

"The very one."

"Then you must have seen the portrait," Jemma said, delighted. "Were the violets just where you might expect? And did he wear his wig? I heard so, but I couldn't countenance it."

Isidore sighed. "I don't know how it happened, but I'm so much more strait-laced than my family. Do you know, Jemma, I really didn't wish to see Lord Jourdain without his clothing?"

"Isidore . . ." Jemma said imploringly.

"Of course he wore a wig. And a patch. I remember being surprised by the size of his—ahem—violets." Isidore picked up her cold tea and drank a sip, put it down again. "Perhaps I should follow Cosway to the country and force the question, Jemma. I can strip myself naked in his bedchamber and see how he responds. *If* he responds."

"It depends on how much you wish to be a duchess,"

Jemma replied. "It could be embarrassing for both of you."

"I *do* want to be a duchess. I've thought of myself as a duchess for years. And all those years I told myself that I would accept whatever sort of man the duke turned out to be. I steeled myself to accept a man with one leg, or any number of vices. I just kept telling myself that I wanted to be truly married, to be able to have children, and stop living this half existence."

Jemma nodded. "I absolutely understand, darling."

"So what's the real difference between a one-legged and a mad husband? I can tolerate this sort of derangement on a daily basis. He doesn't hear voices the way Lord Crumple does."

"Good point," Jemma said. "You're wonderfully brave."

"But if Cosway is unable to respond to me . . . perhaps not." Isidore pushed all her eggs to one side of her plate. "I can't imagine myself choosing a consort simply in order to provide an heir. I'm not a very adventuresome woman."

"Most women would not be in your untouched state, given a husband who didn't return from Africa for this many years. You are, as they say in the Bible, a pearl above price."

"I'm a tedious pearl," Isidore said, moving all her eggs across the plate again. "I realized that during my stay at Lord Strange's estate. I don't want to have interesting conversations about French letters, or watch dissolute plays featuring half-naked mythological gods. And I don't want a marriage predicated on my need to find a substitute in the bedchamber."

"Then you should certainly determine if Cosway is capable," Jemma said. "If he is not, you can annul the marriage. If he is, you can resign yourself to his eccentricities."

Isidore nodded. She had read Tacitus on how to conduct a war, and Machiavelli on how to conquer a kingdom. She could launch a campaign so overwhelming that her husband would never know what hit him. The dowager duchess was almost certainly attempting to convince her son to wear clothing befitting a duke. Well, Isidore was going to spend her time trying to get him *out* of those same clothes.

She pushed her plate away. Advance planning was crucial to any plan of war. "If I send a message to Signora Angelico, she will send me a nightdress on an urgent basis."

Jemma grinned. "That's a brilliant trap. A capable man, presented with such a nightdress and your figure inside, will react swiftly. If not . . ."

Isidore reached up and pulled the bell cord to summon her maid. Cosway's days as a bachelor—and a virgin—were numbered.

Chapter Five

Revels House
February 22, 1784

Simeon's father had rarely made use of his study. He was an outdoors sort of man. Simeon's happiest childhood memories were of afternoons spent tramping through wet forests, looking for game.

It made him uneasy to walk into his father's study and sit down behind his great oak desk. He felt as if his father would erupt back into life, bellowing at him. Simeon shook his head. His greatest teacher, Valamksepa, had taught him the importance of maintaining peace by exerting personal control. He could hear the man's soft voice in his ear, telling him that hunger, pain, thirst, lust . . . all of those things were nothing more than insects biting at the soul.

A man walked through life on the path he created for himself. He did not allow pettiness to lead him astray. Valamksepa's teachings had kept Simeon calm in the face of tribal unrest, the death of half his camel-drivers from intestinal fever, and fierce sandstorms. This was nothing in comparison.

Simeon took a deep cleansing breath and sat down, pushing aside stacks of paper. Then he paused and looked again. An undated bill of trading for purchase of thatchery materials, presumably for mending village roofs. He looked at the next one. An imploring letter from a cottager, requesting winter wheat. His mother's spidery handwriting noted, "Done." He glanced through the first ten or fifteen. Only a very few contained his mother's notations; the rest appeared to have been ignored.

Anger is nothing more than the other side of fear . . . and both drive a man to his knees. *A man never falls to his knees from anger, lust, or fear.* The three most dangerous emotions.

Simeon picked up a few more of the papers and read them. Valamksepa had forgotten to speak of guilt.

Hours later, he raised his head from a stack of papers and stared blearily at his butler.

"Your Grace, would you like me to bring you a light breakfast?"

Simeon ran a hand through his hair. "What time is it?"

"Eleven in the morning. Your Grace ought to go to bed," Honeydew said disapprovingly.

Had he really stayed up all night? He had. And yet more papers awaited, stacked in crazy piles around the desk. He'd found a new cache at four in the morning, letters from solicitors pleading for their clients' payments, letters from his father's solicitors containing information about the estate, about investments . . . The only thing that seemed to characterize this particular pile was that they were written on hot-pressed paper rather than foolscap.

Could it be that his mother hadn't responded because she didn't like the type of paper the writers employed?

The very idea of asking her made him want to groan.

"Breakfast," Honeydew prompted.

"Yes."

"No doubt you would like to bathe before eating," the butler said, "I shall order a footman to prepare one for you directly." It wasn't a hint. It was more like a royal command.

"I have a few more papers to read," Simeon said. At some point people in his household would have to stop treating him like the rebellious sixteen-year-old boy he had once been.

A few minutes later he raised his head. "Ah, Honeydew. I forgot to . . ."

"It is now one o'clock," Honeydew informed him.

Simeon looked with some surprise at the tray next to him. Apparently, he'd eaten all the toast without noticing.

"Those papers have been waiting for years, Your Grace. Surely a night or two won't make any difference."

"Some—nay, many—of these papers extend back into the days when my father was alive."

"Ah." The butler's face was utterly inexpressive.

"Yet my father didn't suffer a long illness; he died in a carriage accident. How could—" Simeon bit off the words. It wasn't appropriate to ask the butler why his father had stopped answering estate mail.

And yet it was true. Incredibly, it seemed that his father had made a practice of not paying bills until he absolutely had to, until letters from solicitors reached hysterical and unpleasant depths. He knew. He'd found all the letters. He even thought there was a system to it:

his father paid after the fourth or fifth dunning letter, and then quite frequently only part of the bill.

Apparently tradesmen were so happy to receive a few pence on the pound that they ceased their complaints. It was inconceivable.

Well, perhaps it was conceivable in the case of a man with no substance. Yet the Duke of Cosway could hardly be described as poor.

Simeon kept turning back to the estate books, neatly kept, neatly laid out. The estate was thriving. He couldn't explain how or why. There had been no improvements made in years. His father had fired the estate manager years ago. But it was. He could pay off all the outstanding bills and feel no pinch.

So why had his father done it?

There was only one person who could tell him, and he didn't wish to speak to her.

"Mr. Kinnaird has arrived, Your Grace," Honeydew said.

Thank God. His father had somehow neglected to fire Kinnaird, the manager of his London properties, perhaps because he didn't see him often. "Send him in immediately, please."

Kinnaird entered, bowing. He was a tall, nervous-looking man with a skinny bottom that showed to no great advantage in his short frock-coat. With it he wore horizontally striped stockings, undoubtedly because his valet thought the effect would give his legs more breadth.

"Kinnaird," Simeon snapped, thinking that the man looked like a fool. And then: *A fool to whom I cheerfully dispatched thousands of pounds worth of fabric and jewels over the years.*

His hand tightened under the table, but he made his voice affable enough. "Please, sit down, Mr. Kinnaird. I do apologize for my brusque greeting just now. I find myself worried by the state of Revels House."

"Entirely understandable," Mr. Kinnaird said, rather unexpectedly.

"Could you tell me where all the fabrics and other items that I sent my mother over the years might be found?" Simeon asked.

"The East Warehouse in Southwark," Mr. Kinnaird replied. He pulled out a small black notebook and opened it. "You first sent ten boxes of stuffs from India in 1776, Your Grace. Those were stored in the upper reaches of the warehouse. As they arrived, succeeding goods were numbered and placed in similar shelving. In 1779, we purchased the warehouse, the better to maintain security. It is guarded around the clock, and all goods are dry and free of infestations."

"And the stones and other nonfabric goods?"

"Jewels were sent on two occasions, arriving in England in March 1781 and in November 1783. On neither occasion did I judge our warehouse to be sufficiently secure. Those materials are stowed at Hoare's bank in London. I have here the bills of deposit, co-signed by the bank manager, myself, and the captain of the vessel in question."

"Mr. Kinnaird," Simeon said, "I have misjudged you. I'm afraid that when I entered this house and realized the state it was in, I jumped to the worst of all possible conclusions."

Kinnaird looked about him. "I cannot take offense, Your Grace. The truth is that the dowager duchess did not welcome my visits, nor did she accept the goods you sent for her personal use. I returned those trunks to the warehouse as you will see on the itemized list."

Simeon sat for a moment. "Did she give any explanation?"

"She is rather set in her ways, Your Grace, as I have noticed elderly ladies often are. Perhaps India and Africa seem too distant for her."

"I gather that she did not allow you to act as a man of business for her, given—" he gestured "—the stacks of papers I find here."

"No, Your Grace. She informed me that she would continue to run things precisely as your father had done. I did inform you of this in a letter, Your Grace."

"Not every letter reached me," Simeon said, staring sightlessly at the piles of foolscap covering his father's desk.

"No, Your Grace. Of course."

"Well, Mr. Kinnaird," Simeon said finally, "could I ask you to return to London and arrange for transfer of the goods I intended as gifts? They can be transported here. I am in the process of directing payment of all overdue bills."

Kinnaird cleared his throat. "I should inform you that Mr. Honeydew occasionally forwarded bills to me that had to be paid and naturally I took care of them."

"You mean he would steal them from this table and send them to you in London?"

"That allowed the household to keep running, Your Grace," Kinnaird said.

It wasn't easy to accept that one's mother has lost her mind. Gone uncooked. Thrown her pancakes to the roof. However you want to put it.

"Very good, Kinnaird," he said. He paused. "Have the servants' wages been raised since my father died?"

"No, my lord. Nor for some years before that sad event. However, I took the liberty of giving each of them a Boxing Day present that brought their wages to near-current rates. Again, Mr. Honeydew was invaluable in this respect."

"As were you, Mr. Kinnaird."

Kinnaird's knees turned inwards and he gave an odd little bob that Simeon thought indicated pleasure. "Thank you, Your Grace."

Simeon felt like going for another run, but instead he made his way to his mother's chambers and knocked on the door.

She was sitting before a small secretary at her window. Simeon realized with a sinking heart that her desk, too, was stacked with sheaves of paper.

He dropped into the bow that she required, waited while she held out her hand to be kissed, waited while she arranged herself in a chair and motioned him to another. Though they were in the country, and surely not expecting morning callers, she wore a high powdered wig hung with teardrop pearls.

"You have come, of course, to apologize," she said, folding her hands. "I expected as much from your father's son."

When had his mother's voice become so high and quavering? When had she developed that slight hitch in her step? When had she become so *old?*

"Mother," he began.

She raised her hand. "I see no reason that you, a duke, should address me by a term suitable for a schoolboy's use."

"Your Grace," he started over. "I am concerned about the state of the paperwork in the study."

"You needn't worry about that," she said, bestowing him with a gracious smile. "I took care of everything regularly. I was brought up to manage a large estate, and I have continued to do so since your father's death. In every case I noted the instructions I gave Honeydew, so that you have a thorough record."

"There are some unpaid bills," he observed.

"Only if the bill was absurd."

"Perhaps I do not grasp the problem. The local candle-maker, for example, does not appear to have been paid in over a year."

"A case in point. How on earth could we have used two hundred tallow candles? Acting as the guardian of your estate, I could not allow chicanery to continue. Either the servants are stealing candles, or the chandler is defrauding us. Either way, the bill remains unpaid until I am satisfied about the matter. Your father was very firm, very firm indeed, when it came to matters of thievery. He couldn't abide a thief!"

"Of course not," Simeon murmured. "Do you have any idea, Mother, why he didn't pay the estate bills? There are a great number unanswered, from well before his death."

"Only the thieves," she said dismissively. "They charge us double, you know, because of the title. They think they can get away with robbery because the duke-dom is so well respected."

He doubted that. In fact, he had no doubt but that the majority of the people living around the duchy loathed the name, seeing that they had been defrauded of proper payments for years.

"And now . . . your apology." She looked at him expectantly.

For the life of him, he didn't know what he was supposed to apologize for.

He cleared his throat.

"You are just like your father!" she exclaimed. "I used to have to instruct him in the precise wording of this sort of thing as well. You have come to apologize for the dissolute manner by which you showed your lower limbs not only to myself, but to the household staff. The lower orders are highly susceptible."

"Susceptible to what?"

"Immorality and vice, of course."

"And my bare knees?"

"Your knees, Cosway, are not only unattractive but uninteresting. I am certain that the footmen would rather not see them, and neither would I."

"And the immorality thereof?" Simeon enquired.

"To be unclothed before the lower orders, except in necessary situations, is to be avoided at all costs."

"I apologize for my bare knees," Simeon said obediently. "Your Grace, would you like me to take care of such correspondence as you are unable to manage?" He nodded toward the desk.

His mother raised an eyebrow. "Do I appear to be an invalid? No? Well, then, why on earth would I wish you to take care of my correspondence?"

"I merely thought—"

"Don't," his mother said magisterially. "There is rather too much thinking going on in this household. Honeydew has always been prone to thought, and I'm sure it's bad for his digestion, as I've told him time and again."

Poor Honeydew, Simeon thought. Probably spent a bit too much time thinking about how to pay bills. Guilt curdled his stomach. "Now you must forgive me," he said, rising.

She shrieked. Simeon dropped back into his seat.

"You may not rise while I am seated," she said, patting her chest. "Nor may you leave until I dismiss you."

Simeon ground his teeth. "I must needs retire, Your Grace."

"Well, why didn't you say so?" She came to her feet nimbly enough. "You are dismissed."

He bowed and left, feeling as angry—and as small—as a schoolboy.

Chapter Six

Revels House
February 24, 1784

The next morning the weather changed, and with it the odor in the house swelled and grew to a stench, the kind that reached out, grabbed a man's breath, and took it away. It wasn't that Simeon hadn't smelled it—or worse—before. But he hadn't expected to smell it in his own home.

He was literally staring down into a pile of shit. He dragged a hand through his hair and turned to Godfrey.

"What the hell is this?"

"The water closet?" Godfrey said.

"I see that." He would have loved to summon up withering sarcasm, but he was too tired.

Godfrey leaned over and showing extreme bravery,

peered down the hole. "Loathsome smell. I hate the water closets. The servants' privy behind the kitchen gardens is much better."

"So you're telling me they're all like this?"

"Yes. They're always worse on damp days and it's raining today. You should smell the house after ten days' rain."

"They're not working," Simeon said flatly. "Water closets are supposed to have *water* running through them. These need to be cleaned out."

The concept had clearly never entered Godfrey's mind. "I don't think Honeydew would like one of the footmen to go down there," he said. "They might never come back up. Do you know what we pay a footman?"

Simeon sighed. He knew precisely how much a footman should be paid for a year's work—and the Cosway estate had been paying approximately half of that amount. "Footmen don't do this sort of work. I believe iron-workers do."

"Iron-workers?" Godfrey sounded puzzled, as well he might be. Clearly, no iron-worker had lifted a finger to the pipes in years.

"We need help." He was going to have to postpone the wedding until the spring. Simeon raked his hand through his hair again. God knows what Isidore would make of that announcement. He could hardly tell her that his mother had become so tight-fisted that the water closets hadn't been cleaned since the days of good Queen Bess.

"Do you suppose," Godfrey said tentatively, "that we could possibly have a proper water closet? Do you remember the Oglethorpes in the next county? Rupert showed me their new water closet. It's all marble. I mean, we couldn't afford anything like that, but perhaps running water?"

Simeon backed out of the privy. "Godfrey, we can have the whole house kitted up in marble if you wish."

Godfrey was at the stage where his legs were almost as long as the rest of him. He trotted along beside Simeon. "What do you mean?"

"We have a large, thriving estate," he said, glancing at his little brother.

His eyes were round and his mouth was open. "Mother said we should never discuss the question of substance."

"Why not?"

"It's not proper."

"It's not proper to have a house stink like a pigsty in summer," Simeon said witheringly. He couldn't criticize his mother to her face, nor yet to her child's. But he could point out the facts. "This is an extremely profitable estate. My wanderings resulted in a second fortune. We can have running water piped into every room, though I wouldn't know why we'd want to."

Godfrey stumbled and almost fell over.

Simeon stopped. "Why aren't you at Eton?" he said, something finally clicking in his brain.

"We can't afford it," Godfrey said. "I've been teaching myself since mother dismissed my tutor."

"Aw . . . *shit!*"

Having left Godfrey wide-eyed at the idea that he would be attending Eton in the fall, Simeon walked back into the study and sat down. In front of him was a letter from a Mr. Pegg, requesting to be paid for the work he did between 1775 and 1780. Mr. Pegg had shoed the duke's horses, as well as kept the carriages in good repair. And while the Peggs had long served the Dukes of Cosway, he was afraid that he would no longer be able to . . .

Simeon picked up the letter and walked upstairs to his mother's parlor. He went through all the elaborate rigmarole that prefaced a simple conversation with her: the bows, the kisses, the request to sit, etc.

"Your Grace," he began.

But his mother raised a hand. "A lady initiates the subject of conversation, Cosway."

He gritted his teeth.

"I want you to promise that you will be on your best behavior so that your wife is not frightened away by your oddness."

"I shall do my best," Simeon said woodenly. "I intend to travel to London tomorrow and beg her pardon; I'm afraid that our wedding celebration must be delayed."

"I shall send a letter with you," she announced. "I shall inform her that you suffered a brain fever. You will do me the great courtesy to confirm this account."

Simeon blinked. "A brain fever?"

"Indeed. Everyone knows that brain fevers are common in foreign parts. It could explain so much." She leaned forward. "Your wife is a kindly woman. It is true that she and I had some difficulties living in the same house; she was a headstrong and sometimes impudent girl with an odd habit of song. I found it onerous to have her about me. But I'm sure all will be different now that she has reached an advanced age."

"A brain fever?" Simeon repeated.

"To explain yourself," she said. Then she added, obligingly: "You." With a wave of her hand.

"Me."

"Look at yourself, Cosway. You don't look like a duke. You look like some sort of minor accountant. You have none of the easy carriage of a true aristocrat. There are dark circles under your eyes, ink on your cuff. You wear no wig and no powder, you are inappropriately dressed, and although I have managed to coerce you into an appropriate level of manners when approaching me, I am not such a fool as to think you would be able to carry off such a trained dog show in front of others.

"In short, I need a story to present to the *ton*." She leaned forward again with an audible creaking of whalebone. "Are you sure that you *didn't* suffer a brain fever, Cosway?"

Simeon wished that Valamksepa were in his place right now. It would be interesting to see whether the guru could maintain his composure. After all, now that Simeon thought about it, Valamksepa sat about in a tent doing his teaching. It was a nice, clean tent, without a duchess in sight. Easy to banish anger in those circumstances.

"No, Mother," he said through clenched teeth. "I was lucky enough to escape brain fevers. This is simply the way I am."

"Indeed, so I thought." An ominous pause: "The brain fever will explain everything."

"There was no brain fever."

"There is now!" She indicated a stack of sealed letters. "I've informed everyone of your precarious health. I'd like you to frank these letters at your earliest convenience. My acquaintances will be kind, Cosway. Noblemen are kind to each other."

"Mother, can you explain why Mr. Pegg's bill for shoeing the horses and maintaining the carriages was never paid?"

"Pegg? Pegg? Who's that?"

"The Pegg family has acted as blacksmiths to the Dukes of Cosway for generations, or so he tells me."

"Or so he tells you!" she said, pouncing on it like a cat on a mouse. "Ay, there's the rub! They'll say anything. Don't pay it! Make him show you the work before you give him a ha'penny."

"The work was done four years ago."

"Well, a good blacksmith's work would endure a mere four years. If it hasn't, then you needn't pay him on the grounds of shoddy work."

"If you'll excuse me, Mother, I must return to the study."

"I shan't excuse you just yet," she said. "Honeydew informs me that you find the water closets inadequate in some way."

"Yes. They stink."

She bridled, but it was his turn to raise his hand. "They *stink*, Mother. And the reason they stink is that Father installed water closets throughout this house and then neglected to have them cleaned out. The pipes must have burst years ago. Water is no longer running through the drains; they must be cleaned."

Her face was rigid with anger. "The duke did everything just as he ought!"

"He ought to have had the pipes cleaned once a year. Honeydew tells me that Father judged it an untoward expense. Why, I can't tell. But the odor that infects this entire house is the result. For God's sake, it smells worse in a duke's house than it does in a Bombay slum!"

"You have no right to speak to me in that pestering fashion! The duke installed the water closets in good faith. The pipes were created of such inferior material that they fell to pieces."

"Why didn't father have them repaired?"

"He demanded the pipes be repaired, naturally!"

"I expect he hadn't paid for the original work," Simeon said.

"He had paid more than a reasonable amount, given the slip-shod work that was done. As witnessed by the fact that the drainage failed almost immediately. He was correct not to pay those thieving rascals!"

"Indeed." He rose, ignoring the question of protocol. "I wish I could find it in my heart to believe that was the truth. You have my apologies." He bowed and left, closing the door quietly behind him.

Chapter Seven

Gore House, Kensington
London Seat of the Duke of Beaumont
February 26, 1784

The carriage drew up at the Beaumonts' townhouse at precisely ten o'clock. Simeon knew because he had timed it to perfection. He was used to planning expeditions like minor military excursions, accounting for wayward tribes, robbers, sandstorms. In England, the road was smooth, the carriage functioned, nary a thief lurked to bring down his horses. He arrived in London the night before, woke up at dawn and waited for the appropriate hour to pay a call on his wife. It was all easy.

And nothing was easy.

For one thing he had to tell his wife, who already

thought he was cracked, that their wedding had to be delayed. Again.

Isidore was undoubtedly contemplating annulment, and perhaps he should just let that happen. They could both find more suitable mates.

She wasn't what he pictured.

When he thought about his wife—and he had, now and then—he remembered a portrait of a sweet-faced little girl, dressed as richly if she were a Renaissance princess. That was why his father had arranged the marriage, of course. The Del'Finos were rich as Croesus and his father wanted her dowry, and never mind the fact that his son was a child when the original contracts were drawn up.

Simeon had readily approved the proxy wedding when he was eighteen and far away in India. He had just begun studying with Valamksepa, and he refused to come home merely so that his father could draw down the second half of a dowry attached to a bride whom he'd never met. He spent the next three years in rigorous solitude, learning endurance, manliness, the Middle Way. He had learned to create an oasis of calm around himself, no matter what happened on his right or his left.

But now that he was back in England, it all seemed complicated. One look at Isidore had dispelled his image of a sweet-faced child bride.

She *was* like a Renaissance princess. Or a queen like Cleopatra.

She was the most sensual woman he'd ever seen in his life, and he had the women of the Sultan of Illa's harem for comparison.

If Isidore put on a gauzy dress and a couple of bracelets, she would have thrown the sultan's first wife into the shade. She was ravishing, with a mouth like a ripe cherry and a body that would make a eunuch weep. She was not what he expected in a wife.

In truth, she was not what he *wanted* in a wife.

Wandering the East for years had taught him a few things about women and men, and all his conclusions led in one direction: it was much easier for a man if he had a docile wife.

Somehow, without even noticing it, he'd fashioned Isidore into the picture of that wife. Shy, sweet, veiled. Of course he'd been offered women—and women had offered themselves—numerous times over his adult life.

But they had never been tempting enough to overcome the teachings of Valamksepa. *Lust,* he had said repeatedly, *is at the heart of many evils.* Simeon had to admit that he probably would have brushed aside the question of evil, except for his inherent dislike of disease. For all he told Isidore that it was a moral decision, he didn't bother with fooling himself.

He liked to be healthy. Very healthy. And a man has only to be in the East for a day before he becomes aware of just what a syphilitic face looks like without a nose. Or he hears a joke about a private member dropping off the body.

He decided early that it wasn't worth it. The women he was offered were members of harems. The women who offered themselves were regularly partaking in all sorts of interesting bedroom activities, with a variety of partners.

He could wait.

And he had waited.

Imagining, all the time, his cool, docile wife . . . the one who would have to be coaxed into kissing him, the one who would scream faintly at the sight of his body. In the month after he decided to return to England, he ran miles across the desert at night, curbing his body, preparing himself for careful, delicate advances to a terrified woman.

Idiot that he was.

His wife burned with sensuality. When he first met her she was wearing a gown that fit like a glove. It was the color of rain in the summer, and it sparkled with tiny diamonds. She had them in her hair too, and on her slippers. Everything about her said, *I am delicious. I am expensive. I am a duchess.*

And everything about her face said, *I don't want to be a virgin.*

The front door to the Duke of Beaumont's house opened and a footman trotted down the steps. Simeon's groomsmen had already leapt down and were surrounding the carriage, rigidly at attention, like tin soldiers.

Isidore greeted him at the door to the sitting room. She wasn't the kind to wait sedately in a chair for a man's arrival. She was dressed in a gown that resembled a man's military costume. Huge flaps at the shoulders narrowed to a point at her waist before the skirts belled out again, over panniers, he supposed. He'd seen a few women wearing those in the last few years—mostly missionaries' wives, trying to preserve a ridiculous way of life while living in the wilds.

But on Isidore he suddenly understood the fashion. It was made to draw a man's eyes to the waist. Her impossibly small, delicate waist. And then above that, to the way her breasts swelled, with no hoops, just delicious, pink flesh against the military braid of her—

He wrenched his eyes away.

What was he doing? He didn't care about women's clothing. Nor the body within. Valamksepa would say such things were mere frivolities.

"Good morning, Isidore," he said, once the door closed behind the butler.

"Duke," she said, with a bend of her head.

"Even my mother didn't address my father with such formality in private."

"Good morning, Cosway," she said, meeting his eyes. Her eyes were almond-shaped, and so beautiful that his heart skipped a beat.

A pulse of annoyance followed directly afterwards.

He didn't want a wife so beautiful that every jackal for miles would be slavering at her heels. No wonder his mother started babbling when she learned that Isidore was at Lord Strange's house party. Every hound in five countries must have been sniffing after her.

One might worry whether she had lost her virginity— but no. Isidore's eyes were clear and true. Disdainful . . . annoyed . . . virginal. She had waited for him. There was something about that fact that gave him a queer feeling.

"My given name is Simeon," he said.

"We hardly know each other." Once you got past her beauty, there was another thing about her. She was angry.

He'd spent years curbing his bodily impulses—but every inch of his body was telling him like a drumbeat, *she's yours, yours, yours . . . take her!* Every bit of native caution, learned from years of dangerous living, was on the alert.

He could do without her.

It would ruin the quality and calmness of his life to have Isidore Del'Fino as a wife. She had turned around and was now sitting down on a little sofa, pulling off her gloves. Her fingers were slender, beautiful, pink-tipped.

"Do you know," he said, sitting down opposite her, "I think we should discuss the question of annulment."

She gasped, her eyes flew to his, and one of her gloves dropped to the floor.

"You must have thought of it," he said, more gently. He picked up her glove and dropped it back in her lap.

"Of course."

"If you would like an annulment, I would not stand in your way."

She blinked at him for a moment, and then said, "I don't understand you."

He didn't understand himself. He'd been offered one of the most beautiful women on three continents, and he was throwing her away. But she was trouble. The skin prickling all over his body told him that . . . as much trouble as he'd ever encountered, and that included the crocodile who almost chewed off his toes.

"I know that I behaved in an extraordinarily ungracious way, wandering around foreign parts and not returning to consummate our marriage. The least I can do is offer you another option, should you wish to take it. My mother has made it vehemently clear that I am unfit to marry a proper gentlewoman."

Her eyes rested on his trousers. He wasn't wearing breeches. He didn't mind baring his lower leg when he was running, but he simply couldn't get used to slipping into stockings. His mother had shrieked, of course. Apparently no one wore trousers except for artisans and eccentrics.

He had replied with the obvious truth: it seemed that he was an eccentric.

"Eccentrics and robbers!" his mother had added. "Yet even they wear *white* trousers!"

"I am wearing a cravat," he said to Isidore now.

He couldn't read her face. She had obviously noted the fact that he wasn't wearing hair powder or a wig. "I tried on a wig with three rows of little snail shells over the ear. I looked like a lunatic."

There was just a suspicion of a smile at the corner of her mouth. If he could find rubies that color, he would . . .

"Do you wear color on your lips?" he asked.

She shot him a look. "Why? Are you averse to women wearing face paint?"

"No, why should I be?" he said, surprised.

She seemed to relax. "There are men who consider themselves an apt judge of what a woman should or shouldn't wear on her face."

"I'm hardly the one to complain," Simeon said, "given as I do not conform to all the customs of an English gentleman."

"Obviously."

"My mother tells me that I greatly underestimated your complaint regarding Nerot's Hotel and that, in fact, ladies stay in such establishments only while traveling outside London. I had no idea from your protest that the experience was prohibited for women."

"Is it my fault, then? I should have been more vehement?"

Simeon opened his mouth. Paused. "I should have listened to you?" he suggested.

There was a hint of a smile on her lips. "You must have worn a cravat at Eton."

"Of course I did. But that feels like a lifetime ago. I am who I am because of the places I have been. And Eton is just a tiny kernel of my past. I'm fond of English seasons. There were times in the midst of the desert when I almost cried to remember how beautiful our rain can be. But the core of me was shaped by the deserts of Abyssinia, by the sands of India."

She sighed.

"I know," he said, nodding. "That's why I thought it was better to bring up the question of annulment rather than let it fester silently between us."

"Why don't you wish to marry me?" she asked bluntly, looking up at him.

He opened his mouth but she raised her hand. "Please don't tell me once again that you are offering me an annulment for my sake. I know precisely the weight you put on my opinion; it was eloquently expressed by your absence in the past years."

He deserved that. And she deserved the truth.

"I am beautiful," she added with a pugnacious kind of honesty that suggested it was second nature to her. "I am a virgin. And we are married. So why would you wish to annul that ceremony?"

"The desert changed me."

She waited, and he had the feeling that it was only by a masterful effort of self-control that she didn't curl her lip. Well, it did sound insane. Put that together with his virginity . . . "I met a great teacher named Valamksepa, when I first traveled to India. He taught me a great deal about what it means to be a man."

"Ah," she said. "A man is obviously not defined by his wig or his legs. So do tell me, what is the measure of a man?"

Her voice was calm, but underneath were banked fires. He was right to annul the marriage.

"A man is measured by his ability to control himself," he said, not allowing the scorn in her eyes to shake him. "I wish to be the sort of man who never falls prey to his baser emotions."

She looked a little confused.

"Anger," he told her. "Fear. Lust."

"You want to avoid anger? How will you do that?"

He grinned. "Oh, I feel anger. The key is not to act on it, not to let it affect me or become an intrinsic part of my life."

"But what has this to do with me?"

They'd reached the stickler. "I was taught," he said carefully, "that a man comes to his life with many choices. Only a fool believes that fate gives him his hand of cards. We make decisions every day."

"And?"

"Marriage is one of the most important. If you and I were to marry—really marry—I would want to undergo the marriage ceremony with you because it marks that important decision. It was something I should never have left to a proxy. Those are *my* vows to make and to keep."

"Or not to make at all," she said flatly. "The fact is, Cosway, that your decision after meeting me is not to make those vows. Am I right?"

"I—"

"You were initially happy to go through with a wedding ceremony," she said. "Yet now you talk of annulment."

She was playing with her glove again, pulling the fingers straight. A flare of fire went up from his belly. That small hand was—*his*. His to unglove, his to kiss, his to . . . His.

He glanced down at his coat to make sure it was thoroughly buttoned. "You are not what I expected," he said bluntly. "My mother sent me a miniature once we were married. That's how I recognized you at Strange's house."

"I remember. I sat for it while I was still living with your mother."

"You looked sweet and docile. Fragile, really."

Isidore's eyes narrowed.

She had suddenly realized precisely why her so-called husband had initiated talk of annulments. He didn't think she was sweet or docile. And he was right.

"My parents had both died several months before the portrait was painted," she pointed out. "Likely I was fragile. Am I to apologize that I have now recovered from that event?"

"Of course not. I was merely explaining my mistaken impression."

Isidore just stopped herself from tossing her head like an offended barmaid. "During my brief time in your mother's house, she continually expressed her doubt that I would develop the qualities of a good wife. I gather you agree."

"I'm afraid that she turned her wish into reality."

"What do you mean?"

"She's written to me regularly over the years, far more so than you have, I might add."

Her mouth did drop open and she leapt to her feet. "You dare to criticize me for not writing you!"

"I didn't mean to criticize—" Simeon said, rising as well.

Isidore took a step toward him. "You? You who never wrote me even a line? You who sent the letters I did write you straight to your solicitors, since I received answers from *them*? You dare suggest I should have written you more frequently?"

There was a moment of silence. "I didn't think of it in that fashion."

"You didn't think of it. You didn't think of writing to your *wife?*"

"You're not really my wife."

With that, Isidore completely lost her temper. "I bloody well am your wife! I am the only wife you have, and let me tell you, annulment will not be an easy business.

What kind of fool are you? When you agreed to that proxy marriage, you agreed to having a *wife*. I was there, even if you weren't. The ceremony was binding!"

"I didn't mean that."

It only made her more furious that he showed no signs of getting angry himself. She took a deep breath. "Then what precisely *did* you mean?"

"I suppose I have a queer idea of marriage."

"That goes without saying," Isidore snapped.

"I've seen a great deal of marriage. And I've spent a great deal of time assessing which marriages are the most successful. It seems absurdly obtuse, but for some reason I thought I had one of those marriages."

"You just said," Isidore noted with exaggerated patience, "that we weren't married at all. With whom did you have this perfect marriage?"

"Well, with you. Except it wasn't really *with* you; I see that now. The combination of that miniature and my mother's descriptions—"

"Just what did your mother say about me?" Isidore demanded.

He looked at her.

"You might as well tell me the worst."

"She never said a bad thing about you."

"Now I am surprised."

"She painted you as the very image of a perfect English gentlewoman: sweet, docile, perfect in every way."

Isidore gasped.

"You are particularly skilled with needlework, and sometimes stay up half the night stitching seams for the poor. But when you aren't engaged in charitable activities, you knot silk laces that are as light as cobwebs."

"What?" she said faintly, dropping back into her chair.

"Light as cobwebs," Cosway repeated, reseating himself as well. "I remember actually considering whether I should request further details. I was establishing a weaving factory in India."

"You were—*what?*"

"Weaving. You know, silks."

"I thought you were wandering around the Nile."

"Well, that too. But I'm afflicted by curiosity. I can't go to a new place without wanting to figure out how things are made, and how they might be made better. That leads to shipping them here and there, generally back to England for sale."

"You're a merchant," Isidore said flatly. "Does your mother know of this development?"

He thought about it. "I have no idea. I expect not."

"I truly feel sorry for her. You do realize that I wasn't even living with her during the time when she wrote all those letters describing my domestic virtues?"

"A revelation I find, sadly, unsurprising. I'm afraid my arrival has been a terrible shock to my mother. All the time she was sending me letters about my submissive, chaste wife—"

"I am chaste!" Isidore flashed.

He met her eyes. "I know that."

A flare of heat went straight down her back to her legs. "So you thought I was a meek little Puritan—"

"Tame," he said, nodding. There was an annoying hint of a smile in his eyes. "Meek and obedient."

"Your mother has much to answer for."

"I formed a picture of our marriage based on that wife."

"Who doesn't exist."

He nodded, but his face sobered. "You're obviously far more intelligent than the pliable woman my mother described, Isidore. So I have to tell you that from what

I've seen in the world, the best marriages are those in which a man's wife is—well, biddable."

Isidore felt her temper rising again but pushed it down. What could she expect? He may not have the outward trappings of an English gentleman, but he was voicing what many a man believed.

"I agree," she said. "Although I would broaden the category. Were I to choose my own spouse, for example, I would like him to be, shall we say, civilized?"

His teeth were very white against his golden skin when he smiled. "Meek and obedient, in other words?"

"Those are not popular words among men. But I could see myself with a husband who was more quiet than myself. I have—" she coughed "—a terrible temper."

"No!"

"All this sarcasm can't be good for you," she said. "You told me in the carriage that you like your every utterance to be straightforward."

He laughed. "I can see you riding roughshod over some poor devil of a husband."

"I wouldn't," she said, stung. "We could simply discuss things together. And come to an agreement that didn't involve my opinion losing ground to his simply because I was his wife."

"That's reasonable. But the truth of it is that you would smile at him, and crook your finger, and the man would come to you as tame as a lapdog."

Isidore shook her head. "It's not the sort of relationship you would understand."

"I shall enjoy seeing you engage in it. *If* we annul our marriage and I can watch some other fellow experiencing it with you. Naturally I would repay your dowry with ample interest."

So he didn't want to come anywhere near her. Isidore was so stoked by rage that she could hardly speak. She was being rejected—*rejected!*—by her husband after waiting for him for years. She got up again and walked a few steps away, the better to regain control of her face.

"I think it's important in any relationship that there be a clearly designated leader," he was saying. "And I would rather be the leader in my own marriage." Then he added: "If you don't mind, Isidore, I won't rise this time."

Cosway would rather annul the marriage than marry her.

She waited for that news to sink in, but the only thing she could feel was the beating of her heart, anger and humiliation driving it to a rapid tattoo.

"As it happens," she said, schooling her voice to calm indifference with every bit of strength she had, "Jemma gave me the direction of the Duke of Beaumont's solicitor in the Inns of Court. I shall make inquiries as to how we go about an annulment."

There was a flash of something in his eyes. What? Regret? Surely not. He sat there, looking calm and relaxed, like a king on his throne. He was throwing her away because she wasn't a docile little seamstress, because she would make him angry.

Angry—and lustful. That was something to think about. She could unclothe herself right here, in the drawing room, and then he would *have* to marry her, but that would be cutting off her nose to spite her face. Why would she bind herself in marriage to a man like this? With these foolish ideas learned in the desert?

"Why don't we make a trip there tomorrow afternoon?" he was asking now.

Isidore refused to allow his eagerness to visit the solicitor to throw her further into humiliation. He was a fool, and she'd known that since the moment she met him.

It would be better to annul the marriage.

She sat down opposite him, reasonably certain that her face showed nothing more than faint irritation. "I have an appointment at eleven tomorrow morning with a mantua-maker to discuss intimate attire."

"Intimate what?"

"A nightdress for my wedding night," she said crushingly.

"If we visit the solicitor first, I would be happy to accompany you to your appointment."

Isidore narrowed her eyes, wondering about the look on her husband's face. She was no expert, but it didn't look like a man who was in control of his lust.

There were three things that no man was supposed to act on, weren't there? Anger, lust . . . and an idea of marriage that included what?

Oh yes.

An intelligent woman within a ten-foot radius.

That must be where *fear* came in.

Chapter Eight

Gore House, Kensington
London Seat of the Duke of Beaumont
February 26, 1784

"Your Grace."

Jemma, Duchess of Beaumont, looked up from her chess board. She had it set out in the library, in the hopes that her husband would come home from the House of Lords earlier than expected. "Yes, Fowle?"

"The Duke of Villiers has sent in his card."

"Is he in his carriage?"

Fowle inclined his head.

"Do request his presence, if he can spare the time."

Fowle paced from the library as majestically as he had entered. It was a sad fact, Jemma thought, that her butler resembled nothing so much as a plump village priest, and yet he clearly envisioned himself as a duke. Or perhaps even a king. There was a touch of *noblesse oblige* in the way he tolerated Jemma's obsession with chess, for example.

Naturally, the Duke of Villiers made a grand entrance. He paused for a moment in the doorway, a vision in pale rose, with black-edged lace falling around his wrists and at his neck. Then he swept into a ducal bow such as Fowle could only dream of.

Jemma came to her feet feeling slightly amused and thoroughly delighted to see Villiers. She used to think that he had the coldest eyes of any man in the *ton*. And yet as she rose from a deep curtsy and took his hands, she revised her opinion. His eyes were black as the devil's nightshirt, to quote her old nanny. And yet—

"I have missed you during my sojourn at Fonthill," he said, raising her hand to his lips.

Not cold.

His thick hair was tied back with a rose ribbon. He looked pale but healthy, presumably recovered from the duel that nearly killed him a few months before. She felt a small pulse of guilt: the duel had been won by her brother, after which he summarily married Villiers's fiancée. Much though Jemma loved her new sister-in-law, she wished that the relation could have been won without injuring her favorite chess partner.

"Come," she said, leading him to the fire. "You're still too thin, you know. Should you be upright?"

"I could challenge you for that insult. I've knocked on death's privy and came back to tell the tale, and you're saying I'm too thin?"

She grinned at him. "Do say that you came to play chess with me? It has been over a month since your fever broke, and that was the length of time for which your doctor issued an embargo on the game, was it not?"

He sat opposite her. She leaned forward, began rearranging the pieces; his large hand came over hers. "Not chess," he said.

"Not—chess?" If not chess, what? She knew him to be a master at the game, just as she was. What did a master do, but play? "I thought your doctor decreed merely a month without chess; have I mistaken the date?"

He leaned his head back against the chair. "I've gone off the game."

"Impossible!"

"Believe it. I missed it at first, of course. I dreamed of chess pieces, of moves, of games I played or thought I played. But then slowly the urge left me. I've decided to take another month at least before returning to the board."

"You're voluntarily eschewing chess?"

His smile was a bit rueful. "I can tell you that it lengthens the days. How do people occupy themselves if they're not chess players?"

Jemma shook her head. "I've never known. So how is the party at Fonthill? Wait! Tell me about Harriet." And she held her breath, not knowing if Villiers was aware that her friend Harriet was having an *affaire* with the owner of Fonthill, Lord Strange.

"Happy," he said, "with Strange. But I'm afraid the festivities are dimmed at the moment, as Strange's daughter is quite gravely ill. I felt it was rude to tax the household with my presence under the circumstances, so I slipped away. I shall return in a day or two when, one hopes, the crisis will be over."

"Oh dear! What sort of illness has she?"

"A fever caused by a rat bite," Villiers said. "But the girl is apparently quite strong, and the doctor is sanguine that all will be well. Harriet is spending her time in the sickroom."

"Of course Harriet would do that," Jemma said. "It's the *affaire* with Strange that I can't imagine. Isidore said that the air scorched around them."

He raised an eyebrow. "I had no idea that the duchess was so poetic in her assessments. I gather Strange and Harriet are in love, a foreign emotion for me." His eyes rested on Jemma. "And how are you?"

She smiled faintly. "Not in love."

"But not unhappy?"

"No."

He seemed to take some answer from that, perhaps to a question he wasn't ready to put into words, for he nodded.

"So what of our match?" she asked, surprised by her own keen disappointment in his refusal of chess.

"One move a day . . . that match?"

"Yes, *that* match," she said. "Do you have so many outstanding matches that you don't remember? To bring it to your recollection, I have won one game, and you have won one game. That leaves one game to break the tie."

"I *do* remember now," he said, watching her under his eyelids. "Let me see . . . if our match went to a third game, the last one was to be played blindfolded and in bed."

"Precisely." Jemma folded her hands. "I'm so happy that it's come back to you. I have been training my maid, Brigitte, so she can stand next to the bed and move our pieces appropriately."

"I did not picture the bedchamber occupied by others than ourselves."

"Life is positively full of disappointments."

"Precisely so. I'm sure your maid could use more training. I'd prefer not to play chess for at least another month. Besides, I must return to Fonthill; I didn't even say goodbye."

"I feel like an old drunk who'd been sitting on a pub stool next to a man for thirty years, only to be told his comrade has chosen sobriety," Jemma said, feeling distinctly nettled.

"Chess is better than alcohol . . . more addictive, more inflammatory, more intelligent."

She looked at him for a moment, and the edge of her mouth curled up. "You'll play again."

"I will trust you to wait for me."

"I was never very good at waiting for men." Jemma was startled to hear the words come from her mouth. In one sense, she meant her husband. She waited three years for Elijah to fetch her from Paris when they were young, after she had flung herself across the Channel in a rage. He didn't visit until the fourth year, and by then it was too late. She had found a lover, and put her marriage behind her.

Villiers's heavy-lidded eyes dropped. "I, on the other hand, am very good at waiting. For you, Jemma . . . I would wait quite a long time."

Jemma woke up. The conversation was happening— perhaps had been happening—on two levels for quite a while and she only now realized it. "Beaumont should be home from Lords within the hour," she said, watching him. "Will the two of you take your *rapprochement* from the sickroom to a drawing room?"

Villiers smiled faintly. He didn't look in the least disappointed by her implicit rejection, which rankled her. Surely he ought to show more response to the invocation of her husband? "Unfortunately, I have a previous engagement. But I wanted your advice. I may have temporarily lost my interest in chess," he said, "but I am compensating by an increased interest in humanity."

"You?" she asked, startled.

"Yes. I, the eternal bystander."

"I always thought you found the affairs of others exhausting and uninteresting. My goodness, Villiers, you're not planning to reform? I shall be so disappointed if it transpires that the only reason to invite you for an evening is because you lend an air of respectability."

"It would be a terrible come-down," he said thoughtfully. "But in truth, I feel no Puritanical leanings." There was a flare of something deep in his eyes that made her want to smile back, reach out her hand . . .

"Do ask my advice, then," she said. "I'm sure I'm capable of wise pronouncements on almost any subject, and yet no one asks for evidence of my wisdom."

"Beaumont doesn't come to you with knotty matters of state?"

"Odd, isn't it?"

"You can mock yourself, Jemma, but he couldn't find a better mind to consider those affairs."

Jemma could feel herself growing faintly pink—and she never blushed. Never.

Of course Villiers didn't miss it. His mouth curled into a mocking smile. "I like blushing," he said. "Women do entirely too little of it, to my mind."

"It can be very useful."

"Useful?"

"There's nothing more disarming than a woman's blush."

"I'll take your word for it. Most women wear so much face paint that blushing is not an option."

"I often wear a great deal of face paint," Jemma said. "Particularly if I think there is the slightest chance that

I shall be shocked. If you are bent on reform, Villiers, I shall take to wearing it regularly."

"Reform . . ." he said. "Or not."

He had so much charm. He'd never wielded it on her like this before. When he smiled at her, it was almost like a caress.

Suddenly she remembered his drawling voice saying that he gave her fair warning that he meant to have her.

She almost shivered. Villiers was beautiful, depraved, tired . . . her husband's enemy, though she never understood precisely why. She had offered herself to him last year and he had refused on the grounds of being Elijah's oldest friend. And then he had changed his mind.

Now Villiers apparently meant to woo her, if that word was appropriate for a married woman.

She swallowed. She had promised Elijah that her scandals were over. She had come back from Paris to give her husband an heir. She felt dizzy.

Villiers didn't seem to notice her silence. Instead he took out a piece of paper. "Read this, Jemma."

She opened it. The letter was headed with the Duke of Cosway's crest. "Isidore's duke!"

"He's back in the country."

"I knew that. Isidore is staying with me at the moment. He left her at a hotel, if you can countenance it, Villiers. A hotel! He left his duchess at a hotel and proceeded to drive to the country to see his mother."

"I find that story unsurprising, given my acquaintance with him. I actually played a game of chess with Cosway on the deck of some rapscallion prince's boat," Villiers said.

"On the Nile river?"

"The same hemisphere. If you can imagine, it was twilight and stiflingly hot, around seven years ago, I suppose. I had decided for a number of reasons that I wished to travel to Arabia—"

She shook her head. "No."

"What?"

"You wanted to play chess, of course. You had no redeeming reason for your journey, such as a love of exploration."

His smile was a wicked thing, the kind of smile that lured a woman. "You have me with a pawn, Jemma. I wanted to go to the Levant and play the chess masters there. But it was so damned uncomfortable!"

"Sand?"

"Heat." He stretched out an arm and looked at his lace. "I am a duke. It has been my charge since I was a mere boy, and while it has undoubtedly spoiled me, it has also marked me. I like to be clean, and I like to dress. Even in my bedchamber, if you can believe it, Jemma, I choose my garments with great care."

She had a sudden entertaining vision of Villiers wrapped in silk. Instinctively, she struck back. "You are so thin after your illness . . . I wonder that you do not need an entirely new wardrobe."

"It is a cruel truth," he sighed. "I seek to build myself up, of course. I am so hopelessly vain that I could never allow myself to visit a lady's chamber until I am more fit."

Perhaps that was why there would be no third game in bed. It was to be a long campaign, she thought. The Duke of Villiers was setting himself out to entice her, before he allowed that last game to be played.

Of all the men who had ever assayed that goal, he was the most dangerous.

"So what happened during the chess match with Cosway?" she said, wrenching her mind away from the question of Villiers's allure.

"Oh, he beat me."

"That must have been disconcerting."

"Very. I played like an idiot, and I knew why. It was just too bloody hot for an Englishman, though Cosway showed no signs of discomfort."

"What kind of man is he?"

"Imagine, if you will, a rather magnificent vessel, belonging to the Bey of Isfaheet. There we sat, with a table of tiger-striped wood between us, the chess pieces carved from the same board. The bishop rode on a rearing lion; the queen was an African princess; the rook was a camel."

"And you were there, in embroidery and lace . . ."

"The picture of a proper English duke. No one else on board had a fifth of the clothes I did. And yet I had forsaken my waistcoat." He opened his eyes very wide. "No waistcoat, Jemma."

"I appreciate the seriousness of your sacrifice," she said, laughing.

"It was twilight and the air lay on the river—for we were on a river wider than I've seen in England—the air lay on that river like a fat whore on a six-penny bed."

Jemma snorted.

He looked at her innocently. "Did I say something amiss?"

He was potent . . . he was so potent in this mood. Wicked and sly and funny. "No," she said. "Please continue."

"Every time I reached out my hand to move one of the pieces, drops of sweat ran down my arm."

"And yet Cosway was not discomforted in the least?"

"Have you met him?"

Jemma shook her head.

"I think it would be fair to say that he's my opposite. No powder. His skin is brown from the sun, of course and he's muscled to a degree that is vastly ungentlemanly. But I think it's the great tumble of inky black hair, unpowdered and not even tied back, that truly marks him. One can easily imagine him fighting off four or five savages at once."

"You could do that," Jemma said loyally.

"I'm not such a fool as to ever put myself in that situation," Villiers said. "As I recall, he wore short trousers that barely reached his knee along with a tunic-like affair, but at some point he removed that and had the boys dunk it in the river. They returned it to him wet. He appeared to be quite comfortable."

"Unfair!" Jemma said.

"Did I mention that he was barefoot?"

"No. And you?"

"Boots. Sturdy English boots made for an exploring Englishman, out to gather useful knowledge of the world's fauna and flora."

"You came home," Jemma guessed.

"I forsook all the chess games I might have won in the palaces of the great pashas . . . I succumbed to the heat."

"Or perhaps," Jemma said wickedly, "to your insistence on dressing like a duke."

"It has occurred to me since. Vanity, thy name is Villiers. Do read his letter."

Jemma had forgotten about it. There was no formal salutation.

Villiers,

I'm having a devil of a time since my return. Would you do me the honor of paying me a visit? There seems to be some disapproval of my ideas. You are, to my mind, the person best suited in the world to advise me on matters of precedence and respectability.

Jemma chuckled.

"I gather you've reached the part when he talks about my ability to arbitrate standards of respectability," Villiers said.

"I was just thinking of you, all booted and laced, on board that ship."

"The letter continues."

My mother assures me that I stand to blacken the title of Cosway throughout England for the next hundred years. If you could pay me a visit at Revels House, I would be most grateful.

Yours & etc.
Cosway

Jemma looked up. "What on earth can he be planning? Isidore said that he'd alluded to a wedding celebration that included some sort of animal sacrifice—but he can't be thinking of enacting a primitive rite here. He would be arrested!"

"Not for animal sacrifice," Villiers said. "As someone who loves sirloin, I can assure you that many cattle have been sacrificed to keep me happy."

"You know what I mean," Jemma said. "And Isidore mentioned *orgies.*"

"Well, that settles it. I knew you were the person to speak to. I shall have to pay him a visit, if only so that I can be part of the orgy planning."

"Have you participated in many?"

"Orgies or weddings?" he asked innocently.

"I doubt you have been in any weddings," she pointed

out. "Your engagement to my ward was your first and last, to the best of my knowledge."

"Alack," he said. "My experience with orgies is just as thin. This will be *such* an education for me, combining two pursuits I have religiously avoided."

"You surprise me," Jemma said. "I would have thought you had indulged in your youth, and then tired of such passionate pursuits."

"The problem lies in my dukedom, I suppose, or in my spoiled nature. I have always thought of orgies as opportunities to share—and I don't do that very well."

"Then I wonder why you have pursued *affaires* with married women," Jemma said.

"Rarely. Very rarely, and only against my better judgment."

"I see."

"Only when the temptation is so great that there seemed no other woman in the world," he added gently.

"Ah."

"In fact, I must tell you that my reputation may be blacker than I deserve. I have, as yet, had no *affaires* of that nature." He rose. "I must continue to my appointment, duchess."

She stayed in her seat for a moment, then looked up at him. "Leopold."

Only the lowering of his eyelids showed that he registered her use of his personal name.

But she wasn't sure exactly what to say.

"I almost forgot," he said. "I brought you a present."

She rose, unable to find words, unsure what her response should be. "A present?"

He took out a fan and laid it on the table. "A mere token, a nothing. It made me think of you." He turned to go.

"Wait—"

He looked back.

"When do you go to Revels House?"

"I shall return to Fonthill tomorrow. If Strange's daughter is still ill, I shall travel on to Revels House in a few days."

She nodded.

"I shall make very sure that you are invited to the wedding, naturally."

"Beaumont and I shall be happy to attend." She wasn't sure why she felt the need to bring her husband's name into the conversation. It wasn't as if Elijah didn't—hadn't—Elijah himself refused to bed her until the chess game with Villiers was over. He understood the potential that she might have an *affaire* with Villiers.

Jemma sat for a long time after the door closed behind Villiers and his rose-colored silks . . . thinking of men. Of husbands, lovers, chess masters, heirs.

Of men.

Chapter Nine

Gore House, Kensington
London Seat of the Duke of Beaumont
February 27, 1784
The next morning

Isidore gave the direction to the groomsman, climbed into the carriage, and started pulling off her gloves.

"Do you always take off your gloves whenever possible?" Simeon asked.

Isidore glanced at him. "You aren't wearing gloves either." Nor a cravat, nor a wig, nor a waistcoat, but why indulge in specifics?

"I dislike gloves, and it seems you do as well."

"Yes," she admitted.

He leaned forward and took her hand, turned it over.

His hand was large and callused, like a working man's hands. He wore no rings, not even a signet.

"Will you tell my fortune?" she asked.

"I don't know how. I had my fortune told once in India. The whole experience scared me to death and I never toyed with such people again."

"What did he say?" It was hard to imagine Cosway, who looked large and fearless, quailing before a fortune-teller.

"He told me that it was up to me to make sure that my fortune didn't turn out as he prophesied."

Isidore succumbed to curiosity. "Please tell!"

He shook his head. "Maybe when we're old and gray."

"*If* we're old and gray together!" she pointed out.

"Are you angry at me because I didn't return when you came of age or because I'm offering you the chance now to annul the marriage?"

"I'm not angry with you," Isidore said, withdrawing her hand. Her voice sounded petulant, but she felt out of her depth with this huge man.

Shamefully, she kept looking at him and thinking *virgin*? How could he be a virgin? He looked all man, all male . . .

She could feel her cheeks getting pink.

"Or are you angry at me because I'm not knowledgeable about conjugal intimacies?"

"No!" she said, turning to the window. "Look, Cosway, we're passing by Somerset House. If you crane your neck you might see the loggia on the south terrace. It was just finished . . . The Inns of Court are very close now."

It was barely an hour before they were back in the carriage again. Isidore was in shock.

"I just can't believe it!" she said. "You ought to be able to annul a marriage easily on the grounds of non-consummation. I'm sure everyone told me so a thousand times over the past few years."

Her husband raised an eyebrow. "I had no idea that people were so interested in the state of our bedchamber."

"Cosway," Isidore said impatiently, "I am twenty-three years old. I've been jaunting around Europe for years. Unless people actually checked their Debrett's, they tended to think we were merely engaged, and I never corrected that impression. Even Jemma, one of my closest friends, thought that for a time. It was less humiliating to let people think such."

"But—"

"But there are plenty who read their Debrett's like a Bible, so they know of the proxy wedding. They would inquire when you were returning. Nonconsummation has been mentioned to me many times. I know Villiers brought it up. And now it seems that it isn't an option."

"I'm sorry," Cosway said. "Even if it were legal, I would have to pass a test of my incapability. I can't."

Isidore made herself say the words, because she had to know: "Are you sure about that?"

"Yes."

"Really sure?"

"No question. Is that what you're worrying about?"

"I'm not worried."

"Because I could show you."

She felt her eyes grow round. "What?"

He had a wicked smile. He started pulling open his greatcoat. "I could show you—"

"Don't!" she snapped.

"The truth is that I find it rather difficult to be around you," he said, leaning back and leaving his greatcoat alone, to her relief.

She felt inexplicably hurt. Of course, he was eager to get an annulment, but there was no need to be so brutal about it. "According to that solicitor, there are other ways to dissolve our marriage," she said a bit stiffly. "So you needn't give up the dream of your docile little hen-wit."

"Hen-wit? Not a kind word, Isidore . . . But I wasn't referring to the question of annulment, but to the state of my cock."

She gasped. "You—"

"Mayn't I use that word in front of a lady?" he inquired, as mild as sweet butter and all the time his eyes laughing at her.

"No!" she managed. "It makes you sound like—like—"

"Tsk, tsk, Isidore. I have the strangest sense that you and my mother are actually quite alike. But how can that be? After all, I rescued you from Lord Strange's notorious house party, did I not? Even I have heard tell of its brothel-like atmosphere. But here you are, quailing at a good, solid Anglo-Saxon word like—"

"Don't!"

"Are you telling me that language like that wasn't flying around Strange's dining room?"

"I tried not to listen to that sort of conversation."

"You did?" He leaned forward suddenly. "Then without inappropriate words, Isidore, may I assure you that when I'm in your presence that part of my body stands to attention?"

Isidore could feel herself growing pink. And she always thought she looked her worst with ruddy cheeks. "Must you say these things?"

"You impugned my manhood," he said. "I couldn't have you thinking that I was a limp lily."

"How would—" she said, and broke off.

"How would I know?" His whole face was alight with amusement. "Really, I do have to show you, Isidore."

"No!"

He barked with laughter. "I can't imagine you at Strange's house. Even in the half hour during which I managed to stay awake, I was told an entirely salacious story about a bishop. And his miter."

Isidore shuddered. "I hated that place."

"Then why were you there?"

She took a deep breath. "To force you to return home, of course."

"That's what my mother said."

"She was right. I had reached the point at which I thought either you came home or—"

"Or?"

Isidore suddenly saw exactly how to get back at him for offering to show her his equipment. She leaned forward and patted his hand. "Jemma told me once that it is a wife's duty to provide an heir if a husband is incapable. Since you showed little signs of returning from Africa, I decided I should begin to explore the possibilities."

All traces of amusement were gone from his face.

"You were going to produce an heir *for me?*"

She shrugged. "And Cosway, if things are not entirely successful on our wedding night, should we decide to stay together, I wouldn't want you to worry. I can always—"

"You will *never* substitute another man for me! I don't know where you got the damned idea that I might be incapable!"

"Neither one of us can know the truth to that," she pointed out. She was dancing on the edge of jeopardy and it felt wonderful.

His mouth opened like that of a fish out of water.

She leaned forward and patted his knee this time. "A

virgin at your age . . . well. I would never tell a soul."
And she beamed at him.

It was a beautiful moment. It almost made up for the
way he was planning to annul their marriage due to her
unsuitability as a wife.

He surprised her.

After staring at her for a moment, he collapsed into a
howling fit of laughter.

She sat silently for a moment, but Cosway had the
kind of laughter that made you want to join in, and she
couldn't keep herself from smiling.

"You think that because I haven't tried out the equipment on a woman, it doesn't work at all?"

"It's a reasonable—"

He started howling with laughter again, and finally
straightened up.

"I don't see what's so funny," she said with reasonable dignity.

"It's you. I suppose it's due to being a lady. One can
only assume from your idea about my equipment that
you yourself have never—" He raised an eyebrow sug-
gestively.

"What?" she asked, completely confused.

"You've never pleasured yourself."

She stared at him. "What?"

"Bloody hell, you haven't."

She felt herself turning pink. "I see no need to engage
in coarse language."

"Shit and dam—"

"Don't!"

"I'm talking about pleasure," he said. "The kind you
apparently have never had."

Isidore kept silent. What pleasure she had had or not
was none of his business.

"I should have known," he muttered to himself. "Now

look here, Isidore. My—well, what word am I allowed to use, then?"

"I don't know. Pizzle, I suppose. Though no one ever talks to me about pizzles."

"They want to," Simeon said. "You just haven't given them the chance. Pizzle, for Christ's sake. Sounds like a word a five-year-old might use when learning to take a piss. Are you sure we can't do with a bolder word, one more in line with the size of the thing?"

Isidore opened her mouth, shut it, opened it again and said: "Pizzle."

"Right. Well, my pizzle is a *pizzalone*, in Italian. A *big* pizzle, Isidore."

He was still making fun of her. She folded her arms over her chest. "There's nothing sadder than a man who feels the need to boast about the size of his equipment," she said sweetly.

"It's not boasting, just stating."

"Hmmmm."

"Want me to prove it?" And he put his hands back on the front of his greatcoat.

"No!"

Simeon looked at Isidore. She was laughing and indignant at the same time. She didn't look docile, or sweet, or biddable . . . she looked like a banked fire waiting for just one spark to flare. She had never pleasured herself . . . she had never . . . she had *waited*.

His blood was pounding through his body, begging him, telling him, commanding him. It took all his strength to resist the impulse to pull her into his arms. "I can completely understand your anxiety," he said.

"You can?"

"You're buying a pig in a poke. Unlike the rest of the Englishmen around here, I haven't been strutting around brothels for the last fifteen years. But if we did marry, I wouldn't bring you any diseases, Isidore."

She nodded.

"You have a reasonable suspicion that my pizzle is not in working condition. Out of shape. Withered from lack of use. Tired from my own handling—"

"That's enough."

"So I would have to prove it to you, obviously, before I could expect you to commit to our marriage."

"But you yourself are not committed, since I'm not a docile little hen-wit."

There was a moment of silence in the carriage. Her summary of his marital ambitions seemed unnecessarily harsh. "It's not that I want to marry an unintelligent woman," he began painstakingly, but she interrupted him.

"You just don't want to marry me."

"It's not a question of *you*, Isidore."

He had that look again, the one of total calm and control. Isidore understood Simeon a bit better now—and pitied him for it. Her husband thought he had anger and lust under control, not to mention fear. He thought he had life under control.

He was a fool, but that wasn't the same thing as being a madman, the way she and Jemma had thought he might be. And from what he was saying, he wasn't incapable. Clearly, she needed to think about what to do next.

"If we call it off, I'll go back to Africa directly," he offered. "Sign the papers and keep out of your hair while you find another husband."

She nodded. "Very generous of you." She looked down and found that her hands had curled into fists. *We* call it off? Simeon clearly thought that he was as much in control of the end of their marriage as he had been of the first eleven years.

"I expect it might put the new husband off his feed to have the old husband hanging around assessing him," Simeon said. "I might want to engage in a pizzle contest, for example."

Isidore smiled stiffly. "What are you talking about?"

"I saw such a contest in Smyrna."

"Where's that?"

"On the Mediterranean sea, part of the Anatolian Empire. I met a vizier and his brother who were traveling to present themselves as possible spouses to a sheikh's daughter. The decisive factor? A pizzle contest."

"Size?"

"Size and endurance," Simeon said. "The sheikh made his entire harem available for the duration of the contest. He invited me to join the contest."

"Was the sheikh just taking anyone? Not that they shouldn't have offered it to you, but you *are* married," Isidore pointed out.

"Oh, the sheikh wouldn't have cared about an English marriage. In order to enter the contest, you had to offer a tiger ruby. And as it happened, I have something of a collection. I do believe that some of the gentlemen in question had no expectation of winning the princess's hand but they were happily offering up tiger rubies anyway."

"Because of the harem," Isidore asked, raising an eyebrow.

"Beautiful women," Simeon said. "Exquisite in every way."

"Wonderful." Her tone could have curdled milk. "How did you ever resist the temptation?"

He grinned at her. "I had you."

"Well," Isidore said, "You didn't—"

"*Have* you," he put in. "You're right. Let's put it this way: I didn't have you. Yet. But you were worth more than a night in a harem and a tiger ruby."

Isidore thought of various remarks she might make, comparing her worth to that of the hen-wit, and stopped herself. "What does a tiger ruby look like? I've never heard of it."

"Gorgeous: rubies with a tawny yellow streak through them. They're tremendously rare. In the end the sheikh was able to garner only eight such rubies even with the lure of his harem."

"How on earth do you know? Did you go to the wedding?"

"Of course! Vizier Takla Haymanot won, and after eleven days of feasting (Takla needed a rest after the contest), he married the sheikh's daughter. Then I bought the eight rubies from the sheikh and we were all happy."

"Will you show me one?"

"Not at the moment. They're in the bank."

"In a bank? If I had rubies like that—though of course their history is rather disagreeable . . ."

"Disagreeable? They were traded for pleasure."

"I doubt the ladies of the harem felt so."

"If they didn't, they did a good job disguising it. They got to choose, you know."

Isidore felt herself turning a bit pink, but she was fascinated. "They got to choose?"

"You have to understand that this particular sheikh had two hundred and thirteen wives in his harem. And he himself was rather elderly. So the young ladies in his harem had little entertainment. The eight suitors were brought forward, and the ladies were allowed to choose. That was another aspect of the contest: if no lady chose to bed a suitor in a given round, he was out of the competition."

"Oh!"

"You would look lovely in a harem veil," he remarked.

If she forced a consummation to the marriage by prancing about wearing nothing but a veil, Simeon would never be granted an annulment. It was something to think about.

"I rather like the way that sheikh managed things," Isidore said.

"Really?"

"Though if I were the princess, I would have talked the sheikh into changing the contest."

"And?" Simeon prompted.

"I think it would be very interesting if the princess too had been able to choose her future consort, the way the ladies of the harem were. I presume the gentlemen in question were not dressed?"

He looked genuinely surprised, which was very satisfying. He needn't think he was the only one who could talk about bawdy things.

The carriage drew to a halt and she automatically started putting her gloves back on.

Simeon reached over and pulled one away.

"What—"

Then he snatched the other. And finally, when the carriage door opened, he flung them straight out into the street. They flew past the face of a startled groomsman, who gave a little shriek and stumbled backward, falling onto his bottom.

"You are utterly deranged!" Isidore said with conviction, leaning forward to look at the street. "I can't go to my appointment without gloves." Sure enough, her blue gloves were lying in a puddle of blackened rainwater.

"You hate them," Simeon said, leaping out of the carriage and holding out his own ungloved hand.

She ground her teeth and then put her hand in his.

The shock of heat she felt was entirely unreasonable.

Chapter Ten

65 Blackfriars Street
February 27, 1784

They were before a row of houses, in a part of London Simeon didn't know. Not that he really knew London. "Doesn't your mantua-maker own a shop?" he asked. The groomsman was standing at the door of a small house.

"We are visiting Signora Angelico's studio, Cosway," Isidore told him. "This is a great honor, extended only to her countrywomen, so please try to behave yourself."

"Couldn't you call me by my given name?"

"It's not polite."

He ignored that. "My name is Simeon. It's a good, workable name and I thank God I didn't end up Godfrey, like my poor brother."

"We're not supposed to call each other by given names."

"I already call you Isidore."

"I didn't give you permission to do so!"

"Every time you call me Cosway, it sounds like cock to me," he said thoughtfully. "Maybe that's not such a bad thing. Maybe you should go right on calling me Cosway, and I'll just—"

Isidore laughed. "Fine. Simeon."

Signora Angelico worked in a large open room on the bottom floor. The first thing Simeon saw were the open shelves that lined the room. Rolled cloth—silk, satin, taffeta—was stacked to the topmost level. It reminded him of souks in Morocco. The colors glowed coyly from the ends of the rolls, deep red silk, lilac shot with silver, the clear yellow of buttercups in early spring. Below the cloth were boxes, filled to the brim and spilling forth their contents: thread, buttons, yards and yards of ribbon. Everywhere there was lace. Lace hanging from wooden poles, lace thrown into piles, thin rivulets of lace and fatter rivers of it heaped on the tables that scattered the room.

Isidore had walked directly into the room, while Simeon paused on the threshold. Now she was dropping a deep curtsy before a woman in late middle age, with a deliciously curvy figure. The mantua-maker was kissing Isidore energetically on both cheeks, calling her *bella*.

Then they both turned and looked at him.

Simeon walked forward and swept into a flourishing bow. "Duke," Isidore said, "may I present Signora Angelico?"

"*Onorato di conoscerla, signora.*"

Isidore raised an eyebrow. "I had no idea you spoke Italian."

"I don't really, but I can improvise from Portuguese." He turned back to Signora Angelico who was declaring herself *felicissima* to encounter, finally, the *marito* of her darling little duchess, whom she had loved since the moment she first saw her.

"Signora Angelico made gowns for my aunt for many years," Isidore explained.

"Your aunt?"

"I lived with my aunt after we married."

"Of course! Your aunt."

"Augustina Del'Fino," Isidore filled in.

So he didn't know every bit of information about what she'd been doing for the last eight years since they married . . . well, perhaps it was more than eight years.

Signora Angelico turned away, her hands in the air, scattering her seamstresses in all directions.

"How long have we been married?" Simeon inquired.

Isidore glanced at him. She would make an excellent politician; she had a way of putting a fellow in his place with nothing more than a raised eyebrow. "Don't you remember?"

"Why would I ask if I did?" he said, surprised.

"We were engaged in June, 1765, married by proxy in June, 1773."

"Of course. You said you were twelve when we actually married."

Signora Angelico was gesticulating madly from the other side of the room.

"And you were eighteen."

"I was in India. How long did you live with my mother?"

"A matter of a few months. I'm afraid that we were not suited temperamentally, and we all agreed that I would be happier with my aunt." She turned away. "*Cara signora, arriviamo!*"

Signora Angelico was chattering away with Isidore in Italian, so rapidly that Simeon couldn't follow. She was pulling bolts of cloth from the shelves and throwing them on the table, screaming at her assistants, waving her hands around . . .

Simeon went back to thinking. So Isidore went to live with her aunt and presumably expected him to collect her up at some point.

Signora turned away so he said to her, "Just when did you think I'd come back for you?"

"When I was sixteen."

"But that was—"

"Seven years ago."

He stared down at her.

"You've been waiting for me for *seven years*?"

"What did you think I've been doing?" And she turned away, cooing over the signora's choice of cloth.

Simeon stared down at the bolt of fabric. It was spun of a material so fine that it looked like cobwebs, and yet he knew he had finer in his warehouses. He had shipped home trunks of fabric.

"Did you ever receive fabric I sent from India?"

She glanced up at him and her eyes were like chips of blue ice now. "They must have gone as astray as you yourself."

With a sinking feeling, he remembered that he sent everything to his mother's direction, who then refused acceptance. It seemed a strange decision on his part, now he thought of it.

He had chosen beautiful pieces and put them to the side, sending them home with instructions that they be delivered to the duchess. It was only now dawning on him that there really were—and had been for years—two duchesses.

The mantua-maker was matching the silvery fabric with a delicate lace tinted a faint blue. Isidore would look like the snow princess in a Russian fairy tale, the ones in which the princess had a heart of ice.

"I don't like it," he said abruptly.

Signora Angelico was clearly not used to being interrupted—nor to being countered. She flew into a paroxysm of exclamations, half in English, half in Italian.

Isidore turned to him and hissed, "You can't say that sort of thing to Signora Angelico! The Queen of France herself has ordered night clothing from signora."

"I don't care whether she sews the king's slippers with her teeth," Simeon said. "This fabric isn't of the quality I'd like you to wear. I may not care much for polite society, Isidore, but I know fabric."

"You wouldn't—"

He turned to Signora Angelico. She was as ruffled as a hen in the rain, her cheeks stained with crimson, her hands waving wildly around her head.

But Simeon had bargained with many a tradesman in places where to lose the bargain was to lose one's head. "This fabric isn't good enough," he said.

"Not good enough!" Signora Angelico's face took on a purple hue. "This is the very best, *magnifico,* lovely in every way, fit for—"

Simeon rubbed it between his fingers and shook his head. "Indian silk."

"Silk from the looms of the Maharaja himself—"

Simeon shook his head. "Signora, signora . . . surely you don't take me for a dunce?" He pushed the fabric to the side and sat on the table.

"Get up!" Isidore said to him in an urgent undertone. "You can't sit before us."

Simeon snapped his fingers at one of the girls, who

were flocking nervously against the wall as if they thought he would faint merely from the signora's frown. "Chairs for Her Grace and Signora Angelico."

Two of them scuttled over with straight-backed chairs, used by the girls while they engaged in hand-sewing. Perfect. Signora Angelico was now seated just below him. He smiled down at her. "I can tell that you are a woman who adores fabric," he cooed. "A woman ravished by antherine silk, so glossy and light, perhaps with a touch of mignonette lace."

Signora's whole face changed. "You know your fabrics, Your Grace."

He smiled at her. "Now this—" he put a finger disdainfully on the silk she proposed. "Paduasoy. A nice strong silk. Perhaps good enough for some. But not," and he gave every word a tiny emphasis, "not for my wife, signora."

"You!" she said. "You are going to lead my poor little duchess on a chase, are you not?" Her black eyes snapped, but he could feel the rigid backs of her girls relax.

"It is a man's duty when faced with such beauty as graces my wife," he said solemnly, reaching down and bringing her hand to his lips. "Of course, had I seen you in my youth . . ."

Signora bounced to her feet. "As if I could have been tempted by such a callow young thing as a raw duke!" She clapped her hands. "Lucia! Bring me that bolt of tiffany."

"Dare I hope the tiffany harks from the looms of Margilan?"

"You will see!" she crowed.

Isidore sat in her chair, stunned into silence. After that, Signora Angelico was putty in Simeon's hands. He rejected the tiffany as too harsh; they finally found a taffeta he found acceptable. It was cherry red, with only a touch of stiffness to it.

"I see it falling to the ground with a froth at the feet and a small train."

"But the color . . ." Signora Angelico shook her head. "If only I had a—"

"Wash it in tea."

"Wash this fabric in tea?" She looked down at the fabric. It looked as if it had been woven by fairies; if you let it fall through your fingers it sounded like a whispered song.

"Of course," Simeon said. He kissed her hand again, and that was that. Isidore was to have a gown of tea-washed taffeta, edged in a thin border of glossy lace made in Brussels.

The signora was drunk with the garment she saw in her imagination. "Coming to the mid finger," she murmured to herself, "*décolletage,* of course."

"Are we finished?" Isidore asked, standing up.

"Tsk, tsk," Simeon said. "These things take time."

"Not for me," Isidore retorted, looking to make sure that Signora Angelico wasn't listening. She wasn't; she looked as dreamy as her aunt had while practicing a new sonata. "The first cloth would have been just fine. I can't imagine why you took such an interest, since the nightdress will presumably be for another's man's pleasure!"

Simeon opened his mouth—and closed it. She had a point. Isidore was intoxicating; he tended to forget everything in her presence.

"We could have been home by now," Isidore said. "I have another appointment." She glanced down at the watch she wore on a ribbon and gave a little shriek. "And I'm late. *If* you please!"

"I must return to Revels House immediately," Simeon

said in the carriage. "There are a few outstanding problems with the estate. I'll return to London next week and we can continue the discussion of our annulment."

Isidore looked at him. "Certainly," she said. "If I happen to be in residence."

He looked absurdly surprised, given that her tone had been quite mild.

Chapter Eleven

Gore House, Kensington
London Seat of the Duke of Beaumont
February 27, 1784

The Duke of Beaumont had had a detestable day. His wife had not appeared at breakfast, and though Jemma rarely made an appearance, he had rather hoped she would. The House of Lords was erupting into all sorts of strange battles to do with Pitt's India Bill and the Mutiny Bill. The king had said Fox was trying to reduce him to a mere figurehead. Fox was trying to force the resignation of the ministry . . .

He was tired. He was so bone-tired that he actually wavered a bit as he descended from his carriage. One of his footmen darted forward as if he were a man of eighty, and Elijah had to wave him away. It was humiliating.

His body was failing him.

Oh, he'd never fainted in public again, as he had last year. Right on the floor of the House of Lords, he had collapsed.

These days, to everyone's eyes, he seemed absolutely fine.

But he knew he wasn't. He felt a clock ticking over his shoulder, and its tick was louder since they'd returned from the Christmas holidays. Perhaps because it had been so relaxing to go to the country for the holidays, to wander through one of Jemma's outrageous masquerades, to play chess with his wife, to bicker amiably about politics with acquaintances who didn't think the outcome of any particular vote was of much importance.

Returning to the seething brew that was the House of Lords was difficult.

No, he hadn't fainted since the first time.

But he *had* passed out, just for a second, now and then. So far he had always been sitting down, and no one had realized.

But the truth—the truth was that he needed to talk to his wife.

Jemma had come back from Paris so they could create an heir. He could hardly bring the words to the surface of his mind. This wasn't the way he wanted to bed Jemma. They had engaged in an elaborate, intricate ballet over the last year. They were beginning . . .

He wasn't sure what they were beginning. But he knew that it was important. More important than anything before.

And still his body failed him.

"You work too hard, Your Grace!" his butler scolded him. "Those rapscallions in the government need to learn to do without you for a time."

Only he knew that he had already cut back his workload. He smiled at Fowle, handed over his greatcoat, inquired of the duchess's whereabouts.

"In the library, Your Grace," the butler said. "With a chess board, and waiting for you, I believe."

He walked into the library and paused for a moment just to savor what lay before him. Jemma was heart-breakingly, astoundingly beautiful. She was sitting in a patch of light cast by many candles, examining her chess board. She had her hair swept up in some sort of compli-cated arrangement, but not powdered. It was the color of old gold, the deep happy color of sunshine. She was wearing an open robe of flowered gauze, worked with gold twists, that came to a deep V over her breasts.

The pulse of longing he felt was for everything about his wife: her wit, her beauty, her breasts, her brilliance . . .

How in the hell could he not have realized it when they first married? How could he have wasted those years, thrown them away on politics and his mistress? Couldn't he have thought—just imagined—that per-haps time wasn't a gift one had for the asking? Couldn't he have remembered that his father had died at thirty-four?

And *he* was thirty-four, as of this month. Time wove its changes, marched apace . . . he would give anything to have back those first weeks of marriage when Jemma looked to him for advice, when she cuddled beside him in the morning, asking questions about the House.

Great fool that he was back then, he had leapt from their bed eager to be at the House, not sitting about with a wife whom he barely knew. Off to his mistress, who appeared during the noon hour on Tuesdays and Fri-days. That was part of his routine: emerge from the House of Lords and exhaust himself with Sarah, right there in his office.

Good old Sarah Cobbett. She loved him; he loved her in a way. One had to hope that she was happy.

He'd pensioned her off after Jemma caught them on the desk in his chambers.

The stab of guilt was an old friend, though it seemed to grow fiercer with the years, not less so.

For her part, Jemma seemed to have forgiven him. Perhaps.

She looked up at him, and her smile made his heart stop.

Life had given him a woman who was—he knew it with a bone-deep certainty—the most intelligent woman in Europe. And he had thrown her away to rut with a kindly woman whose only claim to intelligence was that she was never late to their twice-weekly appointment, not once during the six years in which Sarah was his mistress.

He couldn't even remember Sarah's face now, which just made him feel guiltier.

"Look at this!" Jemma called to him.

He walked over and looked down at the board, rather blindly.

"It's a counter gambit credited to Giuoco. I think I've improved on it. Look . . ." and she moved the pieces so quickly that he almost didn't follow, but of course he did. Their brains were remarkably similar.

He sat down.

"Terrible day?" she asked.

It was almost too much. Her eyes were blue, like the midnight blue of the sky at night. And he wanted—her. Life. To stay here, on this earth with Jemma. To see the child they would create, if they had time.

"Elijah!" she said, startled. Slipped from her seat and sat on his knee. He turned his face into her shoulder. She smelled like roses.

He didn't cry, of course. He never cried. He hadn't when his father died, and he wouldn't cry over his own death either.

But he put an arm around his wife and pulled her closer. She hadn't been this near to him in years.

It felt good.

Chapter Twelve

Revels House
February 29, 1784

Simeon knew the moment that Honeydew opened the study door that there was more trouble. He put down his quill.

The news that the Duke of Cosway had returned, and that he was actually paying the family debts, had spread like wildfire. Half of England seemed to be lined up outside the servants' door, begging five minutes to plead cases, generally to do with bills that his father or mother had refused to pay. Some stretched back twenty years.

"Yes?"

"We have a visitor," Honeydew announced.

Simeon waited, bracing himself for an irate creditor.

"Her Grace, the Duchess of Cosway."

"Oh—" He bit off the curse. He was exhausted, he was dusty, and he could smell the water closets even with the door to his study closed. Isidore would probably take one look at this moldering excuse for a ducal palace and demand the annulment by tomorrow. Which would be a good thing, of course.

Honeydew had become distinctly more friendly, and had even stopped giving Simeon directives regarding his attire and manners. But he didn't seem to be able to stop himself this time. "If you'd like to—"

Simeon looked at him and Honeydew dropped the suggestion. Likely Isidore did think he should be wearing a wig and waistcoat buttoned to the neck with a cravat on top. Even more likely, she pictured Revels House as perfumed and elegant.

He pulled his coat down, straightened his cuffs, noted the ink stain and dismissed it. He could bother with white cuffs and a cravat when he had to go to London and find himself another wife.

"Her Grace is in the Yellow Salon," Honeydew said rather nervously.

"Yellow? Which one is that?"

"The drapes used to be yellow," Honeydew admitted.

"Ah," Simeon said. "The Curdled Milk Salon."

There was actually a smile on his butler's face. "This way, Your Grace."

Isidore was seated on a straw-colored sofa, facing away from him. That straw color had once been lemon yellow, Simeon noted to himself. Isidore looked like a bright jewel perched on a haystack. His wife's hair was the glossy black of a raven's breast; her lips were cherries at their reddest. She looked like every boyhood fantasy he'd ever had about an exotic princess who would dance before him, wearing little more than a scarf.

He glanced down and groaned silently.

He'd tamed his body into perfect submission until he
met his wife. He started buttoning his long coat as he
walked forward, starting from the bottom.

"Isidore," he said, when he had crossed enough of the
faded carpet so that she could hear him without a shout.
The only thing his house had in abundance was space.

She leapt to her feet, turning to face him. She was
wearing a tight jacket over a buttoned waistcoat, with a
tall beehive hat on top of her curls. The jacket was a rich
plum color; gloves of the same color lay discarded on
the sofa beside her.

"Duke," she said, sinking into a curtsy.

He walked toward her and didn't bow. Instead he took
her hands in his and smiled down at her, resisting a sudden temptation to snatch her into his arms and steal a
kiss. One didn't kiss a wife who was not a wife. "This is
a lovely surprise."

When she smiled, her lips formed a perfect cupid's
bow. "I told you I might not wait for your visit to London. I hope I'm not disturbing you," she said sweetly.
She pulled her hands free and sat down.

He sat on the sofa facing hers. It gave a great squeak-
ing groan on feeling his weight, as if it were about to
collapse to the ground. "I am embarrassed to welcome
you here. The house is in a terrible state. This room, for
example . . ."

"It looks clean," she offered, looking about.

It was clean. Honeydew would tolerate no dirt, but
he had the feeling the butler worked to death the few
housemaids his mother had kept in the household. He
might as well get over the rough ground as quickly as
possible. "My mother stopped paying bills a while ago.
And she dismissed most of the household staff."

Isidore had a strange look on her face and he knew

just what she was thinking. The odor had begun drifting through the room like a fetid suitor.

"She didn't have the water closets cleaned, the slates repaired, the house painted, the furniture upholstered, the servants paid, the cottages re-thatched . . ."

Isidore's hand flew to her mouth, and over her nose as well. "Oh, dear!"

Simeon nodded. "That's why I didn't invite you to Revels House. When rain comes, and the wind shifts . . ."

She put down her hand and to his great relief, she was smiling. "You looked tired when I first met you," she observed. "But now you look even worse."

"There is a great deal of paperwork. Unpaid bills, solicitors' letters . . ." He shrugged. "I haven't been sleeping much."

"I have a large estate, and you are my husband, Cosway. It's yours. That is, it should have been yours long ago, but you never appeared to take charge of it so I have managed it."

His heart lightened even further. "The truth is that I have a great deal of money as well. And mystifyingly, so does the duchy. I have no need of substance, though I thank you heartily for it."

"Then why . . ."

He nodded. "Exactly. My mother has long been a mystery to me. Did you understand her during your sojourn here?"

Isidore picked up her gloves and carefully smoothed each finger. "I'm afraid that I was far too young and coarse. Your mother is a woman of great sensibility."

He thought that was a nice way of saying the obvious: his mother was a raving lunatic, if not worse. "She didn't used to be like this," he offered. "I'm afraid the shock of my father's death made things worse."

"How can I help?"

"You can't, but I do appreciate the offer."

"Nonsense," she said, standing up. "You can't manage everything on your own, Simeon." She looked around. "Have you even raised the question of redecorating with your mother?"

He rose, thinking about how casually she said his first name . . . finally. "My mother is having a difficult time adjusting to my presence. She is distressed by the fact that I am paying bills that she considers to have been presented by thieves. But after so much time has passed, I have no way of ascertaining whether the bills are fraudulent, so I am necessarily paying everything in full."

She nodded. "Then I suppose my most pressing question is which bedchamber lies the farthest distance from a water closet?"

Of course she didn't plan to stay in the master bedchamber. Of course not. He'd told her that he wanted to dissolve the marriage. What in the hell had he been thinking?

"I'll ask the butler, shall I?" she said, turning away. The line of her back was straight and incredibly slender. And then her hoops . . . the way her skirt billowed as she walked made him long to follow the line of her back down to her hips with his hand. With a silent groan, he pushed open the door for Isidore and she swept through.

What would Honeydew make of the duchess's request for a bedchamber far, far away? As it turned out, he was in entire sympathy.

"The dowager duchess has her own water closet, of course," Simeon heard him telling Isidore. "And how she can abide the odor on damp days . . ."

"She's probably used to it," Isidore said, reasonably enough.

Back when Simeon was practicing meditation and

first learning to control his body, it had been easy to maintain a manly discretion. When he arrived in Africa, and discovered running, he learned how to control bodily appetites such as hunger.

But England was endangering all his carefully erected barriers. His imperturbable, manly façade was shaken. He was enraged at his dead father for avoiding his obligations. He was irritated by his mother. And worst of all, he was riveted by lust for his wife. If the truth be told, lust was absorbing at least half of his cognitive powers at any given moment, even given that he'd had so little sleep.

He could hear Valamksepa in his mind's ear, intoning that no man need be at the behest of his emotions, and certainly not of his body. The memory sounded like water running over pebbles a long way away.

Isidore put her hand on his sleeve and her touch sent a pulse of fire to his loin. "Simeon, is Godfrey away at school? He was just a toddler when I last saw him. He must be in long pants by now."

Simeon gave her a wry smile. "He's thirteen and nearly as tall as I am. You'll meet him tonight."

She gasped. "Thirteen?"

"I need to find him a tutor. My mother deemed Eton too expensive and yet she never hired a proper tutor. Luckily, he seems very bright and has taught himself, rather eclectically, from my father's library."

"Beaumont is sure to know an appropriate young man. Godfrey taught *himself*?"

Another pulse of shame. He should have been here, making certain that his brother was properly raised. But Simeon made sure his face was impassive. It was weakness to admit weakness. "He will quickly catch up to his peers."

Isidore gave him a quizzical look, but turned away to

speak to Honeydew. "I do not travel lightly," she said. "Several carriages are following more slowly with my clothing."

When Honeydew took her upstairs to explore the most palatable bedchamber—from an olfactory point of view—Simeon returned to his study.

The last thing he wanted to do was be in the same room with Isidore and a bed.

Chapter Thirteen

Revels House
February 29, 1784

Isidore had never selected a room on this basis before: she and Honeydew entered each room and then sniffed. But the stench was pervasive. It followed them from room to room like a friendly dog.

She was beginning to wonder if there was an inn within ready distance when Honeydew suddenly said, "Perhaps the Dower House, Your Grace. Would you consider it? I'm afraid it hasn't been opened or aired, but it's a lovely little house."

"Honeydew, I will consider any place that was not refurbished to include a water closet."

"The water closets in this house might be excellent," Honeydew said, "if only I could have persuaded His

Grace's father, the late duke, to take proper care of the pipes."

"When are they to be cleaned?" she asked.

Honeydew had a look of near agony on his face. "I'm afraid that the duke has encountered some difficulty finding appropriate help, but we should have men here within a day or two. It truly wasn't as bad until this week . . . the damp weather." He wrung his hands.

"I can see that there was little you could do." They walked downstairs and out a side door, and though Isidore would never say so, the relief of walking into the fresh outdoor air, brisk though it might be, was considerable. She saw Honeydew take a lungful as well. "I suppose one gets used to it?" she asked.

"Some do," Honeydew said. It was clear that he had not grown accustomed.

They followed a gravel path around the house. The shambles of a formal garden stretched before them.

She turned to Honeydew, mouth open, but he had the answer. "As of two days ago, His Grace instructed the estate's remaining gardener to hire additional staff as expeditiously as possible. They will bring the gardens back into trim."

The Dower House was not really a house; it was more of a cottage. But it was charming, with a rosebush climbing over the windows. It was like a doll's house.

"What color will the roses be?" she asked.

"Pale pink," the butler replied. "There are a great many of them. The vine hasn't been pruned as it ought, but it puts out a quantity of roses all the same. There are lilac trees around the back, but they won't bloom, of course, until late April."

He took out a huge circle of keys and finally managed to fit one to the lock. "There hasn't been anyone living here since His Grace's grandmother," he said, over his shoulder. "We used to air it out and clean it thoroughly, but in the past few years . . ."

Of course, he hadn't enough staff to spare.

After a small entryway, sunlight fell into a surprisingly large sitting room. The furniture was soft and covered with Holland cloths. There was no attempt at ducal elegance, quite the opposite. The walls were paneled in elmwood, painted a cream color with little pansies scattered here and there. The floor was flagstone, but a cheerful, if faded, rug hugged the middle. Best of all, the house smelled dusty but without even a whiff of sewage.

"How lovely!" Isidore exclaimed.

"The late duke's mother disliked formality," Honeydew said, bustling to pull open the curtains. "Phew! Look at this dust. I'll summon all the housemaids immediately, Your Grace, and we'll have it clean and aired in no time."

Isidore had discovered a charming little bedchamber containing a large sleigh bed and one table stacked with worn, leather-bound books.

"The duke's grandmother was a great reader by all accounts," Honeydew said. "Her own life was quite a romantic tale."

Isidore looked up from a small copy of *Tales of the Nile* that she'd discovered. It was falling apart, though she couldn't tell whether that was due to age or over-reading. "Romantic?"

"Yes, you must ask His Grace to tell you about it," Honeydew said, darting about to throw back the shutters. "There now, if you would be so kind as to accompany me back to the house, we'll get the house tidy for you."

Isidore shook her head. She supposed she would have to reenter the house for dinner. But she couldn't face that yet. She tucked herself into a rocking chair, book in hand. "I am exactly like my husband's grandmother," she said. "A great reader. I shall be quite happy here. When the maids arrive, I'll simply go for a little stroll."

"Will your personal maid be arriving in the later carriages?"

"Yes, Lucille experiences stomach problems when she travels, so she generally follows me in a slow-moving carriage. If it were possible, I would love a bath. I'm quite dusty from the journey."

"I'll set up a hot bath as soon as the maids have finished. If you're quite certain that you're comfortable . . ." He lingered, obviously disturbed by the idea of leaving her.

But Isidore was already opening up a book. "I shall be perfectly happy here, Honeydew. Truly. Please send the dowager duchess my regrets that I cannot greet her due to the absence of my maid."

She had a sudden thought. "Do you know, I believe that I am strangely fatigued by my journey." She smiled at the butler, who had the discretion not to indicate that she seemed in the utter pink of health. "I shall dine here tonight."

He bowed.

"I should be honored if the duke would disrupt his schedule and join me," she added. "Quite informally, of course. He needn't wear a cravat."

Honeydew's eyes were smiling, even if his face kept to a servantlike solemnity. "Just so, Your Grace. I shall inform him." He bowed again. "May I add that your generosity as regards His Grace's attire will be greatly appreciated?"

Chapter Fourteen

Revels House
February 29, 1784

"Her Grace is in the Dower House," Honeydew informed the duke. "The maids have been to clean, and she seems quite comfortable. We started a fire in the grate. The walls are damp, and it should quickly take away the chill."

The duke looked up from the letter he was writing and dragged a hand through his hair. "Really? Because of the stench? I think I must be getting used to it, Honeydew."

"No, Your Grace. The air is somewhat drier than it was this morning and it's not so obvious. But we are due for more rain tonight, or so Mr. Sumerall, the gardener, has told me."

"She's well out of it, then," the duke said, looking exhausted.

"The duchess requests that you dine with her in the Dower House," Honeydew said. In his estimation, the duchess wasn't coming back into the main house until the water closets were cleaned. Even if Mr. Kinnaird managed to find cleaning men in London—and given the amount of money that the duke had given him, he ought to—Honeydew thought that they wouldn't arrive for a day or two.

Besides, Honeydew was discovering he had alarmingly affectionate feelings toward the young duke who worked all day and half the night, and who was paying everyone, honest and true. The whole countryside was talking about it. A year ago he couldn't find a ripe melon without ready money, but now offers were flowing from all sides.

"This Mr. Purfew who claims to have done great service for the late duke," the duke said. "Do you have any idea who that might be, Honeydew?"

Honeydew pursed his lips. "It doesn't ring a bell. There was a Pursloe—"

The duke turned to an enormous ledger that lay open to his right. "I've already noted a payment to Pursloe, made yesterday, for four wigs purchased by my father ten years ago, payment refused on the grounds that they were too old-fashioned."

Honeydew judged it best to be silent.

But the duke smiled faintly. "I suspect my father was buried in one of those old-fashioned wigs?"

"I believe, sir, that there should be a letter thereabouts from a London wigmaker named Mr. Westby, who made the burial wig. It was His Grace's favorite."

The smile fell from the duke's face and he looked to his ledger with a sigh. "I haven't found Westby's letter,

Honeydew. But I attempted to take a nap at one point and discovered a great trove of letters propping up the leg of the sofa. When you get a moment, could you have the footmen remove that sofa? It's beyond repair."

Honeydew saw that the velvet, claw-footed sofa had lurched to the ground, minus a leg. Moreover a sprinkle of straw haloed the floor around it, showing that its innards were openly disintegrating. He felt a rush of embarrassment. "I am sorry that—your father wouldn't—"

The duke held up his hand. "There's no need," he said wearily. "Truly. I am learning the depths of my father's stubbornness letter by letter and I can only admire you for staying in your post. I have instructed Kinnaird to double your wages; consider it hardship pay."

Honeydew drew himself upright. "I thank you, Your Grace." Happy visions of retirement and a small cottage danced before his eyes. Then he returned to the subject at hand. It seemed to him quite odd that the duke and duchess were married, and yet not married. Not to mention sleeping, quite obviously, in different quarters.

What was needed was to create some good old-fashioned propinquity.

"Her Grace has requested supper to be served in the Dower House," he said. "I shall set a cover for you."

The duke nodded. But then, as Honeydew was leaving, he looked up from his desk and said, "Don't forget to ask Godfrey to join us."

Godfrey? A thirteen-year-old joining the intimate dinner between a barely married man and wife? Honeydew could not approve.

"I shall ascertain whether the young master is free to join you," he said, vowing to make quite certain that Godfrey was occupied.

"Of course, I'm free," piped up a voice from the other side of the room.

"Lord Godfrey!"

The boy's brown curls popped up from the far side of yet another faded sofa. "I haven't even met the duchess."

"I didn't know you were still there," the duke said, smiling at his brother. "One hour more and I'm dragging you out on the roads for a run, Godfrey."

Defeated, Honeydew bowed and departed.

Chapter Fifteen

*I*sidore prepared her cottage with great care. A small army of housemaids cleaned it from floor to rafters. Then she sent two of the most capable-looking ones searching all over Revels House for bits of furniture.

By the end of the afternoon, she had her little dollhouse made up a trifle more comfortably. Candles shone all over the room. Upholstered chairs replaced the unpadded armchairs favored by the late dowager duchess. There was a vase of snowdrops that Isidore gathered in the garden, and the bed (large enough for two) was made up with snowy white linens and piled with pillows.

It was still a doll's house, but polished to a high

gleam and smelling deliciously of French lilacs (thanks to some very expensive *parfum*), it spoke of creature comforts.

And seduction.

The footmen arrived with a small dining room table and Isidore had them move it twice before she decided the best place for it was in the corner of the sitting room, where she and Simeon would eat in a mysterious, slightly shadowed intimacy.

She sent a suggested menu to Honeydew, including hot, spiced wine that she could prepare herself at fireside.

She could just picture it: the duke with his broad shoulders, his jacket thrown open and his hair tumbling to his shoulders. She would play the immaculate, utterly delicious wife. If what he wanted was English womanhood in all its delicate docility, she could do that.

It was like a favorite story that she had already read, and now got to enact. The Taming of the Wild Man . . .

Isidore started humming as she dropped into a steaming bath, delicately scented with jasmine. Jasmine had an innocent touch, she thought.

As she sat in the hot water, she refined her story to a trembling virginal bride facing a wild pirate king.

That sounded like just the sort of setting to appeal to Simeon. And he obviously wanted to believe it. Look how he'd leapt at the idea that she'd never pleasured herself.

She found herself smiling. This was going to be fun. She tried out a few sentences in her mind. *Oh dear! It's far too large!*

Or would one say, *You're* far too large?

The etiquette of it all . . . Maybe she could just shudder, throw a hand over her eye and squeak, *No, no, no!*

Of course, the wild pirate would overcome the delicate flower's resistance. The key was to pretend not to enjoy it.

Or perhaps the key was to be afraid?

Simeon wasn't mad. And she had a fair idea that he truly was capable in bed. He was dressed oddly. But he looked male. In fact the very idea of him without clothes made her feel the opposite of frightened.

She got out of the bath and picked up the toweling cloth left for her by Lucille. All she had to do was flirt with him until he took some liberties. Then she would launch into a version of the fragile English rose, and, she hoped, he would revert to wild pirate, and all her worries would be resolved.

Chapter Sixteen

Gore House, Kensington
London Seat of the Duke of Beaumont
February 29, 1784

"What would you like to do this evening?" Jemma
looked down the table at her husband. "We've been invited to Lady Feddrington's soirée in honor of the visit of
the Prussian prince, Duke Ferdinand of Brunswick; or
there is a musicale given by Lady Cholmondelay; and of
course there's the performance of *As You Like It* that we
discussed last week, in which all the women's parts are
played by boys."

Elijah put down his napkin and stood up, walking
around the long table to Jemma. She looked up at him
inquiringly. He looked somewhat better than he had before eating: he was too young to look so bone-tired.

"I am in no mood to watch boys prance about the stage," he said, taking her arm to bring her to her feet, "but I should be happy to escort you to either of the other events."

Jemma blinked at him. She fully expected him to say that he had to work. To read those documents that he was always reading, even at the supper table. "You mean—"

He held out his arm. "I have decided not to work in the evenings. I am at your command, duchess."

"Oh," Jemma said, rather uncertainly.

They strolled toward the drawing room. "I suppose the soirée," Jemma said, deciding. "I should like to dance." She was wearing a new dress, a delicious gown of figured pale yellow satin with a pattern of tiny green leaves. Her skirts were trimmed with double flounces and rather shorter than in the previous year.

Elijah looked down at her with a smile in his eyes.

"Yes, I am wearing a new gown and I should like to show it off," she told him, thinking that there were nice aspects to having been married so long.

"The hem reveals a delectable bit of your slipper," he said gravely.

"You noticed!" She stuck out her toe. She wore yellow slippers with very high heels, ornamented with a cunning little rose.

"Yellow roses," he said, "are not nearly as rare as a perfect ankle like yours, Jemma."

"Good lord," she said, smiling at him. "It must be a blue moon. You're complimenting your wife. Let me find my fan and my knotting bag—"

Fowle handed them to her.

"What a lovely fan," Elijah said, taking it from her. "What is the imagery?"

"I hadn't looked closely," she said, turning away so that Fowle could help her with her cloak.

"Venus and Adonis . . . and a very lovely rendition as well."

She came back and stood on tiptoe to see the fan, which he had spread before him. "Oh, I see. Yes, there is Venus. My goodness."

"She seems to be pulling poor Adonis into the bushes," Elijah said. She loved the dry humor he displayed when he wasn't acting like a hidebound and moralistic politician. "Look at her breasts! No wonder the poor lad looks frightened and titillated, all at once. A tantalizing bit of art, this."

"Surely you don't approve?" she said. "You, the proper politician?"

"No Venus has offered to pull me into the bushes, so I could hardly say." He closed the fan. "Where on earth did it come from, Jemma? You didn't purchase the piece without looking at the illustration?" Fowle threw a cloak around his shoulders.

"Fans are a popular gift at the moment," Jemma said. "This came from Villiers. He gave it to me a few days ago."

"I didn't know he paid you a visit."

Jemma felt a strange qualm. It was all so difficult, having her husband's boyhood friend trying to seduce her. "He came by to tell me of the strange doings of the Duke of Cosway."

Out of the corner of her eye she saw Elijah toss the fan dismissively toward one of the footmen. Of course, that left her without a fan for the evening. No one was ever without a fan. But she could say that she left it in the carriage.

She climbed into the carriage and sank into the corner, suddenly struck by a profound realization. It was too late for Villiers, fan or no. She would never drag him into the bushes. When she first returned from France, she was so angry with Elijah that she thought to have an *affaire* with Villiers, but he had refused her.

And now, now that Villiers had changed his mind . . . it was too late.

Elijah had kissed her a few weeks ago. He had kissed her twice, actually. It was absurd, it was deluded. She was riveted by the memory of those kisses.

He was her first, her only husband, her . . .

Whatever he was to her.

The truth was that she was infatuated. She spent her afternoons in the library, waiting for him to return from the House of Lords. She secretly read all the papers so that she could engage in clever conversation about the events of the day. She thrilled when reading accounts of his speeches, and trembled when he set out in the morning on a day that included a talk before Parliament.

Not that he knew it, of course.

She would rather die of humiliation than let her husband know that she was infatuated by him.

She kept telling herself that Elijah never bothered to come to Paris to bring her home when she had fled there as a young bride. She kept reminding herself of his mistress, but somehow she had lost her rage, or perhaps her enthusiasm for that rage.

It was gone, tucked away in a faded box of memories. And the only clear thing she knew about her marriage was that she was married to a man who was so beautiful, with his sharp cheekbones and English grace, his tall, strong body and intelligent eyes—so beautiful that she would do anything to lure him back to her bed.

She was aware, while dressing, while putting on lip rouge, while putting on her shoes, that she was playing the most serious game of her life. *He* had to come to *her*.

She could not chase him, beg him, or by any means at her disposal make it clear that he was welcome to her person . . . to her heart.

Though he was.

It wouldn't work, not for life.

She wanted Elijah—not the way she had him when they were first married, not with the genial affection and enthusiasm he showed for their awkward couplings. She wanted him, the Duke of Beaumont, one of the most powerful men in government, *at her feet*.

And she wouldn't settle for less.

Villiers would be useful in her campaign. He and Elijah had been childhood friends and were now estranged. Good. She would use him. She would use any man in London who asked her to dance, if it would fan a spark of jealousy in her husband's civilized heart.

But it wasn't jealousy that could do it. It was she: she had to be more witty, more beautiful, more desirable than she ever had been.

Elijah was seated in the opposite corner of the carriage, looking absently out of the window. As always, his wig was immaculate and discreet. Not for the Duke of Beaumont were pyramids of scented curls or immovable rolls perched on top of frizzled locks. He wore a simple, short-cut wig with curls so small they hardly deserved the label.

Underneath, she knew, he had his hair clipped close to his skull. It was a style that would destroy the appeal of almost every man. But on Elijah it brought into focus his cheekbones and the gaunt, courteous, restrained masculinity of him.

By the time they arrived at Lady Feddrington's soirée, the receiving line had broken up and the ballroom was crowded. They stood for a moment at the top of the steps leading down into the room.

"It's a bit overwhelming," Elijah murmured. "How on earth do you ladies manage to move about a room like this, given the width of your panniers?"

Jemma smiled at him. "'Tis only the unfashionable who have *very* wide panniers this season. Look at myself, for instance."

He looked, and she felt his glance as if it were a touch. Not that she showed it. She had spent years in the court of Versailles; if those years had taught her anything, it was that she should never reveal vulnerability.

"Your skirts look as wide as a barnyard door," he said to her. But she saw the laughter in his grave eyes. He needed to laugh more.

She met his eyes with the kind of smile that told a man she liked him. It felt odd to give it to her husband. "Narrower than many," she told him.

"I'm sure you are precisely *à la mode*," he said, taking her arm again. "Shall we?"

They reached the bottom of the steps just as the first notes of a minuet sounded. "Would you like to dance?" he asked her. "I realize it is a great *faux pas* to dance with one's husband, but you could always say that you got it out of the way."

She looked up at him and had to swallow because of the beauty of his eyes. She put her hand in his. "You do me too much honor."

He bowed before her as the music continued, and they moved smoothly, together, into the steps of the dance. It separated them; she felt it as a physical ache.

It brought them back together; she was afraid that her pleasure showed too much in her eyes, and she refused to look at his face. "Look!" she cried, her voice witless, "there's Lady Piddleton, dancing with Saint Albans. He must be gathering material . . . he is always so cruel about her."

Elijah didn't reply. When she stole a look at him, he met her eyes and there was something there.

Surely he would speak to her. Kiss her again. Tell her . . .

The dance ended and he bowed. Saint Albans was at her right elbow, her friend Lord Corbin at her left. Lord Sosney walked up with Lord Killigrew, veritably shouting over the din, "Duchess!"

She caught Elijah's eye for a moment, but he turned away.

And she turned away.

A chess player never shows the moment when she realizes that she might lose a game. That the board has turned against her; the black pieces are clustered for attack. The very best chess players revel in the chance to save themselves.

Jemma reminded herself that she was the very best.

She turned, laughing, to Lord Corbin, holding out her gloved hand to be kissed.

Chapter Seventeen

The Dower House
February 29, 1784

The table gleamed softly with old silver. Honeydew had conveyed Mrs. Bullock's promise that the food would be exquisite. The butler referred darkly to some exigencies in the recent past, but Isidore did not inquire further. She found that a combination of blissful ignorance and high expectations was the best policy when it came to household problems.

She was dressed in an informal open gown of the finest wine-dark silk. The overskirts pulled back into great loops of nearly transparent fabric, tied by forest green knots of silk. It was an unusual and charming garment—and perhaps most importantly, the bodice was cut extremely low.

There was quite a lot of Isidore in the chest area. She generally viewed this feature dispassionately, as an attribute that made certain corsets impossible, and others very uncomfortable. But she wasn't blind to how much men liked to be presented with abundance; if Cosway turned out to be someone enchanted by an expanse of flesh that would suit a worthy milk cow, Isidore was just the right one to enchant him.

In fact, she thought she had the virginal male fantasy in play. Breasts barely covered, with light, billowing skirts that appeared easy to remove, *check*. Unpowdered hair piled in loose curls, *check*. Just a touch of haunting perfume—the sort that smelled clean and innocent rather than French and seductive—*check* and *mate*.

Years of assessing male attraction were coming in quite useful. She thought it was quite likely that the duke, her husband, would experience her femininity like a bolt of lightning.

There was only one thing she didn't envision.

Two males appeared at the door. Make that two virgins. And when they both walked in her front door, Simeon bending his head slightly so as not to strike his forehead on the lintel, it was his little brother Godfrey who looked as if he'd been struck by lightning. He stopped short and Simeon walked straight into him.

His mouth fell open. Strange noises came out, resembling frogs singing on a summer night.

"Good evening, Simeon," she said, moving forward. Didn't he have any sense? Couldn't he have guessed—

Apparently not. Without even a flicker of regret in his eyes, Simeon was turning to his brother and introducing him. "Godfrey, stand tall. You haven't met the duchess for years, but I'm sure you remember her."

Godfrey bowed so deeply that she was afraid he

wasn't coming back up again. He did, eventually, face red and hair on end.

She dropped into a curtsy that unfortunately put her breasts directly under his nose. He turned purple and cast a desperate look at his brother.

"It's my pleasure," Isidore said. She gave him a kindly smile, one that said *calm down.*

But the duke was moving into the room and suddenly it seemed to have shrunk to half its size. Isidore stopped herself from falling back. It was just that Simeon was so . . . male. Very male. Very large.

"What a charming little room this is," he was saying, wandering about just as if she wasn't there, quivering like a jelly tart fresh out of the oven.

"Yes, charming," she said, watching his shoulders. They were broad and beautiful. If he didn't even kiss her good night, she decided, that meant he *was* incapable.

Alternatively, it could mean that he found her unattractive. No. That option was unacceptable.

He pulled out her chair and she sat down, mentally giving herself a shake. Obviously, her earlier plan wouldn't work. But she had once boasted of her ability to make any man flirt. Flirtation was halfway to the bedchamber.

This duke wouldn't see it coming, and Godfrey could take a lesson in adulthood.

She leaned forward, employing the smile that set half of Paris on fire during her twentieth year. That would be the male half, naturally.

"Do tell me about yourself, Simeon?" she cooed. "I feel as if I hardly know you." In her experience, there was nothing a man liked more than to talk about himself.

Simeon put his heavy linen napkin in his lap. "I am so uninteresting," he said blandly. "I would prefer to hear about you. What have you done during the years while I was wandering around Abyssinia and the like?"

He was obviously a worthy opponent. He looked genial, friendly, utterly calm—and about as interested as he would be if she were a nursemaid.

"I traveled Europe with my aunt," she said. "Surely you remember from my letters?" She let just a tiny edge sharpen her words.

The footman was pouring wine and Isidore noticed out of the corner of her eye that Godfrey was drinking with marked enthusiasm. Did boys of that age drink wine? She had the vague idea they were all tucked away in schools; certainly one never saw them at formal dinners.

"I expect that many of your letters did not reach me. I remember getting a note from my solicitor once informing me of some action he'd taken on your behalf."

"Weren't you concerned that I might discuss intimate matters in my letters?"

He looked surprised. "I never considered the possibility, given as we had never met. What intimacies could we exchange? Of course I instructed my solicitors to act on my behalf with regard to any missive from my family that appeared on their desk. One never knew how long it would take to get mail, let alone to return my instructions to London."

"Didn't you ever wonder where your wife was?"

He paused for a moment and then said: "No."

Well, that was straightforward.

"*I* wondered where you were," Godfrey said eagerly. "I still remember your stay at our house, though it was brief."

"Impossible," Isidore said. He was in that gangly stage, where his legs seemed impossibly long. He had the nose of a man and the eyes of a child. "You were only . . . how old? It was '73."

"I was almost three," Godfrey said. "Don't you remember playing peek-a-boo with me? I thought perhaps you had come to live with us."

"I did," Isidore said, seeing no reason to lie to him. "But I caused your mother such discomfort that my aunt decided it was better that I travel with her."

He nodded. "The servants told stories about your visit for years."

She raised an eyebrow.

He had a funny little grin, this brother of Cosway's. "No one before or after has called the duchess a termagant to her face."

"There you see," Isidore said. "What a good thing it was that my aunt agreed to take me with her. The heart palpitations your mother escaped once I left can only be imagined. I trust," she added punctiliously, remembering that she was speaking to a child and should add guidance, "that you did not follow in my disreputable example."

"She's not so terrible," Godfrey said earnestly. "Truly. She gets frightened about money, and that makes her sniffy."

Simeon reached out and knocked his brother on the shoulder in what Isidore assumed was a fraternal gesture.

Honeydew entered, followed by footmen carrying covered dishes. They were placed on the side table, just as she had instructed when she was envisioning a seductive meal. Honeydew waved the footmen outside and served the table himself as the three of them sat in utter silence. Godfrey had finished his wine, so Honeydew poured him another glass before retiring to the great house. Godfrey looked interestingly pink, and Isidore decided he was not used to imbibing.

Simeon's eyes had a kind of ironic laziness to them

that she found rather attractive, given that most men's eyes took on a feverish gleam if she paid them attention, especially with her bosom on display.

"Did you and your aunt live anywhere in particular?" he asked.

He really had ignored all her letters, or not received them.

"We lived in Venice a great deal of the time," she explained, "as my family is from that city. But my aunt plays the violin, and so we traveled to various European capitals and performed in the courts."

"She is a musician? You were travelling around Europe with a performing musician?" Now he looked surprised.

"We always had enough to eat, Simeon. In case you were picturing her playing for pennies by the side of the road."

"Why didn't you inform my solicitor if you were in that sort of situation? It was utterly inappropriate for a duchess and I would never have allowed it!"

Godfrey was halfway through his second glass of wine but paused with the glass halfway to his lips. "Did you travel about in fairs?" he asked eagerly. "I love fairs! One came through the village and my mother allowed me to attend. There was a wonderful fiddler named Mr. McGurdy. Did you ever happen to meet him?"

"No, I didn't meet Mr. McGurdy," Isidore said, enjoying herself hugely. "Why Simeon, are you saying that you would have travelled back to England before completing your investigation of the Nile had you known I was *in extremis?*"

He gave her a sour look. "I would have instructed my solicitors to find you an appropriate situation if you didn't wish to return to my mother's house."

"A nunnery, perhaps?" Isidore asked mockingly.

For a moment his eyes lingered on her chest. "They wouldn't have had you." She felt a flare of triumph.

"Was it hard sleeping by the side of the road?" Godfrey asked. He had finished his second glass and was sawing away at a piece of chicken in a manner that suggested his coordination was impaired.

"I never slept by the side of the road," Isidore said, adding primly, "thank goodness."

"I just don't understand this family!" Simeon said, putting down his cutlery. "Isidore, you had access to whatever funds you wished. Not only did your parents leave you a considerable inheritance, but you could have drawn on my funds at any point. Why were you travelling with fairs? Why is everyone's attitude toward money so peculiar?"

"Mother doesn't know you have all that money," Godfrey said, turning to his brother owlishly. "She thinks we don't have any."

"She knows," Simeon said grimly. "She sees the books. She simply can't bring herself to disperse any of it."

Godfrey frowned. "You mean—"

Isidore shot her husband a look. His little brother had the bewildered look of a child who's been lied to. "Her Grace showed her respect for her husband by continuing to operate the estate precisely as he had done, I have no doubt," she said.

Godfrey brightened. "Yes, of course. Father never allowed any untoward expenditures. He considered it a point of honor."

"There's little honor in not paying tradesmen for their honest work," Simeon said.

Godfrey looked stricken again. Isidore took another try. "When I visited this house many years ago, I remember being rather surprised by your father's frugal attitude.

But in a frank discussion with your mother, she informed me that he considered himself merely the guardian of the duchy and hoped to pass on his estates intact, without wasting his substance as so many noblemen do."

Godfrey reached for the sideboard and the bottle of wine, but Isidore gave him a minatory look and his arm dropped. He picked up his fork, but a moment later Simeon poured wine into all three of their glasses.

"I would greatly appreciate it if you could tell me how you and your aunt were reduced to busking at fairs, given your birth, not to mention our marriage," Simeon said, his voice rather chilly. Apparently, it was her fault that at twelve years old she had failed to voluntarily enter a nunnery while waiting for his return.

"Some say my aunt is one of the greatest violinists ever born," Isidore said. Godfrey had finished his chicken and looked a little dazed.

"She must have been better than Mr. McGurdy, then," Godfrey mumbled. "Though he played a tambourine with his right foot at the same time."

"My aunt played only the violin."

Simeon put down his fork again. "I have felt as if I were living in two worlds for the past week or so, and this only confirms it. Are you saying that your aunt was in great demand, and you did not travel fairs?"

"No, we did not," Isidore said. "She had a long-standing arrangement to join the French court for the Easter season; Queen Marie Antoinette is quite fond of music, you know. My aunt would play solos for her in gardens of Versailles. Sometimes my aunt would steal into the great maze, and then begin to play. The ladies would wander into the labyrinth until they were able to find her by following the sound of her music."

"I'd love to see that," Godfrey said.

"I should like to play a musical instrument," Simeon said. "Once I was in an Indian bazaar and heard an old gentleman play a sort of violin-like instrument so beautifully that I began to weep."

"To *weep?*" Godfrey said, his voice breaking in a high little squeal. "You cried, where anyone could see you?"

Simeon smiled at him. "There's no shame in a man crying."

Nor in being a virgin either, Isidore thought sourly.

"I think it's shameful," Godfrey said. "And do you know, Brother, I think it's a bit shameful that you're sitting down to supper without a cravat. Or a waistcoat. Her Grace—" he stumbled a little and slurred it together—"Her Grace is a duchess, you know. You're not paying respect to her. Or you're not respectful of her." He looked a little confused, but stubborn.

Simeon looked over at Isidore in an inquiring kind of way. "Do you agree with my brother that the size or existence of a cravat determines the respect due a woman?"

"It would be a start," she said sweetly. "After that would have to come respect for a woman's opinions, of course."

She had to admit: he was intelligent. He knew instantly what she was talking about. "It's not that I won't respect my wife's opinions—"

"She is your wife," Godfrey intervened.

"But that when it comes to an emergency, one person has to assume responsibility."

"An emergency," Isidore said, ladling a generous dollop of scorn into her voice. "What sort of emergency are you thinking of?"

"All sorts." He raised his glass, his eyes dark and somber over the rim. "I have been in enough difficult spots, Isidore, to know that dangers flock from every direction."

"For example?"

"Were you ever attacked by a lion?" Godfrey asked. He was definitely slurring his words. He looked terribly sleepy and slightly nauseated.

"Not lately," Simeon said.

"Godfrey, would you like to retire to my armchair for a moment?" Isidore asked.

He just stared at her, until Simeon said, "Godfrey." His voice was quiet, but the authority inherent there was absolute.

Godfrey stumbled to the chair and sat down, his eyes closing immediately.

"Is that your example?" Isidore asked.

"I suppose it could be."

"The situation also could have been avoided had you paid attention. The third glass of wine was too much."

"It was a matter of male pride. I believe this is probably Godfrey's first dinner in which he was offered sufficient wine to make himself ill. It is far better that he overindulge tonight and learn from it, than that he do so on a more public occasion."

"I don't agree with you that there must be a general in every marriage," Isidore said.

"The commonly accepted idea of marriage," Simeon said, "is that the man has to be that leader. I have seen a few successful marriages in which the reverse was true. One of the two people must be accepted as such."

Across the room, Godfrey was making a heavy breathing sound. She would rather assay her first seduction without a drunken thirteen-year-old in the corner.

But Simeon really meant it when he said that they would wait until the night of their wedding. He truly would walk away from her. She had to try *something*.

She leaned toward him so that the lush weight of her breasts hung forward. "Would you tell the footman outside the door that Godfrey has fallen asleep?" she said. "Perhaps Honeydew should escort him to his bed chamber."

"And clear away these dishes," Simeon said. He sounded as if she were a remote acquaintance, who had offered him a boiled sweet. She'd heard that voice before. He had a way of growing even more calm, more distant. She'd seen it before . . .

It meant he felt threatened.

Good.

She leaned back, thinking that her breasts had done their job. "Please," she added.

He rose, opened the door to the outside and had a brief word with the footman. A moment later Godfrey walked unsteadily from the room, looking rather greenish.

"He's going to cast up his accounts in the bushes," Simeon said.

The little house drew around them again, sheltering, sweet, romantic. Then the door opened and Honeydew swept in with dishes of pear stewed in port. He was gone in a moment, leaving them with glasses of sparkling wine.

Isidore had been flirting for years. She let her eyelids droop and threw Simeon a sleepy glance from under her lashes.

He was busy cutting up his pear and didn't notice. She waited a moment but he seemed as concentrated on the pear as if he were boning a pheasant. Fine. She turned to her own pear, trying desperately to think of a seductive topic. Nothing came to mind, so she found herself saying the least romantic thing possible: "When do you think that the water closets will be repaired?"

"Honeydew and I investigated the pipes today," Simeon

said, looking up. "They are completely rotted. If you can believe it, the original piping was done in wood. Naturally the water rotted them through within the year."

"Your father must have been one of the first to install a water closet at all," Isidore said. "That was rather progressive of him."

"It appears from the correspondence I found that he was offered the water closets for a pittance," Simeon said bluntly. "He was supposed to allow the fabricators to use his name and express his approval. I think they probably discarded this idea when he refused to pay that pittance, saying that the pipes didn't work sufficiently. After that, the pipes rotted and there was no one to fix them."

Isidore finished her bite. "It must be quite difficult to be in a position to judge one's parents as an adult," she offered. "Since mine died when I was very young, I knew them only as parents, never as people."

"Were they good to you?"

"Oh yes. They were Italian, you know, so they had a different idea of family life than do many English parents. There were nursemaids, of course, but both of my parents visited the nursery every day. I spent a great deal of time with my mother, in particular."

"And when they died, you were sent here, to my mother?"

"Until my aunt took me away again."

"Probably even if your aunt had been busking at the side of the road, it would have been the right thing to do," he said, putting down his fork and knife.

"The wife of a future duke playing for pennies along with Mr. McGurdy?" she said, laughing a bit.

"My mother has a difficult character," Simeon said. "Your aunt was right. I had no right to criticize her earlier. It is no one's business how you spent your time with your aunt, and certainly not mine, given my lengthy absence."

Isidore was conscious of a warm glow under her breastbone. It wasn't a seductive glow, though, and some time later her so-called husband began making his way out of the cottage without taking even the smallest liberty. In fact, without a single flirtatious comment.

"Wait!" she said, when he had a hand on the door.

He turned.

She walked toward him, not with her signature sleepy look, nor with a little smile of interest, none of the tricks she had used to reduce men to their knees in the past. Instead she just walked to him and looked up, assessing the strong line of his jaw, the slightly wild cut of his hair, the breadth of his shoulders. He looked like a man, an adult. A grown man.

It gave her a little pulse of anxiety, as if she'd been playing with boys up until now. There was something different about the intensity and the fire inside Simeon.

"Will you kiss me good-night, please?" she said.

"Kiss you?"

"Yes. It's customary for married couples."

She thought he would say they weren't married, but he didn't. Instead, he just moved forward and lowered his head, kissed her.

It was over in a second. She had a fleeting sensation of firm lips, a tiny scent of something . . . him . . . male, slightly spicy. And he moved back.

She blinked at him, thinking that kissing wasn't what she expected; it wasn't as good.

"Damn." His voice was quiet, but the night was quiet too.

"What?"

"That wasn't your first kiss, was it?"

"Actually, it was," she said. "Though—" She caught the words back. Why had she waited, evaded so many lips, never allowed herself to be kissed? It was nothing. Nothing special.

But then he moved closer again. "It's all right," she said hastily, sensing that he meant to kiss her again.

This time his arms came around her slowly, and she had time to see the planes of his face, the way he looked straight into her eyes, the way his body loomed over hers . . . This time when his lips touched hers, they didn't slide away immediately.

She had seen kissing. She knew that it was done with open mouths, that it made women cling to their lovers, as if their knees were failing them.

She knew that, all that, and yet—

He kissed her hard this time, not a fleeting caress, but a command. His arms slipped past her, braced against the wall, and his body came against hers. She gasped at the strength of it, the heat, and then their mouths were open together. It was like an open flame that rushed through Isidore's body—the taste of him, the feeling of it, the kiss, his body.

She shivered, made an inarticulate murmur, a noise, a cry. Their tongues met and sang together. Her mind reeled and she wound her arms around his neck. Gone were all her thoughts of seduction, of fragile English brides.

"Yes," she whispered into his mouth, her body against his. Her breasts didn't feel like large objects meant to attract men now. They were on fire, tingling from where they rubbed against his coat. He pulled her tighter, and another little moan came from her throat. He kissed her hard, pushing her against the wall. She wanted to open her eyes, but desire swamped her, betrayed her voice and her logical mind and her plans. She could only cling to him and kiss him back, her tongue touching his and retreating.

Growing bolder, responding to the muffled groan that seemed to come from his chest, not from his mouth.

Finally he pulled back.

"Was that your first kiss?" she asked, when she could speak again.

He stood for a moment, the firelight cascading off the gleam of his hair. Half his face was in shadow.

Finally, he said quietly, "No."

"Ah." She didn't know what she had wanted to hear. Of course he was experienced at kissing. How could he—how could they have—

"It was my second," he said. "The first was a moment or two ago, but I'm not sure they belong in the same category."

And then he was gone, the door closing on a swirl of evening air.

Chapter Eighteen

Revels House
March 1, 1784

The next morning Isidore rose to find a light rain falling. She had a bath, sat by the fire, and read *Tales of the Nile* while Lucille fussed with her clothing.

But it was no good. She didn't want to sit in her cottage while Simeon was off in the main house by himself. She didn't want to wait for him, like a docile little mouse waiting for the cat to pay a call, to find time to discuss the end of their marriage. Besides, their marriage wasn't over, even if he didn't know it yet.

A few seconds later she was shaking the rain from her plumed hat, and handing it to Honeydew. "Your Grace," he was saying. "May I serve you some tea?"

Isidore shook her head. She was looking around the high entrance hall. It wasn't in terrible shape, though the marble was cracked, and the paneling on one door looked scuffed. "What happened to this?" she said, walking over to inspect it before she even off took her pelisse.

"The late duke's dog was a terrible scratcher," Honeydew said. She was getting to know him now, and that quiet tone implied severe disapproval.

"We need some foolscap," she told him, giving her dripping pelisse to a footman. "And a quill. I shall make lists of what needs to be done, and I might as well start with the entry."

She began prowling around the walls, looking at the pictures, the paneling, and the moldings.

"If Your Grace will allow me to act as your secretary," Honeydew said in a tone mingled with astonishment and gratitude.

"Yes, thank you," she said. She had discovered a small painting next to the door leading to the drawing room. It was hanging askew and its frame was broken. But it was a lovely treatment of a dog with a pigeon. "Is this the dog in question?"

Honeydew turned from sending one of the footmen running for paper. "Exactly so, Your Grace. The former duke had his dog painted in a variety of poses."

"This is lovely," Isidore said. "Was the artist ever paid?"

"Yes," Honeydew said, rather surprisingly.

Isidore nodded. "Is the duke in his study?"

"He is working. I'm afraid that the maids discovered a great nest of papers in one of the cupboards in the master bedchamber," Honeydew said. "It appears they include some bills in arrears."

"And the duke's mother?"

"Her Grace rarely makes an appearance before late morning," Honeydew said. "She spends the morning in prayer."

Isidore tried to imagine Simeon's mother praying, failed, and walked into the largest sitting room.

"The Yellow Salon," Honeydew named it. In truth, the previously buttery upholstery had faded to a grayish-cream. But the room's proportions were beautiful. At one point, there had been an exquisite band of blue and gold plaster around the cornice at the top of the walls.

"New drapes, obviously," Isidore said. "This sofa looks quite good and merely needs reupholstering. I very much doubt that all this work could be done locally in a timely fashion; shall we ship the lot off to London? I seem to remember that the Duchess of Beaumont made use of Mr. George Seddon's workshop."

Honeydew beamed. "I agree, Your Grace." He lowered his voice. "If I might suggest that we send payment along with the furniture. I'm afraid that the duke has a reputation to overcome."

"We'll pay double," Isidore said. "I would like the furniture reupholstered as soon as possible." In fact, the more she thought about last night and that kiss . . . "I believe I would like this house to be shining and habitable in ten days, Honeydew. What do you think?"

The smile dropped from his face and he looked a bit winded. "That is hard to imagine."

"I find that ready money does wonders. Do we have a cart for all this furniture?"

"Yes, Your Grace," Honeydew said. "We do, but—"

Isidore smiled at him. "I have absolute faith in you."

Honeydew pulled himself up and nodded. "I shall do my best."

"Let's put those yellow sofas and that large piece there on the list. Goodness, is that a harp?"

Honeydew nodded.

"Missing all its strings," Isidore said. "We'd better make two lists. One set of furniture should go straight to London, with instructions that it be either repaired or reupholstered. The remainder can retire to the attics, the harp among them. We need a plaster-worker as well; the bones of the room are lovely but the walls need redoing. The criss-cross gold and blue around the top merely needs freshening."

Honeydew scribbled at his list. "Yes, Your Grace."

"Thank goodness this mirror isn't broken," she said, stopping before an eleven-foot-high mirror set into the paneling. "Whose portrait is set at the top there, in the medallion?"

"His Grace," Honeydew said, "as a young boy. The chandelier," he added, "is only missing one strand of glass pearls."

"Make a note of it," Isidore said. "I am monstrously fond of the new embroidered chairs, Honeydew, and they would look lovely in this room . . . perhaps with cherry blossoms on a pale yellow background?"

The door behind them opened suddenly and Isidore turned about. In the doorway stood the dowager duchess. She looked pinched and faded, and yet the same pugnacious light that Isidore remembered shone in her eyes.

Isidore immediately dropped into a curtsy that nearly had her sitting on the floor. She didn't raise her head from its respectful position for a good moment before murmuring, eyes still lowered, "Your Grace, what an honor. I had not thought to disturb you at such an early hour."

"Honeydew," the duchess said, "I'm sure that you have much to do."

Isidore turned to Honeydew. "If you could arrange for the cart as we discussed, I shall rejoin you shortly." The dowager seated herself on one of the sofas, so Isidore followed.

Her mother-in-law didn't bother with preliminaries. "We never could abide each other," she said grimly, "but need comes to want, and we have to work around that."

"I am truly happy to see you in such good health, Your Grace."

The older woman waved her hand irritably in the air. "My generation doesn't care so much for that sort of flummery. You don't give a damn about my health, but I imagine that you're as interested in my son's as I am. Have you spent some time with him?" She narrowed her eyes.

"I have. We dined last night with Godfrey."

The duchess's face softened. "Godfrey is a good lad. My elder, on the other hand—" she shook her head. "I'm not of a generation to beat about the bush, so I'll tell you, he's unhinged. I thought at first that I might be able to keep it from you, long enough to head off an annulment, but I realized that talk of brain fever is impossible between a man and a wife. I would have known if my husband grew unhinged, and I expect you know as well."

Isidore cleared her throat. "He is certainly original in his thinking."

"He's mad. Cork-brained. He'll cause you many a humiliation if you stay in the marriage."

It was no more than Isidore herself had initially thought.

"*But,*" Simeon's mother continued, "he's a duke. That's a fact and no one can take that away from him, whether he looks like a common thief or not." She threw Isidore an icy look. "You're on the old side to catch another husband, may I point out? You'll never find one at the level of a duke. Your being Italian and all, you'd be lucky to catch a baron."

Isidore didn't bother to answer.

"He's a duke and that makes you a duchess," she continued. "It isn't trivial to be a duchess. You'll be among the highest in the land. People may talk behind your back about your husband's proclivities, but they won't do so to your face. And who gives a fart what they say behind your back?"

Isidore managed to close her mouth with an effort.

"Don't look so mealy-mouthed!" the duchess snapped at her. "I've never lost a moment's sleep thinking about what little people say behind my back. I advise you to do the same. You're not born to be a duchess, but we chose you carefully enough."

"You chose me due to the dowry my father offered," Isidore put in. She was starting to feel a rising wave of fury. How could a mother speak about her son in such withering terms? True, Simeon was unusual, but—

"He promised you were a biddable girl," her mother-in-law said crushingly.

"He was mistaken," Isidore said, showing her teeth in an approximation of a smile.

"I realized that the moment I saw you," the duchess said. "Only twelve years old, and as saucy as a lower housemaid. I thought then that it would fall apart before the wedding and likely it would have but for my son's refusal to return to England. Of course he was suffering from brain fever."

"He didn't have brain fever," Isidore said.

"Put your gloves back on!" the duchess barked. "No duchess would show her ungloved hands in public. I can see that making *you* into proper duchess material is going to be as hard as bundling my son into acceptable shape."

"Your son is more than acceptable," Isidore said, placing her gloves on the table before her with some precision.

It was a signal of war. The duchess, who had up till now resembled an elderly bulldog, suddenly straightened and took on the air of a mastiff. "I foresee the long lineage of the Cosways dragged into the dirt."

Isidore smiled kindly at her. "I will do my very best to get the dirt out of this room, not to mention this *house*, which smells worse than most slums."

"A duchess does not lower herself to such inconsequential matters."

"Your—and I use the word advisedly—*your* house looks like the tumble-down shack owned by an impoverished peasant. The house stinks like a privy, the furniture is falling apart, and the servants haven't been paid. I may not have been raised by a duke, but my father would have been ashamed to treat his dependents as you have routinely treated your staff."

She paused, but the duchess didn't seem ready to take up her side of the argument yet, so Isidore continued. "My father would also have been ashamed to allow the house of his forefathers to fall into such disrepair."

"It is not in disrepair," the duchess said, her voice a growl. "There might be a piece of rackety furniture here and there that could use repair, but problems with the—"

But Isidore was just beginning. "Broken windows," she said. "Warped wood that will need to be replaced. The chimney in the west wing seems to have toppled in on itself, from what I could see. My father, Your Grace, would call it a *disgrace*!"

Silence followed.

Her mother-in-law was red in the face and seemed to have blown up slightly, as a frog does before croaking. Isidore reached out and picked up her gloves. "You might be more comfortable retiring to your chambers," she said, her voice even. "All the furniture in the down-

stairs rooms will be removed in the next few hours and
sent to London for refurbishing or replacement."

That goaded the duchess into speech. "By whose authority do you dare that action!" she shouted.

Isidore stood. "By my own." She pulled on her gloves,
snapping them onto each finger. "That of the Duchess of
Cosway."

"You'll bankrupt the estate!"

"Nonsense. The Cosway estate is one of the richest in
the kingdom, and even if it were not so, I inherited my
father's entire estate. *I,* Your Grace, am likely the richest
woman in this kingdom, barring their royal highnesses.
Not to mention the fact that your son brought back a fortune in tiger rubies from Africa. If we wish to gild this
entire house so that they can see the glow from London,
we can afford to do so."

"So that's the way of the world! The young waste the
substance that the elderly worked so hard to build up, on
fripperies, trivialities, gilded walls . . ."

"In this case," Isidore said briskly, "the young make a
necessary outlay of funds to repair the neglect and damage by the uncaring—"

"Don't you call me uncaring!" the duchess said, leaping to her feet with a great creaking of corsets. "I may
not have thought that the broken window was terribly
important, and I certainly never prided myself on being
one of the richest women in the kingdom, the way you
do, but I cared for this estate. I love it. It's—"

She turned, very precisely, and walked from the
room, closing the door behind her.

"Oh . . . *hell,*" Isidore said. Obviously she had bun-
gled that. "It's my temper," she said out loud, staring
down at her gloves.

The door opened again to Honeydew, ushering in a
bevy of strong-looking men. "If Your Grace would help

us select furniture for the cart, that would be most kind."

By the end of the morning, the downstairs had been emptied. Even the dining room table was gone. "It's scarred," Isidore told Honeydew. "I love that black oak, but it needs work. And frankly, I would prefer a table with more graceful lines. I have a mind to order a complete dining room set by Georges Jacob. He created a beautiful set for Queen Marie Antoinette in her Petit Trianon."

Honeydew gulped. "From France, Your Grace?"

"Yes, of course," Isidore said. She was ticking off a mental list on her fingers. "The furniture is dispatched to Mr. Seddon's workshop. This afternoon I'll send to Signora Angelico about an appropriate person to sew new curtains, and another to Antoine-Joseph Peyre about the broken statuary in the ballroom." She paused because Honeydew looked confused. "Monsieur Peyre did some work on my palazzo in Venice, and it so happens that he's in London. I'm sure that he will help us."

"Palazzo?" Honeydew enquired.

Isidore smiled at him. "If only it were closer, I would have furniture shipped from there. Monsieur Peyre worked all my walls in Venice with delicious flowers, in the style that I most prefer."

"By next week?" Honeydew said faintly.

"He won't finish by then, of course."

She turned about as she heard the study door open: the study was the only room on the first floor that they had not yet stripped of its furnishings. Simeon walked out. His hair was standing on end and there were dark circles under his eyes. "Honeydew," he said, apparently not even seeing her, "have you ever heard of the Brothers Verbeckt?"

Honeydew frowned.

"They are asking for a large sum and though the reference is rather obscure, they seem to be talking of hunting. I thought perhaps the author was German."

"That would be Verby, down in the village," Honeydew said, his face clearing. "Now that's a pack of nonsense! For hunting, does he say? Verby used to go along with your father as a gun-cleaner now and then, and only when the duke had no one better to take with him. Brothers Verbeckt indeed!"

Simeon turned to Isidore and bowed. "Forgive me, duchess; I didn't see you were there."

That was a lie. Isidore knew the moment his door opened. She could feel his presence even behind the door, as she made her lists. And the moment they were standing together in the same room, desire strung between them like an invisible thread.

But she smiled at him. He wanted to preserve the illusion of his life without desire, without fear. "Good morning."

His eyes drifted over her and even though she was rather dusty and tired, suddenly, under his gaze, she felt all curves and female beauty.

"I've heard mysterious thumps," he said, recovering first. "What on earth has been happening, Honeydew?"

"Her Grace has sent all the furniture to London," Honeydew said. He was no fool, and was backing toward the hallway. "If you'll forgive me, Your Graces, I must see to luncheon." He stopped. "The table!"

"We'll eat in the Dower House," Isidore said soothingly. "Her Grace will undoubtedly wish a light luncheon in her chambers, just as she did last night."

"What happened to the table?" Simeon asked, once Honeydew disappeared. "Did a leg fall off?"

"Oh no," Isidore said. "I've sent everything to London, just as Honeydew said. Wouldn't you like to see?"

They walked into the dining room. Without furniture, and with the moldering curtains torn down, it was a wide, echoing room. Honeydew had sent maids in the moment the furniture was gone, and even the walls glistened.

"The house should be ready to receive guests in a few weeks at most," Isidore said, since Simeon seemed to be silenced by the total lack of furniture.

"You got rid of all the furniture?"

There was a kind of controlled anger in his voice that made Isidore's eyes narrow. "I didn't get rid of it," she said. "Well, I got rid of some it. But everything that could be refurbished has been sent to London."

Simeon walked to the door leading to the great sitting room and stopped. Isidore knew exactly what he was looking at: the empty, stained floor where there had been two threadbare Aubussons and clusters of furniture in various states of disrepair.

"You sent away all my furniture," Simeon stated. He ran a hand through his hair.

Isidore stared at his back. His shoulders seemed very tense. "It is presumably my furniture as well," she told him.

"If we remain married," he said. Then he whirled about. "You have no right to send away every stick of furniture in this house. People live here. I live here. You could have done me the nominal courtesy of asking my permission."

"Your permission?" Isidore echoed. "Your permission for what? Would you have said that you wished to keep the rug that your father's incontinent dog chose as his private privy, or the one with a rip down the middle?"

"Do you mock me?"

Surely there were women who would have cowered at this point. But Isidore had never cowered at anyone, including Simeon's mother, and she wasn't going to start now. "Absolutely," she said. "Mock where mockery is due, I say."

"*You*—" he said violently, and broke off.

"Yes?"

And then, when he didn't answer: "Are you sure you don't want to characterize my heinous crime? That of sending the furniture out to be repaired so that this house is livable, if not hospitable?"

"Where is my mother to eat dinner?" he asked.

Isidore opened her mouth—and paused. "In the Dower House?"

"All four of us, happily crowded in the corner?"

"Honeydew will find a larger table," Isidore said.

"Could you please consult with me before you embark on projects such as emptying out the house?" he asked.

He had himself under control again. Isidore almost sighed. There was something magnificent about Simeon in a rage. Not that she wished to court that condition, she told herself. "Of course," she said. "Instantly. Every time. I'll ask you so many questions that you'll grow tired of the very sound of my voice."

He shot her a sardonic look, but at least his mouth relaxed.

"What on earth could have happened to this wall?" he asked, wandering over to examine a gap in the paneling.

"Your father kicked it," she said, answering his query.

"My father—"

"Your father apparently kicked the paneling after a game of cards. The strength of his leg was such that he remained stuck with one foot in the wall and the other on the floor, until the footmen could extract him."

Simeon turned around and ran a hand through his

hair. "Isidore, have I lost my mind? Is this normal behavior for an English family?"

She smiled at that. "How would I know? I'm Italian, remember?"

"I spent the entire morning going through a most unpleasant stack of letters. They are all dated from six to eight years ago, and not only did each of them ask for money, but each had been denied by my father."

He was a beautiful man: spare, large, wild-looking. Even his eyes were beautiful, filled with disappointment though they were.

He ran his hand through his hair again. "Am I truly mad, Isidore?"

"No," she said promptly. "I should tell you that I had an argument with your mother this morning."

"I apologize for my mother's undoubted vehemence." He leaned against the wall next to her.

"I lost my temper," Isidore said, meeting his eyes. "I spoke in a most inappropriate manner. And I said things that I wish I hadn't."

"That pretty much sums up my experience of England," he said, looking down at her.

Isidore suddenly felt as if her knees were weak. He was going to kiss her—he was—he did. His lips felt more familiar now. He licked her lips and she almost giggled, but then she put an arm around his neck and drew him close.

Thoughts fled as their bodies met. He was all hard muscle, and she melting softness. They both smelled of dust. But under the dust and faint smell of ink, she could smell the spicy cleanness that was Simeon. It made her tremble. It made her put both arms around his neck and hold on.

Chapter Nineteen

Revels House
March 1, 1784
That afternoon

Simeon was conscious of savage disappointment: in his father, every time he leafed through sheaves of rejected bills, in himself. He had returned from the Dower House the night before and retreated to the study until numbers swam before his eyes.

Yet his father wasn't the heart of his problem. *She* was. He could fix the house, and pay the bills. He couldn't fix what happened to him when he was around Isidore. He felt like a hunting animal seeing her, as if even the hairs on the back of his neck knew where she was in the room.

Finally, at this late date, he understood all the poetry

of desire and lust that he had ignored before. Valamk-sepa used to recite the poetry of Rumi, a poet from 500 years ago; Simeon had exulted because he was free from the embarrassments described by the poet. And yet, Rumi was right: reason was powerless in the face of the lust he felt for Isidore. All he wanted to do was retreat to a bedchamber and—and rut.

Like an animal.

Not like a principled, thoughtful human being, like the kind of man he had always believed himself to be.

Except he was starting to worry about that too.

Finally he put down his quill and realized exactly what he feared: by marrying Isidore, he would be giving up himself. He would be giving *in* to violent tempests of emotion. His house would be shaken by screaming fights between his mother and his wife. He would be unable to withstand her, because he lusted after her to the point of being unable to think.

He felt ill—the kind of sick airy rush in his head that he used to feel when he and his men were being stalked by a tiger.

Danger . . .

His wife was equally worried. Isidore wanted to be a duchess. She had thought so before her husband appeared, and she thought so even more so now that Simeon turned out to be so knee-weakeningly appealing.

And yet life with him was going to be humiliating.

She could survive any amount of public embarrassment. He could go about London without a wig, and run through Hyde Park in a nappy. The problem was that he didn't really like her very much.

She could see it in the way he fought his attraction to her, in the veiled coolness of his eyes when she described the changes she planned for the house. Simply in the way he looked at her.

A husband who didn't like her. It wasn't what she expected, though she couldn't say that she ever gave it a thought. Women liked her. Men desired her. She admired some and tolerated most.

Isidore sat down on one of the few chairs left in the house. She probably merited the scorn she saw in Simeon's eyes. After all, she wasn't what he wanted.

But what could she do? How do you make a man like you? *Like?* What did husbands like about their wives? A sense of humor, a partnership—

Partnership. She could help him more.

She leaped to her feet. He kept asking the butler questions about various bills. If there was one thing Isidore was good at, it was making inquiries.

"Honeydew, I should like to visit the village," she said a few minutes later. "If you would have a bath drawn for me, I shall change my clothing."

"When would you like the carriage, Your Grace?"

Isidore looked down at her dusty skirts. "It will take me at least two hours to make myself presentable."

It actually took three, but when she climbed into the carriage, she felt fairly certain that she was perfectly attired: duchesslike, yet not too grand. She brought along Lucille and a footman carrying a thick purse. If there was one thing she was *not* going to do, it was order on credit.

The village consisted of six or seven establishments: baker, butcher, smithy, pub and a shop that seemed to sell everything from cloth to ceramic pitchers. Plus a church. She hesitated for a moment, thinking that the vicar was undoubtedly important, but what did she have to say to a vicar?

Two seconds later she was inside the general shop. It was rather dark because the ceiling was hung with a maze of objects. A table was jumbled with fabric, ribbons, buttons, cooking implements, a butter churn.

"Your Grace," Lucille whispered, "what on earth are we doing here?"

Just then a lean-faced man, with such pronounced hollows in his cheeks that they looked like small caves, came forward. He bowed deeply.

Isidore pulled off her gloves.

"May I help you?" he asked.

"Yes, I would like to buy something."

His expression didn't change. "A ribbon?"

There was something just faintly, faintly insolent in his tone. As if a duchess would only want a pretty ribbon, like a small child, or perhaps as if a duchess could only afford a ribbon.

"A bolt of woolen cloth," Isidore said, picking the largest and most useful thing she saw. She needed to buy something large, something that would give the shopkeeper confidence that the Duchy of Cosway was solvent.

"A bolt of cloth," he said. "Of course, Your Grace."

So he did know who she was. There was an odd sucking sound and the man's cheeks suddenly popped inward. Then he turned around, plucked up a bolt of russet wool and thumped it down before her. "Will this do? It's eight shillings a yard. How many yards would you like? I accept only ready money in this shop."

Not enough. Not nearly enough. "I'd like more," Isidore said.

"More cloth?" He sucked his cheeks in again, with an audible pop. "I have blues, grays, greens, and more russet. How many yards would Your Grace need this morning?"

He was mocking her. Isidore's eyes narrowed. "A great deal," she said, giving him a blindingly cheerful smile. "Probably every yard you have. I do like cloth."

"Wool," he said, "is a universal taste." He turned around and bawled, "The bolts!"

Isidore took the purse from her footman. "How many houses are there in the village?"

"Twenty-three."

"I'll have five yards per household."

"There are a few huts down by the river."

"I shall buy for twenty-seven households, then, which would be 135 yards, if I'm not mistaken." She opened her purse.

"Over one thousand shillings," the storekeeper said, his voice a bit strangled.

"One thousand and eighty," Isidore said cheerfully. "Or fifty-four pounds." She counted them out, then deliberately put a guinea on the counter. "For delivery to each house in the village." The shopkeeper almost smiled.

She put down another guinea, and his eyes widened. Another. They formed a small golden pile. Deliberately, she built it into an unsteady mountain.

There was an audible pop. No one made a sound; even the footman seemed to be holding his breath.

"There are twenty-seven houses," she said. "I shall add an extra guinea, so that you might provide some thread and needles to go with the fabrics."

"Yes," the man said, his voice half strangled. "Though there's no need—"

"I am the Duchess of Cosway. I always pay for the value of the merchandise I buy, and naturally, for its delivery as well. There is nothing more valuable than your time, Mr. . . ."

"Mr. Mopser, Your Grace, Harry Mopser."

Isidore held out her hand. "Mr. Mopser, it has been our pleasure to frequent your establishment."

"Ba, ba—" he said, but finally managed to say, "Yer Grace."

She swept from the store, hiding a smile. In the bakery, she ordered twenty-seven meat pies. In the church, having come up with something to say to the vicar after all, she promised a new steeple.

By the time she reached the smithy, Isidore felt like an ambassadress to a foreign country. The vicar had welcomed the idea of giving each household in the village a measure of wool with great enthusiasm; the baker had confided that she sent up a few pound cakes to Revels House weekly, in memory of the late duke's mother; Isidore promptly paid for five-years' worth of pound cakes.

The smithy had a low door and a pungent odor, like sulphur. "There's nothing to buy here," Lucille protested.

"Then we'll just greet the smith," Isidore said cheerfully.

Once inside the smithy, all she could see was a low ceiling, blackened beams, and the dim glow of the fire. Before she could say anything, her footman called, "The Duchess of Cosway."

There was a clatter and a man rose from the hearth. He didn't bow, or even smile. He just put his hands on his hips and stared at her, and it wasn't a nice look. He had a crooked nose and his eyes looked like the sunken coals of his own fire. "The *new* duchess, I suppose," he stated.

Isidore blinked.

"A newly minted duchess," he drawled. "Flanked by a footman, the better to protect you in case a starving villager manages to sling mud in your direction."

He had the air of someone of incredible strength and yet he was surprisingly gaunt. Behind her, Lucille made a little sound, as if she were a mouse scurrying away.

"Do you wish you had some mud to hand?" she asked, meeting his eyes.

"A duchess who's not afraid of an insult . . . how peculiar."

"Not that I've noticed," she said, putting out a hand as her footman took a menacing step forward. "No one is as impolite to each other as equals, in my experience."

"Do they chide each other with talk of starving children, then? Of fields rotting at the stalk due to bad seed? Of betrayal and coarse unconcern at the hands of those who should take the greatest care?"

Isidore's heart was beating fast. *This* was the heart of the matter. She looked around and saw a three-legged stool, covered with dust. With no hesitation she walked over, sat down, and folded her hands. "Lucille, I'll thank you and John to wait for me in the carriage. I'll sit for a moment and talk to Mr. . . ."

"Pegg," the smith said. "Silas Pegg."

"Oh no, Your Grace," Lucille moaned, looking toward the door as if it was heaven's gate itself.

Isidore fixed her with a duchess stare and a moment later the smithy was empty.

"You may sit down," she said.

He just looked at her.

"If you wish."

"I only sit amongst my equals." His teeth were very white. "Duchess."

Isidore had the distinct impression that she had been deemed lower than an equal. "Please tell me about the children," she said, "and the fields."

He curled his lip.

"Unless you wish to be counted amongst those who

should indicate concern and haven't bothered," she pointed out.

"I heard that the young duke is paying overdue bills," Mr. Pegg said.

"Every bill," Isidore said. "He is paying every bill that the duchy owes."

The smith grunted.

Isidore let the silence grow between them.

"We need a midwife and an apothecary," he said after a time. "The bridge over the river is cracked and dangerous, so the post stopped coming to the village."

"A midwife?" Isidore said. "Is there a surgeon?"

"Pasterby, in the next village," the smith said. "I can't think of anyone who can afford him." He turned to the side and plucked a horseshoe from the fire with a pair of tongs. It glowed red and smelled like hell's own furnace, to Isidore. Then, as if she wasn't there, the smith placed it precisely on his anvil, picked up a hammer, swung it over his head and brought it down with a precise clanging sound.

"Is there a school?" Isidore asked, timing herself between swings of the hammer.

He scoffed. "A school? You must be joking."

She waited.

"Schools are at the behest of the duchy," he finally said, turning the horseshoe over with long tongs.

"Was there ever a school?"

"Not in my lifetime."

"What about a midwife?"

His hammer must have come down slightly askew because the horseshoe suddenly whipped past her cheek and clanged against the wall of the cabin.

Isidore didn't turn around, just gazed steadily at the smith. He looked a bit white. He put down his hammer very precisely, picked up a stool, and sat down on it facing her.

"What happens if a man kills a duchess?" he said. Almost friendly.

Isidore let her eyes smile, but not her mouth. "Hanging," she offered.

He put his hands on his knees. "The old duke chose a neighboring smith to put up the standards on the bridge over the river, after I wouldn't work for him any longer. The man mixed sand with the iron to save money, thinking to charge the duke twice as much and perhaps end up with his expenses."

"Why did he do it at all?"

"If you didn't accept the duke's custom, he'd have you arrested for something. At least, that's what folks thought."

"And yet you're not in jail," she said. "How astonishing."

"He was like a very small dog: all bark, no bite," Mr. Pegg said flatly. "After I refused to do any more work for him, he never entered here again, but nothing the worse happened for that. Nothing that—"

He stopped.

"What?"

"No midwife," he said. "She couldn't stay because no one could pay her. I've done all right because horses always need shoeing, and the baker's all right too, because people need bread. But almost all the other merchants are gone. People don't understand how much the great house matters, out here in the country. They stopped paying servants, you know, or paid them only once a year. No one could manage on half wages. The local people couldn't work there any longer."

"So who is working at Revels House now?"

"The desperate. Honeydew is a good sort, and he's kept out true criminals."

Isidore nodded. "The bridge," she said. "The wages, the school, the apothecary, the post road. And the midwife?"

His eyes went blank. "Yes."

She looked around the smelly, dusty smithy again. There was a cot against the wall, with a gray blanket cast over it. This was no house. It was just a place to be. And yet it looked as if he lived here.

"Did your wife lose a baby?" Isidore asked.

"That depends on how you see it. She kept the baby with her, so I never saw the child."

Isidore looked at the dirt floor because there was too much pain in his eyes. But: "So the baby wasn't born?"

She didn't glance up, but his voice continued, rough with that sort of male anger that accompanies pain. "Joan labored for two days. I found the surgeon from the next village, Pasterby, forced him to come. It was too late." Still not looking, she heard him get up and clump to the wall to fetch the horseshoe.

He put it down on the anvil and struck it with the hammer, a gentler, quieter blow than earlier. "She might have died, even with a midwife here." Another thump of the hammer. "But she died alone and in pain, while I was riding over to the next village. And for that—"

"She knew you were coming," Isidore said. "That you were trying to help."

"For that I pissed on the duke's marble coffin," the smith said. He turned to her. "And for that I almost killed his daughter-in-law."

Isidore nodded.

"Aren't you going to have a hysterical fit and scream your way out of here?"

"I'm learning so much," Isidore said. "I'll send Honeydew to polish the family tomb directly."

There was a moment of silence and then he made a strange barking sound. Isidore was trying to blink away an errant tear and didn't realize what the sound was, until she understood he was laughing. And laughing.

Isidore rose and brushed off her back of her pelisse. "Mr. Pegg, I need someone to help me."

He stopped laughing and looked at her. "I suspect you would not be surprised to hear that I require all duchesses to pay beforehand."

"The vicar reports that he has many graves without stones, as people haven't been able to afford them. I told him that the Duke of Cosway would be righting the cemetery, and making sure that each grave has a proper memorial."

He looked at her. "My Joan has a stone."

She nodded. "Will you help me make sure that everyone who was not as lucky as Joan gets a stone?"

"Lucky?" he said. And snorted.

"Lucky," she said. "Unlucky in some ways, lucky in others."

"Christ," he muttered. "A philosophical duchess. That's just what this village needs."

"Philosophical and rich," Isidore said.

He got to the door before her and pushed it open. "As I said, Your Grace. Just what this village needs."

Chapter Twenty

Revels House
March 2, 1784
The next day

The man from London had bulging eyes that reminded Simeon of a tree frog he'd seen in Morocco. He had on a wine-red velvet waistcoat that must have belonged to a nobleman at some point. It strained over Mr. Merkin's impressive stomach.

"Yer Grace," he said, bowing as much as his stomach would allow.

"I am very grateful for your assistance with this problem," Simeon said.

"Sewers is my business," Mr. Merkin said. "There's no one who knows the inside of a sewer better than I do."

"It's not really a sewer," Simeon said. "My father put in a water-pumping system—"

"Sewer," Mr. Merkin said cheerfully. "Just because it don't work so well doesn't mean it's not a sewer. I can smell its perfume, so why doesn't your butler here show me the place and I'll do an assessment."

Simeon stood up. "I shall accompany you myself. I am curious about the solution."

"I can tell you on the hoof," Mr. Merkin said, taking a generous pinch of snuff as he led the way out of the room. "I've seen this over and again. It's meant to flow, and it ain't flowing. You could do dirt, but you han't done dirt."

"Ah," Simeon said.

"Have to pipe it," Mr. Merkin said.

"I'm not sure I follow the question of dirt?" Simeon said.

They arrived at the door to the first-floor water closet. Honeydew, with a look of fastidious agony, directed a footman to remove the felt blanket that had been tacked tightly to the wall so as to cover the entire door.

"This'll be the heart of it," Mr. Merkin said. "The rest of the closets feed into the pit here. I'll send the men in. We'll have to clean it all out; you do realize that."

"I had hoped so," Simeon said.

"We have to take it out through the front door," Mr. Merkin said. "There's them as has palpitations at that thought, but there's no other way to do it. The pipes are blocked; we need to clean it out right good and then pull all the pipes and replace them. They'll have fallen to bits."

"Perhaps we should simply—"

The footman pulled down the last corner of the green felt and opened the door; without thinking, Simeon fell back a pace. The smell reached out to greet them, as thick and loathsome as a London fog. It felt like something that had weight and mass. Perhaps even life.

Mr. Merkin walked forward as if he smelled nothing.

"Your Grace need not follow," Honeydew said, with a note of conscious heroism in his voice. "I will accompany Mr. Merkin and ascertain if he needs assistance."

"Could it be that something died there?" Simeon asked, feeling himself turn pale. "I once came on a village ravaged by the plague and the odor is disconcertingly similar."

"Always a possibility," Merkin called back. "Rats need air like anything else. If one fell in, it'd be dead within minutes. I'm just—" there was the sound of wood shattering—"removing the seat so I can see the size of it." He backed out a moment later and Simeon was oddly gratified to see that he was mopping his forehead with a red handkerchief. "That's a bad one, that is."

"How can you possibly clean the pit?" Simeon asked.

"Oh, my men will do that. We'll set up a dumbwaiter and take it out in wheelbarrows. Your man said you wanted the best, and you've got them. I brought the Dead Watch with me."

Simeon backed up as Honeydew closed the door to the water closet, with the air of someone shutting the door on a wild animal. "What is the Dead Watch?"

"The Dead Watch," Merkin repeated. "London's finest. You're paying them double, of course, but it's worth it. Penny wise, pound foolish, I always say. The lads will be down there in a thrice and clean it until it sparkles like a plate. You'll have to maintain it, of course, Yer Grace. No more of this foolishness. You'll need me to check your pipes every three months; fresh water twice a day. I can lay it all out with your butler here. If you love your sewer, it'll love you back."

Simeon could hear Honeydew making a sound like a rusty grate, which he thought indicated some reluctance to love the sewer. "The Dead Watch?" he persisted.

"The part of the Watch that cleans up the dead," Merkin replied. "The floaters, in the river, of course. But there's them as get stuck in a house and no one finds them. There's the murders, of course. The Dead Watch doesn't do your ordinary killing. But a truly nasty one? They're the men for the job!"

His cheerfulness made Simeon feel a bit ill.

"I always use them for this sort of thing," Merkin continued. "They're down at the pub, waiting for me, Yer Grace, and if you'll excuse me, we'll start on the job."

"Of course," Simeon said.

"I'll be putting a pipe down there first. I have to get the gas out, or me lads will keel over. No air. Then yer butler and I will be figuring out the way to get the muck out of the house with the least fuss. And I'll be asking yer Grace to leave."

"Leave? I can't leave, I—"

"Leave," Mr. Merkin said. "You seem to be stomaching the smell all right now, but this is nothing. You'll have to be out of the house tomorrow morning and not come back til the day after, Yer Grace. And that goes for all the maids and everyone else as well. The butler can stay with me, and make sure that the silver stays in its place."

Simeon heard a little groan from Honeydew's direction.

"We'll open the house up and pipe all the gas out. It'll take a day and a night, maybe two days. We'll go down there, empty it out, and wash it. Then I'll replace the pipes, but that's a different matter."

"Will you go down in the hole yourself?" Simeon asked, unable to imagine the gaudy Mr. Merkin making his way down into a pit.

"No, no," Merkin said impatiently. "I've the Dead

Watch for that. In the normal run of things I use a couple of mud larks. Now I need to take my leave, Yer Grace. If you'd be out of the house by morning, I'd be obliged. As you can imagine, the Watch may well be needed in the city any day, so I need to start."

He paused and hauled down his waistcoat so that it covered his stomach better. "Now I've one more thing to tell you, Yer Grace. The Dead Watch ain't my servants, and I can't speak for their behavior."

"What worries you about them?" Simeon asked.

"Thievery worries me. I know my mud larks."

"Mud larks?" Simeon interrupted.

"Lads who grow up in the mud of the Thames," Merkin said impatiently. "I pick the best of the lot and my lads don't thieve. But the Dead Watch are pirates. They go where no one else in the city will go. They do the tasks that no one else will do. They think themselves as outside the law, see?"

Honeydew made a groaning sound.

"You need them, Yer Grace, cause I ain't going to get anyone else down there to clean out that muck. They're the only ones."

"Even if we paid—"

"There ain't enough money in the world. Besides, chances are if I sent one of my larks down there, the poor fool would die and then I'd have to cope with a dead body on top of it all, *if* there ain't one down there already. That's a worrying smell you have down there, I don't mind telling you." He swung about and peered at Honeydew. "Anyone missing from the household in the past few years? A housemaid run away without notice, that sort of thing?"

Honeydew drew himself upright. "Absolutely not."

"Good. There's gas down there, understand? Not air. The Dead Watch, now, they have lungs made out of steel. I've seen them in action and they go where no one can go, down in the Thames, for example, holding their breath longer than a man should."

"Honeydew," Simeon said apologetically, "we need that pit cleaned out, no matter how much it disturbs the household."

"They're used to going into a house where a man has been dead for a month or two," Merkin continued, hooking his thumbs into his waistcoat pockets and rocking back and forth a bit. "They take whatever money's on the corpse, and see it as their due. Same for a floater. If they pick up a knickknack or two in a house of that type, who's to bother? There's no relatives, see? Otherwise they would have found the poor dead soul before he moldered away."

"Absolutely," Simeon assured him.

"I'll move everything to the barn," Honeydew said. "And guard it."

"That'll do it," Merkin said. "They're not really robbers."

"Just thieves," Honeydew put in.

"They might pick up a thing here or there, something left before their eye, but as I say, Yer Grace, they're doing a job as no one else will do." He turned. "Now, if you'll forgive me, I've got to make arrangements. Mr. Honeydew here showed me where the pipes come out on the hillside. We'll be pulling them from that direction, at least till they break in our hands, while the Dead Watch is doing their job." And with that, he left.

"I'll stay in the house, Honeydew. You can put the silver in my study. I'm just turning the tide with my father's papers."

"There's a nice desk in the Dower House," Honeydew said soothingly. "I'll have all your papers transferred there immediately. If Your Grace would excuse me, I have a number of arrangements to make. I don't trust those miscreants anywhere near the silver. It must be removed from the house. That and everything that could be fenced."

Simeon walked back into his study and sat down. He had left a complicated letter from Mr. Kinnaird open on his desk. He tried to return to its detailed description of the state of the townhouse on St. James Square. Water had broken through the roof and seeped into the attics; rats had made nests in the kitchen . . .

The smell of the sewer seemed to cling to his skin. He sniffed his sleeve, but it was his imagination. Or—

He stood up. He had had a bath two hours ago, but it was time for another.

Chapter Twenty-one

Revels House
March 2, 1784

*I*sidore entered the house in the late afternoon to find servants scurrying this way and that, their arms full of ornaments and small statuary. Finally she discovered Honeydew, directing traffic. "What is happening?"

"The sewer will be cleaned," Honeydew said. "By people from London who have requested that we vacate the house. The dowager duchess refuses to leave."

"Ah," Isidore said.

"Master Godfrey has been dispatched to spend a night or two with the vicar. The vicar is a Latin scholar, and Master Godfrey needs to refresh his skill since he will be going to school."

"Should I speak to the duchess?" Isidore asked, only

belatedly thinking that it was an odd thing to ask a butler. But Honeydew was something more than a butler.

"I believe that would be inadvisable," he said without blinking. "If Her Grace has decided not to leave her rooms, she will not leave her rooms. If you will forgive the presumption."

"I'm sure you're right," Isidore said. "Where might I find my husband, Honeydew? I want to speak to him about my trip to the village yesterday." She loved using that word, *husband*. It made her whole tenuous situation seem less so, though how the use of one word could do that, she didn't know.

"In his chambers, Your Grace."

"Oh." She paused.

"He's merely checking on some papers," Honeydew said. "You may enter at will, Your Grace, and you won't disturb him. Now if you'll excuse me." A footman struggled by with a tub filled with silver candlesticks. "We're removing everything for safekeeping. I must supervise—" And with a hurried bow, he left.

Isidore walked up the stairs, came to the door of the master bedchamber, and pushed open the door. Simeon wasn't working on papers.

He had his back to her. It was naked.

It was a beautiful back: strong and muscled, and that same golden toast color as his face. Isidore froze in the doorway. As she watched, he reached out for a ball of soap perched on a small table to his left. Water slid over his skin, chasing the hollows of muscles as he flexed, running his right hand up his left arm. Individual bubbles slid over his skin like small kisses.

The air smelled spicy and sweet. She'd never smelled perfume on his skin, not that she'd really had the opportunity to smell—

He ducked his head forward and then raked his fingers through gleaming wet, clean hair. Isidore didn't breathe as he braced his hands on the sides of the tub and stood up.

His body wasn't at all like hers. She was all curves, the gift of her Italian mother. Depending on how tightly she laced her corset, her waist was small, and then her breasts and hips swelled above and below—not gently, not in a slim, English style, but with a lush Latin bountifulness.

Nothing was lush about Simeon's body. It was all rippling muscles, even his bottom. As he stood, the last bubbles ran down his back, down his legs. His bottom was hollowed on the sides. Her fingers twitched and she suddenly realized that, in her imagination, she was tracing the bubbles, down over the muscles of his back that rippled as he reached for a towel. He bent forward . . . perhaps it was the running that gave him such large thighs? She'd heard of men padding their pantaloons to give themselves bulk. Simeon had the muscles of a dock-worker.

He had one foot out of the bath now, and was drying off his second leg. She started to move soundlessly backwards.

"Don't leave," he commanded, not turning his head.

He must have noticed the door open, and probably thought she was a footman. She stepped back again and began to ease the door shut.

"Isidore."

Her mouth fell open.

Moving with his usual thoughtful control, he wrapped the towel around his waist and turned around. Isidore snapped her mouth shut.

"I am sorry to have disturbed your bath," she said, keeping her voice even. "I wished to speak to you about your mother's refusal to leave the house." She swallowed.

He didn't have a mat of hair on his chest. She could see the shape and size of each muscle, see the way the human body was designed to be.

"How did you know I was there?" She forced herself to meet his eyes. Of course, they were utterly calm, unreadable.

"Your scent," he said.

She cleared her throat. "Your soap has a very interesting odor." That was such a stupid thing to say. The words fell into the air between them. Obviously, this was a perfect opportunity to seduce Simeon.

"Cardamom," he said.

"I suppose you found the soap in the East somewhere?" She sounded like a fool, Isidore thought desperately.

"India," he said. "It's a spice used in cooking as well."

"Interesting," she managed.

The white towel settled a little lower on Simeon's hips and without thinking she looked toward the movement and then jerked her eyes back to his face. He was just looking at her with a pleasant inquiry, as if they were in the drawing room, and he'd asked whether she would like a cup of tea.

She couldn't seduce him. She didn't have the faintest idea how to go about it, and what seemed easy when she was in London wasn't easy at all. He didn't seem the least interested in the fact that she was in his bedchamber while he was nearly unclothed.

Besides . . .

He was so large. Everything about him was big, from his shoulders to his feet.

She dropped a curtsy, taking refuge in formality. "I beg you to forgive me for interrupting your bath," she said, backing up one step and then whirling so she could leave. She shut the door so fast that it slammed a bit, the sound reverberating down the corridor.

Inside the room, Simeon unclenched his teeth and then threw away the damned towel with a muffled curse. She hadn't seemed to notice the way it tented in the front, though she had certainly seen how close he was to utter loss of control. She had fled as if a horde of desert tribesmen had brandished their swords at her.

He glanced down at his personal weapon and then dropped into a chair. Christ, this was a mess. He didn't dare touch himself for fear he would explode. He had been sitting in the bath, thinking of her: the way her hair gleamed like rumpled strands of black silk, waiting to be woven into the kind of garment a man could bury his face in, stroke his cheek, other parts of his body . . .

His blood had been raging through his body already when he heard that light knock and then, before he could gather his wits, the door opened and it was she. He knew instantly, of course. Who else in the household smelled of jasmine, like a poem in flowers? Even with the house reeking of sewage, he knew when she was near because her scent came to meet him.

But Isidore's real scent wasn't jasmine. Her scent was under the fresh, clear call of the flower, something that teased his senses more than any perfume, made him think deliriously of burying his face in her hair, of kissing her skin, licking her from head to foot.

Embarrassing. That's what it was.

She was like a firebrand, burning more brightly than any woman he'd ever known. He could accept this marriage—and spend his life circling around her, like a tribesman with a precious donkey, trying, trying to keep her from being stolen.

Did he have any choice?

*A man always has choices. If you tell yourself you
have no choice, you lie . . . you lie in the worst possible
manner: because almost always a man who tells himself that he has no choices has already made up his
mind to the wrong choice.* Valamksepa's voice sounded
hateful in his ears, even as he recognized the truth of it.
Of course, he had a choice. He knew that he could have
the marriage annulled, just as the solicitor admitted,
and damn the laws of England. He wasn't a duke for
nothing. As the highest in the land, just under royalty,
he could wield his money and power like a club and
achieve what other men were unable to do.

But was that the right thing to do? Was it the ethical
thing to do? Isidore would no longer be a duchess. But
then, it rankled him to hear that she had ever introduced
herself as Lady Del'Fino. She was—

He pulled himself back together, realizing that he
was clenching his teeth. She was only nominally his.
Nominally.

Chapter Twenty-two

Mansfield Place, Number One
London Seat of Lord Brody
March 2, 1784

𝕴t was Lord Brody's soirée in honor of his nubile daughter—a spotty little horror with frizzled hair—and Jemma was wandering the various rooms, trying to look as if she were not searching for her husband.

Madame Bertière hailed her. "Your Grace, do come see who's just arrived from Paris. Of course, you two know each other so well."

Jemma's heart sank. It was the Marquise de Perthuis, one of her least favorite people in all of France. Jemma and the marquise had been viewed as great rivals in the French court, though Jemma was never quite sure what they were competing *for*. But their undoubted dislike for each other kept people like Madame Bertière happily gossiping.

As always, the marquise was dressed in such a way that she took up more space than the Tower of London. Just to make a point, Jemma looked slowly, deliberately, up the wadded length of the marquise's wig, pausing on each of four stuffed birds. They were rather charming little birds, black and white, of course. The marquise wore only black and white.

Jemma sank into a deep curtsy. "But of course I am acquainted with the marquise," she said, her smile hitting a perfect register between indifference and recognition.

The marquise had the near expressionless countenance of a woman who understood face paint and used it with consummate skill. In fact, she would have been alluring except that her penchant for black and white drew attention to her costumes rather than her face. Those affectations, Jemma thought uncharitably, made her appear much older than her twenty-seven years.

"Ah, the *délicieuse* Duchess of Beaumont! How happy were all the ladies of the French court when you returned to England. As you know," she said, turning to Madame Bertière, "the duchess provides such formidable competition for the gentlemen!"

A nice hit, Jemma thought. She managed to praise me and yet note my adulterous tendencies. She unfurled her fan and smiled over the edge of it. "What a delightful costume you are wearing, madame. I wish I had the courage to go against fashion the way you do. I'm sure I would be sadly clumsy if my hips were quite as wide as yours, and yet you manage with such grace."

The marquise was far too sophisticated to stiffen; instead, she threw Jemma a sweet, roguish smile. "And I adore those delicious little flowers on your gown, duchess. I can certainly understand why you keep your panniers so small . . . when a woman has been gifted with such an ample bosom, large panniers inevitably make her look like an hourglass. Or a haystack. Your skill in dressing is *so* admirable!"

"Do you intend to pay us a long visit?" Jemma inquired.

"Ah, one travels to escape the *ennui* of life," sighed the marquise. "In truth, without your entertainments to enliven Paris, it is a tediously puritanical place."

Another hit, Jemma thought. Not as potent, though. There was something a little tired about the marquise, as if she had lost interest in the verbal fencing matches, the flares of witty comments, that had shaped her days in Versailles.

In fact, now that Jemma looked beyond her face powder, she saw that the marquise's cheeks were rather gaunt.

Jemma slipped her hand through the marquise's, an action she would never have taken in Versailles. She waved off Madame Bertière. "The marquise and I will take a turn or two and allow everyone to admire us. 'Tis an act of great kindness on my part, given the marquise's elegance will so put mine in the shade."

Previously, the marquise would have laughed in a way that indicated her complete agreement. Now she said nothing. It was almost unnerving.

They walked through the crowd, lowering their chins at acquaintances. Jemma made her way unerringly toward the ladies' salon. They entered to find three chattering debutantes, who wisely fled. Jemma turned to the attending maid. "I am feeling quite faint. Please stand outside the door and make certain that no one enters."

The maid whisked herself through the door.

The marquise sat down heavily, as if the weight of her enormous panniers dragged her to the ground. She had aged from the woman Jemma knew two years ago, the woman who snapped and laughed her way through the French court, grinding insouciant courtiers under her jeweled heels, making—and destroying—a lady's reputation with one mocking glance.

She had never been a nice person. But all the same, she had been a strong person.

"And now," Jemma said, sitting down opposite her, "are you quite all right, Madame la Marquise? You do not seem yourself."

The marquise started to laugh, her response to everything. But it broke off, and the sound that emerged sounded like a violent hiccup instead. Jemma waited.

"Have you seen my husband?" she finally asked. Her voice was hoarse.

"No," Jemma replied. "He is not in London, to the best of my knowledge." She hesitated.

But the marquise intervened before she could think of a tactful question. "He left. He followed *une femme* to England. He said it would be a brief visit, some weeks. It has been eight months."

"I did hear such a rumor," Jemma said cautiously.

The marquise had a delicate lace handkerchief clutched in her hand. For a moment Jemma thought she was going to start tearing it apart, ripping it to shreds like a madwoman in a play. But no: she opened her hand and let it fall to the ground.

It lay on the floor, crumpled, and their eyes met over it. "That is how he treated me," the marquise said. "Like a piece of dirty linen, to be thrown to the side after it has been soiled."

"Oh—"

"I must find him. I must." There was some sort of

suppressed rage about her that made Jemma twitch, and long to leave the room.

"Do you wish him to return to you?" Jemma asked.

"That—that *salaud*! Never. But I want to tell him to his face what sort of man he is. I want to tell his *petite amie* what sort of woman she is. I want—I want to—"

Jemma reached forward and put a hand on her arm. "Forgive me," she said gently, "for my impertinence. But what will the conversation change?"

The marquise raised her head. "He left me."

Jemma suddenly remembered that the marquise was the daughter of a duke, and connected to French royalty. She looked, in that moment, like a queen whose subjects had inexplicably snuck away and crossed a border to another kingdom.

"He had no right to leave me!"

"Men are prone to extreme foolishness," Jemma said.

"He has humiliated me in front of the court. He has—he has caused me great distress."

For the marquise, Jemma thought that was probably close to saying that her husband had beaten her in the open marketplace.

"But what do you hope to—"

"Repentence," the marquise said, "is too much to ask. No one repents anymore. It is as out of fashion as fidelity. But he has degraded me, brought me to his level. He must—"

She stopped.

Jemma nodded. "I faced the same problem, many years ago. My husband had made clear to me his utter lack of respect, his love for another woman. I lived in France for years as a result. It took me a great many years to understand that marriage lines do not control the heart."

The marquise's face twisted.

"My husband was in love with someone else," Jemma

repeated. "There was nothing I could say or do to change that circumstance. My advice, and I mean this seriously, is that you do not choose to follow him. Fashion a life of your own. I was not always happy in Paris, but I was often content."

The marquise snapped open her fan, but not before Jemma saw the glint of tears in her eyes. Jemma rose to her feet and held out her hand.

"We must return to the ball. It is too demoralizing for the men to discover that women are talking amongst themselves. Their fear of conspiracy moves them to overprize virtue in the female sex. They grow more conservative as a result."

The marquise chuckled. It wasn't the laughter that Jemma remembered, but it was a reasonable approximation.

Elijah was leaning casually against the wall just outside the door when they emerged. Jemma couldn't help it; a smile leapt from her heart to her lips. The marquise threw her a sour look. "It seems that men are not the only ones with ambitions to virtue," she said. "Beware lest you grow conservative, duchess."

It was almost worthy of her former waspishness.

Elijah was bowing before the marquise, taking her hand to his lips. "You are as exquisite as ever," he said, using his politician's voice, the one that sounded as sincere as if he were prophesying rain while drops fell on his hat.

The marquise sauntered away. She looked back, over her shoulder, and caught Jemma's eye. There was something like envy—or rage—on her face.

"Do not ever imagine yourself comfortable, duchess. A mistake I committed."

Then she turned with a swish of her skirts and disappeared into the ballroom.

"Dear me, what an uncomfortable woman she is!"

Elijah says. "All in white and black like that. She reminds me of a chess board."

Jemma closed her fan. "She's beautiful, though. Don't you think?"

"Undoubtedly." He hesitated. "Villiers is here. He asked me whether you and I had begun our third game in the match."

"And you told him?" She looked up at Elijah's face, at his stark cheekbones, deep eyes, tired intelligence.

"I told him that I only wished I had you blindfolded and in bed," he said, looking down at her. It should have been a joke . . .

It wasn't a joke.

His eyes were serious.

"You do?" she said. It was hard even to force the air into her lungs to say that.

"And I told him that I would prefer that he complete his game immediately, under the circumstances."

"You mean because if people suspect that I am having an *affaire* with him, they will not countenance our child as our own."

He nodded. But there seemed to be so much more going on in the conversation, so much that was unsaid. Jemma's heart was beating rapidly in her throat. "I don't . . ." She cleared her throat and tried again. "I don't wish to play that final game."

His face went utterly still. He stayed there for a moment, looking down at her. Then his utterly charming smile appeared and he bowed.

"In that case, my lady, I certainly will never urge the unpleasantness on you."

He was gone, Jemma staring after him.

"The game with Villiers," she clarified. But he was gone.

Chapter Twenty-three

The Dower House
March 2, 1784
Early evening

Simeon's papers had been transferred to the Dower House. He was seated at a small desk and stood up when Isidore entered, keeping one hand on the desk, a sheet of paper in his other hand.

Isidore sat down, trying very hard to forget that the last time she saw him, he was naked. "As you didn't join me for dinner last night, I had no chance to tell you that I went to the village. I bought one hundred and thirty-five yards of wool, and twenty-seven meat pies."

He blinked and put down the paper. "Do we have a sudden need for meat pies? Or wool?"

"They are gifts from the duchy to the villagers, to

mend relations. Everyone in the village will receive a meat pie and five yards of wool, courtesy of the duke and duchess."

"Ah." He looked down at the sheet before him. "Did you go into Mopser's shop?"

"Yes. He sold me the wool."

Simeon's jaw clenched. "I have a letter from him demanding back payment for candles."

"I can imagine there must be many such letters. People apparently believed that your father would have them taken up by the magistrates if they failed to provide the duchy with his requests, even when he didn't pay," Isidore said cheerfully. She pulled off her gloves and smoothed them on her knee.

Simeon's eye rested on them for a moment and then he said, "Isidore, I am having to pay bills that I am certain are fraudulent."

"Oh."

"I briefly calculated Mopser's request, for example. In order to use the number of candles that he says he sent to the house over the last five years, we'd need seven to nine candles burning at all hours of the day or night in every room in this house."

Isidore bit her lip. "But the candelabra . . ."

"That's calculating a rate of burn at about four hours, although most candles actually burn in approximately six," he said, folding his hands. "Honeydew says that the candelabra haven't been lit for years."

"Mopser was probably trying to make up for other bills that your father didn't pay," Isidore pointed out.

"Or he's a rascal taking advantage of the situation."

"I truly don't think so," Isidore said. "In any event, I asked him to deliver five yards of wool to every house in the village. That's well over one hundred yards, given that we have twenty-seven dwellings."

"Did you say twenty-seven?"

"Including the huts down by the river," Isidore said.

"There are nineteen houses in the village," Simeon said. "Thirteen are occupied. There are indeed two hut-like structures by the river, but they are counted among the nineteen. He's a thief."

"Everyone in the village has suffered horribly because of your father's peculiarities," Isidore protested. "They have learned to scramble and perhaps to prevaricate. The smith, Silas Pegg, told me that the bridge is extremely unsafe, as there is dust mixed with the steel. Pegg himself refused to fulfill your father's request due to previous unpaid bills, and so the smith in the next village did it, but only after he charged the duke twice as much to try to get his expenses . . ." Her voice trailed off.

Simeon's was frowning so hard that his brows almost met in the middle. "You're telling me that the smith in the next village sent in a false bill."

"He had to!" Isidore said. "He calculated that your father would pay at most fifty percent, and so if he made the bill for twice as much, he might end up with his expenses."

"This is the kind of thing that clearly drove my father into madness."

"Mad—" Isidore stopped.

"He must have been mad," Simeon said, moving the papers about on his desk. Isidore's attention was caught for a moment by the beauty of his long fingers. He plucked out a sheet of paper. "From a seamstress in the village, asking for remuneration for two christening gowns. *Christening* gowns. Never paid."

"I assume the bill is thirteen years old, given your brother's age," Isidore said.

"A long illness," Simeon said. "It's the only thing that explains it."

"Did your father note why he refused?"

"He said that he didn't care for the gowns, and that she should take them back again. The note is undated, but my guess is that he rejected the gowns only after the christening."

"I don't think that Mopser could be charged with your father's madness, if we call it that."

Simeon's jaw set again, Isidore noticed. "He was plagued by false invoices. He felt that he was beset by criminals asking for money, and so, to some extent, he truly was."

"They were desperate."

"I suppose." He straightened the papers again. "There's nothing that can be done now, except pay these requests, fraudulent though they might be."

"The most important thing is that we establish ourselves as honorable," Isidore said. "That we make it clear that we will pay our bills honestly and on time."

"I am not convinced that giving money to a thief like Mopser is the way to reestablish that confidence."

"He won't be able to fool you," Isidore pointed out. "From what you describe today, you could enumerate every candle burned in the future."

His hands stilled. "That doesn't sound entirely complimentary."

Isidore got up and drifted around the corner of the desk. She reached out and drew a finger down his thick, unpowdered hair. She had to admit that it was enticing without powder. She was so used to men with little piles of white on their shoulders, with hair stiff with unguent, curled, or powdered. But Simeon's hair shone with health as it tumbled around his brow in disordered curls.

He looked up at her inquiringly and their eyes met. Her finger wandered from his hair to his strong forehead, down the bridge of his nose, to his lips.

"Are you trying to distract me?" He sounded mildly interested.

Isidore promptly sat on his knee. "Is it possible?"

"Yes."

"Then I am." She put her arms around his neck, but disconcertingly, he didn't embrace her back. In fact, there was a look in his eye that was not—

"Why so condemning?" Isidore inquired. "Is it forbidden to kiss one's wife, even if she might not be your wife for long?"

"I am attempting to see whether I discern a pattern," he said.

Isidore sighed inwardly. He smelled like plums, spicy and clean. If she stayed close enough to him, she couldn't even remember what the water closets smelled like. His lips were beautiful, so she reached up to touch them with her own.

He brushed her lips, only to firmly move her back.

Isidore was aware of a flare of hurt inside. Her eyes fell while she tried to think of a graceful way to clamber off his lap without looking as if she were offended.

"Oh, *hell*," he growled. And then suddenly he kissed her. Really kissed her. She had just brushed her mouth with his, but he didn't bother with anything light and teasing. Simeon kissed the way he spoke: in a forward attack, in an utterly direct, heartbreakingly honest way. His kiss said, "I want you."

Their teeth bumped together, and he changed the angle of his neck, and suddenly his kiss was saying, "I have you. You're mine."

Isidore's head fell back and she clung to him, letting the touch of his mouth shimmer through her body like shards of fire. She pressed closer to him, knowing that what she was feeling was lust. Good, old-fashioned lust. Lust, she discovered, made her tremble and melt inside. It made her forget that he was showing signs of being as tight with money as his father.

Lust made her mind reel and the only thought that went fuzzily through her head was some sort of repetition of *don't stop*.

Of course, he stopped.

"I spent all these years avoiding kisses because I was told they led to nothing good," she managed, pulling herself together. She kept her tone light, as if she wasn't struggling to keep her spine straight.

His eyes were fierce, like a preacher's eyes. She groaned and let her forehead fall onto his shoulder. "Don't tell me you're going to apologize."

"For what?"

"For kissing me. You have a look about you as if you thought you'd committed a sin."

"No." But she thought he sounded unconvinced.

"Do you ever lose control?" she asked, suddenly interested.

"In what way?"

Even his responses were cautious and thought out.

"Do you swear?" she asked hopefully. "Take the Lord's name in vain? Become blasphemous?"

He thought about that.

She thought about the fact he had to think it over, and decided to try to stop using her favorite epithet, *bastardo*. Though it reminded her of her mother, a good Catholic woman . . .

"On occasion," he decided.

"What sort of occasion are we talking about? Is this a lion-chasing-man occasion, or a hit-elbow-on-doorframe occasion?"

There was a glimmer of a smile in his dark eyes and she thrilled to it like an Italian hearing an opera. "Lion-catches-man occasion."

She quirked up the corner of her mouth. "I thought so."

Just like that, his eyes went serious again. "If you're prepared for all eventualities, there's no need to react with fear or anger to the unknown."

"Because there is no unknown?"

"Exactly."

"So you'll never shout at me?"

"I hope not. I would be ashamed to shout at my wife. Or at an underling of any kind."

Isidore's brows snapped together and her back straightened all by itself. "An underling of any kind—one of those kinds being the spousal variety?"

"There's nothing unusual about my position on marriage, Isidore," he said. "I do not mean any lack of respect. From what I've already learned of you, I think that you are better at managing people, better read, and more generous than I am. I would be honored to serve under you, were you the captain of a ship."

Her eyes narrowed.

"But I am worried." He seemed to be picking his words carefully. "It would not have been my choice to throw money in the direction of Mopser's store."

Isidore stood up and then said, "In addition to paying him for the wool, I also gave him twenty-seven guineas."

Simeon's mouth fell open for a moment. "You—what?"

"I gave him twenty-seven guineas. For delivering the wool."

"You—you mean ha'pennies, don't you? You gave him a—*you gave him twenty-seven guineas?*"

Being a great screamer herself, Isidore had never believed anyone who claimed never to shout. She whipped around. "You're howling at me," she pointed out, with some satisfaction.

Simeon had surged out of his chair, but he caught himself. His voice calmed, but his eyes were searing with anger. "Do you know how much money twenty-seven guineas is?"

"You never returned to claim me as your wife," she said. "Therefore I took over management of my estate when I turned nineteen."

Simeon stared at his wife. "I'm proud of you," he said woodenly. This was a disaster. A total disaster. Isidore was like a walking version of a succubus, the kind of woman who twisted a man's resolution and manliness and turned him into porridge.

"You're not proud of me!" she shouted at him. Suddenly she sounded much more Italian than she normally did.

He pulled his mind away. So what if her voice had a kind of husky tinge that made him quiver, like a dog hearing its master? That was it, exactly. She was going on about her dowry.

Simeon took a deep breath, centered himself, reminded himself that he was nothing more than a small pebble on the shores of eternity.

"I apologize for not returning and taking care of your dowry myself," he said.

"It wasn't just my dowry!" she shouted.

"You're raising your voice."

"So are you! And it wasn't just my dowry. I inherited my parents' estate, you cretin."

"Cretin?" he said slowly.

"*Cretino!*" she said. Clearly, she had completely lost control. There were inky black curls flying around her head, and she actually pointed a finger at him, as if she were his governess. "Just what do you think I'm talking about?"

"Your dowry," he said, pulling his mind back on track.

"Thirteen vineyards," she said, walking a step toward him. "A palazzo in Venice, on the Grand Canal, a house in the mountains outside Florence that my mother inherited from her grandfather, a Medici duke, and a house in Trieste that belonged to my great-grandmother on my father's side."

Simeon opened his mouth, but she walked another step toward him. Her eyes were glowing with rage. "In all, I employ over two hundred *underlings.*" Her voice was scathing. "None of them live in houses filled with the stink of excrement! None of my houses are surrounded by withered lands. None of my bills are unpaid! *None of them!*"

The truth of it felt like a blow. "You're right."

"Those bills should be paid as a gesture of good will, and because at this point you cannot ascertain who is swindling you and who is not. And let me remind you, Simeon, that your father is the swindler in question: it was he who ordered goods and services, and never paid for them."

"I never—" He stopped. "I didn't think of it in that light. I should have known that my mother was unable to run this estate. Had I paid more attention to my solicitors' letters, I probably would have discovered that my father had lost his mind."

The anger in her eyes turned to sympathy. He hated that. In fact, he hated her. He bowed. "If you'll forgive me, I have an appointment." Then he turned and left, not waiting for her permission.

He headed straight outside. It was raining, but the air smelled sweet and clean. Birds were ignoring the rain and singing anyway. A footman tumbled through the door behind him, bleating something about his greatcoat. He ignored him and headed into the dilapidated gardens.

There was a scamper of feet behind him and he turned around, ready to snap a reprimand. Honeydew had to learn his place—

But it was Isidore.

She was trotting down the path after him, holding an absurdly coquettish, pink, ruffled umbrella in the air. Her hair was still in disarray, and little ringlets bobbed on her shoulders as she ran toward him. He almost stepped off the path, behind a bush, but he stopped himself.

She skidded to a halt in front of him. He braced himself, but there was no sympathy in her eyes. Instead, she looked rather annoyed.

"I think we have to make a rule," she said.

"What?" His lips felt numb. He felt slightly unbalanced. He often felt like that around Isidore. "What sort of rule?"

"No walking out and leaving a person in the midst of an argument." She tucked her arm into his and cocked her umbrella. Her face was shiny with rain. A drop ran down her cheek.

Simeon put a finger on the raindrop and brushed it away.

"I'm sorry," she said.

"So am I."

"I expect it was wonderful in Africa, away from here," she said.

Simeon sighed inwardly. From the sympathetic strain in Isidore's voice, she was clearly coming to understand the reasons that he fled to the East the moment he turned seventeen.

"I don't walk out in the rain," he said, all evidence to the contrary. "I am practical, thoughtful, and controlled."

She laughed and it was terrifying how much he liked the sound.

"I myself never walk in the rain, and particularly never sit down on wet benches," she said, plumping herself onto a wrought-iron bench shining with water. She laughed up at him and he sat down beside her.

The rain was merely sprinkling now, rolling down his neck in an unconvincing, yet cold, manner.

"When my mother died," Isidore said, "I was so afraid that I couldn't breathe correctly."

He stopped thinking about how cold his bottom felt and curled his hands around her fingers instead. They were small and warm.

"I used to lie awake at night and think that my breath was filling the room, so there wouldn't be any air left for me to breathe."

Simeon thought of saying the obvious, that her fear didn't make sense, but choked it back. Isidore was not a person who appreciated the obvious. "When did that feeling go away?" he asked instead.

"I finally told my aunt."

"And she was able to reassure you?"

"No. She couldn't convince me that I wasn't right." He turned to see her smiling up at him, her lips soft and ruby-colored, like a flower on the banks of the Ganges River.

"Ah," he said hopelessly, falling into that longing state that gripped him around Isidore. She was right in her initial assessment of his sanity. He'd waited too long to sleep with a woman, and now he'd lost his wits.

"My point is that I am not very good at changing my mind," Isidore said. "I am trying to tell you . . ."

"How did you get over it?" he asked abruptly. "Was

that happening when you were brought here to live, to this house?"

She nodded. "I really was a little crazed. I used to lie in bed and hold my breath, hoping to save enough so that I wouldn't die before morning."

He dropped her hand and put an arm around her. "Isidore."

She sighed and put her head on his shoulder. He smelled flowers and that other thing: Essence of Isidore.

"What did your aunt say?"

"She told me to sing. She said that singing actually created air, that when you filled your lungs and let it out in song, the air in the room expanded." She looked up at him. "Aren't you going to tell me that the whole idea is deranged?"

He kissed the end of her nose. It was a small, straight nose. A very beautiful nose. He was aware of a feeling in the back of his head that said that lust for a woman's nose was probably the beginning of a long list of absurdities. "No."

She put her head back on his shoulder and he tightened his arm. "I sang and sang. Your mother found it particularly difficult when I sang at the table. But you see, I had to sing because every time that I felt a tightening that meant there wasn't air enough in a room . . ." Her voice trailed off. "I know it's crazy."

"I never grieved for my father," Simeon said. "I don't think I really believed in his death until I came back here, and found the estate as it is."

"You must be very angry at him." She said it matter-of-factly.

"I am angry at myself," he said. "Obviously he was losing his mind, and I never came home to find out. Had I been in England, I would have realized. I would have known."

"You couldn't have done anything, though," Isidore said. "I saw your father at the opera four years ago. He was perfectly sane."

"To all appearances, perhaps," Simeon said, rather bitterly.

"And in his own mind. What could you have said to him? *Father, I think you're mad; why don't I pay the bills?*"

Simeon thought about that. Then he thought about how cold his bottom was and pulled Isidore to her feet. She twisted about to look at her backside.

"You're wet," he said, and then shocked himself. He put a hand directly on her wet skirts. "And cold."

She was wearing petticoats under her skirts, of course. And some sort of apparatus that kept her skirts billowing out at the sides. Her skirts were all wet, though, and they collapsed against her skin. He could feel a round, warm curve of flesh under his palm.

With a groan, he put both hands there and pulled him against her, taking her mouth.

"What—" she said, startled, but he took the word away from her, kissed her until she was pressed against him, arms around his neck.

But he didn't move his hands. He didn't think he could. She kissed him and talked at the same time. He could hear little bits of words, here and there, his name, a phrase, a little moan. He tried nipping her lip and she pushed against him . . . she liked it.

Suddenly she put her lips around his tongue and sucked and his blood flared in his body. From some distance he heard the groan in his throat, and ignored it. He was intoxicated by the plump sweetness under his hands. His head was swimming and his blood was on fire. He could take her home now. He could take her to the bedchamber and throw her on the bed. She was his wife, his wife, his—

The word beat sanity into him He forcibly uncurled his fingers and let her dress fall free. She murmured something and pulled him even closer. He waited for one heartbeat and then raised his head.

She looked up at him, her eyes hazy with desire.

"I think you're right," he said. "I waited too long."

She blinked at him. "To bed a woman," he clarified.

Her arms fell to her sides. A raindrop ran down her cheek. "Why do you say that?"

He answered her honestly. "I don't feel sane when I'm kissing you." She liked that. The bleak look went away and her dimple appeared, like a gift. He wanted to kiss it, but stopped himself.

"Perhaps that just makes you one of the family?" she suggested.

He was caught watching her lips and didn't understand.

"When I was singing all over this house and half the night, I was cracked," she said, a smile teasing her lips. "When your father was refusing to pay bills, he was cracked."

"My mother?" he said, raising an eyebrow.

"Grief," Isidore said. "Grief. She's not cracked, but she honored his memory as best she could."

"Ah." There was something important there, but he couldn't think about it now, so he took her arm and turned back to the house. Raindrops were caught on her long eyelashes. He could see them shining like shattered diamonds. "What did you sing?" he asked, rather desperately. Of course he couldn't stop here in the path and lick her eyelashes. He was losing his mind.

"Whatever came to me," Isidore said cheerfully. "I

wasn't very musical, you understand. I wouldn't want you to think that I added to the general charm of the house."

"Did it already smell?" he asked, aghast.

"Oh, no!" Isidore said. "Not at all. Didn't Honeydew say that the water closets were put in five years ago? This was eleven years ago. I remember that your mother was particularly vexed when I would sing a ballad about a forlorn lady who jumped from a cliff because she found herself with child. I learned it from my nanny at some point, but your mother considered it quite indelicate."

"I can imagine," Simeon said, feeling slightly cheered.

"Your mother did not feel that I was very ladylike. And I'm not, Simeon. I still sing in the wrong places and at the wrong times. Even if you don't swear, I do. I take after my mother, and she was a passionate Italian woman."

"I know." Simeon knew he should probably take this moment to point out that she wouldn't want to be with a dried-up old stick like himself, that she would be happier with someone more passionate. But instead he said, "I'm so sorry about your parents, Isidore." And he put his arm around her again.

She didn't say anything, and they walked home through the rain. By the time they arrived at the cottage it had turned into a proper English downpour, the kind that slants sideways.

Honeydew met them at the door to the Dower House and said, "The silver has been removed, as have all small movables, the smaller pictures in the West Gallery, and the Sèvres china."

"Where have you put them?" Simeon asked, watching Isidore walk away from him. Her skirts were wet and clung to her legs in the back. Now that he knew what she felt like under his hands he would never be the same again.

"The west barn," Honeydew was saying. "The footmen will sleep there, of course. The maids have all been sent home for a few days. The cook will be in the village, as the bakery kitchen has been kindly opened for our use."

Simeon dragged his eyes away as Isidore closed the bedchamber door. "My mother?"

"The dowager duchess refuses to leave Revels House. She also refuses to allow her jewelry to be removed; nothing in her room has been touched."

"I'll stay with her, of course," Simeon said with a sigh.

"I took the opportunity of sending all the furniture in the master bedchamber to London for refurbishing," Honeydew said smoothly. "You and the duchess must stop here in the Dower House. It will be rather intimate quarters, I'm afraid."

Simeon looked sharply at Honeydew, but his face was impervious.

"Set up a bed in the sitting room," he said. "I trust you can find me something of that nature, Honeydew?"

He could tell the butler didn't like it, but Simeon merely left. It would be a sad day when he cowered before his own butler.

Chapter Twenty-four

Gore House, Kensington
London Seat of the Duke of Beaumont
March 3, 1784

Jemma stared sightlessly into the glass above her dressing table. Then she pulled open the crumpled piece of foolscap and read it again.

It read precisely as it had a moment ago.

His Grace the Duke of Beaumont asked to be remembered to the duchess, and apologized for the fact that the note was written by his secretary, but he was unavailable today. And unfortunately tomorrow looked just as busy. With regrets, etc. Signed Mr. Cunningham, Elijah's secretary.

Elijah had never done that before, never actually written her through his secretary, when they were living in the same house. The note had been delivered, along with a letter from her sister-in-law and an invitation to dine from Lady Castlemaine, as if her husband were no more than another acquaintance.

He had withdrawn. Elijah had retreated back to his chambers in the Inns of Court.

Obviously he had misunderstood her.

Not seeing him was a torment. She'd just come from breakfast, and Elijah wasn't there. And she had driven her maid to distraction, trying on two breakfast gowns before she chose just the right one, before she tripped into the room looking as fresh and elegant as she possibly could.

Only to be told by the butler that His Grace had eschewed breakfast. Jemma had pretended total indifference, naturally.

Can there be anything more humiliating than living out one's life in front of servants who are both observant and intelligent? Sometimes Jemma felt as if she were acting in a play, and she seemed to have lost her ability to dissemble. Brigitte, her maid, surely suspected. Her butler, Fowle, quite likely.

It was humiliating to hanker after one's husband. To be dazzled by his eyes and his attention, until he suddenly withdrew it.

Perhaps Elijah has an appointment with his mistress, she told herself, just to test the pain of it. But she was no better at believing in mistresses now than she had been when they were first married. She would never, ever have thought Elijah had a mistress. She couldn't have imagined that he rose from her bed only to welcome the woman to his chambers at noon.

Even now . . .

Even now she couldn't believe it.

She stared unseeingly into her glass. Was it that she

thought she was too beautiful to be scorned? The only person who had ever scorned her, so to speak, was her own husband. Perhaps the right way to put that was that the only person who had ever shown indifference was her husband.

For a moment, an image of Villiers flashed across her eyes. Her revenge was ready at hand. She needn't watch as her husband turned from her company to the House of Lords, with as much interest as if he had selected a game of billiards over one of macao. She could turn to Villiers. All of London would know within hours of their first public appearance together.

Elijah would be humiliated and it would serve him right.

But she knew even as she envisioned it that she couldn't—or wouldn't—do it. Villiers was no pawn; he was a man. A dangerous man: beautiful, witty and easy to love. That was where the danger lay, in the fact she could fall in love with him.

Then her marriage would truly be over.

Somehow, it had never been over in her mind, not even when she fled to France and Elijah didn't follow, nor the first time she found herself in bed with another man. Even when she tormented herself with remembering Elijah's declaration of love for his mistress.

He never said he loved *her*, Jemma, his wife. Surely that in itself was enough to end a marriage?

The invisible bonds had grown thin over the years that she lived in France without him. Attenuated by memory and her dalliances with other men.

But they never broke.

And all those memories were fresh to her now: of their wedding, when she hardly knew him, and yet her heart thrilled at the sight of him waiting for her in St. Paul's Cathedral. Of their wedding night, when she was so awkward and he thoughtful, if (she thought in retrospect) rather reserved. But of course he was in love with another woman. Still . . .

There was a habit of mind, a way of thinking and talking, that came from being married to someone. A sort of bone-deep intimacy that survives even blows such as their marriage had taken.

Love, it could be called.

Odd, fugitive, undeserved. She had done nothing to deserve his love, and she rather thought he hadn't given it. Sometimes she thought, recently, that she saw something tender in his eyes, almost longing, but . . .

But somehow she had poured out her love when they first married, and there was no taking it back, no matter how she tried.

And no matter how he rebuffed her.

Perhaps . . . perhaps she was making a mountain from a mouse. Elijah worked too hard. He always worked too hard; that was why he had fainted in the House of Lords last year. Overwork and lack of sleep.

Perhaps he needed to be reminded that life was not work. She could . . .

But the idea of going to his chambers in the Inns of Court made her physically ill. She could remember what his mistress's hair looked like, flowing over the edge of his desk. Surely he still had that desk. It was a large solid oak one, good for the weight of a sturdy woman.

It hadn't been making a creaking sound as she entered, though he was surely thrusting with some strength . . .

It was all so far in the past, and yet close enough to touch.

She couldn't go to his chambers. What if she did and there was some evidence of his current mistress, if he had one?

Or had he told her that he had no mistress these days?

She couldn't even remember: such a crucial detail and it was gone.

Jemma rose to her feet; her letters fell to the carpet. She was not a woman, she told herself, to sit around bleating and wringing her hands. She was a person who—

Who went and *got* a man if she wished.

She wasn't a mere lass anymore. If she wanted to see her husband, she would do so. And of course she would have his clerks properly announce her, so that in the remote chance he was entertaining a woman, he could bundle her out the back door.

She needed an excuse for paying a visit. In vain she tried to think of something important. Why would she stop by his office? Why would any wife? Only to announce an immediate change of plans. If one, for instance, had suddenly decided to leave London for a few days, and go to the country. She could go to their country house and check on the renovation of the North Wing.

Suddenly a letter on the floor caught her eye, and it came to her: she knew where she was going. Her sister-in-law, darling Roberta, had written her a letter full of laughing, rueful details about Roberta's father, who was marrying a woman he met at Bartholomew Fair. That might be bad enough, but the woman apparently earned her money by donning a fish tail and speaking in verse—and Roberta's father was a marquess.

Naturally she had to stop by Elijah's chambers and tell him that the Marquess of Wharton and Malmesbury had lost his heart to a mermaid, and that she meant to pay Roberta a visit and see the mermaid in person. Perhaps she would force Elijah to take her to luncheon, or a ride in the park. She glanced out the window and saw it was drizzling.

A ride in the rain.

She, Jemma, was not leaving London without another kiss.

Sad, but true.

Her husband had kissed her twice in the last nine years, both recently. And she had kissed him once. Stupid beggar of a woman that she was, she treasured those kisses.

There. It was settled. She would instruct Brigitte to pack for a short journey, and meanwhile she would go to Elijah's chambers. If he wasn't there, she would wait. And when he finally arrived, she would kiss him goodbye.

The smile on her lips had a spice of joy about it that made her nervous, catching a glimpse of herself in the mirror.

When had all this happened?

When did . . .

She turned away. There was no accounting for the human heart, or so her mama had always said.

Chapter Twenty-five

The Dower House
March 3, 1784

It was still raining. Isidore sat at her window, watching rain slide off the thorns of the rose briar circling her window. She could live without being a duchess. It would prickle, if she were honest. True, she had thought of herself as a duchess for years, whether she called herself Lady Del'Fino or no.

But what was a duchess, after all?

Just a title. Simeon was merely the only man for whom she'd allowed herself to feel desire. There were likely hundreds of desirable men waiting for her to discover them. She could direct the solicitor to unravel the weave of their marriage lines, go to London, and begin flirting with every man she met.

She felt as sad as the raindrops.

When Lucille appeared, full of excitement about the dismantling of the house, she put on her clothes without saying more than a word. Why should she seduce Simeon as she had planned? Surely that would be the worst possible footing on which to start a marriage. Likely he would blame her thereafter, thinking her a Jezebel who lured him into a marriage he didn't want.

She rejected the delicious gown her maid suggested and pointed to a blue-black one, sprigged with blackberry vines. It was sedate; it was proper. She wore it to go to church.

By the time she emerged from the bedchamber, Cosway was already seated at the desk in the sitting room, a stack of papers before him. Isidore felt a flash of irritation at him, for being so beautiful, so restrained, so not in love with her.

Not that it was his fault.

"If you will forgive me for my intrusion," he said, rising, "I thought we might break our fast together. The Dead Watch apparently have entered the pit and cleaning has commenced. Honeydew asked that we serve ourselves, as he has the entire household staff guarding the silver, at least those who are not consigned to guard parts of the house."

"Goodness," Isidore said, seating herself at the table before he could help her. "Are we giving hardship pay to those assigned to the fumes?"

"An excellent suggestion."

She picked up a muffin and buttered it, very precisely. They could be friends. There was no reason for her to feel melancholic. A whole world of men lay before her. "What work need you do today?"

"I have left the most difficult letters for the end," Simeon said.

"Difficult in what sense? Are their requests unlikely?"

"No. I took your advice and paid all those about which I had doubts."

She put down her muffin and felt her smile growing. "That was very generous of you, given your fear of being swindled."

"I didn't do it out of generosity," Simeon said. "In fact, I don't think I am particularly kind."

She couldn't think what to say to that, so she took a bite of her muffin.

"I like to keep what is mine," he continued.

I was yours, she thought, somewhat bitterly.

"These are letters that hint at other transgressions," Simeon stated.

"Of what kind?" Isidore asked interestedly.

Simeon rose, extracted a sheet of tinted note paper, and handed it to her. It was written in a sloping, elegant hand and still smelled faintly of roses. It wasn't long, though bitterness made the phrases pungent.

Isidore looked up. "Your father's mistress, I presume?"

"One of them."

"One? How many are there?"

"There are four such letters. Then there are five or six of a less imploring nature."

"Five or six! That's—"

"At least ten women," Simeon said flatly.

Isidore bit her lip. "As I understand it, it is a common practice. Ten may seem a great many, but your father was a man of many years, and he—"

"The ten letters are all dated within the last six years of his life."

"Well," Isidore said, thinking frantically, "he certainly was a *virile* man."

Simeon's jaw tightened. Clearly he did not appreciate his father's virility.

"At least your mother doesn't know," Isidore said, looking for a bright side.

"Actually, she does."

"How do you know?"

In answer, he got up and fetched another piece of paper, handing it to her. This letter wasn't quite so bitter: it mournfully requested that the duke fulfill at least some of the promises he had made, for a small cottage, the writer noted, and a pension. At the very bottom, written in the duchess's spidery handwriting was a note indicating a payment of four hundred pounds.

"Four hundred pounds!" Isidore said. "At least *she* got her cottage."

"Yes." His voice was so uncompromising and rage-filled that Isidore fell silent again. "Did your father have a mistress?" he asked, finally.

"I don't believe so. My mother . . ." Her voice trailed off.

"What?"

"Would have killed him," she said. "You said that I was uncomfortably emotional, Simeon. I got it from my mother. She had a terrible temper, and occasionally she would erupt into rages and scream." She smiled, thinking of it.

Simeon looked appalled.

"My father would argue at first," Isidore said, "and finally he would start laughing. Then she would laugh too, and it would be over."

"I feel as if I returned home to a family I never knew," Simeon said. "I had no idea that my father swam in a sea of deceit, cheating everyone from the tradespeople to his intimates. I fear that debts of honor will be called in at any moment."

"Was he a gamester?"

"I have no idea. To this point, no one has approached me about gaming debts left unpaid. I didn't know him."

"It could be that no one really understands another person," Isidore offered.

Simeon put down his knife and fork with sharp little clicks. "I am a man of restraint and habit, Isidore. I do not like chaos."

"I know," Isidore said, feeling her melancholy almost like a friend at this point.

"I dislike—I truly dislike—this feeling that at any moment, unpleasant truths about my family may appear. I wasn't observant as a child and I noticed little beyond my parents' arguments. Even those I paid scant attention to. I was utterly riveted by my dreams of travel."

She had to smile at the idea of that. "Ever since you were little?"

"I left the country at the earliest possible age. My father thought I would be travelling for a year. I knew it would be far longer, though I didn't emphasize the point. Yet I would have come back if I'd known the family was unraveling at the seams."

"How you've changed," Isidore said. "You used to long for adventure, and now you seem to want the quiet life you once despised."

"There's such a thing as too much adventure," he said dryly. "Near-Death-by-Privy is a good example of what adventure often looks like, up close."

"Once you pay the outstanding bills, you won't be buffeted by chaos." It had to be said, so she said it. "I have been thinking about your reluctance to marry me, Simeon, and I think your initial instinct was right. I am not the proper wife for you. The solicitor made it clear that we could end the marriage, and I think we should."

He had picked up his knife but he put it down again,

very precisely. He didn't seem inclined to speak, so she continued. "You will be much happier with someone like yourself, someone restrained and organized. I am not very restrained, Simeon. And you haven't even seen my worst side. I would make you uncomfortable in the long run."

"I begin to question my concept of marriage," he said, but his voice was wooden.

"I know I would," Isidore said, pushing away her plate. "We've turned into friends, don't you think? Perhaps because we are both people without experience. But you called lust a transitory emotion, and I'm certain that you're right. Previously, I never allowed myself to feel anything of that nature."

"I should hope not."

"Why not?" she asked. "Wouldn't you rather that I *had* felt lust and had restrained myself? Not that it matters," she answered herself. "I think you will be much more comfortable with someone as composed as yourself."

"She sounds like a personal secretary," Simeon observed.

"No, not at all," Isidore said, warming to the task. "We'll find you someone sweet."

"Docile?"

"Well, that's such an unattractive word. Perhaps not docile, but you would be more comfortable perhaps with someone more biddable. I am not biddable, Simeon. Not in the least. I have made my own way for too many years. I never really realized it before, but I fear I have become a virago."

He gasped, but she saw the amusement in his eyes. "No!"

"Laugh as you like," she told him. "You're grateful I'm saying this, and don't pretend that you're not. As I said, we'll find you a charming English girl to whom restraint and prudence are second nature."

"Like my mother?"

"Your mother?" she repeated, losing track of the conversation.

He looked at her thoughtfully. "My mother learned my father's lessons so well that she maintained his deranged method of paying bills for years after his death. The only hint of rebellion I can find is that she paid his mistress so generously. He would have hated that. But that in itself indicates a certain lack of passion, don't you think? I find it hard to believe that she was not aware of the existence of all these women."

Isidore really didn't know what to think of Simeon's mother. "You don't like passion," she pointed out. "It is uncomfortable. Your mother likely feels the same way. After all, if one's husband is determined to stray, what can one do?"

"What would you do? If I took a mistress?"

Isidore didn't even need to think about that. "I'd kill you," she told him, smiling to soften it a little. "So you see, Simeon, I would be a very uncomfortable wife."

"I don't intend to have a mistress, or mistresses," Simeon said.

"That's very admirable of you. I'm sure your wife will be much happier."

"I feel queasy at the idea of you choosing my bride."

"Of course," Isidore said brightly. "I didn't mean to intrude in any fashion."

There was a beat of silence, so she added, "I shall naturally be looking for my own spouse so I wouldn't have to time to search out the proper damsel for you. We both must manage the task on our own."

"Won't you mind not being a duchess?"

"Oh, no," she said airily. "Titles are not very important to me."

"You might not feel that way after more reflection."

"If that proves to be the case, I shall simply set my cap at a duke," Isidore pointed out. "The Duke of Villiers is surprisingly attractive. He and I accompanied my friend Harriet to Lord Strange's house party. I had no idea that Villiers was so witty."

"The problem is not you, Isidore, but myself."

"You said that before," Isidore pointed out, feeling irritated. "I entirely understand that you find me unrestful. I accept it; in fact, as I've just said, I've come to agree with you. After all, what if I wanted a husband who would show passionate interest in *me*?"

His eyes were impenetrable. "Yes, what then?"

"I do not want a spouse who will be always calm and ordered," she told him. "My father cared deeply about my mother."

"I'm sure he did."

"He never would have taken a mistress, not because he was afraid that she would scream at him, but because they were a pair. They faced the world together. Even—" her throat was tight a moment, but she said it anyway—"even though I couldn't bear it, I was glad they died together. I simply couldn't imagine one without the other."

"They were fortunate."

"You wouldn't have thought so," she said. "They did fight. Sometimes my mother won, and sometimes my father won. On balance, I think my mother won more often. I remember finding them kissing. And I remember my mother sending me to the nursery, and pulling father off for a nap as well."

Simeon's mouth curled in a smile.

"I thought for years after that that all grown-ups slept

in the afternoon. Unlike myself, my father didn't protest."

"I expect not."

"I want what my parents had. In a queer way I'm grateful that you didn't come home promptly when I was sixteen. I'd been telling myself that I just wanted an acceptable marriage. But now I understand that I was settling for whomever emerged from the desert because I didn't really have a choice."

She stood up and walked a quick step to the mantelpiece, turned and looked at him. "I have to thank you, Simeon. I never thought I had any choice, so I didn't allow myself to think about what *I* wanted in a marriage."

"And what do you want?" He had stood as soon as she had. His voice sounded a bit queer, rather stifled, so she peered at him. But he looked exactly the same: passionless, calm Simeon. At least he was polite enough not to break into celebration at her announcement.

"I want to be liked," she told him, feeling more cheerful by the moment. "I think I'd like to fall in love. Oh, and I want to be courted. Many men have tried, you know."

"I have no doubt." His face did look a bit cross.

"Flowers and such," Isidore told him. "Even jewels, sometimes, if they didn't yet realize what sort of person I am. I'd like a marriage in which—" She stopped. "Do you suppose it's too much to hope that my husband will listen to my opinion all of the time?"

"Yes."

She wrinkled her nose. "Then most of the time. And I'd like all the passion that you don't want. I don't wish for a calm and contained life. I'd rather have some adventure." In fact, Isidore felt quite cheerful even thinking about it.

Suddenly he was standing just before her. He moved like some sort of predator, but then he didn't seem to know what he wanted to say.

"Simeon?" she asked.

He didn't kiss her, even though her knees weakened at the look in his eyes. "I just want you to know that I like you, Isidore."

She couldn't think what to answer.

Chapter Twenty-six

Number Four, Gray's Inn
The Duke of Beaumont's offices
March 3, 1784
That afternoon

Jemma arrived at Elijah's offices in the Inns of Court feeling reasonably certain that she looked exquisite. That is to say, she was as certain as a woman could be who had just spent three hours putting on a gown of amber silk embroidered with sprigs of white flowers. Her shoes were trimmed with dark gold braid and finished with a jeweled buckle. She wore her hair up and lightly powdered, with jewels that matched her shoes.

Elijah likely wouldn't note the details, but a woman feels more confidence when she is perfectly attired from head to toe.

When Jemma had visited Elijah's offices for the first time, just after their marriage began, it was the middle of the day and the offices had been empty. She had strolled through a series of rooms noting the dark wood paneling and serious portraits of plump men, until she wandered into Elijah's inner sanctum. This afternoon, the scene was utterly different. She pushed open the door to Elijah's outer chamber to find it crowded with men shouting at each other.

There was a brief silence as they twisted their necks to look at her, and then the noise erupted again. But she noticed a nervous clerk scuttle into the inner offices after a glance at her, so she stayed where she was.

Before her were two worthy London merchants, or so she would guess from their clothing, arguing with a third man, surely a government official, about what they termed a "nest of pestilence." Jemma hadn't figured out where the nest might be located before Elijah's private secretary appeared, looking harassed.

Mr. Cunningham wove his way through the knots of gentlemen and burst into an apologetic speech the moment he arrived at her side.

"It's quite all right," Jemma told him. "I am finding it interesting."

"It's Wednesday, Your Grace," he told her, leading her toward the door from which he had emerged. "I'm afraid that Wednesdays are rather chaotic. Well, as are Tuesdays. And—"

"All other days," Jemma filled in. "Who are all these gentlemen?"

"Petitioners," he said. "As you may know, the East India Company has a great many men in its employ whose only business is to inform members of Parliament just what the company would like to have done. There are always more than a few of those in His Grace's offices, hoping for a word. Lately there have been a great many people offering various solutions to the current wave of depredatory robberies."

"I've read about them," Jemma said, "but what on earth does Beaumont have to offer to the poor robbed people?"

"Oh, it's not the victims we bother about," Mr. Cunningham told her. "It's how to cope with the criminals once they're caught that's on the government's mind at the moment. We used to banish them all to the colonies, but the American war stopped that."

"Of course," Jemma said. "It's as if the rat-catcher suddenly left town. There's no one to cope with the rats."

"We've tried settling them in West Africa, and it doesn't work," Mr. Cunningham said, weaving his way through a second room just as teeming with gentlemen, if not more so. "We have a great number imprisoned in the hulks, decommissioned warships moored in the Thames, if you can believe it."

"I expect they attempt to escape daily." They entered a third room filled with chattering petitioners. "Mr. Cunningham, is there a better time to visit my husband?"

"Oh no, it's like this from dawn to dusk," Mr. Cunningham said over his shoulder.

"Goodness. I haven't visited in years, but I had no idea . . ."

"Due to the fact that he is favored by Mr. Pitt, but also respected by Mr. Fox, His Grace finds himself in the unenviable position of brokering compromises."

Finally they reached a room in which resided only a number of weedy-looking men scratching busily at sheets of foolscap. "If you will step this way, Your Grace," Mr. Cunningham said, "the duke will be happy to greet you in his private chamber."

Jemma stepped through the door; Mr. Cunningham melted away behind her.

Elijah's office was beautifully appointed, with a rococo fireplace of just the sort that she most admired, and a lovely group of chairs clustered before it. He was already on his feet, out from behind his desk, and moving toward her. But her heart sank when she saw the look of cool reserve in his eyes.

"We need to speak," she said. "I am sorry to bother you when you have so many people clamoring for your time." She could hear a faint roar of voices through the closed door.

"Please," Elijah said, guiding her to a small sofa.

She raised an eyebrow. "Cherry twill? Very nice." It looked precisely like the chairs that graced her salon in Paris.

"I admired them in your house," he said simply. And then: "They made me think of you."

Jemma didn't know how to take that. Did she really want her husband to remember her due to a pair of chairs? He sat down opposite her, rather than beside her.

"I received an amusing letter from Roberta, saying that her father is marrying his mermaid," she said. "I can't resist the idea of paying her a visit and meeting the mermaid myself. I thought to leave this afternoon or at the latest, tomorrow morning, so I wanted to let you know."

"It was very kind of you to tell me yourself," he said. "A mermaid. I should like to meet a mermaid."

"I had hoped to see you this morning." That was too blunt, but the sentence just jumped from her mouth.

He was silent for a moment. "I'm been—"

"I know you're busy," she said, cutting him off. "We have been married too long to lie to each other, Elijah."

"I would have thought that the longer a marriage survived, the more the untruths accumulate."

Jemma hated the fact that her heart lurched at the very sight of his smile. "I would prefer the opposite. I thought your note might have resulted from a misunderstanding about my last words to you."

Obviously, he was a master of the art of silence.

"I told you that I did not wish to play the last game in my match with the Duke of Villiers." She held her breath.

His expression didn't change, and she dropped her eyes to her gloved hands. Fool that she was, she'd probably created the situation out of thin air. Look at all the petitioners he dealt with. He could not come home because he was busy. She was a *fool*. Her heart beat in tune with her self-recriminations.

He cleared his throat. "May I sit next to you, duchess?"

Jemma could feel a smile curling her lips. It was the gentleness of his tone. "Yes," she said, rather breathlessly, adding: "Duke."

"I thought you indicated a wish to discard *our* last game," he said, seating himself next to her.

She pulled off her gloves and then reached up to touch his cheekbone. "You look tired again, Elijah."

"Not *our* last game?" he said, showing the polite persistence that likely got him to the top of the government.

"Villiers's," she said. "I intend to relinquish the match to Villiers without playing the third game."

"He won't take that well."

Jemma laughed. "Pity for your rival?"

"Leopold has always been unlucky in love."

"I shall play him other games," she said, "but not blindfolded. And not in bed."

His lips barely touched hers, just brushed her mouth, but the very touch made Jemma shiver. It wasn't the sensuality of it, but the affection that was heart-breaking. There had been so much anger between them.

"I have to leave London as well. Pitt has called a meeting in his country house, since Parliament is in Easter Recess for a few weeks."

The regret in his eyes was deep and unfeigned. "How long?" she asked, wondering if it were possible for married couples to feel as excited as new lovers.

"I'll tell him that I must return for the king's fête on the twenty-sixth," he said, kissing her again. But it wasn't the kiss she wanted, so she wound an arm around his arm and brought him down to her. He smelled like Elijah. He tasted . . . oh he tasted like complexity and power and something that seemed awfully suggestive of—

But that thought was gone in the way his lips moved over hers, powerfully, commandingly. There was such a potent sense of homecoming that Jemma felt tears prick her eyes.

He didn't touch her in any way. Her hands didn't stray over his shoulders or disrupt his wig. They only touched in that most intimate, most silent of fashions.

They were still kissing when a hard rap sounded at the door and Mr. Cunningham poked his head in. Jemma saw utter surprise cross his face. Of course, Mr. Cunningham was probably more acquainted with the crumbling state of her marriage than she was.

But Elijah didn't even turn around. "What is it, Ransom?" he said. He kept looking down at her, smiling an odd little lopsided smile.

"There's been another breakout from the convict ship moored in the Thames near the Blackfriars Bridge," Cunningham said, whisking himself back out the door.

"I told them it was a damn fool idea to house people in the hulks," Elijah said.

"Housing criminals on warships? Or the part about the Thames?"

"Did you know about that? You're a constant surprise to me, Jemma." And he bent his head again.

"I'll be gone by the time you come home," she said, some time later. She was breathless and happy and frightened, all at once.

"I shouldn't let you leave," he said.

To Jemma's mind, it seemed as if the muffled uproar in the outside chambers was growing louder by the moment.

"They'll want me to address Lords about what to do," he murmured, cupping her face in his hands.

"What will you say?" she managed.

"I've always—" he brushed his lips over hers—"said that the use of warships"—another kiss—"was an outrageous mistake."

The noise outside rose to something of a crescendo, and Jemma, pulling herself free, stood up. But she couldn't bear to leave just yet.

"Why?" she asked.

Being Elijah, he took her question seriously. "Most of the convicts are unemployed veterans of our various wars. Unable to find work, they turn to robbery and worse. The warships make terrible prisons: the men spend most of their time trying to escape. And one in four dies during his first three years there."

"The nests of pestilence," Jemma said with a little gasp, "I heard men talking about them in the outer chamber."

Elijah nodded.

"You are a good man," Jemma said, straightening his cravat.

He caught her hands, turned her right one over and kissed her palm. "Not always."

"When it's most important," she said.

"I begin to think the opposite. It could be that *you* are most important, Jemma. To me." He held her hands for a moment, and then let them go. "I shall come directly to the king's yacht on the twenty-sixth, Jemma. And I shall look for you."

Jemma never really understood the description of a singing heart until that moment, but as she threaded her way out of the crowded chambers, every man arguing over issues of clemency to convicts, deportation to foreign lands, banishment, execution, hanging . . . She couldn't stop the foolish smile on her lips.

Or the song in the general vicinity of her breast.

Chapter Twenty-seven

The Dower House
March 3, 1784

*I*sidore did not want to have an intimate meal with Simeon. It was too heart-wrenching. After having thought of him as her husband for so many years, some parts of her couldn't stop thinking of him that way. Mostly, if she were strictly honest about it, her body.

She only had to see him to want to kiss him. If they ate together, just the two of them, she might embarrass herself somehow.

They had spent the afternoon working through the final stack of papers. They had an argument over one of the letters. It talked of love, rather than money. That made it worse, to Isidore's mind, and she thought that the woman deserved more than the standard four-hundred-pound gift they had agreed upon.

"She may be in no need of funds," Simeon pointed out. "She doesn't mention his promises, unlike the rest of them."

"But she knows he is married. He is a duke, and she addressed the letter to him. Why would she write if she didn't need funds?"

"She loved him."

Isidore took the letter back. "She does address him by his first name."

"She asks him to visit her. She says she misses him."

"Your poor mother," Isidore said.

Simeon blinked. "I was just thinking that it was nice to find that my father didn't wheedle his way into this woman's bed with financial promises and then disappear. She doesn't sound angry."

"No, just lonely. Your father may have acted honorably toward her. Perhaps this mistress is in comfortable circumstances."

"Perhaps she's a rich widow," Simeon said. There was something longing in his voice.

"I'm sorry," she said quietly.

"As am I." And that was the end of that.

All afternoon, as the light coming into the room turned from pale yellow to gold, it played in his hair. She was developing a foolish love of unpowdered hair. The light made Simeon's hair look as if there were streaks of near blue among the curls. When he pushed it back with his hands, one ringlet always fell back over his brow.

She kept shifting uneasily, aware that her body was sending her all sorts of treacherous signals, signals that didn't agree with her newfound resolution to find a man who would court her.

Because for all Simeon was polite enough to say he liked her, that wasn't good enough.

She wanted to be loved.

After all the years in which she'd schooled herself into cheerfully accepting whatever type of man her duke turned out to be, she'd discovered that if she had the choice, she would like to be loved with a deep passion. The kind she had seen in her father's eyes when he bent to kiss her mother.

Why had she never before realized how important love was?

The last thing she wanted was to be betrayed by an unruly lust for unpowdered hair into some sort of indiscretion with Simeon, something that would turn their marriage into a *fait accompli*.

Chapter Twenty-eight

Revels House
March 3, 1784

After hours of sorting though the late duke's delinquencies, Isidore felt as if she were going as mad as her former father-in-law. "I think your mother must be suffocating in that house," she announced. "I shall see if I can tempt her into joining us for supper."

Simeon looked up, obviously startled. "You will?"

"I'll try," she conceded. "You might clear away those letters, just in case she agrees."

"She has been adamant in her refusal."

"It's not right that she should be in a house full of fumes." Isidore stood up.

"I'll lend my voice as well, if you will allow me to

finish this note and clear away any letters that might distress my mother."

"You don't think I'll be successful on my own?"

"I'd be shocked, but that's a commentary on my mother's stubbornness, not on your persuasive skills. But I'd prefer to accompany you, given the fumes."

Isidore went outside to wait for him, but after five minutes, she was too restless to wait. She wouldn't be felled by the smell. Her house in Venice had persistent odor problems, emanating from the canals, and she had never succumbed to the vapors.

She entered the house through the ballroom and was immediately met by the stench. There was a racket in the main hallway, and she cautiously opened the door. A man was trundling a wheelbarrow past her. Isidore's eyes fell to the barrow, and then she wished they hadn't.

He didn't see her, so she slipped up the stairs. If anything, the smell was actually stronger as she climbed the stairs. Her knock on the dowager's door was met with something resembling a bark. "Your Grace?" she called. "It is the duchess. Would you open the door?"

A moment later the dowager did open the door, the better to glower at Isidore.

Isidore fell into a deep curtsy. "Did the duke not leave a footman to guard you?"

"The fool began to vomit," the dowager said irritably. "What on earth are you doing here? The stench is enough to make any person vomit, not merely the lower orders. You must leave at once."

"I came to ask you to join us in the Dower House," Isidore said. Truly, she did feel a bit faint at the odor. "Supper is being sent from the village. You can't possibly eat here."

"I doubt that I could eat."

Isidore realized that the dowager was distinctly white, with patches of rouge standing out like poppies on her cheeks. "Your Grace, I insist that you accompany me out of this house. You are faint from lack of air."

"I am faint from the stench," the dowager said. But she put out a hand to the back of a chair. "I thought I would—"

Isidore took her arm. "You may return to your chambers as soon as they are habitable," she said coaxingly.

"You needn't treat me like a child!" the dowager snapped, but she did take a step toward the door. "I can't leave my jewels."

"They'll be—"

"I go nowhere without my jewels. No one understands my attachment to them."

Isidore nodded. "We'll take them with us."

"And I was working on letters," the duchess said. "I must have them as well. I must finish my correspondence."

Isidore glanced over at the table stacked high with sheets of stationery. "We can't carry those. Is this your jewelry box?" She picked up an exquisite little box, rosewood with silver hinges.

"One of them," the dowager said. "The other is there." She nodded toward a much larger box, made of leather and trimmed with faded velvet.

"Goodness," Isidore said a moment later. "It *is* heavy."

"I shall carry the smaller one," the dowager announced. "Give it to me. I suppose all the footmen have fled the house."

"They're in the barn," Isidore explained.

"Stuff and nonsense," the dowager said, taking the rosewood box. She opened the door of her room and the smell came to meet them, like a blow. The dowager fell back.

"Steady," Isidore said. "Your Grace, why don't I fetch your son? Footmen could carry you outside."

"I am tired of being old," the dowager stated. "I shall leave this room under my own two feet."

They started down the stairs. When they reached the bottom, the hallway held a couple of men so filthy that Isidore had never seen the like. Dirt was caked on their legs and splattered on their shirts. Their faces were partially covered with red kerchiefs, but their hair and skin was caked with excrement.

The one closest to the bottom stair grinned, his teeth startling white against the kerchief covering his nose.

The dowager made a strange gulping noise, and her grip on Isidore's arm weakened. "Your Grace!" Isidore said sharply, pulling her mother-in-law off the final stair.

The dowager opened her mouth, like a fish out of water. "This is—this is—"

"I agree, but we must continue."

"Oh dear, oh dear, ladies as is seeing what they shouldn't," a cheerful voice said.

Isidore looked up and met the eyes of a third man, who had just emerged from the water closet. She knew in an instant that this particular member of the Dead Watch was an utter rogue, due to the peculiar flatness of his eyes, and the way he was smiling without smiling. "Jack Bartlebee, top of the Dead Watch," he said to her. "And you two must be duchesses. I've a tenderness for the nobility. Really I do. When the king passes in his carriage of a Sunday, I always bobs me knee. Don't I, lads?"

"That you do, Jack," one chimed in.

"Ain't it a shame, yer duchess, but Mr. Honeybutt

went down the hillside to deal with a little problem with the pipes. We'll have to help you."

The closest man held out his hands, caked with brown.

The dowager made a choking sound and clutched her jewelry box.

"Tush, tush," Bartlebee said. "You're affronting the ladies, Wiglet. You was always too forward in your approach. Ladies like the gentle word, the sweet tongue, ain't that right?"

"Sir," Isidore said, "if you would move to the side, I would be grateful to take my mother-in-law into the open. She faints for lack of air."

"I'll help you," Bartlebee said genially. "Of course I will. I'll take that wee little box that the lady is holding—"

"Don't touch it!" the dowager said, her voice a strangely airy version of her normal peremptory tone. "I can't have you touch my—"

All three of them had their hands stretched out. Isidore took a step to the side, dragging the dowager with her. She could leave through the ballroom, rather than out the front door. The men were enjoying causing fear. Their faces were alight with some sort of strange pleasure.

"How dare you terrify an old woman!" she shouted at them, suddenly furious. "You've frightened her!"

Bartlebee just laughed at her, and even his eyes, those horrible flat eyes, looked amused. "It's a valuable lesson she's learning. Duchesses shit as well as everyone else. And once you've been in the shit as much as we have, you learn that the color of the stuff is the same, ain't it, lads?"

There was a chorus of agreement.

"Let's cut the sauce," Bartlebee said suddenly. "We're only halfway through these privies, duchess. You wouldn't want us to leave the job undone, would you? Because no one else is going down into that pit. No one in England. So we'd like a little present to keep us going."

"No," Isidore stated. "You've been well paid."

The dowager was utterly silent, staring at the men with horrified eyes.

"The young lady don't even look frightened," Bartlebee said, turning to his men. "That's unusual, that is."

"I'm not frightened," Isidore spat. "I'm disgusted by your lack of kindness. Have you no grandmother yourself?"

"Is that a grandmother?" Bartlebee asked, interestedly. He moved closer to the dowager, who cowered away with a stifled little moan. "Oh, I see. It must be the wrinkles, am I right, Wiglet? The more wrinkled you are, the older you are? I've heard of that. Course, we on the Dead Watch don't generally live to collect all that many wrinkles, so we don't bother. We don't have families in the regular way of things."

They all guffawed.

"You'll excuse me for not pitying you," Isidore snapped. "If you have no families, it's due to your criminal tendencies. Doubtless, no woman will have anything to do with you."

"Doubtless, doubtless," Bartlebee said. "But just to make you feel better, miss, I will tell you that Wiglet here married Betsy as does behind the livery stables on Pond Street. Now there, does that make you feel better?"

Isidore looked at Wiglet. He had no teeth and a leer.

"Did I express any sorrow over your lonely condition?" Isidore asked, politely enough. "If I did, I assure you it was an error."

"Enough of this charmin' banter," Bartlebee said. "We'll be having a jewelry box, since you was daft enough to bring it into the shit, if you'll pardon my plain speaking. And just as payment for this delightful little chat, we'll be having the large box, not the smaller."

"The duke will have you all thrown into jail," the dowager half screamed. Her fingers were digging into Isidore's arm like small talons.

"That he won't," Bartlebee said. "I'm happy to reassure you there. Where the Dead Watch go, nobody sees. That makes us above the law, as they'll be happy to tell you in London."

"No one is above the law!" Isidore snapped. If she could just keep the conversation going. Simeon would finish his letter. Honeydew would return. She took another cautious step to the side, dragging the dowager with her. She almost had her back to the ballroom door.

"Now if I murdered someone," Bartlebee said, with that horrible mirthless grin of his, "I reckon you'd be right. A parish constable might knock on my door, if he could find it, of course. It's such a temptation sometimes. All you'd have to do was tip someone into a pit, and they'd fall into a permanent sleep due to a sad, sad accident. Ain't it a temptation, lads?"

Only Wiglet answered: "Ay!" Bartlebee was grinning, but his other man didn't look as comfortable.

"You should all be ashamed of yourselves," Isidore said, schooling her voice to a clear, high severity. "We're paying you a fair and honest wage for the work you're doing. And how do you repay us? By frightening an old woman half to death."

As if on cue, the dowager groaned and sank against Isidore's shoulder, though Isidore noticed that her mother-in-law kept tight hold of her jewelry box. Now the door was directly behind her.

Bartlebee stepped smartly forward, and she realized

that she was going to have to give up the jewelry box, that all the jewels in the world weren't worth one touch from his finger. She couldn't turn around to open the door without letting go of the dowager, or letting go of the box.

Just then she heard a voice behind her, like a thread of sound. "Isidore."

It was Simeon. The door at her back started to ease open. Bartlebee was reaching toward her, grinning; any moment he would see the opening door.

Without hesitation, Isidore shrieked "Now!" Then she lifted the box she held and dashed it to the ground at her feet. With an ear-splitting crack, it opened and jewels skidded across the floor.

The door behind her whipped back and Simeon leapt forward. He landed between his mother and the men, standing in the midst of a pile of dusty-looking necklaces.

"What is this, gentlemen?" Simeon asked. His voice was as calm as if he were conversing with Honeydew.

Isidore's heart skipped a beat when she saw that Bartlebee was utterly unafraid. And his men stopped looking abashed as their eyes brightened at the prospect of a fight.

"It's the duke himself!" Bartlebee said, delighted. "See, gents, he'll know about the law of the land. He'll know that we're doing a loathsome job, and all we're asking for is a bit of a treat. And as we just told the duchess here, we might not be able to finish the job if we're not given something to lighten our labor." He suddenly kicked Wiglet, who was on his knees, scrabbling amongst the jewels. "Hist now! There's no need to act undignified-like!"

It all happened so fast that Isidore couldn't follow it. One moment Simeon was standing perfectly still before her, and the next moment his foot connected with Wiglet's jaw. He whirled, and Bartlebee's head snapped back. He whirled once more, and kicked the third man in the jaw.

He turned to his mother. "I do apologize, Your Grace," he said, his voice as tranquil as ever. "I was reluctant to use my fists given their lack of cleanliness. I hope my delayed arrival didn't cause you any undue alarm."

All three men were on the ground. Wiglet and the other were struggling into a sitting position, but Bartlebee just lay sprawled on the marble, mouth open and eyes closed. Unconscious, he didn't look nearly as menacing. His jaw was narrow and his teeth jutted up like white turnips overgrowing their planting.

"Dear me," Simeon said. "I do believe that Mr. Bartlebee may have suffered neck damage. It's always a possibility with Eastern arts of defense." He prodded Bartlebee with his foot and the man groaned but didn't move. "He seems to be alive," Simeon said, turning to the two men climbing to their feet. "As I believe he himself said, it's so easy to kill people. I always have to remind myself not to strike too hard."

"You'll have to make a note of it," Isidore said, keeping laughter and triumph out of her voice with an effort. Then she readjusted her hold on the dowager, who was still sagging against her, and skewered Wiglet and his compatriot with her glare. "You're lucky the duke *didn't* lame you for life after the way you frightened his mother!"

"Bartlebee will be dazed for a time," Simeon told them. His tone was quiet, not at all triumphant. "I suggest you leave him here and finish the task you have at hand."

Wiglet hesitated.

"Need I repeat myself?" Simeon's voice was utterly

calm, but Wiglet quailed as if he'd leveled a weapon at them.

He swallowed and then opened his hand. A dusky ruby rolled onto the ground and bounced once, rolling to a rest next to Bartlebee's elbow.

"Are you second in command?" Simeon asked.

"Yeth," Wiglet said. His lip was already swollen to twice normal size.

"Right then, get on with it. You'll know in an hour or two whether your commander will ever walk again. I do hope that there'll be no further reason for me to feel concern about my safety, or the safety of my wife, my mother, or my possessions."

Wiglet backed away quickly. "Never, Yer Grace," he gobbled. "Not in the least. I mean, never." He and the other man stepped through the door into the water closet, presumably throwing themselves down the hole in their fervor to get away from Simeon.

The dowager pulled herself to a standing position. "My jewels!" she said. "On the floor with those filthy, ravening beasts. I shall never feel the same about them, never!"

Simeon bent down to pick up the stones.

"Get up!" she shrieked, her voice suddenly strong. "That's a job for a servant, as I shouldn't have to tell you!"

"Your Grace!" Isidore said, "Let's—"

Simeon dropped the ruby into the cracked box on the floor and straightened. "Would you prefer that we leave the rest for Honeydew to collect, Mother?"

"I would prefer never to have been born," his mother said on a gasping breath. "You—you have humiliated me one too many times. One too many times!"

Isidore's mouth fell open.

"Your father would have taken those ruffians out with

a blow to the jaw, like any respectable Englishman," the dowager said. But her voice cracked on a sob. "You—my son—with his feet—"

Isidore met Simeon's eyes over his mother's head.

"We'll go outside now, Your Grace," she said, lifting the remaining jewelry box from the dowager's arms. "Follow me, if you please."

They left Simeon there, the marble around his feet littered with tarnished jewels, in settings popular a half century ago. Isidore turned around once, but he was staring at the ground.

Chapter Twenty-nine

Gore House, Kensington
London seat of the Duke of Beaumont
March 3, 1784

The Duke of Villiers handed his cloak to Fowle, the Beaumonts' butler, pausing at the news that Jemma was out, but that the duke was in.

He and Elijah had to talk.

It had been years since they had spoken properly, although his valet Finchley babbled of how Elijah saved Villiers's life when he was in a fever. Since Villiers had no memory of that, he could hardly savor the reunion.

The truth was that Villiers was currently doing his best to seduce Elijah's wife, and yet apparently he owed him gratitude for the said life-saving.

What was all that between old friends?

"I'll announce myself," he told Fowle. As he entered the library, he saw Elijah's profile around the side of a high-backed chair. He seemed to have closed his eyes. Villiers loathed naps. But then Elijah spent his adult life saving the world, or at least the English parts of it, while he himself concentrated on frivolities like chess.

As always when he observed differences between his life and another man's, he paused to consider whether he would prefer to order his world on Elijah's model.

No. He had no wish to take up his seat in the House of Lords. In fact, he had a positive revulsion to the idea.

Villiers walked noiselessly across the wine-colored, flowered carpet. It was as glorious as one of his own coats. He rounded the chair.

Elijah was indeed asleep.

Or not asleep.

There was something odd about the immobility of his face, about the way his body was slumped in the corner of the chair.

"Duke," Villiers said sharply, bending over. Could Elijah have fainted? His face was rather white. "Elijah!"

His eyelashes were dark against his face. He had been beautiful even back when they were both clumsy puppies and Elijah was the only person in the world that Villiers loved. Villiers himself had had a big nose, and uncontrollable hair that wouldn't stay tied back properly, nor yet fit under a wig. Then Elijah had the white-blond curls of an angel, and the perfect profile of a young Gabriel.

Villiers reached out, touched Elijah's shoulder.

Shook Elijah.

Shook him again.

Chapter Thirty

Revels House
March 3, 1784

The last thing that the dowager said to Isidore before she left for her sister's estate was that she wanted every jewel cleaned before they were returned to her.

"He gave them to me *every time*," she said to Isidore. "I'm sure you know what I mean."

"No."

"Then you shall. After all, you have married a Cosway. I never liked those necklaces, but they remind me of my husband." She had the smaller box, the older one with silver hinges, beside her on the carriage seat. "These were my mother's. I don't mind if you keep some of the others; after all, you're married to the duke. But these I shall keep and give to my sister's children. You may inform my son so."

"The duke is bathing," Isidore said. "Could you please wait until he is able to bid you goodbye?"

"No. I shall stay at a neighbor's and be at my sister's estate by tomorrow at dusk. You can tell him where I've gone. He's no son of mine, I'm convinced of that."

Isidore frowned.

"Oh, don't be such a fool," the dowager said, in her cracked, breathy way. "He's my blood, God knows it to be so. And Godfrey as well. But Godfrey is off to Eton, and I'm tired of all this. I did my best!"

"Of course—"

"I was a good wife, a proper wife. I never questioned the women. The jewels were given to me from guilt, you know. At least he felt *that*." She looked at Isidore accusingly. "That was something."

"Yes."

"I don't want to be in this house full of memories, and letters I haven't answered, and the stupid, *stupid* things he did." Her voice was savage. "That stink—it's the stink of stupidity."

Isidore nodded.

"My sister, the Dowager Countess of Douglass, keeps an old-fashioned house, perhaps, but it's the sort that I'm comfortable with. This son of mine, with the way he looks and he acts . . . I can't do it anymore. I can't be here and pretend that I don't care when traditions are violated, and stupid, *stupid* men do just as they wish. He runs about the country naked."

"Not precisely," Isidore managed.

"They live to humiliate us. Over and over. My husband never trotted about in diapers. But when I think of it now,

he might as well have been naked. You may leave now."
She waved her hand.

Isidore backed out of the carriage.

"You'll find out," the dowager said. Her gaze was not
unkind. "Send my things after me once the maids are
able to enter that wretched house. I'll write Godfrey
with my consolations and instructions for his future
welfare. You'll have to cope with the duke's unkempt
ways and his foreignness. God knows I tried but he was
never mine. Not really mine."

Isidore curtsied, the deep, respectful curtsy that one
gives to a deposed queen.

The queen didn't notice.

Chapter Thirty-one

Gore House, Kensington
London Seat of the Duke of Beaumont
March 3, 1784

𝐼t was as if the world froze for a moment. He shook Elijah—and Elijah's head flopped forward, like a poppy on a broken stalk.

"No!" Without even thinking, Villiers shook Elijah again, hard. "Wake up!" Fear suddenly wrenched his gut.

Elijah woke up.

For a moment he stared straight ahead, as if into a country no one else could see. Then his eyes slipped to Villiers and he smiled. "Hello."

Villiers stumbled backwards, feeling for a chair, and fell into it. "Christ and damnation."

Elijah's smile faded.

"What was that?" Villiers said. "What just happened?"

And, when there was no answer: "*Elijah!*"

They hadn't used first names with each other since they were both fifteen, sixteen . . . whenever that was that they quarreled over a lass and never spoke again.

"I collapsed," Elijah said bluntly. "I must have fainted. It's my heart. I'm thirty-four."

"Thirty-four?" Villiers shook his head. "Thirty-four? What's that, a terminal date for hearts?"

"My father died at thirty-four," Elijah said, putting his head back on the chair and looking up at the ceiling. "His heart failed him. I had hopes of surpassing his span, but I have, increasingly, these small episodes. I see no reason to fool myself."

"Oh, God."

"Not quite yet," he said, that beautiful half-smile of his quirking the corner of his mouth. He shook his head. "There's nothing more to say about it all, Leo."

Villiers hated being called Leopold. He hated being anything other than Villiers, and he never was, to anyone other than Elijah. The very sound of the name made him feel unbalanced, as if nearly twenty years had vanished.

"I don't accept that," he said. The words felt harsh in his throat. "Have you seen a doctor?"

Elijah shrugged. "There's no need."

"You blacked out."

He nodded.

"Damn it!"

"Yes."

"I've been trying to seduce your wife and you never said a word."

Elijah smiled at that. "What difference would it make?"

"All the world," Villiers said. His voice grated in his

own ears so he got up and walked to the side of the room and stared unseeingly out the window.

"I don't see why it should. You and I have always had disagreements over women."

"The barmaid," Villiers said, making a vain attempt to get hold of himself and yet keep the conversation going.

"You chided me with it when you were in the grip of fever. You told me that I had the barmaid, the dog, and Jemma. I couldn't make you understand that the dog was long dead. But I could certainly understand why you'd like to take Jemma."

Villiers turned around. Elijah was still seated, looking at him with that patient, courteous curiosity that was a hallmark of his dealings in Parliament. "Damn it, aren't you angry?" he demanded.

"Because you allowed my old dog to die while you saved my life?" Elijah raised an eyebrow. "I was angry when I was sixteen and foolish. I'm sorry I retaliated by stealing your barmaid away."

"Not that. Aren't you angry about your heart failing?"

Elijah fell silent.

Finally Villiers said, "I am sorry that your dog died."

"She was all I had, and all that really mattered to me."

Villiers moved sharply, then forced himself to be still.

"Except for you, of course." Elijah raised his eyes. "You were my dearest friend, and I stole your mistress and pushed you away because you were ungracious enough to save my life in a river, and not manage to save that of my dog as well."

"We were both fools," Villiers muttered.

"There were few things that I treasured in life, and I threw away one. Then I sated myself with government and flurries of power, and I threw away my wife. It seems a remarkable waste of years; I certainly agree in your judgment of my foolishness."

"I won't go near Jemma again. It wasn't for revenge; truly, it wasn't. It was just that—"

"She's Jemma," Elijah said simply.

"Yes. Does she know that you're ill?"

"No! And she mustn't."

"That's not fair."

"There's no fairness in life," Elijah said, his voice heavy. "I'll be gone whether she has time to grieve and fear for it, or not. I want the time I have left with her without grief."

"Of course." Villiers cursed himself for ever trying to entice Jemma.

"I'm winning, you know." Elijah's smile was a beautiful thing. It had helped him triumph during many a difficult battle in Parliament, that smile. It had won the heart of a prickly, ugly young duke by the name of Villiers, back when they were both nine years old. "She's planning to concede the remaining game in your match when she sees you next."

"You are winning," Villiers said. "You are."

"I've been very slow, very tactical," Elijah said. "I wasted so much time in my life. I've planned this like a campaign, the most important campaign of my life. And you played a part, Leo."

"I—"

"I needed formidable opposition," he said. "You provided it."

Villiers sat down opposite Elijah again. "You must tell her. How often do you have these spells?"

"Oh, once a week or so. More frequently of late."

"Do you have any idea how much time you have?"

Elijah shook his head. "I don't want to know."

"I'll leave," Villiers said. "You'll have an open field. God, I . . ."

"Don't leave. I wish you would play chess with me. Now and then."

"I would be honored."

There was a silence during which, had they not been English noblemen, the men might have embraced. Might even have cried. Might have said something of love, of friendship, of sadness. But being English noblemen, they didn't need to say those things: their eyes met and it was all there. Their boyhood friendship, their childish rages, the blows they dealt each other.

"I won't go anywhere near her," Villiers said. It sounded like a vow.

"You must."

"No—"

Elijah smiled at him, but his eyes were shadowed. "You have to be there for her, Leo. I need to think you will."

"You want me to continue to woo her so that . . ."

Sometimes even an English gentleman feels sorrow catch him like a wicked pain in the back of the throat. At times like that, he might walk to the window and look out at a garden in the first stages of spring.

Until he was sure he wouldn't be unmanly.

But then, being English, he would eventually turn around and find his oldest friend sitting in the same place, waiting. And he would pull over a chess table and start laying out the pieces.

Chapter Thirty-two

The Dower House
March 3, 1784

As the dowager's carriage drove away, Isidore walked back to the Dower House with one thought in her mind. She was a fool. Simeon may not love her, but he was the man she had. And she could not allow him to be in this fetid, empty house by himself. He could learn to love her. She thought of the way he whirled and struck, and knew the feeling in her heart for what it was. She was halfway to being hopelessly in love with him, for all the same reasons that drove his mother to despise him: for his strength, for his uniqueness, for the Simeon-ness of him.

Simeon rose from the desk when she entered. "You

entered Revels House without my permission," he stated, by way of greeting. "I asked you to wait for me because I knew those men posed a danger."

"I thought you were accompanying me in order to add your voice to my entreaty."

"And you thought that my participation would be a disadvantage," he said. His jaw was set, his shoulders rigid.

"Yes."

"I commanded you."

"I don't recognize commands," she stated, making sure that he knew exactly what she was saying.

"I didn't want to frighten you by mentioning the Dead Watch."

"I don't frighten easily." But she didn't feel like squabbling, so she said, "Simeon, I just want to say that you were *magnificent*!"

"That is very kind of you."

"I think your mother was flustered by the shock, the horror of all that had happened," Isidore said, galloping on without any encouragement from his expression.

"She was horrified by my exhibition of foreign skills," he said. But his voice was dry, and not wounded.

"I thought the way you whirled and struck was amazing."

He met her eyes, and she could read them, if no one else could. "She'll never like me."

"That is her weakness and her loss," Isidore said firmly. "As Honeydew may have informed you, she left to stay with her sister. I think she will be much happier for a visit."

"Honeydew does not believe she is ever coming back. She asked for all her things, including the furniture in her bedchamber."

"Then we will be happy to send it along," Isidore said. "That will save it a trip to London, though it may fall apart on the journey, of course."

"If you entered my aunt's house, you might think you'd stepped back two hundred years."

"In that case your mother's furniture will feel right at home." Isidore drifted closer. Yes, she deserved love and courtship. But sometimes a woman had to take what she could get, especially if it came in a muscled, beautiful, and entirely desirable package.

"Doubtless."

Isidore took a deep breath, remembering Jemma's various lessons regarding men. Then she reached down and pulled off one of her slippers. Simeon watched as she dropped it on the floor. She pulled off another and placed it precisely next to the first.

"Isidore?" he asked. Naturally, his voice held the kind of mild curiosity with which one might inquire if the vicar was staying for supper.

She didn't answer. She pulled up her skirts and snagged one stocking from its garter. It flowed to the ground and pooled at her ankle. She put out a toe and the stocking rolled off of its own accord. She thought that Simeon's eyes looked less calm, so she made an event of the second stocking.

"Isidore," Simeon repeated. "What are you doing?"

"Undressing myself."

"Honeydew will likely enter at any moment."

Isidore pulled up her skirts and undid the little ties that held her panniers around her waist. They collapsed silently to the floor and she stepped out of them. "You had better send him away," she said. "I wouldn't want you to be embarrassed by your wife."

"You don't want to be my wife," he said, but his voice had a husky undertone.

"No, I don't," she said agreeably. She was wrestling with her petticoat now. "I deserve better than you."

"You do."

"I deserve to be courted." Her petticoat fell and she kicked her way out of it. "With flowers, jewels, and poetry written specially for the occasion. I deserve to be adored. Someone should be kneeling at my feet." She looked pointedly at Simeon, but he showed no signs of abasing himself, so she began unlacing her bodice.

"I deserve," she finished, "to be loved."

"Yes," he said. Still he didn't move.

Inside, Isidore felt as if a drop of ice water was running down her back. He wasn't panting at her feet the way Jemma had promised. Perhaps he thought her thighs were too plump, but men liked plump thighs, didn't they?

He just stood there, saying nothing although she had finished unlacing her bodice. She could back silently into the bedroom, pretending that none of this had happened, or she could drop her gown. She looked at Simeon again. He could have been carved out of wood.

Like a flash flood, Isidore felt a wave of red coming over her face. Her bodice was open all down the front, though of course her breasts didn't show due to her chemise. That was one saving grace.

A second later she had fled into the bedchamber and closed the door. She tripped on the threshold and fell to her knees with a hard thump. A sob was rising in her throat but she cut it off. She would pretend that nothing happened. Nothing. She just happened to partially undress before him, and if he heard even a whisper of a sob, then he would feel sorry for her and—

Though she hadn't heard the sound of footsteps, he spoke just outside the door. "Isidore?"

"No," she said, thankful that her voice didn't tremble.

She knelt on the hard wood, her hands shaking, holding her bodice together.

"No?"

She cleared her throat. "I'm not available at the moment."

"Why aren't you available?"

A flash of rage had her off her knees. "Why? What did you think I was available *for*?"

There was silence. He was a gentleman. It wasn't his fault that she had listened to Jemma and thought that all men were at the mercy of their loins. Obviously, she had the remarkable bad luck to be married to the one man who was in control of his body. Wonderful.

Though, of course, it was likely that men controlled their bodies best when they didn't feel true desire. A tear slipped over her clenched fists.

"Isidore, I'm coming in."

"I'd rather you didn't," she snapped. "This was all a misunderstanding, and may we *please* just forget it ever happened?"

"No."

She swallowed. "Just go away, please."

There was a muffled thump. But it wasn't the door. He was probably leaving. Isidore sat down on the bed, her back to the door. He could go to blazes, for all she cared. Any number of men in London would look faint when she took off a glove, never mind dropping a petticoat.

"Isidore, will you open the door?"

"For God's sake," she shouted back, losing her temper. "Will you leave me alone? Haven't you embarrassed me enough?"

"How much revenge do you intend to take?"

What a stupid question. "You are quite safe. Now if you would just please *leave*!"

"I can't. I took my clothes off."

"You—"

"I'm quite naked. And while it's not very chilly today, there is a good likelihood that Honeydew will enter at any moment."

Isidore's hands fell from her mouth. Being Simeon, he sounded entirely practical. "I think I hear voices on the garden path," he added.

"No, you don't," Isidore said, but her voice was weak. She was consumed by a blaze of curiosity. "You're really naked? *Naked*?"

"I've never stood naked in a sitting room before," he said.

"Well, enjoy it," she said weakly.

There was a moment's silence while she thought about the fact that Simeon was out there without clothes. He had taken his clothing off?

"Isidore," he said quietly, "Honeydew is walking toward the Dower House. I can see him through the window."

She threw the bedchamber door open, grabbed his arm, and jerked him forward.

There he was.

Afternoon sun was slanting onto the wide planks, stained dark with years. At first Isidore just saw his feet. They looked just as large and male as they had after his bath. He dropped the clothing he held on the floor.

Her own toes curled. Of course she should meet his eyes. She should look higher than his knees. But—

She was staring at his thighs when they suddenly moved in her direction. "I suggest," came a voice somewhere above her ear, a rather strained voice, she thought, "that we retire to your bed."

His voice had no semblance of control. It was rough

like velvet and his eyes were half closed, but not slumbering. It was as if the beast inside him had woken up. "I never meant to embarrass you," he said.

She smiled, a bit tightly.

"I don't think very quickly," he said. "No, listen to me, Isidore."

She raised her eyes. Truly, it was rather fascinating—

"When things happen quickly, as when you took off your clothes, I can't think what to say. It wasn't that I didn't—"

"It's all right," she said.

"I want you. Desperately."

"Oh." He was making her feel embarrassed now.

"I'm not good at talking." When he moved it was so sudden that she didn't even know what was happening until she felt the bedcover at her back, and he reared over her, gently pulling her bodice apart.

It occurred to her that she was supposed to squeal with fright but instead she arched her back so that he could pull off her sleeves. The muscles in his shoulder bunched as he gently untied her chemise and pulled it over her head.

"What should we do next?" she asked. He seemed to know. He lowered his long body on top of her, balanced on his elbows.

Isidore gulped. "Aren't you going to—"

But he was kissing her, deep boneless kisses, the kind that made her wind her arms around his neck, and pull his body down onto hers.

Her hands slid down his back and onto his bottom, curved over warm muscles, slipped between his legs. "You—" His voice was pained. He arched his back. "Oh God, Isidore, that feels so good."

She started laughing and his mouth came down on hers with desperation. And then he pressed against her.

It was extremely odd. Like a door opening, Isidore thought. First there was only herself, and then somehow there was room enough for him as well.

He made a rough sound, low in his throat and pressed deeper. Isidore waited for the pain that was supposed to come, but nothing happened.

Well, that was good.

He pulled back and then thrust forward again.

It felt good. It did. Well, perhaps it didn't feel that good. There was a little pulling feeling that she didn't care for all that much. Isidore tried to push away that disloyal thought. He was supposed to do whatever, and she could just do what she wished. And what she wished was to touch him.

Stroking his back felt like nothing she'd experienced before. It was all rippling muscle, ridges and curves that moved under her fingers as he—

He did that thrusting thing.

The truth was, she didn't really care for it all that much.

But he did. That was the wonderful thing about it— there wasn't an ounce of composure about Simeon now, nothing of the controlled man. His face was alive with pleasure. She ran her hands over his cheekbones and he thrust forward so hard that she actually gasped and raised her knees.

Which felt better, for some reason.

He made another sound in his throat, as if he were dying, and that made her smile. "Isidore," he said. "Are you—are you—"

"Yes?" she said helpfully.

"I can't control myself much longer." His voice sound dark and anguished.

No wonder women love bedroom activities. "That's just as it ought to be," she cooed. Every time she moved, he gasped, so she arched her back again. It felt better that way for her as well. If she moved, he lost control. Which was exactly what she wanted, Isidore thought. He pulled back and gripped her hips so hard that it was going to leave bruises, pulled her up and toward him. He was definitely out of control.

Simeon's head was roaring, his body rejoicing in a rhythm that he felt as if he'd known for years. It was like a glorious race. It was pure physical joy. Isidore's body was soft, warm, wet—

He couldn't wait much longer. And yet it was like seeing the finish line and not wanting to reach it. He didn't want to come.

He didn't want—

Pleasure was roaring in his legs, and Isidore was meeting him now, raising her hips in a way that made him want to bite her on the collarbone, act like a rampaging beast.

His vision was almost black by the time he let himself go, wild and fierce. He thrust forward, dimly hearing the bed frame pound the cottage wall, dimly sensing Isidore's little laugh, dimly—

He was outside himself. The smell of Isidore and her curvy little body, her laugh, the sound of her voice, the way she touched him without fear and without shame, took him to another place.

He threw his head back and roared like a man who was never quiet, like a lion claiming his mate.

Chapter Thirty-three

The Dower House
March 3, 1784

Simeon came back into his body very slowly. Valamk-sepa used to talk about a noncorporeal experience that fasting monks experienced. Simeon never thought it sounded like an appealing prospect, but he might have to rethink that naïve supposition.

He was covered with sweat, panting as if he'd had a long run, and happier than he'd been in years. Isidore had her eyes closed, so he drank her in: the slightly exotic tilt of her eyes, her little nose, her creamy skin. She was exquisite. She was his. She was impulsive and infuriating and all too emotional, but she was his fate.

There are exquisite aspects to surrendering to one's fate.

"Did it hurt, Isidore?" he asked, suddenly remembering that she too had been a virgin, and rolling off her body.

She opened her eyes. "No, not at all. Did it hurt for you?"

"No, but no one says that it ought to."

"It was not terribly uncomfortable," she said, coming up on her elbows and peering down her body.

He followed her eyes. She had the most curvy, creamy body that he could have imagined.

"No blood," she said relievedly, flopping back down again. "A few bruises on my hips. So what did you think?"

Simeon had never been very good at explaining things. How could he explain a rush of pleasure so acute that it felt as if his skin were alive, as if he knew her body as well as his own, as if he was seeing the world in color after being blind?

"I liked it," Isidore continued.

That was good. Simeon lay back because if he didn't stop looking at her, he would leap on top of her again. His rod stirred at the thought.

"It's not something I would want to do every day," she continued, "but from what I hear, people don't do it all that often anyway."

Simeon turned his head.

She was looking at him, rather shyly. "Do you mind that we consummated our marriage, Simeon?"

It didn't sound as if Isidore had fallen out of herself while making love to him. In fact, now he thought about it . . .

Not that he knew much about women's bodies. He'd always avoided salacious campfire talk. She didn't experience great pleasure.

That was entirely unacceptable.

Likely she wouldn't wish to try making love again for a time. That too was unacceptable. He made a plan and implemented it, all in one second.

"We weren't very good," he said, propping himself up on an elbow, ignoring her question.

She blinked. "We weren't?"

"No."

"I thought—"

"We need to work on it. You shouldn't like to be a failure, would you?"

She didn't respond as impulsively as he hoped. "I don't think I was a failure," she said. "Nor you either. What were you expecting?"

"More," he said, though he wasn't actually sure there could be anything *more* than what he'd experienced. "It's because we're beginners," he added hastily.

"I suppose that could be true," Isidore said. "What do you think we did wrong? How did it feel for you?"

"Short," he said, realizing that was true. "Surely it should take longer than a few minutes."

"I don't know," Isidore said. "You're—you're—" She waved her hand.

"One of the things that's odd is that we were so intimate," Simeon said, realizing he really meant it. "We joined our bodies together, and yet I don't truly understand your body."

"How could you understand it?"

"Well," he said, reaching out delicately, "how does it feel to have breasts?"

She started laughing, a delicious low gust of laughter. "How does it *feel*? Simeon, do you think that you're a normal man?"

"It seems like a logical question to me. I don't have

anything of that nature standing out from my chest. Are you aware of them all the time? Do you know they're there?"

"Do you know that your knees are there all the time?"

"Only when I use them. But those don't have any use. That is—"

"Of course they have use," she said, sitting up. "I just don't have a baby to use them yet."

"Will you nurse your own children?"

"My mother nursed me," Isidore said. "Italian gentlewomen nurse their own children. My mother believed that babies are less likely to survive if they're given to a wet nurse."

Simeon didn't want to talk about babies. "I just thought," he said slowly, "that women's breasts felt good. For example . . ." He reached out his hand, realizing with a certain remote part of his brain that his fingers were trembling, and cupped the sweet heaviness of her breast. "What does that feel like?"

"Fine," she said. "My goodness, it's strange to think that you can just touch me like that. No one touches me."

"But I'm your husband now. In truth and in law." He let his thumb wander in a little caress.

"I suppose."

"And how does this feel?" He rubbed his thumb over her nipple.

"Oh—"

He did it again. "Isidore?"

She opened her mouth but no words emerged. "I have heard that women find this quite pleasant as well," Simeon said, feeling more cheerful. He bent his head and put his lips to her breast.

She cleared her throat. "Simeon, you're not a child and—"

His lips closed around her nipple. Children had nothing to do with the way desire coursed through his legs, through his heart.

Her hand fell from his shoulder onto the bed, bone-less. He started suckling her, and her head fell back. Harder, and a muffled little sound hung in the air. His body was rigid, throbbing. But he was in control.

He pulled back. "See?" he said, talking around the tightness in his throat, the groan that wanted to come out. "We're not there."

She opened her eyes. They were a little dazed, sweet, unfocused.

"Where?" There was a tremor in her voice.

Simeon forced himself to roll away, sit up casually. "We don't know anything about each other's bodies," he said over his shoulder. If he looked at her any longer, he'd leap on top of her. "We'll have to practice."

"Practice?" Isidore's voice was husky and a little irri-tated. He loved it.

"Tonight, perhaps." He pulled on his shirt, still not looking. "If we feel like it."

There was a sudden motion and she was sitting up. But the next thing she said was a mile from the husky nymph he was imagining.

"Simeon!" A shrew would be proud of that squeal. "What did you *do*?"

He swung around. "What?"

She was staring down at her legs. "You—you peed on me!" She swallowed. "*In* me!"

"Any blood?" He bent over and peered interestedly.

"That's not blood." She hastily wiped off her leg, and jumped off the bed. A second later she had her chemise over her head. He'd ripped it, so it fell open in the front, but she didn't seem to notice.

"It's not pee. Didn't anyone tell you about bedding?"

"My aunt forgot to mention this charming detail."

"It's just a little fluid, carrying my part of a baby."

She looked down at her legs, now decently covered.

"I'll show you tonight," he said, pulling on his trousers.

"Show me what?" she asked suspiciously.

"How my body works."

In the back of his mind, he was thinking about the way she touched his body. Even now her eyes seemed to be drawn to his body, so he slowed his fingers, pulled his trousers up the curve of his arse slower than he needed to.

"I can demonstrate without making love," he said casually, meeting her eyes when she finally looked up again. "Since you didn't find it entirely pleasurable."

"Neither did you," she said defensively.

"We'll improve."

"Of course," she said. "Good."

"Tonight," he said, throwing his coat over his shoulder.

Chapter Thirty-four

The Dower House
March 3, 1784

Tonight? What did he mean by that? Isidore wasn't at all sure that she wanted to repeat bedding so soon. She felt slightly tender. And she felt odd. Disappointed, which was stupid. Besides, Godfrey was returning from his stay at the vicar's, which meant that there couldn't be any marital intimacy. Godfrey would be sleeping in the sitting room of Dower House. She didn't want anyone in Revels House until the Dead Watch were safely back in London.

She wandered out for a walk. It was the kind of day that pretends spring has come, even though it hasn't. The air smelled sweet, and the sun was shining. A blackthorn tree in the garden had already bloomed and was scattering seeds everywhere, like a child feeding birds in a dizzying circle.

Simeon would be a quite good husband. He was thoughtful and caring. His rueful little smile made her feel meltingly affectionate. He was so lovable when he wasn't in control, when he admitted that he wasn't sure what to do next. This afternoon was a perfect example. And he had admitted himself that the whole matrimonial experience wasn't quite all it could be. In fact, he was devastatingly attractive when he—

She stopped. It would be easy to love a man who admitted his faults, who threw off his clothes when he realized that he'd embarrassed her. When Simeon was spontaneous, he was irresistible.

Yet when she was spontaneous, it drove him to distraction. He shouted—and then he kissed. In short, he lost control.

"Godfrey will be staying in the Dower House, of course," she told Honeydew on her return. "I am convinced the air is unclean in the main house and he is a growing boy. Besides, we emptied his room of furniture," she added. "He can sleep in the sitting room."

Honeydew didn't react by so much as a twitch to the news that, apparently, the duke would be sleeping with his wife. Likely Simeon's eyes would narrow a bit when he heard how she was rearranging his life, but the Middle Way would stop him from making too much of an outcry.

Pah! That's what her father would have said. Take the left way, or the right way. The upper way, the lower way . . .

She couldn't help grinning, thinking of his body. The lower way was likely something that no proper English gentleman would take. Yet even thinking about his body made her legs prickle and her breath feel short.

When he arched over her, his eyes grew smoky and dark. They looked almost anguished.

She started wondering again what he meant by showing her how his body worked. Worked? She knew how it worked. That part grew stiff.

His body was long and lean, like a man who could run twenty miles to save his beloved. Like a man who fought off ruffians without even dirtying his hands.

Yes, she would quite like to know how his body worked. The thought made her smile.

It was precisely the smile that irritated Simeon during supper. Isidore kept looking at him in a certain way, and before he could stop it, his blood would flare through his body and he would start shaking. Just a little, but still— shaking.

Shaking!

The thought of the Middle Way came into his head and he actually pushed it away. It seemed irrelevant when he was with Isidore, with that bubbling joy in her eyes and the way her hair curled so sweetly, and the impudent little way she would glance at him . . .

He liked to think that every time she smiled *that* way, she was thinking about him. Intimately.

It wasn't right to contemplate control. Not when Isidore was thinking about something else.

Besides, it was taking all his control to keep a calm conversation going through dinner. Isidore wasn't wearing anything like the provocative gown that she wore the last time the three of them dined together. And he himself had put on breeches rather than his inappropriate trousers. The stockings didn't seem to bother him so much this time, probably a sign that he was turning into a proper Englishman. But no proper Englishman would be ravished by lust, the way he was.

The only thing he wanted was Isidore, warm and sweet under him.

Honeydew poured lemonade for Godfrey. No wine, even though he threw Simeon an imploring glance.

Simeon found himself grinding his teeth.

Couldn't Godfrey have been housed in the barn? Did Isidore have to be so kind to his little brother? He had—

He had plans for this evening.

He shifted in his seat. Surely this was just what Valamksepa talked about. Lust as a poison in the blood, a wild, insurgent storm carrying reason before it. He had no reason. He just wanted her.

It wasn't the Middle Way. God knows what kind of way it was. A bad way. He drank his wine and brooded about her breasts. The whole Middle Way concept ignored the fact that a man's blood went on fire around his wife.

And Isidore was his wife.

Surely . . .

No.

At the end of supper he rose, ready to go somewhere. He seemed to have no bed, so he would presumably be housed in the barn with Honeydew.

But then it became clear that Isidore had different ideas. The meal was over, and before he knew exactly what was happening, she was in front of him, like a little whirlwind of silk and the sweet smell of her skin, saying this, saying that. She put everyone in their place, ordered Honeydew around in the sweetest of ways, directed Godfrey into his bed and he, it seemed, was to accompany her on a stroll through the gardens.

"It's a lovely night," she said, smiling up at him. "The moon is out."

She had long eyelashes that curled upward so delicately that they distracted him. "Hmmm," he said, unable to formulate even a simple sentence.

A moment later they were strolling down a path. It was actually quite warm in an early spring sort of way.

"Where shall we go?" Isidore asked. Her voice was bubbling, like a child at a party.

"For a walk?" he suggested. His mind felt like marmalade. All he wanted to do was drag her behind a tree and cup his hands around her bottom. How could he have made love to her and not spent an hour on each breast? It felt as if those lost moments were mocking him now.

Something in her expression dimmed a little and he wrenched his mind away from her bodice. Cleared his throat. "Shall we visit the summer house?" he asked, desperately.

"A summer house! You have one?"

He would do anything for that smile. The certainty of his vulnerability was so dangerous that he just walked beside her, silent as the grave. They walked toward the bottom of the formal gardens. "It's more of a folly than a true summer house," he said finally.

They rounded a last turn.

"As you see."

Her mouth fell open.

"It wasn't meant to be a ruin," he told her, deciding honesty was the best policy. "Although I understand that ruins are becoming quite fashionable." He cocked his head and tried to see it through her eyes. A romantic heap of stone, supposedly a disintegrating medieval castle? Or what he saw: another of his father's imprudent failures, a building that was to be a proper summer house of stone, fallen to pieces after the builders were left unpaid?

Isidore walked ahead of him. She wasn't wearing

panniers tonight, and her gown followed the curves of her own delectable hips.

"Have you been inside?" she said, turning and looking at him. He could barely focus on what she was saying over the roaring in his blood. She was his, and he had to have her, to own her, to touch her, to kiss her, to . . .

She leaned back against the fragment of a stone wall and smiled at him. Was that an invitation? Who gave a damn?

With a muttered curse, he strode forward and picked her up, as smoothly as if he carried damsels on a regular basis. "The grass might be wet," he said, hearing the roughness of his own voice.

She didn't say anything, but she wasn't struggling to get away. She just nestled there in his arms, a curvy perfumed bundle. He rounded the building and headed straight for the broken arch. Where the courtyard was supposed to be . . .

Yes. Tiles gleamed faintly in the moonlight. Fallen walls protected them from view . . . not that anyone was out wandering his gardens at this hour of night.

He put her down and stripped off his coat. He still couldn't meet her eyes. She would be horrified if she knew what he was like, how mad in lust he was, mad enough to howl at the moon, to pounce on her like an animal.

"Simeon?" she asked. Her voice didn't sound frightened. It was husky and caught a little on his name. There was something about it that made his groin clench. And then she combed her fingers through her hair, almost shyly, and he broke, lunged at her and yanked her against him. If he'd thought, he might have considered a gentleman's kiss, a sweet meeting of mouths that would tempt her into opening her lips . . .

He ravaged her, took what he wanted, took her sweetness and the taste of her, the smell of her, the way her body swayed under his fingers when he kissed her, the way she murmured something, or perhaps moaned.

But in the back of his mind a voice was shouting for attention. He couldn't just—he couldn't just do what—

She was moaning, she was, just a little sound in the back of her throat but it was enough to make him mad. Surely he could just put her down—

Gently, of course.

On the ground? Cold and damp?

His bad angel spoke up again, telling him that his coat was as good as a blanket. For a moment he managed to look down at Isidore with a modicum of logic.

Her eyes were dazed and she had her hand wrapped in his hair. She looked like a woman in the grip of desire. She would . . .

No.

His good angel screamed so loud that even his most diabolic self shuddered. "I promised," he said, and had to stop for a moment. She licked his lip, and it sent a stab of desire to his loins that could only be responded to in like manner. He had his hands around her again, lifting her slightly so that she fit snugly against him.

No.

"I'm going to show you how my body works," he said, pushing her away.

Isidore's mouth was slightly puffy, bruised. Her eyes were like shadowed wells. "Tomorrow," she said, drifting toward him. "For now, let's just kiss."

He had to take charge. He had to be in control. He stepped back and ripped his shirt over his head.

There was an audible gasp and then a giggle. He risked looking at her.

"Simeon! You're taking your clothing off—"

He leaned over and pulled off a boot, and the other boot. The stones felt cold under his stocking feet.

"I can hardly see you!" she protested. "The moon isn't that bright and—" Her eyes were large and shining. She could see him well enough. He could see every shadow and curve on her, every inch of skin he wanted to kiss and lick . . .

He pulled down his breeches, paused for a moment and pulled off his stockings as well. If you're going to be naked in the garden, you might as well *be* naked.

Then, finally, he met her eyes.

Her hair was tumbling around her shoulders, falling around her face in a way that made her look shy and retiring, like the girl he thought he wanted. Back when he didn't know anything. Isidore might look shy, but it was a trick of the moonlight; her eyes were ranging all over his body, pausing here and there, sticking at his midsection until he almost started to grin, but he stopped. Waited.

She needed to *know* him in order to want him, he had decided.

"You have so many muscles," she said finally. "Why?"

"Because I run."

She came closer until she was a fraction of an inch from his skin. It was incredibly erotic, standing there naked before her in the moonlight. She reached out a finger and touched his chest. Her touch burned and he had to clench his fists to stop himself from reaching out to her. She rocked back on her heels and he felt her touch leave him.

"So how *does* your body work?" she whispered. But she wasn't looking in the right place any longer.

His erection was standing out from his body, straining in her direction. He wrapped his fingers around himself. Her eyes flickered, darkened he thought, though it was hard to tell in the moonlight. "This is designed for your body," he said. "Man and woman are designed to fit together." He let his hand fall away.

Of course she was no timid miss. She wrapped her fingers around him and his head fell back. He caught a groan back at the last moment. "I'm glad it's not hairy," she said thoughtfully. "You don't have very much chest hair, do you, Simeon?"

She loosed her grip and then just as he was about to answer, swept her fingers down the length of him. The words died and he couldn't stop the muffled sound in his throat. She liked that; he saw a gleam in her eyes.

And that was what he wanted, wasn't it? Wasn't it? Because she was experimenting now, holding him close, sliding—

"No," he managed.

"Yes," she said, tightening her hand, sliding . . . And her other hand, it was—

Fire raced up his thighs. He put his hands on her wrists and pulled them from his body, holding them for a moment before he let them drop.

"No."

She pouted and her lips were so plumply alluring that he forgot his plan and pulled her into his arms. She gasped and then fit herself to him perfectly, like parts of a piano coming together to make music. Like a violin reunited with its bow.

"You're mine," he said. His voice was guttural and not calm. Not soothing. Not in control. He didn't even care. She put her lips against his chest and gave him a little kiss, and another. The touch of her lips burned. He couldn't remember what the next phase of the plan was. But that part of his brain was still beating out the same reproach: gentlemen don't make love to their ladies out-of-doors. It's not proper. It's not *right*. It's not calm and collected.

It's—

"I'll show you," he said, his voice catching because her hair against his cheek was as soft as spun silk and he just wanted to eat her. To lick her. It could rain on them and he would lick every drop from her body and keep her warm.

But the gentleman in him was shouting *No*. Still.

"Show me what?" Her whisper was languid, sweet. "Simeon?"

"Yes."

"Don't you want to help with my lacings?"

Madness fought with the plan, fought with civility, fought—and lost. "No."

That was definitely disappointment in her eyes.

"When I—" What word was he supposed to use? Not cock and not pizzle. "This is is my prick." The word fell harshly from his lips.

She surprised him; she'd probably always surprise him. She laughed. "*The bawdy prick of noon!*"

"Shakespeare was very fond of punning and pricks."

"I like that word," she said, reaching out. It was unfortunate that his brain stopped working the moment her cool fingers began running over him, touching him, tightening.

He tried. "When I—" The words were lost in a groan.

"*Your naked weapon is out,*" she said, gurgling with laughter. But he couldn't join her in a game of Shakespearean quotes, not when his body was on fire. He jerked in her hand and she laughed again, the triumphant sound of a woman who's discovered a power she didn't understand she had.

"When I come—" he said, pulling himself together.

"When you what?"

"Come. Oh God, Isidore, if you keep doing that I *am* going to come." He leaned into the pillar at his back. The marble was chilly and gave him some sanity.

"Do," she breathed, swaying closer to him. Her hand was trapped between the silk of her skirts and the rough hair of his belly. But he didn't want to frighten her, to have her disgusted.

He pushed her back. "Just watch, this time."

Her eyes were huge, excited. He managed to pull his thoughts back from his groin. "In order for us to be successful between the sheets, we have to understand what makes the other person feel pleasure."

She opened her lips but said nothing. Still, there was something in her eyes that made him keep going. "Tomorrow, I'll ask you to show me."

"Show you what?"

"What you find pleasurable," he confirmed. "My body isn't nearly as interesting as yours, but there are points that—" He put a thumb over his own nipple. "This isn't as beautiful nor useful, but it feels pleasure."

Her mouth curled in a little smile that affected him much more than his own touch on his body. He moved his hand down, deliberately, slowly, wrapped his fingers around his length. Slid his hand. Took his pleasure from the way she shifted back and forth, as if she was feeling heat between her legs, as if she were remembering the afternoon.

"It looks larger than it did earlier," she whispered.

His body moved instinctively toward her, passionate to establish a rhythm that would satisfy and daze her, drive her to the pleasure he had felt.

"So when you lose control, what happens?"

The question hung on the air. He cleared his throat. "I eject fluid that contains my contribution to a future child." And: "I wouldn't describe it as losing control." He let his hand fall away from his body.

She put her hand on him, and he instantly shuddered. The fire touched his spine, raced down his legs like a premonition of the future. "If I keep doing this—" she demonstrated—"wouldn't you lose control?"

"No." But it was a gasp.

"Because you never lose control?"

"Because that's not—" he drew in a breath—"an accurate description."

Her fingers dandled him, stroked him, fired him. "Are you sure that I couldn't make you lose control?"

"You could give me the greatest pleasure," he said. "As I will give to you."

She smiled, lopsided, let her hand fall. "What else feels good?" He blinked. "Only those two parts of your body? That's it?"

"That's enough," he told her.

She was smiling again. "Can I show you now what pleasures me?"

"The night and this place are too dark and cold for a lady," he said, pulling his shirt over his head. His body was thrumming to a rhythm of its own, madness flaring in his blood.

"I thought our bed, perhaps . . ."

"But Godfrey is in the sitting room."

"We shall have to be quiet," she said, turning to walk out of the courtyard. The moonlight caught her hair, turned it to darkened spun silver, precious liquid light chiseling the curve of her cheek, the plumpness of her bottom lip, the wry wit in her eye.

He was just pulling on his boots when she paused.

"Of course," she said, "it's a good thing that all of this doesn't mean losing control, Simeon, don't you think?"

"Yes."

"Because while I might be worried that *I* would make some sort of untoward noise and wake young Godfrey, I would never have to worry about you."

He followed her. Years in the desert had taught him a number of survival lessons.

One of them was never to ignore a gauntlet thrown at your very feet.

Chapter Thirty-five

The Dower House
March 3, 1784

*H*oneydew greeted them in the entryway to the Dower House, as if disheveled dukes were all in a day's work. "Your Graces," he said. "If you would be so kind as to keep your voices down, the young master is asleep."

Isidore took off her wet pelisse and handed it to him. "My goodness, Honeydew," she said, "you must take yourself to your bed. It's begun raining again."

"There appears to be some small chance of flooding," Honeydew said.

"Nonsense," Simeon said. "We're on a hill."

"The bridge leading to the village," Honeydew clarified. "I took the liberty of sending your lady's maid to temporary lodgings in the village; if the bridge went out, we'd have to house everyone in the barn and Miss Lucille would not be pleased."

"Are you staying in the village as well?" Simeon asked.

"I shall retire to the barn again tonight, Your Grace. We need to keep an eye on the silver."

"Good man," Simeon said briefly. "We won't keep you." He closed the door behind his butler, thinking that Honeydew was a man he'd always want at his back, whether on a camel or in an English countryhouse. He was loyal and honest, through and through.

Isidore had vanished. Simeon poked his head into the sitting room. The fire was burning low, so he threw on a couple more logs and walked over to look at his brother. Godfrey was lying flat on his back. In the blurry firelight he looked unnervingly like their father. He even snored like their father.

Simeon listened to the noise for a few seconds and then began to grin.

The little bedchamber wasn't directly off the great room; there was a small passageway, almost a hallway leading to it.

He paused for a moment, wondering if husbands knocked at their wives' bedchambers.

Isidore heard him outside the door and her heart leapt so high it felt as if it were in her throat. What on earth was he doing? He wouldn't go to the barn with Honeydew, would he?

Would he?

She looked down at herself, reclining on the bed. "Come in!" she called.

The door opened and she saw him in the doorway. She gave him a moment, looking down at herself, trying to see her body through his eyes. She was plump in the right places, she thought, and sleek in others. She'd lit candles, and the reflection of small flames darted over her skin, making her look like a marble statue, the naughty Roman kind. Her hair tumbled around her shoulders, and Isidore had arranged it so that one of her breasts showed and the other didn't.

"You may come in," she said, feeling a nervous giggle in the back of her throat.

He closed the door with great precision and then put his hands to his coat.

"No!"

He raised an eyebrow.

"It's your turn to learn about *my* body."

He walked over to the bed. "May I sit with you?"

"No!" He looked so large that he made her feel dizzy. He sat down in a chair and crossed his legs. The look on Simeon's face made him look younger than she'd ever seen him. There was devilment in those eyes. You couldn't look like that when you were buried in a smelly old house, surrounded by bills.

"I want you to pay very close attention to this lesson," she told him, propping herself up on one elbow.

He had to wrench his eyes away from her breasts, but he finally looked up. "I do. I mean, I am."

She couldn't help grinning. She sat up all the way. "These are my breasts." She actually never touched them very much. But his eyes made her bold. She let her hands curve around her breasts, sweet and firm, the way she would like to be touched. "This afternoon . . ." She shook her head.

His eyes were wide and clear. "Not right?"

"Your hands are very strong. I had bruises on my hips."

"I apologize." The look of desire disappeared from his eyes and he stopped looking at her breasts.

"That wasn't what I meant!" she said hastily. "I liked it, but . . . I would like this even more." She smiled at him and, just like that, all the desire came back into his eyes.

"I didn't hurt you, did I?"

"No!"

"Just tell me if I'm ever holding you too hard," he said. "I didn't know. I need to practice." Without even seeming to move, he was sitting at her side. But he didn't touch her, just watched her hands, still holding her breasts.

Isidore felt a flush and she dropped her hands to the bed. "So lovely," he murmured. He reached out with just one fingertip and ran it over the curve of her breast. "Beautiful." The finger trailed over pale pink, touched her nipple and she jumped.

She couldn't stop looking at his face. He was beautiful, not *for a man*, just beautiful. His eyes were fringed with thick lashes, still a little spiky from being in the rain. His cheeks were lean and he had the chin of a man who would always protect you, never leave you.

She murmured something that even she couldn't hear and leaned into him so that his hand, his large calloused hand, curled around her breast. His palm came hard against her nipple and made her shiver.

"Does that feel good?" he asked. His voice had changed. It was deeper. Not tired or strained, the way it sounded when he was talking to Honeydew about the drains, or his mother about anything at all.

She nodded. He did something else with his thumb and she flinched back.

"Too much?"

She pulled away. "It's stupid, but I feel . . ." She looked down. "They feel as if they're just too sensitive. It feels good, but then it hurts."

"But first it feels good?"

She smiled at him, loving the way his eyes were dark with desire, carefully thinking at the same time, watching her, learning. "So this is the time to learn about my body," she said almost chattily.

He nodded.

"I've never been with a man before you, but I've thought about it."

"Tell me what you thought about, sweetheart."

"I'd like to be kissed, not just here." She put a finger to her lips, waited until his eyes followed her finger. "But here." She touched her shoulder, her neck, the curve of her breast, the side of her waist, the inside of her thigh. "Everywhere," she whispered.

That was laughter in his eyes. It made her almost embarrassed—except that embarrassment made her feel obstinate.

"I'd like to be kissed *everywhere*," she repeated. Why not? It was beyond scandalous. But she was three-and-twenty, and she'd heard stories. The stories about what men did—sometimes, with some women.

She'd always thought that those stories sounded like heaven.

From the smile curling Simeon's lips, he didn't think it was a terrible proposition.

"Gently," she added.

"Did you enjoy this afternoon?"

Isidore blinked.

"The truth," he clarified.

"Not very much." He flinched. "But you knew that," she said, puzzled. "You didn't enjoy it either. Remember, you told me that—"

"What in particular didn't you like?" he asked. "We won't do it again."

She cleared her throat. "I think I'd prefer kisses to some touches. Your hands are very strong."

He smiled slowly. "Kisses. Anything else you'd like to show me?" His eyes moved over her slowly, like a caress, and Isidore suddenly felt naked. Which she was. His finger slid down the pale skin of her stomach and paused, pulling out a little ringlet of hair. "What about here?"

"A *very* delicate area," Isidore managed. She felt as if she were getting a fever. His leg, clothed in fine woolen breeches, brushed against the naked skin of her leg; it was unbearably erotic. She reached out and wound her hands into his hair.

"You don't like my hair unpowdered," Simeon said, as if he were promising something.

But it was thick and silky under her fingers, strong as he was. It didn't smell like violet powder, but like that indefinable smell of clean male. "I like it now," she whispered.

His mouth lowered to hers but hovered without touching her lips. That finger was still—

"What are you doing?" she whispered. The fever was spiking, focusing between her legs in an embarrassing way.

"Kissing," he said calmly, looking straight at her.

"That's not—"

"Think of it as pre-kissing."

Isidore couldn't even think, not with that finger touching her so sweetly. It was completely unlike the way he gripped her the previous night . . . She anchored her fingers in his hair and pulled his mouth to hers. "Kiss me!"

He kissed her deep and soft, and at the same time, his fingers just kept wandering, kissing in their own way, a kind of finger kisses that made her shiver and feel a singing heat down her legs. He pulled his mouth free and licked her lip; to her embarrassment, Isidore's head fell back and a hoarse little sound came from her throat.

"Does that feel good?" he whispered. He was kissing her jaw, and gave a little nip to her ear lobe, but frankly, Isidore wasn't paying much attention. It was what he was doing with his hand that was making her hips rise into the air and little moans fly from her mouth. Dimly she was aware that he was kissing all the parts that she had indicated. Unfortunately, she didn't care anymore.

She only realized that he'd stopped kissing when his hand stopped moving.

"Sweetheart?"

She frowned at him. Simeon didn't say that sort of endearment to her. Nor did he smile like that, a kind of wide, joyful smile like a child in a playground.

"You're gripping me very tightly," he said, sparks of mischief in his eyes. "I might have bruises on my arms." He moved his fingers again and she arched backward with a gasp.

She showed her teeth in a warning. "Simeon . . ."

"Enough pre-kisses," he muttered. Before she knew what was happening, there was a warm wet tongue where one finger had been, and still his hand was there, filling her, making her shake all over until she finally dug her fingers into his arms and threw back her head and screamed.

Thirty seconds later she remembered where she was. "Godfrey!"

Simeon cocked an ear. "Still snoring," he said cheerfully.

She fell backwards.

"No thanks to you," Simeon added.

"Oh . . . my," Isidore said. Her body was slowly coming back to earth. The pleasure felt as if it were still trembling in her toes, singing in her fingertips.

Simeon stood up and started taking off his clothes. He was as methodical as she would have expected. He neatly aligned his boots by the wall. He took off his neckcloth and hung it over a chair.

If Isidore hadn't been feeling a kind of outrageous, limp pleasure, she would almost have been annoyed. But then she kept looking at his front, and she couldn't get annoyed. He wanted her, yet there was a part of Simeon that resisted chaos so strongly that he couldn't rip off his clothes and fall on her like a ravening wolf.

That didn't mean he wasn't strung as tightly as a drum. His eyes were glowing with a combination of controlled power and pure lust. Her body stopped being quite so limp and a prickling awareness overtook her.

Naked now, Simeon bent over to place his carefully folded breeches on the old rocking chair. The line of his flank gleamed golden in the firelight.

So what if he were an example of control and methodical thinking? He was gorgeous, and he was hers.

She rolled over on her side and propped up her head with one hand, checking to make sure that her breasts were not flopping inelegantly. They looked quite delectable and round, thank goodness.

He stopped and put a log on the fire.

She bit back a smile. He was afraid. Making love didn't suit Simeon's wish to be in control. To be in charge. In fact, she would guess that the parts of it that she most enjoyed, he most disliked.

What she wanted was to see that look on his face again, the one which surrendered to the moment, to the pleasure, to *her*.

Simeon straightened from the fire, turned and started to sit down next to her, probably intending, gentleman-like, to ask her what she would prefer. Or something like that.

"My turn," Isidore said, putting her hand over his mouth before he could speak. She was getting feverish again. She pulled him and pushed him until he was lying flat on the bed. Of course, he was too much of a gentleman to resist, though she could see he didn't really like it. Simeon wanted to be in control. He felt too vulnerable, lying on his back.

She smiled at him, a sweet, dangerous smile. He was just where she wanted him. Then she reached out to touch him. He was hard, like a marble statue, but burning hot. Smooth and erotic. Made to stroke. He didn't move while she explored him, soothed him, coaxed him.

He didn't even make a sound until her hand closed around him again and she made an experimental move—

And then he uttered an odd strangled noise that made her head jerk back. But she knew, she knew that it wasn't pain, and her fingers curled even tighter.

Then she started all those pre-kisses he had perfected, using two hands instead of one. And she followed them directly with real kisses, dusting his golden skin with the press of her lips. When she reached his nipples, he surged up under her. She looked up to find his eyes wide, full of passion, with no thought of control or order. It was hard to smile and kiss at the same time, but the taste of his skin calmed her giddy pleasure, brought on another kind of wildness. She tasted him, bit him, sipping his skin and his smell. Of course he didn't scream, the way she did. But his breath came quickly, forcefully, especially the lower she went on his body.

And lower she went.

He tasted like soap, and felt soft and hard at once. He said "No, Isidore," seeming to wake up, so she put her lips around him.

He fell back then, surrendered, gave in. She played

with him, teased him, loved him, until he suddenly surged from beneath her and flipped her over.

"Isidore," he growled. There wasn't a bit of control in his eyes, or his hands, or the way he was holding her hard, at the hips. She arched toward him, loving it. He lowered his head to her breast and she started to whimper, almost to scream, except he was—

It felt different this time. She felt softer, welcoming, wetter. The largeness that had felt intrusive earlier felt delicious. She gasped and instinctively tightened around him.

"Don't ask me to stop," he said, and the catch in his voice filled her with joy.

"Don't stop," she cried. "Don't . . ."

He thrust forward, and again, again, again, until she started to give little screams every time. His eyes flared and he smothered her pants with the taste and the shape of his mouth. She thought he was going to stop, but he didn't, he kept going, and going. Every stroke made the fire burn higher until she was breathing as hard as he was, moving with his body as if they were one.

Finally she tore her mouth away from his and flew free, shuddering against him, crying out and as if Simeon had waited for her, he surged forward, desperate, violent, free . . .

Then they sank together back onto the bed. It was different, it was all different. They were two bodies, and yet one body.

He rolled them to their sides. She slid her arm around him, still trembling a little, and didn't say a word.

When a man like Simeon lost every vestige of restraint, it wasn't ladylike to show exuberance.

Chapter Thirty-six

The Dower House
March 4, 1784
The next evening

"You see, Princess Ayabdar is an extraordinary woman. She is the granddaughter both of the empress and of Ras Michael. And she married Powussen, the Governor of Begemder. I had the privilege of spending quite a good deal of time with her."

"Why did you do that?" Isidore asked suspiciously.

"Because I was appointed a royal magician."

"*What?*"

"I demonstrated that I could break through three shields with a mere tallow candle."

"How did you do that?

"I loaded my gun with powder and a farthing candle

and it went through three leather shields. And I had a magic weapon."

"Which was?"

"My virginity." He laughed at the look on her face.

"And here I thought you were saving it just for me."

"Virginity is a very useful thing. The fact that I was a virgin, attested to by my men, and more seriously, by a court magician who read it in my palm, meant that I was allowed to converse with the princess."

Isidore snorted. "How many other virgins did she have speaking to her?"

Simeon leaned over and nipped her lip. "I was the only one. There are few grown men who can claim the status."

"Who would know? I've never met anyone who announced it as freely as you do."

"I had my palm read on entering the Court, and the court magician shrieked it aloud for all to hear."

"Were you embarrassed?"

He shrugged a little.

Isidore nodded. "I would have been humiliated too, were I you. It was becoming embarrassing to be a virgin wife at twenty-three. You can't imagine how many men thought that was a tragedy."

"Yes, I can."

"I was starting to think that I'd never make love."

"There were days when I thought I couldn't bear it any longer," he confessed. "Instead of a lion, some poor woman would find me leaping out at her from behind a bush."

Isidore started giggling. "But it turned you into a magician. Did you think about bedding this princess?"

"You couldn't *not* think about it," he said, a little smile curling his lips. "She is so utterly brilliant: she can speak five or six languages, and quote Hindu poetry for hours."

Isidore decided she didn't like the princess. "Hindu? But she's Abyssinian."

"She has sent men to India to bring poetry back, which she translates, preserving it for the pleasure of her people and their culture."

"Admirable," Isidore said. She forced herself to relax. The princess was back there in the sand somewhere, living in a hut. She could afford to be generous.

"And her palace," Simeon said dreamily. "You can hardly imagine, Isidore. It's made entirely of pink marble, and it looks over the banks of a huge rain plain. Sometimes the plain fills with white flowers, thousands and thousands of them. If there's rain, the plain forms a great blue mirror to the sky."

"That sounds lovely," Isidore said, despite herself.

"I've never met a woman more intelligent. We argued for hours. She managed to change my mind about several ideas."

Clearly, to Simeon, changing his mind was practically an unheard-of experience. Isidore sighed and changed the subject. "I am curved in all the places where you are straight," she said, caressing the line of Simeon's hip. Their arms brushed for a moment as he reached out to touch her as well.

"I can't stop touching you," he said. "I can't stop thinking of you. The idea of returning to Revels House is inconceivable."

Isidore laughed and rolled on her back. "Now that the odor is gone I feel much more inclined to consider the possibility. But meanwhile . . ."

He accepted her invitation, of course.

It was an hour later. The sheets were rumpled, and Isidore was sweaty in places she'd never considered before, like the backs of her knees. If she lay absolutely still, she could feel tiny quivers in the sweetest parts of her body. She felt like the air did after her aunt put down her violin, as if it were still singing, but in silence.

"Do you suppose it's like this for everyone?" she asked.

"The poets sing of it," Simeon said lazily. He was lying on his back, one hand over his head, the other on her hip. "There's an ancient Sufi poet named Rumi . . . he spoke of desire as a sickness bringing joy."

"But this pleasure," Isidore said. "If it always feels this pleasurable, why don't people do it all the time?"

Simeon stretched. "I think we waited so long that we were like volcanoes waiting to explode. I know that sometimes bedding can be very, very unpleasant," Simeon said, turning over to face her. "We're lucky, you and I. Sometimes people just don't fit, as I understand it. There can be discomfort. Or one person might not find the other attractive." His sleepy smile said that wasn't a problem for him.

It wasn't a problem for Isidore either. Sometimes it felt as if her heart opened up when they made love. Love . . .

"But do you think it feels like this if the people aren't married?" she asked, unable to bring the word *love* to her lips. Did she love him?

He laughed at that and she wrinkled her nose at him. "You are asking whether a wedding certificate increases pleasure?"

"Stupid of me," she said.

Yet she felt somewhere deep inside her that he was missing the point. Though she wasn't sure what the point was.

"We do need to talk seriously, Isidore," he said.

"Hmmm?"

"We have to have a plan."

"A plan?"

"A plan for our marriage. Neither of us is precisely what the other envisioned as a spouse. We'll simply have to try to change. As much as we can. That way we won't find ourselves at odds. So if I hadn't been me, if you were able to pick any man in the *ton,* what kind of person would you like him to be?"

She giggled. "Red-haired?"

"Seriously."

"Must we be serious?" she moaned. "It's far into the middle of the night. I'm tired."

"We can sleep late in the morning. No one will dare wake us. It's important, Isidore."

She tried to pull herself together. "Seriously? What sort of man would I have chosen?"

"I suppose the more proper question is how would he have differed from me?"

She hesitated.

"Isidore," he said patiently. "I'm not a fool. I'm the man you've got and I just made you very happy. I'm not going to feel insulted if you wish I wore a cravat more frequently."

"Well, now that you mention it . . ."

"But not a wig," he said, alarmed. "I'm not sure I could tolerate a wig."

"How about a little powder for important occasions?"

"Such as going to Court?"

"More than going to Court. Balls in London. Places where your head would be the only unpowdered one in the crowd."

"Just not a wig. I cannot wear those little rolls of snails over my ears. But I can powder. What else, Isidore?"

"Could you look a bit more respectable?" She grinned at him. "You are *mine*, which means that not all the ladies get to enjoy the image of you naked."

"I like that," he said with a slow smile.

"I'd rather they didn't have quite such a chance to see your legs in those short trousers of yours."

He looked alarmed. "I can't stop running, Isidore. It's part of who I am."

"Perhaps in longer trousers?"

He nodded. "What else?"

"I can't really think of anything," Isidore said. The most delicious languor was stealing over her.

"I haven't told you my wishes for marriage yet."

Sleep was like a gorgeous warm blanket, hovering at the edge of her vision. "Um . . ." she said. "Whatever you want."

"That's it," he said.

"What?"

"You said what I want."

"I did?" Isidore struggled to wake up enough to remember what she just said.

"You said, whatever you want."

"Umph."

Simeon pulled himself to a seated position. "I had a great deal of time over the past years to analyze marriage. That's really why I thought we should probably annul our marriage, Isidore: we don't suit the pattern of successful spouses."

"We don't? Didn't you tell me this before?" she said sleepily.

"Would you describe yourself as docile and meek in every way?"

She snorted.

"Biddable and likely to listen calmly to good advice?"

"Yes to the second part, no to the first." But he was obviously going down the mental list he had been cherishing for years.

"Willing to allow your husband to command you on occasion?"

"Sometimes . . ." she said.

He eyed her.

"In bed?" she offered hopefully.

"What about if you're in danger?"

"Ah."

"I'm worried that unless we have a system of command set up, such as I had with my men, this marriage will founder or, worse, in a moment of crisis, I won't be able to save us."

"But Simeon, there aren't moments of crisis in England," she said painstakingly. "The things you likely envision—attacks by lions, sandstorms, marauding tribes—they simply do not happen here in England."

"The Dead Watch had a remarkable resemblance to a mangy pack of starving lions."

Isidore nodded. "If I encounter the Dead Watch again, or if there is an attack by a marauding lion, I promise that I will accept your commands."

He smiled. "We have to know where the ultimate authority lies."

Isidore didn't like the sound of that. "If it's not a moment of immediate physical danger, I would most biddably listen to the reasons behind the advice you're offering."

It was his turn to scowl. "I have to know that you're mine, Isidore."

"I am. According to English law, I am one of your possessions, just like a cow or a privy house."

"You see? You don't really accept it."

"Well, I can hardly change the entire system of government in England. I've always known that once you came home I would have a husband."

"It's important," he said earnestly. "I have to know you respect my opinions, that you'll obey me without a moment's thought. Otherwise our marriage will never work."

She shook her head. "What if you said, *pour that cup of coffee over my hand*—and it was burning hot?"

"Why would I want coffee poured over my hand?" He had a typically male, confused look on his face.

"It's just an illustration."

"Pour it," he said decisively. "If I say such a thing, it means I've lost my mind and returned to my second infancy. You'll have to teach me the way we teach children, by example."

She sighed. "What if you command me to do something that I consider truly foolish? What if there is an obviously better way to handle the given situation?"

"Why would I do that?' "

She resisted the temptation to say, *Because you're not God Almighty!* And said, "Let's just pretend that the situation arose."

"Sometimes I make mistakes," he said, surprising her. "There was a time when I bought a vast number of red and green flowered beads to trade. I thought they were far more beautiful than the small sky-blue ones that the merchant in Jidda told me to buy. I thought he was trying to trick me. Once we had hauled those beads far into the deserts of Abyssinia, they were rejected by everyone."

"Why on earth did you bring beads with you?"

"They were much easier than carrying food or water," he explained. "I always carried a quantity of beads."

"Why not money?"

"Money is local to a given district. But the female

desire for beautiful things . . . universal." He grinned at her.

"So where are my sky-blue beads?" she said, giggling.

He rolled over on top of her. "So will you listen to me if there's a dangerous situation?"

She looked up at him. "Not if you're choosing the wrong kind of beads. But I don't mind obeying you if you're right."

"Someone has to be the *capo,* to put it in Italian, or our marriage will be like a failed expedition. It will fall apart."

Isidore stopped herself from rolling her eyes. It was as if Simeon was haunted by the memory of wild beasts jumping at him. It might take a few years, but he would come to learn that the English countryside held no dangers she could think of. "In cases of danger . . ."

"What if we had a signal between us, and when I included the signal in something I said, then you obeyed me without a second thought?"

She nodded. "As long as you didn't abuse your privilege."

He was braced over her, on his elbows, his lips deliciously close to hers. Who could have thought that a large male body lying on top of hers could feel so good, against all reason?

He leaned down and brushed his lips with hers. "If I say, *now,* Isidore, you have to obey."

"You say *now* a hundred times a day," she said.

"You would know the difference if I really meant it."

"Danger," she prompted him. "Danger, remember? I might not be listening all that closely to your tone of voice."

She gave a little wiggle to remind him about the other things he was getting with this marriage along with a bad-tempered Italian wife. Sure enough, his eyes glazed a little.

"How about something in a foreign language?" she suggested.

His face cleared. "If I say, *As your Baalomaal*, Isidore, then you obey me without question."

"And what does *Baalomaal* mean?" she asked suspiciously.

He leaned down again, a wicked smile in his eyes. "As the Lord of your Bedchamber, Isidore, I command that you kiss me now."

She drew his head down to hers. "As you wish," she said, as demurely as any husband could wish.

Chapter Thirty-seven

The Cricket and Song Inn
West of London
March 4, 1784

Jemma, the Duchess of Beaumont, allowed herself to be handed out of the carriage only to discover that there was an acre of mud covering the inn yard. She halted on the bottom step of her carriage and surveyed her grooms- men, trying to estimate their general strength. Unfortu- nately, the two standing at her carriage door looked suspiciously weedy. The last thing she wanted was to be dropped into the muck.

"Your Grace," came a drawling voice.

She jerked up her head to find that the only other car- riage drawn up in the yard had just flung open its door, revealing the Duke of Villiers.

"Villiers!" she cried, "Do tell me that you have a husky footman who can get me into that inn. I'm feeling extreme trepidation, as I'm sure my poor groomsmen are as well."

He stepped down into the mud as if it didn't exist. He was dressed exquisitely, of course. His cloak was a ruby red so dark that it seemed nearly black. Its capes lay over his shoulders with the sleek elegance that comes from the very finest wool.

Jemma couldn't help smiling at him. Villiers was so dramatic, and yet now that she had come to know him, his elegance and drama seemed to fade in relation to the rest of him. He walked over to her.

"I hope you don't expect me to put down my cloak," he said in his usual drawl. "I've worn this only once, and I am inestimably fond of it."

She laughed. "I expect you to lend me a strapping footman, Villiers! I must needs get to that inn. I've been on the road for hours and I'm famished. I set out yesterday from London, if you can believe it. We lost a wheel, and I had to spend the night a mere hour from the city."

He held out his arms. "Come, then."

Jemma froze. "You're convalescing."

He scooped her off the step as if she were no more than a girl of five. "I'm feeling better. Of course, it could be that I've miscalculated my abilities." His steps slowed. "Oh—"

She shrieked as his hands suddenly gave a little and she dipped toward the ground. "No!"

"Oh, all right then," he said. There was a dark strain of laughter in his tone.

"You're evil," she accused him.

"And you're not the first to tell me so," he said comfortably, putting her down within the door of the inn.

"Well," Jemma said, shaking out her skirts. "I do

thank you, Villiers. Naturally I would have preferred to walk on that cloak of yours, but I'll take what I can get."

"A sensible notion. Life is, alas, full of compromises."

Jemma felt a bit strange about the whole thing.

"Your Graces," the innkeeper was gobbling, "I'm afraid that I have no private rooms at the moment. The south chimney has collapsed."

Villiers turned his cold eyes on the innkeeper and a moment later it transpired that the public room had no other customers, and the innkeeper would take it upon himself to keep out any who might appear.

"Until the duchess has had some tea," Villiers said gently.

Jemma felt so oddly unbalanced that she found herself chattering as they walked into the room, telling him that she was on her way to pay a visit to his one-time fiancée. "Roberta's father, the Marquess of Wharton and Malmesbury, is marrying a mermaid he met at a public fair."

"My joy at the dissolution of that engagement deepens by the moment," Villiers said languidly. "Does the mermaid come with piscine *accoutrements*?"

"Naturally," Jemma said. "I believe she straps on a tail and speaks in verse for a few shillings."

"Just what one wants in a mother-in-law. Yes, I truly made a lucky escape."

"I should like some tea, please," Jemma told the innkeeper. "And something to eat as well, if you would be so kind." She had a strange uncertainty in her stomach, and it was always best to eat in those circumstances. "How odd that we should meet at the same inn."

"I'm off to pay the Duke of Cosway a visit, as I told you I would," Villiers said.

The innkeeper put down a tea tray and she busied

herself with pouring. It was rather awkward to find herself in an inn with Villiers. Why, it was almost like an assignation, though of course it *wasn't*. Would Elijah believe that, though?

It was entirely surprising how strongly she wanted to believe that Elijah would not think it an assignation. An *affaire*.

"The fact that you and I have both been summoned to the side of errant people of our rank may be tedious," Villiers pointed out, "but entirely unsurprising. To whom could they turn?"

"Anyone," Jemma said, wishing that she had paid no attention to that letter from Roberta.

There was a great commotion in the innyard. "The innkeeper said that he would keep this room—" Jemma began, but before she could finish the sentence the door swept open. She looked up to find the Marquise de Perthuis, dressed in a black travelling gown badly splashed with mud at the hem.

"What a remarkable pleasure," the marquise said, strolling forward. "My carriage has been stuck in the mud for an hour, and I was feeling miserably tedious. What a *delight*, an absolute delight, it is to find you here, my darling duchess!"

Jemma ground her teeth and swept into a curtsy that was just a shade on the disrespectful side.

"Along with the Duke of Villiers," the marquise trilled. "What extraordinary luck to find that we are all stranded at the same time."

The worst thing Jemma could do would be to emphasize the truth of that account. No one would believe that she and Villiers had found themselves at the same inn by mere happenstance. So with a nicely calculated twist of indifference, she said, "Not so strange, after all. After all, we are surely all going to the same event?"

The marquise's face stilled. "No," she said, but now her smile had a drop of ice to it.

Jemma paused just long enough to indicate a touch of embarrassment that the marquise was without an invitation. "It's nothing, of course," she said, just hastily enough. "I'm quite certain now I think of it that the ceremony was to be a *very* small one. Didn't the Duke of Cosway say as much to you, Villiers?"

"So small as to be infinitesimal," Villiers drawled, which was really quite wrong of him.

"What ceremony is in question?" the marquise said, accepting a cup of tea. She had lost the delighted glow she had when she walked in and found them together, and Jemma's stomach relaxed. It was better for the marquise to feel unpopular, than for her to be overjoyed by the discovery of Jemma's supposed *affaire* with Villiers.

"Oh, a wedding," Villiers sighed. "Cosway's wedding."

The marquise knit her brow. "Dear me. I am so ignorant about the English . . . who is this Cosway?"

"I believe it was Henry VIII who elevated the Earl of Cosway to the rank of duke, did he not?" Villiers said.

Jemma never paid any attention to that sort of thing. "The current Cosway was wed by proxy. He has now returned from years travelling abroad and plans to reconsecrate the marriage."

"Dear me, how peculiar," the marquise observed. "In my experience men are so very willing to break the marital bonds, rather than renew them."

There was something bleak in her eyes. "Whom are you visiting, Madame la Marquise?" Jemma asked.

The marquise fiddled with her sugar spoon, and Jemma wished she hadn't asked. Then she shrugged, a little, helpless shrug. "I am the fool everyone thinks I am," she said, sighing. "I heard that perhaps my Henri is to be found in Lincolnshire and I travel there to find him."

"The Marquis de Perthuis?" Villiers said. "In Lincolnshire . . . the wilds of the British countryside? Surely not."

"Perhaps no," the marquise said, putting another spoonful of sugar in her cup, although it was already, by Jemma's reckoning, sickeningly sweet. "I cannot sit about London and be pitied." Her voice was calm but her eyes weren't.

Villiers met Jemma's eyes over the tea tray and she read in his the pity she felt. In Villiers's eyes! Was that possible? The duke was known for his cruel indifference.

The marquise stirred and stirred her thickened brew of tea, as the three of them sat in silence and stared at her spoon. Then she raised her head and looked to Jemma. "Would you do it again?" she asked. "Your marriage, if I remember correctly, was arranged for you. If you were given the choice, would you marry your duke?"

"Yes," Jemma said without hesitation.

"Then you're a fool in love," the marquise said bitterly. "As was I. They say—" her voice was savage—"that it's better to have loved once and lost, than never loved at all. They are wrong. You should warn this Cosway, if he's a friend of yours."

"I don't believe he's in love," Villiers said tranquilly, "which should protect him from any storms of emotion. The marriage was arranged in his youth."

"When I have children, I shall establish all their marriages at an early age," the marquise said, still stirring. "I shall choose their spouses on the basis of ethical worth."

"Are you so sure that Cosway is not in love, Villiers?"

Jemma put in. "I had a letter from his wife-to-be that suggested otherwise, if one read between the lines."

"Who is this wife?" the marquise asked. "Has she ever travelled to France?"

"She lived in Paris for some years. Lady Del'Fino."

"Ah, yes." The tea stirred faster. "Henri took some pleasure in her company."

"As does every man," Jemma said. "Yet Isidore has waited patiently for her duke to return from his excursions about various continents."

"I have never heard otherwise," the marquise allowed.

"Cosway is not in love," Villiers said. "In fact, I believe there may be a question about whether he will go through with the wedding." The marquise put down her spoon, and sadness fled her eyes immediately. "The marriage is, of course, unconsummated."

"Ah," the marquise breathed.

"Though I tell you this in the strictest confidence."

"Of course!"

Villiers leaned toward the marquise. "I really mean that, Louise."

Jemma blinked in surprise, but Louise—the marquise—merely rapped him on the hand with her spoon. "I beg you to tell me the details, Villiers. I am quite languishing for something interesting to think about."

"I noticed," Villiers said, sitting back. "You must practice putting your husband out of your mind, my dear marquise."

My dear marquise? Louise? Jemma couldn't remember ever hearing a shred of gossip to do with the Marquise de Perthuis and the Duke of Villiers.

The marquise started giggling. "Do you know what I thought when I entered the room?"

"If only the duchess would grant me an indiscretion," Villiers said with a comic emphasis. But there was something serious in his voice, and the marquise's eyes narrowed. "The dear Marquise de Perthuis is my second cousin twice removed," Villiers said, turning to Jemma. "We were thrown together on more than one occasion as children."

"Hardly children," the marquise said, shrugging. "Infants more like. My mother never let me near him after I reached a certain age." She smiled, and Jemma realized that she was likely quite beautiful when happy.

"Base rumors," Villiers said tranquilly. "May I trouble you to pour me another cup of tea, duchess?"

"Rumors!" the marquise said, chortling. "Since we are so very intimate, my dears . . . you were rumored to have a by-blow at the tender age of eighteen, Villiers. It cannot be so many years ago that you have *quite* forgotten?"

"Rank gossip," Villier replied.

"How old were you when you had this child?" Jemma asked curiously. It fascinated her, the way men sprinkled illegitimate children around the countryside.

"Something over two-and-twenty. A distasteful subject, and redolent of my many youthful stupidities," Villiers said. "Please, may we speak of other subjects?"

"Yes," the marquise said. "You can tell me why the Duke of Cosway wishes to dissolve his marriage. After all, Lady Del'Fino is quite lovely. I cannot conceive of the man who would not wish to marry her."

"I'm not sure that Isidore wishes to marry Cosway either," Jemma said, feeling that she should defend her side of the conundrum. "He picked up some disagreeable habits while living abroad."

The marquise wrinkled her nose. "Did he lose the inclination to bathe?"

"No, but he trots around the countryside in a pair of short trousers," Jemma said, "and no stockings."

"Does he display himself for a reason?" the marquise enquired.

"I believe he considers himself to be taking something of a constitutional," Jemma explained.

"I look forward to seeing it," Villiers put in.

"At any rate, Cosway is being a fool. Of course he must consummate his marriage," Jemma said. Her tea was cold and she put her cup down untouched.

"I don't agree," Villiers replied. "If he feels no touch of partiality for the lady—and he has suggested to me that he does not—then it would be better for both of them if they seized the opportunity to dissolve their union, such as it is."

The marquise opened her mouth to say something and thought better of it.

"He has no right to talk of love and such foolishnesses," Jemma said, rather more vehemently than she intended. "He agreed to marry her years ago. She waited for him and very kindly did not create a scandal. He has no right to back out of the agreement now. None!"

"It would not be the most honorable thing to do," Villiers said. "But honor is not always the best criterion by which to judge a lifetime's worth of happiness."

"If he does not honor his wife," the marquise interjected, "the marriage will not be a happy one."

"Perhaps marriage is not meant to be a happy state," Jemma said. "When did we all become so foolishly emotional, so childish in our thinking? Cosway has an obligation to marry Isidore and follow through with his promises."

"It is not as if Lady Del'Fino will lack for a spouse," Villiers said. "She is both beautiful and rich. She will not be left at the wayside."

"That is hardly the point," Jemma snapped. "Will she be a duchess? Will she regain the years that she spent waiting for him to return from his explorations?"

"I agree absolutely," the marquise said. "An arranged marriage, in which neither member feels an embarrassing excess of emotion, is a thing of beauty. Never will Cosway feel anxiety about her whereabouts. Or vice versa."

"But you were in love with Henri, Louise," Villiers said, going on the attack. "I remember your wedding, and you were every inch the enchanted—and enchanting—bride. Would you tell Cosway that he has no right to that joy?"

Jemma met Louise's eyes over the table in perfect agreement. Never having married, Villiers had no idea what he was talking about. "We must wait until Villiers marries," Jemma said to the marquise, ignoring his naïve question entirely.

"Yes," the marquise replied, her smile widening. "A perfect revenge! Perhaps there will be someone at Cosway's wedding, if it takes place. My cousin will fall helplessly in love."

"Then, alack, she must wait for me," Villiers said.

Jemma raised an eyebrow.

"I just remembered an appointment in London."

"How peculiar of you, Villiers," Jemma said. "You remembered this appointment just now?"

"He is afraid," the marquise said, stirring her tea. "Afraid he'll be overcome by sentiment during this touching reconsecration and end up married himself."

"I believe that it would take more than an idle threat to frighten the duke," Jemma said. "Do tell, Villiers. What earth-shakingly important appointment slipped your mind until this very moment?"

Leopold Dautry, Duke of Villiers, would have been

the first to say that idle threats were not enough to frighten him. But he had just discovered, to his discomfort, that fear is part of the human condition.

If Jemma were on her way to visit her sister-in-law, then Elijah would be alone tonight. And Villiers found that intolerable. It was foolishly emotional, and yet he was helpless to dismiss the feeling. Elijah would not die alone, not as long as his oldest friend could prevent it.

"Nothing earth-shaking," he said, putting his spoon precisely by his cup. "Nothing more than a game of chess promised to your husband, m'dear."

"To *Elijah?*"

"Precisely."

"You're turning back to London and ignoring the missive sent to you by the Duke of Cosway for fear of missing a game of chess with my husband?"

"Ah, but I have known Beaumont nearly all the years of my life, and Cosway a mere dozen or so. I had no idea that you too were travelling and that Beaumont is alone. It behooves me to keep my appointments."

"Is it because the two of you were estranged for so long?" Jemma asked. She turned to the marquise. "I think it is hardly a secret; my husband and Villiers were boyhood friends and then fell out over some foolishness when they were striplings."

"Over a dog," Villiers explained.

"Exactly! The stupidity of men never ceases to amaze me," Jemma said. "At any rate, they have only recently mended their fences."

"Naturally," Villiers drawled, "I should hate to insult him in any fashion. Such a touchy fellow, your husband."

"Elijah? Nonsense! I don't believe this tarradiddle, Villiers, not for a moment. There must be something else . . ."

"Villiers remembered the sudden appointment after my question about his children," the marquise said, raising an eyebrow.

"There is nothing there to make me return to London," Villiers said. "Although . . ."

"I knew it," Jemma said. "Out with it! What of those poor misbegotten children of yours, Villiers?"

"I promised a young woman who nursed me during my illness that I would take a more fatherly role than merely pay for their maintenance," Villiers said, offering up the story as bait to distract Jemma.

"Goodness," the marquise said. "She must have been a Puritan. What on earth did she expect you to do? Raise them yourself?"

"I believe," Villiers said, taking a final sip of his tea, "that she meant just that."

"An ill-bred notion," the marquise said flatly. "Were you to take your bastards under your own roof, Villiers, you would have the greatest difficulty fixing an alliance with a respectable woman."

He looked at her with a little smile in his eyes. "Do you really think so?"

"You're challenging him," Jemma said, laughing a bit. "Do go ahead, Villiers. Start your own orphanage and then announce your candidacy for marriage."

"Those of the highest blood can be remarkably vulgar," the marquise said, in a tone that suggested she was thinking of her own spouse.

"I suppose my vulgarity is evidenced by the existence of the children themselves," Villiers said. "But I am giving serious thought to the question. An excessive regard for public opinion is not congenial to my sense of self."

"Naturally the children must be well cared for," the marquise said. "If they were not, it would be morally reprehensible on your part. But I see no duty that requires you to admit children of a base union to your own household."

Villiers merely smiled.

"I must be on my way," the marquise said, coming to her feet. "I hope to make at least four hours in my journey before evening."

They parted at the door, the innkeeper having cleverly placed wooden rondels as stepping stones to the three carriages.

"It's too late for my boots," Villiers said. He waited until the marquise was climbing into her carriage, and then leaned close to Jemma. "And I am sorry about that wooden pathway for other reasons as well."

His breath stirred the hair at her ear and he saw her turn faintly pink.

"Goodbye," she said, turning away. "Do give my best to Elijah."

"I shall," Villiers said. "I shall."

He watched her all the way to her carriage door, but she didn't look back.

Chapter Thirty-eight

The house's lack of odor was almost miraculous. Simeon walked through the front door taking deep breaths, and even opened the door to the downstairs water closet. The pit didn't smell.

"Are the Dead Watch gone?" Simeon asked Mr. Merkin, who was pointing out the sparkling nature of said pit. "I gather that Mr. Bartlebee is walking again."

"It will be a lesson to him," Mr. Merkin said. As he would tell his wife later, it was none of his business how a duke of the realm protects his own property. "Now I've made a very pleasant discovery, Yer Grace."

Simeon raised an eyebrow.

"The way your river runs down there," Mr. Merkin

explained, "I believe that we can simply divert a portion of it to flow continuously through the central pit. Revels House will have a drainage system *like no other*! Nary an odor, even on the rainiest of days!"

"Where will the flow emerge?" Simeon asked cautiously.

"We'll dig a pit on the far side of the hill. In ten years, that will be the most fertile land in the duchy," Mr. Merkin said, pulling down his waistcoat. "We're replacing the rotten pipes with the very best, but I know that you and the duchess are of one mind on this, Yer Grace. *Spare no expense,* the duchess said to me. It may take a bit of an outlay, but this house will be odiferously pure!"

An odd phrasing, but Simeon understood exactly what he meant.

Honeydew walked into the study with a stack of Simeon's papers, a footman at his heels with more papers. But Simeon froze on the threshold. The room had no furniture other than half-filled bookshelves. Honeydew was arranging stacks of bills and letters in neat piles on the empty shelves.

"Where are my books?" he said, hearing the sharpness in his own voice. "Where is my father's desk?"

"The duchess had me send the desk straight to London the day you moved to the Dower House," Honeydew said. "We are expecting all the furniture back in a matter of days. The duchess was quite right, and an offer of double payment in ready money has effected miracles."

Simeon digested that. "The books? Have they gone to London as well?"

"Only the ones which were falling to pieces," Honeydew said. He pointed to the ceiling. Simeon looked up and saw a dingy stain that stretched from one corner over approximately a third of the room. "I'm afraid that when the water closet pipes leaked, they inundated the study, causing the rot of a number of books. On the duchess's instructions—"

Simeon cut him off. "I see." He felt that familiar swell of anger against his father. Some of those books were among the first books printed in England. He remembered an edition of John Donne's poems signed by the poet himself ... likely merely a moldering heap of pages now.

"The duchess believes that the books can be restored," Honeydew said. The consolation in his tone just made Simeon more irritated.

"Of course," he snapped.

A footman appeared with the small desk from the Dower House and placed it precisely in the middle of the echoing study. Honeydew immediately lifted a pile of papers from the bookshelf and moved it to the desk. "There, Your Grace," he said soothingly. "Peters will fetch a chair and you'll be as comfortable as can be. At least that odor's gone!"

The demise of the odor had obviously made Honeydew giddy with pleasure.

When the chair appeared, Simeon took a seat and began looking over the letters delivered the previous day. Four new bills had arrived, for various expenses incurred by the duchy in the last ten years, along with a letter from another woman who had apparently been promised riches by his father in exchange for access to her bed.

Why did his father bother making huge promises to women, promises he obviously never meant to keep? There was something pitiful about the pattern of it. Invariably his father swore that he had fallen in love at first sight. Then he promised to support his "beloved" for the rest of her life, generally offering a small cottage as well as a cash payment. After, one must assume, enjoying himself, he would return home, thereafter ignoring all future communication.

It didn't sit well with Simeon. The truth of it soured in his stomach and made him . . . irritable.

Honeydew appeared at the door. "Mr. Pegg would like to see you, Your Grace. Mr. Pegg is—"

"I know who he is," Simeon said. "I already directed that he should be paid for his smithy work."

"He is here about the cemetery," Honeydew said. He advanced somewhat into the room, lowering his voice. "Her Grace seems to have effected a somewhat miraculous transformation in Mr. Pegg. He's acting as the mayor of the village. The kitchen staff reported last night that on discovering that Mr. Mopser had been charging double to villagers living by the river, Pegg stormed into the shop and forced a promise that the practice would stop."

"Show him in," Simeon said.

Pegg looked sand-beaten, like a man who'd been driving a camel caravan for far too long. But his back was straight, and the spark in his eye was honest. Simeon got up and came around the table. Isidore was obviously a good judge of character.

He felt less magnanimous toward his wife by a quarter of an hour later. Some repairs Pegg itemized for the village were acceptable: a widow needed a new roof, the church needed a new privy, etc. The village green was to be opened for use by the villagers, and six fowl provided to each cottage. Likewise, villagers were to be allowed to hunt rabbits and small fowl in the duke's forest, without risking arrest from the gamekeeper. Not that there was a gamekeeper; his father dismissed him several years ago.

But two hundred pounds to refurbish the cemetery?

And another two hundred pounds to be given to Henry Wissner, thatcher, as a fee for accepting Martin Smith as an apprentice? Three hundreds pounds for John Phillipson and Christopher Sumerall to oversee the construction of a new spire for the village church?

He and Pegg argued a bit, jostling back and forth over the steeple and the cemetery. At the end of another half hour they were both satisfied. Admittedly, Isidore had chosen well. Pegg cared for the village and its people. He would keep Mopser's conniving nature under control. Simeon just wished that Isidore had consulted with him beforehand. Not that he would have disagreed with her, but . . .

It was perhaps unfortunate that the next visitor Honeydew ushered into the study was another stranger. "Monsieur Antoine-Joseph Peyre," Honeydew announced.

Simeon had perfected a sympathetic smile, meant to defuse the frustration of those presenting bills older than their children. But Monsieur Peyre did not present himself with the abject mien of the duchy's many creditors. He bowed with the poise of a man who enjoyed perfect self-confidence. He was attired in a coat of flaring orange, adorned with large buttons and embroidered with fleur-de-lis in silver thread. On straightening up, he pulled a small scent flacon from his pocket and sniffed loudly.

"Monsieur Peyre," Simeon said, bowing. "How may I help you?"

Peyre lowered his eyes from the frieze-work surrounding the study and said, "The question, Your Grace, is not how *you* can help me, but how *I* can help you!" Without further ado, he began to stroll about the room, his open perfume bottle trailing a potent scent of flowers.

Simeon waited, suppressing a grin. Monsieur Peyre resembled nothing so much as a bright orange rooster, proud of his plumage and certain that his crowing alone made the sun rise. He felt rather less amused when it transpired that Peyre had arrived with nine plaster-workers in tow and fully expected to be working in Revels House for at least ten days, if not longer.

"It depends, of course, on how elaborate you would like the walls," Peyre said airily. "In the duchess's abode in Venice, the formal rooms are covered with a perfect fantasy of gilded plants, blossoms, and the like. It is—" he kissed his fingertips—"exquisite! But here we are in the English countryside, and one does not feel the same exuberance, the same delightful sparkle. I think perhaps a more classical look might suit. I see this room with pale panels . . ."

While Monsieur Peyre rattled on, Simeon brooded about Isidore summoning plaster-workers to redo his house without mentioning the fact to him.

"Your Grace," Peyre announced, "I do not find an objectionable smell here."

Simeon turned around to find that Peyre was recorking his little flacon of perfume. The bottle was surrounded by an absurdly elaborate golden cage worked with enamel flowers.

"The water closets have been repaired," Simeon explained.

"The duchess's missive warned me to be prepared for an odor," Peyre said with a shudder. "I contemplated refusing her invitation. But—" he opened his eyes very wide—"who can refuse Her Grace anything?"

"Indeed," Simeon said. Then he heard an echo of his mother's sour tone in that word and softened it with a smile. "Please continue as you see fit, Monsieur Peyre. We have the utmost trust in your judgment."

"Naturally," Monsieur Peyre said. "Naturally!" But he was pleased.

He left in a cloud of perfume, and Simeon turned to sit down at his desk, paused, and looked through the window at the garden. He had left Isidore in the Dower House. A good proponent of the Middle Way would surrender his anger, perhaps running an extra mile or two. He would center himself in the universe, remember that anger is a force for evil and that the waters of the ages washed against the pebbles of eternity.

Simeon strode out the door and into the ballroom. Monsieur Peyre was in the center of a cluster of men, pointing to the frieze-work at the top of the room. He caught just a word or two, in French. The place would probably end up looking like Versailles, he thought.

He left through the ballroom door and headed for the Dower House. He would merely request that his wife consult with him before making large decisions to do with the house. Of course, he would remain civil. He would avoid anything akin to an argument.

Those predictions might have come true, if Simeon hadn't been so angry. "The problem," he said painstakingly, "is that you never think before you act."

"Yes, I do!"

"You sent away all our furniture, never thinking where my mother would eat her nightly meal. You bought bolts of cloth from the village thief and paid him a small fortune to deliver them. You anointed a bad-tempered smith as the mayor. You nearly instigated a robbery and assault on my mother because you couldn't wait five minutes for me to finish my letter."

"That's not—"

"You are irresponsible and heedless in your actions toward others," he said steadily. "You are used to getting your way in all things—"

"So are you!"

"Be that as it may, you have constantly forced my

hand." She looked a bit white, and more than a bit angry, he noticed dispassionately. "I dislike having a wife who has no respect for my opinions."

"*That* is a different matter," she said, cutting across his voice like a knife across butter. "You may disparage me for acting as you see it, without foresight. It may be simply that I think faster than you do. After all, my bolts of cloth managed to salvage relations with the village. My anointing of a mayor assuaged a man who hated your father due to the deaths of his wife and baby."

Simeon narrowed his eyes.

"There's no medical help in this village," she said. "I'm sure I need not detail the reasons for the village's impoverishment. The smith drove to the next town to beg for help from the surgeon; by the time he returned, his pregnant wife was dead. You may think that my methods are unorthodox, but they are effective."

"I want to make those decisions," Simeon said stubbornly.

"And your wife has what role in your life?" Her face was now utterly white, and Simeon knew that he was seeing Isidore at her most furious.

His *wife* had always been an illusory, shadowy creature, the docile sweetheart whom his mother had created in letters, the lass who sat in the corner of the room weaving lace as delicate as moonbeams. *That* maiden wouldn't want to make decisions. She chose to sit in the corner of the room and be as fascinating as dirt.

"I don't know," he admitted.

"I do. You want your wife to be nothing more than a child who listens without question to your every word. In fact, I think it would be better if your wife didn't even speak your language. I can't imagine why you didn't marry some foreign lady you encountered in Abyssinia, perhaps the princess you told me about."

He felt his face freeze, just for a second, but Isidore was smarter than any woman he'd met, smarter by far than the princess, for all that lady's ability with languages. She actually laughed. "You did! You thought about marrying a woman who didn't even speak your language. That's just perfect. She could sit in the corner translating poems, while you rampaged about making all sorts of asinine decisions. Luckily she would never question you because she wouldn't even understand what you were doing!"

"What makes you think that I make asinine decisions?" he enquired.

There was a moment's silence.

"Have I put you in harm's way?" he said mildly. "Taken the furniture out from underneath you?"

"You're trying to make me into some sort of silenced African princess, and you're asking *me* if I think you make asinine decisions?"

Well, that was clear. Simeon thought he'd heard enough. His jaw tightened, but before he could say a word, she took a deep breath. "This marriage will never work. Never."

He opened his mouth again, but—

"I thought if I could help you, that you would grow to like having me as a partner," she said. "What a fool I was! It matters to me to be with a man who respects my opinions, who actually wants to be with me, who—"

Simeon met her eyes. "I do like you, Isidore."

"You know, I really wish I believed you. Alternatively, I wish that it didn't matter to me. But it does. Somewhere in these last ten years we spent apart when we should have been married, I kept thinking about whether I'd like you, but I never considered you not liking *me*, who I am. I suppose it was vanity."

"I do like you," he said.

She went on without even hearing him. "It's probably my fault. Maybe I would have been more docile when I was sixteen. But it's too late now. I can't stop being a person just because you want a wife who doesn't speak English." She whipped around. "What stopped your marriage to the princess?"

"I was promised to you."

"Correction," she said scathingly, "you were married to me. But that's all right. As the solicitor so obligingly told us, we *can* have this marriage dissolved."

"No, we can't. We've consummated it."

"I am not pregnant," she said, through clenched teeth. "Not pregnant."

He almost asked how she knew and the words died in his throat. "Oh."

"No one need ever know that I foolishly—impulsively as you would no doubt characterize it—took off my clothes before you, inspiring an ill-advised intimacy. My next husband will be understanding, I'm sure."

"Your *next*—"

Her eyes met his. "You don't want to be married to me, Simeon."

"I—"

He was destined never to finish a sentence around her. Her eyes were as fierce as those of a trapped animal. "I don't want to have to earn love by giving up my ability to make decisions that determine how I live."

What could he say to that?

Her lip curled. "There's a woman out there for you. I would say that youth should be a prerequisite for you. Perhaps your mother can find you someone, rather than making up stories about me. I'll leave tomorrow morning."

"What?"

"In London, I'll inform the solicitor that we're going ahead with the annulment, on whatever grounds he feels will be the most timely."

"Is there a need to be so hasty?" Simeon said, feeling peculiarly sick.

"Yes. I'm twenty-three," Isidore said. "Most brides are sixteen, Simeon. *Sixteen*. I'm twenty-three. You'll forgive me if I make haste."

He grabbed her arm. "You must be insane."

"Undoubtedly," she snapped. "Why I didn't annul this marriage years ago is beyond my understanding."

"You are *mine*."

"Don't try to act as if I'm a desert princess you can scream at." Isidore jerked her arm out of his hand.

"You and I—"

"There is no *you and I*."

"You didn't think so last night."

"Neither one of us knew anything about bedding until recently," she said, rolling her eyes. "It's nice that we learned to be together and share reasonable pleasure, but let's not pretend that it was unique, shall we? Likely the next time will be even better."

Next time? *Next time*? There was a howl in Simeon's soul that would terrify Isidore if she knew. He felt his teeth baring, like some sort of wild animal. She had no bloody idea what they shared. None.

"I don't understand why you're so quick to leave," he said. "I think you don't like the way you feel about me."

Her lip curled. "I don't. You're right. I want to admire my husband."

He ignored that. She had the tongue of an Italian fishwife, but her eyes were saying something else. "You're singing," he said suddenly.

The note broke off.

"You love me."

"I don't."

"You do. You love me." The certainty of it was in his heart.

When she finally spoke, her voice was gentle. "You probably thought that the princess loved you too, didn't you, Simeon?"

He blinked at her, having forgotten what princess they were talking about.

"Some men are just like that," she said, almost to herself, her voice lilting as if she were singing, a sad little song in a minor key. "They think everyone loves them."

"And sometimes a woman thinks that no one could love her," he said, catching her again as she was about to slip through the door.

"I haven't allowed any men to know me," she said. "Except you."

"I love you." He said it, and knew it was true.

But she didn't act as if she heard. "I'll be in London," she said. "I'll ask the solicitor to write you directly, Simeon." Then she brushed off his hand as if he were no more than a passerby and left the room.

He stood there for a long time, thinking about a little girl who had just lost her parents and sang instead of weeping. And a grown woman who didn't believe he loved her, and sang while she spoke. But never wept.

She would understand once she got to London. She would see what they had together.

As for Isidore, she retired into the Dower House's bedchamber and indulged in an angry fit of tears. Why did Simeon have to have those dusky brown eyes, which were too damn beautiful for a man? Somehow it was even more of an affront that he had decided to dress like an English gentleman that morning. It made it harder to think about him as an object of ridicule, a man who trotted around the countryside dressed in short trousers, talking about the Middle Way.

It made it harder to scorn him, when he bowed with such easy and impersonal formality, held her gloved hand for just the right amount of time, as if he'd never told her to throw away her gloves.

He was in control again. Hatred of that fueled Isidore all the way to London the next day, all the way to Jemma's house.

Where she discovered a houseful of servants, but no Jemma.

Chapter Thirty-nine

Isidore spent the two days before Jemma returned unsuccessfully attempting not to think about her marriage. Or, to be more exact, the lack thereof.

"Simeon doesn't like me," she told Jemma, once she finally came home. "Well, he may be right. That is, he likes things to be calm and ordered. And I'm afraid I don't take directions—"

"Take directions?" Jemma said, sounding rather stunned. "What sort of directions? And what do you mean, he doesn't like you?"

"He wishes I were someone else," Isidore said, looking about for her handkerchief. "You see, he had the idea that his wife would be sweet and docile."

Jemma snorted.

"His mother wrote him bundles of letters describing me as some sort of virtuous seamstress, even though I had left her household years before."

"Lies are never helpful in a marriage," Jemma observed.

"I suppose not," Isidore said, wiping away a tear. "But it wasn't my lie. At any rate, I've been a terrible shock to him. I make decisions quite quickly, you know, and I don't always think beforehand."

"You are darling, if impulsive," Jemma said.

"That's a nice way to put it. I think Simeon's assessment is more harsh."

"He's a fool," Jemma said, interrupting. "But darling, you're going to have to forgive him for that sort of foolishness. It's endemic in the gender."

Isidore pressed her lips together. "I wouldn't mind, but—"

"He hurt your feelings," Jemma said.

Tears fell on Isidore's hand. "I've been so stupidly foolish, Jemma, and I think I fell in love with him. But he doesn't even *like* me, I mean, the kind of person I am. And I just can't take that. I feel so hurt."

Jemma wound an arm around her. "Quite rightly, darling. I like you and love you too, and so does every sane person in Europe."

"Every time I want to—you know—I feel as if I'm having to seduce him. You can't imagine what that's like, Jemma. It's so humiliating!" Her voice trailed into a sob.

"You mean he doesn't approach you?"

"No. The fi-first time was because I took off my clothing in front of him."

Jemma laughed.

"And that was your fault! You told me that men don't—well—I can't remember, anyway, you were absolutely right. I took off my clothes, and he couldn't resist me but then he wasn't happy about it afterwards."

"He wasn't? Are you sure?"

"Well, he was, but then he wasn't. The second time, his brother was staying in the Dower House, so I asked Simeon to go for a walk with me."

"And you took off your clothing again?" Jemma sounded fascinated.

"No, but I made it quite clear . . . I mean, *I* had to ask him to go for a walk!"

Jemma was tapping her lips with one finger. "Very unusual."

"He didn't really ever want to make love to me, but I forced his hand. And now he says that I'm impulsive and I don't obey him. I really think he'd be happier with someone far more docile," Isidore said. "He would. And he doesn't—"

"Don't tell me again that he doesn't like you," Jemma said hastily. "I don't believe it for a moment. It sounds to me as if he lost his temper."

"Oh no, Simeon never loses his temper."

"Never?"

"Not even when workmen attacked his mother and myself. He didn't show a bit of passion. He was absolutely calm, and he simply knocked out two of them and kicked down the third and—"

"He did?"

Isidore twisted her handkerchief. "And then he said it was all my fault because I hadn't waited for him."

"How very unpleasant. It sounds to me as if the duke needs to lose his temper, so that he descends from his sanctimonious heights."

"Oh, he never will," Isidore said dispiritedly. "Why, I expect that I could kiss another man directly in front of him, and he would just watch me in that unemotional way he has."

"I'd like to see that," Jemma said. And then, thoughtfully: "I truly would."

"What?"

"See you kiss another man in front of your husband—that same husband who thinks that bedding is all a matter of the body and not the heart."

"He'd probably just turn away. And that would—" Isidore sniffed.

But Jemma's eyes were shining. "It will be good for you too. I think you're letting that husband of yours get away with far too much. He's making you feel small, and less than your wonderful self. He needs a lesson."

Isidore raised her eyes. "You think—"

"I think," Jemma said firmly. "It'll be a matter of one beckoning glance and you'll have all the gentlemen you want on their knees before you."

Isidore sniffed again. "Then why isn't my own husband that way, Jemma? I've tried kissing him, and putting my arms around him like the most frightful hussy, and he just pushes me away."

"I don't know," Jemma admitted. "I've never encountered anyone precisely like your husband, Isidore."

"I suppose I should be glad he's unique."

"It would be much easier if he weren't," Jemma pointed out. "I prefer the lapdog model of husband myself."

Isidore managed to smile at her. "The kind of husband you have, you mean?"

"I didn't say I had one of them. Just that they were enormously appealing." Jemma's smile was a rueful acknowledgment that her husband, Elijah, had never come at her whistle.

"Lady Farthingward is having a ridotto tonight," Jemma said. "You can bask in adoration."

"But Simeon won't be here to see me get kissed. He bid me goodbye, in the politest of fashions. It's been two days and he hasn't come to London."

"Perhaps not tonight," Jemma said. "But soon. It won't take him long to think through your final conversation, Isidore. He'll be here."

Simeon didn't come to London that night. Nor the night after, nor the night after.

A whole week had passed.

Fine, Isidore told herself. It was fine. She wanted a man who would care about her. Simeon said he loved her, but she started to doubt her memory. Had he said he loved her? Was it a fevered creation of her brain?

Probably. Because if he loved her, he wouldn't have let her go. He would lie awake the way she did, thinking about the way he smiled, or the way his brow furrowed when looking at one of his father's absurd letters. He would wake damp with sweat, the sheets twisted around his legs, having dreamt that she was caressing him.

She longed with an ache that seemed not in the heart but in the bones, for something she couldn't have.

For a husband.

For wasn't that what she always wanted from him? To be a husband. To come back from Africa, bed her, love her, acknowledge her.

After another week she set her jaw and started looking at men in earnest. There were men, lots of them. All of England seemed to know that her marriage was to be annulled, thanks to the dowager duchess's vivid descriptions of her son's brain fever. Isidore hardened her heart against worrying about what Simeon thought about his mother's betrayal.

He had made his own bed, as the dowager had said. He must lie in it. Alone. Of course, he was likely happy, practicing the Middle Way, organizing the household . . .

Another week passed. He was never coming. Jemma finally admitted that she must have been wrong.

"It's not his fault," Isidore said helplessly. The nights of lying awake had clarified things. "He really can't help being a person who hates disorder. I think it must be because he sensed what his father was like, even as a boy."

"How could he not, given the stench of the sewer?" Jemma said. She had taken a sharp dislike to the entire family. "His mother is extremely common, given those letters she is writing." The dowager had not been sparing in her description of Simeon's fighting skills. "His father was a complete rotter and cracked to boot. And he is—"

"Don't," Isidore said swiftly. "Don't."

Jemma sat down on the bed. "Marriage is an enviable state," she said. "You will enjoy it, the next time."

"I've thought so for years," Isidore said.

"How long will this annulment take?"

"The solicitor says that since His Majesty himself has taken an interest, it should take only a month or so. He already met with the Archbishop of Canterbury, given the king's request for prompt action. Lady Pewter annulled her marriage in a month once her husband started dressing in women's clothing on the open street. The solicitor sent a note that he will like to visit tomorrow. I expect he has news on that front."

Jemma nodded. "Is Cosway aware that matters are moving so quickly?"

It was all so humiliating. "I expect so."

"Then it's over."

Isidore could feel her body drooping, like a plant without water. Which was foolish, foolish, foolish. "I feel like taking to my bed and never getting out," she whispered.

"I can understand that," Jemma said.

They sat in silence for a while.

"It smells," Jemma said, finally. "I don't mean the water closets, Isidore. I mean your husband. There's something off here."

"You know what I don't understand?" Isidore said. "He said that he loved me. He *said* that."

"You never told me that before!"

"I didn't believe him."

"You should have believed him," Jemma said. "Men never say that sort of thing unless they mean it. They have rigid defenses prohibiting displays of emotion." She was smiling. "He is just being a fool."

"He's not a fool," Isidore said.

"He doesn't know what he wants. Well, I expect he knows just what he wants, but he's afraid to reach out and take it."

"Simeon is not afraid of anything," Isidore said, almost sadly.

"He's afraid of you."

Isidore snorted.

"He's afraid of you because his mother is an old cow who is telling all of England that he's crazy. And his father was even worse, with all his mistresses, and irresponsibilities."

"That has nothing to do with me."

"Then why didn't he come back, all those years, when his mother was writing him letters describing the paragon waiting for him at home?" Jemma pounced.

"Because he was looking for the source of the Nile," Isidore offered.

"Nonsense! Years passed. He could have nipped back here, snatched you up and taken you back to die of a Nile fever. He could have come back here, annulled the marriage, and returned to paddle around the river some more. He never came back."

"I'm aware of that," Isidore said, thinking that Jemma could be awfully dictatorial at times.

"I think that he's afraid to own you. To own anything."

"He doesn't *own* me," Isidore said, with dignity. "I am a human being, not a heifer."

Jemma waved her hand. "Think like a man, Isidore. Think like a man! I expect he never really wanted the paragon. You saved him from the tiresomeness of perfection."

"I'm too much," Isidore said glumly.

"I think you may have been just a wee bit overbearing," Jemma said. "Men like to conquer, you know."

"It's so stupid," Isidore said, feeling tears prick her eyes. "If I understand you, you're saying that he's throwing me away like yesterday's tart simply because he finds me too overbearing. I—I—" She meant to say that she deserved better, but she forgot the sentence and floundered into tears instead.

"He needs to take charge. That's why he tried to redo the wedding. That's why he hasn't come to London, because it would mean following your whistle. He's no lap dog."

"No," Isidore said, sniffing.

Jemma was smiling. "We have to make him understand what he might lose."

"What do you mean?"

"When I found that my husband had a mistress, I packed up my bags and fled."

Isidore narrowed her eyes. "I'd kill him first and then flee."

"That's always an option, of course," Jemma said.

"But with the wisdom of hindsight, I think I should have just given Elijah a taste of his own medicine."

"You should have taken a mistress? Or a—what would the word be?"

"A lover. I have decided in the years since that perhaps had I flaunted a lover before Elijah in the early days of our marriage he might have cared."

"Why?" Isidore bit her lip. "It doesn't seem logical, Jemma, though I wish it were true. If the only concern your husband had was to do with his heir, I really don't see how three years one way or the other would change things."

"I know much more about men than I did. I was *his,* when we lived together in London and were first married. Three years later, he'd practically forgotten about me. Men do that. If you allow Simeon to return to Abyssinia and start rootling around looking for another river basin, he'll forget you."

Isidore felt tears welling up in her eyes.

"And you don't want that," Jemma said gently.

"It's so awful!" Isidore said, drawing a ragged breath. "I—I—"

"I fell in love with Elijah, who didn't show any interest in returning the favor. It took me forever to get over it."

"I'm afraid I never will," Isidore said shakily. "It's the most ridiculous thing in the world. It's just that I love the way he's taken on the house, and doesn't even blame his rather hateful mother, or his father, who was a positive criminal! I know he didn't like the way I dashed into things, but I thought . . ."

"I expect he's madly in love with you," Jemma said consolingly. "Who could not be?"

"I just can't let him return to Africa," Isidore said. "And I don't want to marry anyone else!"

"Then you won't," Jemma said. Against all reason,

she was smiling. "We'll arrange it so that he comes to his senses. Do you know that when people are knocked silly by a blow, sometimes a second injury puts them back into a sane mind? That's what we'll do."

"I don't want Simeon hit on the head," Isidore said, alarmed.

"We won't *hit* him," Jemma said. "We'll just do something to throw him out of his complacent frame of mind."

"What?"

"It's not a question of what," Jemma said, smiling. "It's a question of whom."

"Then?"

"Villiers."

Chapter Forty

Revels House
March 26, 1784
Early in the morning

The Duke of Villiers paused before entering the house. If the truth be told, he was remarkably fastidious. Sometimes he embarrassed himself by his dislike of bodily functions. Other men seemed to love sweating and generally rolling around in their own muck. He did not, and a sewer was perfectly emblematic of the sort of bodily process he would prefer to be invisible and certainly inoffensive.

But the butler was waiting, so Villiers climbed the stairs with a sigh. How he had become such a slave to his acquaintances, he didn't know. Though he had the idea that Elijah would correct him and say, *slave to his friends*. One cautious sniff within the hallway, and Villiers felt more cheerful.

He turned from handing his cloak to the butler. "I heard tales that Revels House had been conquered by a terrible odor," he told the butler.

The man beamed. "No longer, Your Grace. If I might show you into the Yellow Salon, the duke will join you shortly, I'm sure."

Villiers no sooner entered the salon than he stopped short, staring at the rug stretched at his feet. It blazed up at him, an extraordinary dancing pattern of cherry red and deep crimson that covered the entire floor. Stags bounded in incredible detail around the border. "My God," he said. "I've never seen anything like it."

"There are only two or three such in the world, as I understand it," the butler told him. "His Grace bought it from a Mongolian king. It is knotted in wool and silk, with gold and silver threads."

Villiers had an enormous estate, but he thought he might be treading on something of comparable value. It made him feel almost queasy to walk on it.

Cosway stamped right over the carpet when he entered. "I'm sorry to have written you that letter," he said without further greeting. "I've called a halt to my marriage ceremony." He looked tired. Disheveled, but not nearly as extraordinarily odd as his mother's letters had promised.

"So what got you into breeches?" Villiers asked, skirting the question of marriage. "According to various reports, you were shocking the countryside in your trousers."

Cosway shrugged. "It wasn't worth the amount of anxiety it seemed to cause my acquaintances. Not to mention my household."

"No powder," Villiers observed. "But breeches, and a decent waistcoat. We'll make a duke of you yet."

Cosway smiled faintly. "I even have a valet."

"Can you be ready to leave for London in an hour?"

"What?"

"In an hour," Villiers said agreeably. "You might want to tell your valet to begin packing."

Cosway's smile grew. "No."

"Tonight the king holds a party on board the royal yacht, the *Peregrine,* which has been moored in the Thames, just outside the Tower of London."

"Fascinating," Cosway said. "I hope you enjoy yourself."

Villiers dropped into a chair, taking a moment to deliberately rearrange himself. Then he said, as casually as possible: "The king has interested himself personally in the dissolution of your marriage on the grounds of your insanity, and has ordered the matter expedited both in Parliament and with the church. The duchess—that would be, *your* duchess—has been invited tonight. It is my distinct impression that the king will personally grant her a dissolution of her marriage."

It was a blow. Villiers could see that. Then Cosway's jaw set and his back straightened.

"I can't stop her," he said. "She deserves to choose her own husband."

"She's already being courted by every fortune hunter on three continents."

"Yes, I expect that is the case." Cosway sat down and crossed his legs as if they were discussing tomorrow's weather.

Another man might have believed Cosway's uncaring voice. But somehow Villiers had learned to recognize the signs of anguish, even buried deep in a man's eyes.

"Ah well," he said. "I just thought I'd let you know. I must say, I'm glad to hear that you're so uninterested."

"Why is that?"

There was just a shade of suspicion in Cosway's tone, but Villiers was too good an actor to start laughing. "Well, I don't know if I've ever mentioned it to you, but I have a number of illegitimate children," he said.

Cosway's eyebrows flew up. "Do you find that inconvenient?"

"I haven't," Villiers said feelingly, "but I am beginning to. You see, I have decided to gather these children into my own household."

"And the number is?" Cosway asked.

"Six." Villiers sighed. "I can hardly believe it myself. The sins of youth become the burden of old age."

"You're hardly old," Cosway objected. "What are you, thirty? I suppose you could sprout a full dozen if you put your mind to it."

"Thirty-four," Villiers said. "And my soul is much older, I assure you. At any rate, six illegitimate children do pose something of a problem for my matrimonial prospects, as you can imagine."

Cosway snorted. "You won't be—" He broke off.

Villiers watched with satisfaction as the truth dawned.

"I need to find them a mother," he pointed out. "Women of my own rank are unlikely to take me, under the circumstances. But a divorced woman? And Isidore is very delectable." He said it gently, but apparently not gently enough.

He could have sworn that Cosway didn't even move, but the next moment there was a strong hand around his throat. "She is no mother for your misbegotten brats," Cosway snarled. The tight thread of rage in his voice would have made Villiers smile, but he had a suspicion he might die for it. "She's mine." He threw Villiers backwards. The chair nearly tilted and went over, but held.

Villiers delicately felt his throat. Jemma would owe him for this one. Friendship was one thing; physical assault was not as appealing. He coughed. Cosway didn't seem to be impressed, so he coughed again, harder.

Cosway was still standing over him, staring. "Damn it," he said, turning and throwing himself down into a chair. "You lied to me. Bastard."

"In what way?" Villiers asked cautiously.

"You don't intend to marry Isidore, do you?"

"Not if it drives you to assail me, no."

Cosway's face was as foul as any pirate captain Villiers had had the good luck not to meet. "I'd probably rip your guts out at the altar."

"Charming," Villiers said. "What happened to all that Middle Way business that you regaled me with when we were on board ship together? Aren't you a calm pebble on the shores of eternity any more?"

"I met Isidore," Cosway said through clenched teeth.

"Women," Villiers sighed. He got up and rang the bell.

The butler appeared immediately. "May I bring some refreshments?"

"A wet cloth for my throat," Villiers said. "And tell the duke's valet that we're leaving for London within the hour. We'll be on the royal yacht tonight and the valet needs to pack accordingly."

"Damn it," Cosway said behind him.

"You're just rediscovering your manhood," Villiers said soothingly. "All that pebble business wasn't good for you. The question is, how are you going to win her back without getting yourself thrown in the Tower for murder?"

"She said she wants to pick her husband," Cosway said. "She wants to be wooed. Flowers. Poetry."

"Jewels," Villiers said. "Skip the flowers; they just die. Do you have any jewelry?"

"Tiger rubies. I just had them transferred from Hoare's bank."

"Excellent."

"But Isidore is not really interested in that sort of thing," Cosway said, slumping back in his chair.

"What is she looking for?"

"A lapdog," Cosway said. "Someone who will allow her to make all the decisions and believe everything she says."

"She'll adjust," Villiers said, getting up and wandering over to examine the wall paneling. "You have some lovely frieze work here, Cosway. Was this original to the room?"

"No. Isidore brought someone in, but she left before seeing what he did."

Villiers turned around. "Here's my advice, for what it's worth. There's been nothing romantic about your marriage."

"What marriage?"

"Exactly. She went off to London to have it annulled and you didn't even bother to follow."

"I'm not a damned dog to follow at her heels!"

"Exactly," Villiers said. "You're more of a pirate."

Cosway narrowed his eyes. "A—"

"A man who slashes his way to his lady's side," Villiers said, almost dreamily. "Beating all the odds, including causing grave bodily harm to those highest in the realm (for which he could be hung, mind you), he makes his way to his chosen bride and slings her over his shoulder, heading for the freedom of the open—"

"I have it," Cosway said, cutting him off. "I suppose you write melodramas on the sly?"

"Do you think I ought to?" Villiers said, widening his eyes. "I'm so pleased you think I have talent."

"God," Cosway said. "If I didn't know you were one of the best fencers in Europe, I'd wonder about your manhood, Villiers."

Villiers shook down the lace at his wrists. "I've only lost one duel. And that was to a man in love."

"Ah."

"So you see," he continued gently, "I have a great respect for the condition. I would put myself in danger from such a man only under the strongest persuasion."

He could see Cosway thinking, accepting it, learning to live with it. He even smiled, a moment later. "So who forced you to come here?"

"Jemma, Duchess of Beaumont," Villiers said. "Now we must leave. It will take me at least three hours to prepare for the king's festivities tonight." He eyed Cosway. "Depending on the skill of your valet, it should take you at least four."

Chapter Forty-one

The Peregrine
Yacht to His Royal Highness, George III
March 26, 1784

*I*sidore knew it was a silent, defiant gesture. Her solicitor assured her that the king himself intended to speak to her that very evening about the dissolution of her marriage; she chose to wear the dress in which she first met her husband. She had a strong feeling that the majority of men on the royal yacht would not react to her presence by querying whether her taste ran to the unorthodox.

"Lord," Jemma said, coming up behind her. "You look astonishing, Isidore."

"It's something of a debutante ball for me," Isidore

said, smiling at her in the mirror. "I intend to impress all available men with my attributes."

"No debutante could wear that gown," Jemma said, "given your meager bodice and less-than-meager curves. The design is so beautiful: I love the blue watered silk petticoat underneath the silver. Gorgeous! Especially with the diamonds sewn all over it . . . You look like a fairy."

"I think of fairies as small green creatures with transparent wings," Isidore said dubiously.

"A fairy queen," Jemma amended. "One look at you and mortals lose their wits, forever wandering in the depths of the forest."

"You are rather odd, Jemma, do you know that?"

"I accept that about myself. And I'm not the one with diamonds pasted everywhere from her bottom to her heels."

"I just want to make it clear to everyone that I'm—it is ridiculous, isn't it?"

"Everyone knows how much you're worth, darling," Jemma said soothingly. "I like the glittering look. It's a public service. You'll reflect the candlelight so no one falls overboard. You know, last time the king had a gathering on his yacht, Lord Piddle tripped over his own feet and somersaulted into the water."

"Did he come back up again?"

"Naturally," Jemma said. "He floated like a cork."

"If I fell overboard," Isidore said, "I would sink like a stone. These diamonds are quite small but put together, they're quite heavy."

"I suggest you sit in a throne to receive the admiring hoards."

Isidore bit her lip.

"Villiers went to fetch him," Jemma said, guessing exactly what she was thinking.

"What if Villiers can't convince him?" Isidore said, fear welling up in her heart. "What if Simeon is perfectly happy without me, and has decided I'm just too much trouble?"

"Then we'll auction your dress in the marketplace and you can buy yourself a new husband."

By ten in the evening, Isidore was beginning to accept that even the Duke of Villiers couldn't work miracles. King George III had come and gone, giving his assurance that the bill of divorce her solicitor had submitted would be approved speedily. It should have warmed Isidore's heart to realize that even a happily married monarch found her bosom appealing, but it didn't.

Why didn't Simeon come? She stood up listlessly and put her hand into the hand of some gentleman. She couldn't even remember his name. There had been so many suitors that she'd taken to describing them to Jemma by their clothes. This one wore a turquoise coat with green buttons. *Not* a good combination. She managed to find a smile for him.

Turquoise Coat bowed with a great deal of unnecessary hand flourishing, and they eased their way onto the crowded floor. The yacht was ample for a boat, but the king had been lavish with his invitations and there were (in Isidore's opinion) far too many people onboard. Her panniers kept knocking against those of other ladies, necessitating a constant flow of apologies. What's more, the gentle rocking motion of the river made dancing all the more difficult, especially when dressed in perilously delicate heels and a cumbersome gown.

She was just twitching her hem out from under the clumsy feet of one of the royal dukes when there was a sudden thump and the entire yacht bounded in the water, as if a giant's hand had thrown it in the air an inch or two.

The duke frowned as though her gown were to blame and lumbered off to the deck, followed by most of the dancers.

"Peculiar," her partner remarked. "I wonder what that was about. I suppose we could go look at the water." The musicians produced one screeching discord, and then settled back to finish the measure.

Some people continued to dance, though most had drifted through the doors that opened onto the deck. She could hear a few shouts from outside. Jemma appeared at her shoulder, her eyes sparkling. "I think another boat has hit us," she cried over the noise. "I'm looking for Beaumont!" And she was gone.

Turquoise Coat started a running complaint. Drunken river boat captains presented a hazard to everyone on the river . . . Isidore had a headache, and it wasn't getting any better listening to prognostications about the rightful punishment that would be meted out to the drunken captain who struck the king's own yacht.

"If you'll forgive me, my lord," she said, "I must retire to the lady's salon for a moment."

"I doubt if that is entirely safe," Turquoise Coat said. "What if the boat has suffered some damage? We should make our way outside."

"If the boat were damaged, we would be listing," she pointed out.

"I do hear some shouting and such."

Isidore slipped her hand out of his arm. "It has been a pleasure, my lord."

He said something, and she turned about. "Excuse me?"

"I'm not a lord," he snapped, looking distinctly put upon.

She turned away without answering, which made her feel guilty all the way back across the now empty ballroom floor. The boat was still rocking from side to side. Her guess would be that it had burst free of its moorings and was drifting in the Thames. Which meant that it would strike one or the other bank in a matter of five minutes. Hardly anything to worry about.

At any rate, she didn't see any reason to join the crowds on deck, where doubtless her gown would be trod on and she might even fall overboard, given the fact that the heels of her diamond-encrusted shoes had proved to be far too high for comfort. She teetered across the polished floor and finally made her way into the ladies' salon.

The maids had deserted their posts, naturally. She sat down on a chaise-longue and stared at the opposite wall.

She loved him, and she'd lost him. She'd lost him by being a peremptory dragon. "Arrogant," she muttered to herself. "Fool." She'd dropped her handkerchief somewhere so she resorted to pulling up her jewel-encrusted skirts and wiping her eyes on her chemise.

"Lost your way?"

She hadn't heard the door open. She hadn't heard any footsteps, or sensed eyes watching her. She hadn't planned anything to say, which was almost the worst of it.

He looked like any other duke of the realm, dressed in a gorgeous coat of dark blue satin, embroidered with pomegranates.

"That's not your coat," she said.

"It belongs to Villiers." He didn't take his eyes off her.

"You look like a duke," she said, sniffing a little.

Being Simeon, he didn't bother with flummery about clothing. "You are free to choose a husband, or so they tell me," he stated.

She swallowed. Her heart was beating so fast that she could hear it in her ears. "Yes."

"I could offer myself as part of the horde that Villiers assures me is sniffing about you."

A tiny tendril of hope sprang up in her heart.

"You could," she said, nodding. "You're wearing breeches. I'm sure that was one of my requirements."

"And powder," he said, "for meeting royalty. But—"

"But?" she whispered.

"I'm not offering myself."

Her stomach twisted on a great wave of nausea and shame. "I see," she said faintly. He was looking at her closely so she couldn't, she couldn't cry. She mustn't. She didn't.

"Surely that doesn't surprise you," he said, moving into the room and closing the door behind him.

"This is the ladies' salon," she said. Her voice cracked, which was stupid. She was swamped by a feeling of bewilderment, like a child who just lost both parents in one moment. She had believed him when he said he loved her. Her eyes blurred and she had to bite her lip hard. She turned away from him. "I think it's time to leave," she said, forcing the words out of her throat. "Jemma will be wondering where I am."

He didn't answer, so finally she turned back. Simeon was busy jamming a gilt chair between the closed door and the dressing table.

"What are you doing?" she whispered.

"I'm not offering for your hand," he said, walking over and towering above her.

"There's no need to emphasize your decision!" she snapped. "I fully understand your reluctance."

"Do you, Isidore? Do you really?"

She lifted her chin. "Of course I understand. I gave you scant courtesy when I made those decisions about the house, for which you were justly angry."

"No."

"No?"

"I'm not offering for your hand, Isidore, because I'm taking it."

She blinked at him.

"I'm not a tame dog to follow you to London and paw at your skirts. I want you," he said fiercely. "Because I love you, and you love me. And damn it, you're going to be the very devil to live with. But you're *my* devil, and I can't let anyone else have you, and I can't imagine life without you."

Isidore took one sobbing, song-filled breath. "I thought—"

"You thought I didn't love you enough to stay with you," he said. "And you tested me by taking off to London and expecting me to follow."

She lurched to her feet like an ungainly adolescent, literally throwing herself into his arms. "I love you," she said, her voice breaking.

"I thought I couldn't follow you because it meant I was your inferior."

"I never thought that!" Isidore said.

"I couldn't accept the truth," he said. "You rule my heart, Isidore, and there's no shame in that."

She took his face in her hands. "I love you," she whispered.

He kissed her so hard that her hands slipped around his neck. He kissed her so sweetly that her heart was never the same. And he kissed her so fiercely that she knew that a lion had voluntarily walked into the circle of her arms. Isidore Del'Fino, Duchess of Cosway, never forgot that last lesson.

His hands were roaming. "You can't," she said breathlessly, thinking of all the people on deck—and he did it anyway. "You shouldn't," she gasped a few minutes later—but he already was.

Her bodice was designed to cover her breasts, no matter the circumstances, but it gave way before Simeon's
determination. The breath caught in Isidore's throat
when she saw his face.

"You're so beautiful," he said. His voice was hoarse
and his hands hovered above her, as if he were afraid
to touch her. "Ripe and delicate and as beautiful as a
rose."

They didn't have time for poetry. So Isidore caught
him by the hair and said, "*Simeon.*"

He looked at her, his eyes dark as a moonless night.
"Kiss me," she commanded.

"Like this?" he asked, a glimmer of laughter in those
wicked eyes of his. He dropped a polite little kiss on her
nipple.

She shook her head.

"Like this?" he inquired, giving her a tiny lick.

Her hips bucked, but it wasn't enough. "*Simeon.*"

So he laughed and suckled her, shaping her other
breast with a rough hand. All thought of possible inter-
ruptions flew from her head.

It wasn't many minutes later that Simeon found himself on his knees before Isidore. Her skirts were thrown
up and she was lying back on the chaise-longue, making
the sort of moans that only a woman in a very, very
pleasurable state might make.

She was so beautiful. Her hair had toppled out of its
coiffure of elaborate curls and puffs, and fell about her
shoulders. Her lips were a deeper red than any ruby; her
skin was peaches and cream. She tasted like nectar, but
the true aphrodisiac was the look in her eyes.

He drew his fingers down over creamy flesh and began sweetly circling a bit lower. She trembled and then
begged, finally propping herself up on her elbows and
scowling at him, which was just what he wanted.

He loved her scowl. So he dipped his head and gave her exactly what she wanted, drove her to the very edge of abandonment, kissed her until cries tumbled from her lips like a song . . . and pulled back.

Sure enough, he got the scowl back. "You're trying to make me addled," Isidore said, catching her breath.

He soothed her with his fingers until she writhed under his touch. "I'm just making sure that you know who I am."

"Simeon," she breathed. "My husband."

It was at that moment he heard a dim banging noise behind him. He ignored it, concentrating on giving Isidore exactly what she wanted. Sending his beloved toppling into the kind of chaotic bliss that poets dream of. Except—

It was more than a distant annoyance. There was a chaotic shouting and crashing from the boat deck. And then the pounding was on their very door. "Come out!" a voice called out, high and alarmed. "The prison ship, the hulk, hit the yacht and prisoners—"

"What?" Simeon said sharply, lifting his head. One had to expect that at some point the king's servants would desire entrance and he meant to deny them. But this sounded more serious.

"He said something about prisoners," Isidore said, her breath catching in a little pant. "A prison ship. Simeon . . . don't stop, please don't stop!"

But his entire body had gone on alert in the time it took for her to say the sentence. "Up," he commanded, jerking down her skirts as he spoke.

"What?" Isidore stood up, but her legs were wobbly and she clung to his arm.

"One of the prison boats moored in the Thames must have struck this yacht. Or we struck it." He wrenched on his breeches.

"Oh." Isidore stood for a moment, trying to catch her breath. "I suppose we'd better leave then." She found one of her shoes and turned it right side up.

"Can you run in those?" Simeon was listening at the door.

"No."

"Leave them." He tossed Villiers's beautiful coat into the corner.

"But the diamonds—" Isidore looked about swiftly, and then flung her shoes under the sofa. She could always retrieve them later.

Simeon pulled the chair out of the way. "I think from the noise the prisoners have escaped and are getting onto the yacht," he said. "We need to get out of here."

"Couldn't that chair protect us?" Isidore asked longingly, running her hands up his chest.

"Not if they fire the vessel."

Isidore's eyes rounded. "I can't swim in this gown, Simeon."

"Do you remember that conversation we had, back when I was afraid of crises and you told me there weren't any in England?" He couldn't help it; she was so delicious that he had to kiss her again.

"You're my *bally*-something," Isidore said a moment later, looking a great deal less frightened. "Just tell me what to do, *capo*."

"We're going overboard," he said. "We can't stay here, with you in that gown. And we need to get off as quickly as possible."

Isidore nodded and put her hand in his. He pulled the door open cautiously and looked out. There was no one in the ballroom. But with the door open, the sound from the deck swelled. There was screaming and the unmistakable sound of swords clashing. "They're fighting," Isidore breathed.

"The king's own guard is likely here. Not to mention parish constables, the Watch, and guards from the prison ship." But he didn't really give a damn about that. The only thing he cared about was the most precious bundle of his entire life, her hand trustingly clasped in his. "Don't worry," Simeon said fiercely.

The smile she gave him blinded him. "I'm not."

They walked silently into the ballroom, keeping to the edge of the wall, heading to the doors on the other side of the room, away from the deck. Once through the door, Simeon made his way swiftly through the corridors until he came to the staircase at the very end of the yacht.

"We'll go up here," he said in her ear. "We have to go straight over the railing, Isidore. If they see you, they'll fight to the death to have you."

She nodded. He wrapped his hands around her and gave her one last, fierce kiss.

"I'll go off the railing to the left and distract them. I doubt they can swim, and at any rate, I don't think they'll bother. But they'll certainly come to the railing on that side." His voice was just a thread of sound. "Stay behind this door and count to twenty. Then run through the door and over the railing to the right without pausing to think or listen. Promise?"

She nodded again.

He eased open the door and launched himself through it. Isidore began to count. Don't listen, she told herself. You said you wouldn't listen. You just count to twenty, and then run. That's all—

She couldn't help it. Ears were made for listening. She heard Simeon's footsteps and a splash and then shouts. Happy shouts in rough accents. With a leaden feeling of terror, she realized that Simeon had dived overboard but that a ruffian already in the water had grabbed him instantly.

She crept to the door and peered through it. A few ragged men were hanging over the railing, then a head appeared and they were hauling up Simeon, dripping and furious. They had his arms behind his back.

The prisoner who'd caught Simeon climbed over the railing. "Kicked me right good, he did," the man said, adding a word that Isidore had never heard before. "I'll have my own back for that." And before Isidore could draw a breath he pulled back his arm and socked Simeon in the cheek. Simeon fell backward against the deck, pinned by the two men holding his arms.

Isidore almost screamed, but stopped herself. Simeon didn't deign to say a word in response to the blow. He just looked deliberately from face to face, studying the five men clustered around him.

"Here, what you doing then?" one of the prisoners said, obviously uncomfortable that Simeon didn't make a sound.

"Memorizing your faces," he said. The rage so potent in his voice made Isidore shiver.

"I'll just give him two black eyes, why don't I?" the man snarled. "That'll stop him."

Isidore's stomach lurched. She couldn't stay here, hidden, while they beat Simeon. She had to startle them enough so that they would drop his arms, because then he could knock them all out with his kick. Soundlessly, she crept back down the stairs. She needed a weapon. Unfortunately, the king's yacht didn't seem to have any weapons. She couldn't even find a heavy candlestick.

Suddenly, she had an idea, and flew back into the ladies' salon, retrieving her diamond slippers. These should get their attention. She ran up the stairs again, breathing hard, and found that not much had changed.

The same two ruffians were clutching Simeon's arms, though thankfully he didn't seem to have taken any more blows. From what she could understand, they were going to bargain his life for their freedom.

She waited for the right moment, eased open the door, and tossed out the diamond shoe.

It somersaulted in the light of the torches illuminating the deck and landed just in front of the group. For a moment they all stared at it, as if a bird of paradise had landed on the deck. The shoe glistened with jewels.

Then, with a muffled shout, all five men dove for it.

Simeon kicked the man closest to him so hard that the convict flew back against the wall of the yacht. In a swift, swirling circle he sent the other four spinning to the deck, one after another. Isidore wrenched open the door and flew at Simeon. His muscled arms closed around her and he threw himself backward, overboard.

They struck the water with such force that Simeon's arms spun away from Isidore's waist. Icy water closed over her face and her heavy skirts pulled her down into the acid-tasting water as effectively as if she had stones in her pockets.

Something brushed her face and she thought of water-logged corpses rescued by the Dead Watch. Frantically, she beat her arms, trying to rise to the surface, but she couldn't counteract the plummeting weight of all those diamonds.

Then, like a benediction, like a prayer, Simeon's strong arms closed around her and he pulled her upward with a strong, smooth stroke. Isidore broke the surface, choking and gasping for breath.

"Easy," he said, holding her up. "I've got you, sweetheart. I've got you."

"I—I thought—"

He gave her a hard, swift kiss. "I want you out of the river." And without another word he began towing her through the water as if she were no heavier than a babe.

Isidore had just enough time to be confusedly grateful for Simeon's passion for running and the strength it gave him. (Turquoise Coat would have left her to sink or, rather, he would have plummeted down right next to her.)

Then they were at the shore, where a hundred helping hands reached out to them. Simeon was up in a flash, turning around to pull Isidore up the bank. Her skirts seemed ten times heavier than they had been, and the weight of water and jewels made the silk of her over-skirts stretch past her feet, tripping her. Finally Simeon just bent down, picked her up in his arms and walked up the slope.

Everyone on the bank was screaming and howling "Hurrah!" The noise was deafening. Isidore felt a sudden breeze, took one appalled glance down, and realized that the diamond-encrusted cloth of her bodice had given up its battle with gravity and had fallen below her nipples. She looked up, horrified, and met Simeon's eyes. He was laughing.

A second later they were on the bankside, and Simeon wrapped a coat tightly around her. "I can't let *all* of London know what they're missing," he said into her ear.

"Oh, Simeon," she said, hiccupping, half-crying. "He struck you, Simeon. He struck you and I couldn't do anything to stop him."

"You did stop him," Simeon said. "I might have died, but for you."

"And then we were in the water," Isidore said with another hiccup, "and I was going down, and all I could think of was the Dead Watch and how they would gloat when they were sent to find my body."

"Never," he said, his arms tightening around her. "I would never allow that to happen."

"Don't ever let them be the ones to rescue my body, Simeon," she said. "*Promise* me."

"You're not going to drown. Ever."

She put her head against his chest and listened to the strong beat of his heart. They were safe. Tears slid slowly down her cheeks.

He said something she couldn't hear.

"What?"

"Don't you see how lucky we are, Isidore?"

"Yes," she said, a little damply. Her heart was still pounding with fear, even now she was in the warm circle of his arms.

He pulled back and cupped her face in his hands. "We're like your parents, sweetheart. If one of us is going to be lost, both of us will go. I would never, ever stop searching for you if our boat overturned."

Then he was kissing her, the kind of possessive, loving kiss that she'd seen her father give her mother a hundred times. Tears welled out of her eyes, and Isidore wound her arms around Simeon's neck and held on as tightly as she could, even as her tears made him a little wetter than he already was.

It sounded as if the cheers grew even louder when he lowered his head to hers again . . . but maybe that was just her imagination.

Two minutes later, Simeon picked her up again and carried her through the crowd, regardless of her wet, heavy dress trailing behind them. Isidore hadn't paid much attention to what was happening around her, but when the groomsmen closed the carriage door behind them and Simeon deposited her on a seat, she looked about. She was placed in the most luxurious carriage she had ever ridden in, upholstered in red velvet with gold coronets sprinkled everywhere. The horses started and she could hardly feel the motion, so sweetly was the coach designed and calibrated.

"Where are we?" she asked, half laughing.

Simeon was wrestling off his wet shirt and didn't look up. "The Duke of Buckingham's carriage."

"A royal carriage," she said, watching him under her eyelashes. Her breath felt hot in her chest. Surely he couldn't mean to . . .

He did mean precisely that.

Because a second later Simeon was tenderly peeling her drenched bodice down to her waist. There were red marks on her skin left by the diamonds as she struck the surface of the water. He kissed every little bruise, moving down her body like a man who knew exactly where those kisses were most needed.

And though Isidore had never imagined such a thing was possible—making love in a carriage, let alone a prince's carriage!—she found herself laying back on red velvet upholstery as her husband deftly woke her body into the same trembling, vibrating state she had experienced on the yacht.

"We shouldn't," she whispered at some point, and lost her train of thought when a wave of pleasure swept her into a place where words were impossible.

And when he thrust into her, she plummeted into a state where she could do nothing but sob for the pure pleasure of it.

Simeon's body begged him to follow her, but instead he chose to make love to Isidore slowly. It was only by kissing her, by stroking her, by stroking in her, that he could tell her in a way that scorched the truth into both their hearts.

Finally, he couldn't keep to his slow rhythm. He began pumping hard and fast, keeping his eyes open so he could see the way she strained to meet him, the way she gasped and cried out, the sheer beauty of her eyes and mouth.

The carriage rocked as it rounded a corner, and the sensation just increased their pleasure. "Simeon," Isidore gasped, "we must be nearly home."

"I told them not to open the door," he said, but he could feel his control slipping away.

"Simeon!" Isidore cried, pulling his body even deeper inside her own, forcing him to throw away the remnants of his control and surrender to something wilder and more beautiful. Something that left Isidore crying (just a little), and Simeon's eyes misty (just a little).

In the moments that followed, broken only by their whispered endearments, he realized something his heart already knew. They were partners. She would always make impulsive decisions and he would make slow, reasoned ones. He would always be a little terrified that she would look at him with the scorn he saw in his mother's eyes. And she would always be a little terrified that he would look at her and not love her enough.

In short, they were made for each other.

He thought of eloquent things he should say, all the tenderness and passion and hope in his chest, and distilled it to one sentence. "I love you."

She kissed him. And kissed him.

"Whither thou goest," he said to her, in a voice so quiet that she could hardly hear it over the clattering wheels. "There will I go too."

Chapter Forty-two

It wasn't until two weeks afterward that Isidore understood the whole of what happened. She hadn't realized that most of London saw their daring escape, and Simeon's rescue of her. Nor that the King himself watched Simeon carry her from the water and kiss her afterwards, and then swore that he would never listen to another solicitor bleating on about one of his noblemen being mad, let alone annul a marriage on those grounds.

She didn't understand that by knocking out the ringleaders of the prisoners' rebellion, Simeon had enabled the king's guards to trounce the uprising. And she certainly didn't envision her husband being summoned to

St. James's Palace for a public proclamation of the nation's gratitude, during which the Duke of Cosway declared that any success was the result of working together with his duchess.

It was the ball following the king's declaration, and Isidore hadn't seen her husband for at least an hour. She kept glancing over her dancing partners' shoulders, wondering where he might be. She had developed a horror of the silver gown, and so Lucille had carefully removed all the diamonds—the ones that weren't left behind in the mud of the Thames—and sewn them onto a presentation gown.

But she hadn't chosen to wear that tonight; in fact, she thought it might be a long time before she chose to wear diamonds again. Her gown was a pale rose-colored velvet with Chantilly lace, and she wore it with a fortune in tiger rubies.

Her former suitors were out in force. Most of them hadn't lost hope that she would find herself disaffected with Simeon. Even if she weren't planning to annul her marriage, they hoped that she might turn to one of them by way of consoling herself for her husband's eccentricities. They smiled, capered and bowed . . . She felt overwhelmed by their florid scent, by the way they "accidentally" brushed her chest, by the way their teeth showed when they smiled.

Somehow she'd decided that a man should smile gravely, smell faintly like cardamom soap, and touch her breasts only in the privacy of the marital bedchamber.

The nature of marriage is such that a woman no sooner formulates rules of this nature . . . than they are broken.

The Earl of Bisselbate was just bowing before her, flourishing his hand as if he were a peasant sowing seeds (Isidore thought uncharitably), when suddenly another hand touched her shoulder. She jumped and turned. Simeon. She smiled up at him, not even noticing that the earl had straightened and was expectantly holding out his hand to lead her into the dance.

"Simeon," she breathed. "Where have you been?"

"The king had a private request," he said, smiling down at her. "It seems the queen has taken a liking to tiger rubies."

The earl cleared his throat.

"Do forgive me," Isidore said, turning reluctantly back to her escort. "I—"

"As your *Baalomaal*," Simeon said . . . His voice was low and meant for only her ears.

Without a second's thought, Isidore sank backwards, throwing a hand to her brow, knowing that Simeon would catch her, feeling his arms go around her. "Oh!" she cried. "I feel so faint! It must be the heat."

Simeon was laughing silently. He carried her swiftly through the chattering nobles, out the door and down one of the myriad corridors of St. James's Palace.

Isidore lay her head against his chest, loving the strong beat of his heart, not bothering to ask what the danger was. Simeon was with her. All would be well.

A few moments later he whisked her through a door. It was a velvety dark space. He put her on her feet.

"Simeon?" she asked. It felt as if they were in a very small room. "Where are we?"

"A closet," he said. "But there's room to lie down . . . in case you felt like it."

She laughed, but he fell to his knees, and pulled up her skirts. She put her hands on his powerful shoulders, bracing herself against the intoxicating little kisses that were burning a path up her legs.

"But, Simeon," she gasped, feeling her knees weaken,

knowing that in a moment she'd be lying on the floor of a broom closet in the king's own palace. "I thought you would use that word *baalomaal* only in moments of great danger."

He didn't choose to answer until her breath was coming quickly and she was leaning against the wall, uttering broken little moans. Then he stood up, stripped off his coat, and put it on the floor. It was a magnificent coat, worked by Villiers's own embroiderer, black roses on deep brown . . . It was also soft and made an excellent improvised bed.

A moment later Simeon was kissing his wife's inner thigh again, and Isidore was having trouble keeping her mind on the conversation.

"There *was* danger," he said, but only when she wasn't sure what he was talking about anymore.

He waited until her breath was coming and going in unsteady little pants, and he was poised above her in the velvety darkness, feeling her twist up against him, begging, pleading . . .

Then he entered her in one swift stroke, savoring the exquisite beauty of sharing her body, her breath, her love. "Because I love you," he said, his voice rough, the voice of a man who was come to understand that control is only worth having if it's worth throwing away—at certain moments.

"I love you too," she breathed, arching toward him, urging him on.

"It was a matter of some danger," he told her.

He could feel her giggle. "Hmmm."

The time for talking was over but he had to say it first. "Those men were in danger, Isidore. In grave danger. It makes me ache just to look at you. It makes me enraged to see other men look at you, let alone touch you."

Her hands were sliding over his rear, inflaming him.

"You're *mine*," he said fiercely, taking her mouth in a kiss as possessive as he felt.

"I'm yours," she said, kissing him back. "And you're mine."

An Epilogue
in Two Parts
Part One

The Bishop's Study
Canterbury Cathedral
A month or so later

The Archbishop of Canterbury had to admit that the rules surrounding the reconsecration of a marriage were vague, even to him. It was hardly his fault; no one ever requested the ceremony. He spent a great deal of his time putting together couples whom he knew perfectly well were not bound for matrimonial bliss.

Now this couple probably would be blissful. Or perhaps it was better to say that they *were* blissful.

They had said their vows, holding tightly to each other's hands. They'd said "I do," with commendably loud voices.

But even so they didn't seem to want to stop vowing things to each other.

"I'll always love you," the groom said. "You're the ballast to my soul."

"I promise to be less impulsive," she was saying. The bishop knew what that meant. His mother had been impulsive. He sighed and wondered if they were ever leaving.

"I adore you just as you are," the groom whispered.

Oh really.

Kissing again.

He poured himself another glass of sherry. It was going to be a long evening.

Epilogue
Part Two

Revels House
A year or so later

There was a baby crying. Simeon staggered to his feet, shocked out of the sleep of the truly exhausted. Isidore lay next to him, not even stirring. He spared a lopsided smile for his wife, loving her tangled curls and long eyelashes, the arm flung over her head, even the dark circles under her eyes.

He made it to the door, banged a knee on the bedside table, and swallowed a curse. Life seemed more chaotic all the time, and his ability to remain calm in the eye of a storm wasn't any stronger. As he opened the door, the nanny was already halfway down the corridor. "Here's Lucia," she said, handing over a warm little bundle.

A small red face ringed in soft black curls looked up

at him for one moment, registered that he wasn't the milk-providing parent, and erupted back into a howl. There was no telling Lucia that she was a pebble on the shores of eternity. She was a living, breathing, adorable source of chaos, and he loved her so much that it felt as if his heart were beating outside his body.

"Hush, sweetie," Simeon said to her, running a finger down her passionate little nose. "Mama's sleeping . . . won't you let mama sleep for just another moment or two?"

She looked at him with her mother's huge, almond-shaped eyes. But she knew exactly who she was in life, and exactly what she could command. She was the lady of the bedchamber, and the sitting room, and the whole of Revels House, so she opened her mouth again to make that quite clear, just in case her papa mistook the situation.

He kissed her, and gave her a last cuddle, and handed her over to her mother. Who didn't bother with endearments, just propped herself up against the headboard and tucked Lucia exactly where she wanted to be. Simeon just lay back down when he cocked an ear, sighed, and swung his legs off the bed again.

"It hasn't been a terrible night," Isidore offered sleepily. "I think we had at least three hours."

"Lovely," he said, trying to sound grumpier than he felt.

"Dante," the nurse said cheerfully, handing him over. "*And* Pietro, but he's still half asleep and won't mind waiting for a moment or two."

Simeon walked back into his bedchamber, his arms full of the reasons why he had given up an attempt to remain calm. He kissed little Dante (the smallest of the three) on the nose, and handed him over.

Then he sat down holding Pietro, who opened his

eyes and blinked about a little before deciding to try out his newest, most precious accomplishment.

A smile.

That was the problem with living in a clean tent on the banks of the Ganges River. There were no gummy smiles, no warm little bundles, no beautiful, impetuous wives, no responsibilities . . .

No life. Real life.

In other words, no love.

Historical Note

The foremost subject of this historical note must be the intrepid traveler who served as the loose model for my hero. James Bruce, a laird from Scotland, was an extraordinary Georgian gentleman who travelled throughout many remote African states, returning home to publish multiple volumes of his *Travels to Discover the Source of the Nile*. Among his other accomplishments, he discovered the source of the Blue Nile in Ethiopia (not to be mistaken with the White Nile, to its west). While I made up many of my duke's experiences, Bruce did indeed meet the Bahrnagash, whom he describes as a small man in short trousers with bare feet and a knife stuck in his girdle, and he attended the festive marriage of Princess Ayabdar, a ceremony notable for including animal sacrifice and communal sex. (Bruce had trouble believing his own eyes; he insists that the ladies were "women of family and character.") My duke wins Bahrnagash's respect through a race; Bruce appears to have won his approval due to his expert handling of a black steed. If you are interested in reading more about a man who is definitely an early prototype for Jack Colton, the hero of *Romancing the Stone*, I recommend J.M. Reid's life of Bruce (*Traveller Extraordinary: The Life of James Bruce of Kinnaird*) along with Bruce's own *Travels*, which is still available through print-on-demand.

One significant difference between Bruce and the Duke of Cosway is Simeon's faltering adherence to the Middle Way. I make no claim whatsoever to historical verisimilitude in Simeon's recollections of Valamksepa's teachings. The term "Middle Way" is drawn from Rudyard Kipling's novel *Kim*, in which the titular hero meets a Tibetan holy man who seeks freedom from the "Wheel of Things." Had Simeon been lucky enough to meet the guru of *Kim,* he might well have been better prepared to encounter the mire that awaited him in Revels House. But I drew Valamksepa's wisdom from the flotsam and jetsam of bowdlerized Eastern teaching, and they have no basis in reality.

I'll finish this note with just a word about water closets, since their development (and failure) lie at the heart of Simeon's greatest challenge. The 1770's were an exciting time in the history of modern toilets; between 1775 and 1785, inventors created the S-trap (preventing the escape of foul air), the "plunger closet," and the float valve system. None of these new inventions were yet in use in country houses, but water closets were definitely gaining dominance over outdoor privies and old-fashioned close-stools.

Look for
Jemma and Elijah
Beaumont's story
in the next installment of

ELOISA
JAMES's

acclaimed Duchess series

Available June 2009 from

Avon Books